The
Deadliest Sin

The Deadliest Sin

CAROLINE RICHARDS

KENSINGTON PUBLISHING CORP.
www.kensingtonbooks.com

BRAVA BOOKS are published by

Kensington Publishing Corp.
119 West 40th Street
New York, NY 10018

All Kensington titles, imprints and distributed lines are available at special quantity discounts for bulk purchases for sales promotion, premiums, fund-raising, educational or institutional use.

Special book excerpts or customized printings can also be created to fit specific needs. For details, write or phone the office of the Kensington Special Sales Manager: Kensington Publishing Corp., 119 West 40th Street, New York, NY 10018. Attn. Special Sales Department. Phone: 1-800-221-2647.

Brava and the B logo are Reg. U.S. Pat. & TM Off.

ISBN-13: 978-0-7582-4275-4
ISBN-10: 0-7582-4275-1

First Kensington Trade Paperback Printing: September 2010

10 9 8 7 6 5 4 3 2 1

Printed in the United States of America

Chapter 1

"Oh, do come with me, Julia. Those dusty tomes can wait—it's glorious outside!" Rowena's voice was clear and true as the first birdsong of spring.

Dear God, her sister.

Julia Woolcott's eyes flew open, widening in the darkness. She blinked. How long had she been asleep, outside the reach of her senses? The darkness was total and she wondered if her eyes were really open. Perhaps she was blind. The blackness was as final as a closed coffin lid.

Thoughts were slow in coming. Counting her breaths, she ignored the burning sensation in her lower limbs. Panic closed her throat, but she knew screaming would do little good. No one would hear. She swallowed back the terror that was more powerful than the scalding pain enveloping her right leg.

More than anything, she needed to know her sister and Meredith were safe, far away at Montfort in the Cheviot Hills. The high stone wall and thick hedges surrounding the sixteenth-century estate would protect them. Let them be safe, she prayed beneath her breath.

The shores of madness had never seemed closer. But as always, the wall of silence appeared when she needed it most, shutting out the world, keeping her safe.

She would not think of that. She would think of Rowena wrinkling her nose at the smells emanating from her older sister's warren of rooms above the stables at Montfort. It was where Julia played with light and dark, with her daguerreotypes, capturing images with her camera obscura and then fixing them to copper plates with iodine.

"They're gorgeous, Jules, simply magic!" Julia heard Rowena's unabashed enthusiasm and imagined her pulling at Julia's elbow, tapping a riding crop impatiently on the edge of the scarred table where the exposed copper plates lay. Her younger sister could never be kept indoors; it would be as cruel as pinning a butterfly to a board. Closing her eyes in the darkness, Julia imagined the spirit of Rowena captured on one of the copper plates, hair flying in the wind, riding at reckless speed toward Montfort's endless horizons, and drifted off in slumber.

Awakening again she experienced another sinking recognition that she was no longer asleep but locked away in a layer of shadows, gradations of thick, muffling darkness. Julia attempted to shift her weight from beneath a leaden heaviness but nothing moved save the stiffness of crinolines and whalebone. Heading off panic, she sifted through the images colliding in her mind's eye. The footman and the knife. The tall man, his face in the shadows, the one who had shut her in that suffocating place.

Then she was calm. Her aunt's still-beautiful countenance shimmering before her, a picture she had captured many times with her camera, that newfound miracle. Unlike her sister Rowena, brazen and bold, Aunt Meredith would always turn her pure profile away from the camera lens, as though its penetrating gaze would rob her of her secrets. And Meredith had so many secrets.

The air was like a heavy linen sheet pressed against Julia's face, yet a cold sweat plastered her chemise and dress to her body. It was peculiar, the ability to retreat into herself, away from the pain numbing her leg and away from the threat that lay outside that suffocating room.

A few moments, an hour, or a day passed. She found herself seated, her limbs trembling from the effort. Guilt choked her, a tide of nausea threatening to sweep away the tattered edges of her self-regard. Why had she ignored Meredith's warnings and accepted Wadsworth's invitation to photograph his country estate? Flexing her stiff fingers, Julia felt for the ground beneath her. A film of dust gathered under her nails. If she could push herself higher, lean against a wall, allow the blood to flow . . .

The pain in her leg was a strange solace, as were thoughts of Montfort—her refuge and the splendid seclusion where her life with her sister and her aunt had begun. She could remember nothing else, her early childhood was an empty canvas, bleached of memories. Lady Meredith Woolcott had offered a universe unto itself. Protected, guarded, secure—for a reason.

Julia's mouth was dry. She longed for water to wash away her remorse. New images crowded her thoughts, taking over the darkness in bright bursts of recognition. Meredith and Rowena waving to her from the green expanse of lawn at Montfort. The sun dancing on the tranquil pond in the east gardens. Meredith's eyes, clouded with worry, that last afternoon in the library. Warnings that were meant to be heeded. Secrets that were meant to be kept. Wise counsel from her aunt that Julia had chosen, in her defiance, to ignore.

She ran a shaking hand through the shambles of her hair, her bonnet long discarded somewhere in the dark. She pieced together her shattered thoughts. When had she arrived? Last evening or days ago? A picture began to form. Her carriage had clattered up to a house with a daunting silhouette, all crenellations and peaks. Chandeliers glittered coldly into the gathering dusk. The entryway had been brightly lit, the air infused with the perfume of decadence, sultry and heavy. That much she could remember before her mind clamped shut.

The world tilted and she ground her nails into the stone beneath her palms for balance. She should be sobbing but her eyes were sandpaper dry. Voices echoed in the dark, or were they footsteps? She strained her ears and craned her neck, peering into the thick darkness. She sensed vibrations more than sounds. Footsteps, actual or imagined, would do her no good.

She felt the floor around her, imagining rotted wood and broken stone. Logic told her there had to be an entranceway. Taking a deep breath, she twisted onto her left hip, arms flailing to find purchase to heave herself into a standing position. Not for the first time in her life, she cursed her heavy skirts, entangling her legs. If she could at least stand . . . She pushed herself up on her right elbow, wrestling aside her skirts with an impatient hand. The fabric tore, the sound muffled in the darkness. The white-hot pain no longer mattered, nor did the bile flooding her throat. Gathering her legs beneath her, she pushed herself up, swaying like a mad marionette without the security of strings.

She held her breath. The silence was complete. Arms outstretched, her hands clutched at air. No wall. Nothing to lean on. Just one small step, one after the other, and she would encounter a wall, a door, something. She bit back a silent plea. Hadn't Meredith taught them long ago about the uselessness of prayer?

Suddenly, her palms were halted by the sensation of solid muscle. Instinctively, she stopped, convinced that she was losing her mind. She felt the barely perceptible rise and fall of a chest beneath her opened palms.

Where there had been only black, there was a shower of stars in front of her eyes and a humming in her head. She saw him, without the benefit of light or the quick trace of her fingers, behind her unseeing eyes.

She took a step back in the darkness away from the man who wanted her dead.

Chapter 2

"Who are you?" Julia asked.

He went by many names in many languages, one more profane than the next, and every last one deserved. He listened to her staccato breaths, and breathed in the faint scent of her perspiration and floral toilet water mingling with her panic. The darkness suited him perfectly. He found daylight generally unhelpful in such endeavors.

He didn't answer her question. "Unfortunate, your outburst last evening. There was little choice but to place you here, where you wouldn't attract undue attention." The outrageousness of his statement rang in the enclosed space. He knew the power of fear, that great equalizer. He couldn't see her, but imagined her expression of anger and dread. His ears picked up a hesitation as though she was trying to find words that wouldn't come.

"What did you expect? For me to simply acquiesce, follow you blindly into that den of iniquity? How long have you been in this room, alongside me?" Her voice was halting, with a slight hoarseness to it, as though weakened from disuse.

His ear, trained to exotic languages, detected the faint tremor. He remembered her eyes from the night before, wide and shadowed under the brim of a spectacularly ugly bonnet. "It's of no importance," he said finally, feeling her balled fists leave his chest.

"To you."

He shrugged his shoulders, well aware that she couldn't see but surprised by the spirit of her rejoinder. She was disoriented, a good thing. He knew the feeling, having once spent three days in complete darkness in the caves of Pashtun after running afoul of a caravan and a sheik who had misinterpreted his interest in the sheik's cargo. Miss Woolcott, he'd wager, was not seasoned in quite the same way, despite her momentary bravado.

He had been expecting a spinster, redolent of moth balls and camphor oil, a type with which, despite his travels, he'd had mercifully scant experience. "I believe we're well beyond niceties such as formal introductions," he said. He'd always felt a certain tedium when it came to women of his own class, who, for the most part, believed the world extended no further than the Thames. But then again, he should probably be grateful. Thus far Miss Woolcott had substituted a surprising penchant for violence for the more predictable histrionics. The footman had not emerged unscathed in their scuffle.

"You are entirely too cavalier," she said, sharply. Her voice was uncommonly low with none of the breathlessness so common to young women. "You will have to forgive my earlier behavior," she continued, and he wondered briefly how she was going to explain her surprising attack on the footman. In his experience, Englishwomen dealt with the unwelcome by reaching for the smelling salts rather than the pointed end of a letter opener. "I'd been led to believe that I was to meet with Sir Simon Wadsworth, to take photographs of his estate, his gardens. Instead, I find myself here." As far as she was concerned, she might have found herself in the steppes of Russia instead of a windowless, cork-lined room in the English countryside.

He took a step toward her, knowing the impact enforced proximity carried. He didn't have to touch her, not yet, at least.

She did not back away. Bolder than she had any right to be, she continued undaunted. "There was obviously some mistake." She was dissembling but it was of little import in the grander scheme of things. "I wish you to clarify this situation or at the very least offer an apology. A case of mistaken identity, perhaps?"

His silence was worse than any answer.

It must cause her some pain, he acknowledged impartially, the gash in her leg. Unfortunate, that injury, but she had struggled more than anyone had anticipated, regrettably attracting the attention of the overzealous footman. He couldn't really fault the man when she'd seized the letter opener in a pitiable attempt at self-defense. Entirely unexpected.

Her voice shook. "You're clearly unwilling to provide me with answers."

He smiled in the dark.

Her skirts rustled, as though she was drawing herself up straight. The small movement made her wince. "I've spent the last I don't know how many hours in this suffocating room. All I can recollect is receiving Sir Wadsworth's commission, making arrangements to travel to his country estate, arriving and then—" She broke off mid-sentence.

"And then?"

She let out a hiss of breath. "I refuse to put into words what I saw."

"So you do remember. Fortunately, I *can* put it into words, if you feel it beneath you."

More silence, although her breathing had accelerated.

"I take it you're appalled, Miss Woolcott." He could just picture the thinning of her lips, the tensing of her shoulders. In general, Englishwomen were willfully ignorant of nature and its carnal imperatives. He, however, was not discomfited in the least, with the tenor of that discussion.

"I should like to leave this place."

"I'm certain you would. And to have your injury seen to."

No tears. No importuning. Interesting. Miss Woolcott appeared to have been hiding a spine under all the hectares of gray wool, not to mention some spirit under that singularly heavy bonnet that had shielded her face from his eyes. For some reason, he remembered the feel of her thin shoulders, like bird bones, beneath his hands.

"Where is my photographic apparatus? It is of great value to me." Her tone had taken on the impatience of a stern governess.

He'd rather face a stampede of wildebeests. And had, as a matter of fact, not so long ago on the shores of Lake Tanganyika.

The heap of chests, bandboxes, and her camera, like a giant spider on three legs, had been swept from the main hall, along with its owner. "It is secure." *Although you are not. Far from it,* he wanted to add.

"As though I should believe you." She paused in the darkness. "If you refuse to give me answers, I should like to leave now," she repeated, as though to a child reluctant to give up his toy. Her low voice vibrated with suppressed fear.

"My apologies." He didn't attempt to keep the sarcasm from his voice, nor his desire to shock. It had been some time since he'd had direct contact with the rarified, hot-house type of well-bred Englishwoman. If he listened carefully, he could hear the pulse of narrow-mindedness throbbing. "I am clearly remiss in my duties. Therefore, you may like to know this room where you have spent the last five hours was constructed by the great grandfather of our present host, Sir Wadsworth, who, when not disporting himself at debauched masked balls over which he presided with salacious enthusiasm, spent time here. History tells us the illustrious Lord Edgar Wadsworth provided the most exacting specifications for this project. He preferred to partake of his pleasures in sound-proofed surroundings. One can only speculate as to why."

Her breathing stilled. He wondered whether she was a virgin. It would make things somewhat more difficult.

She digested his statements before adding a challenge of her own. "Before setting out on my journey, I made some of my own inquiries, learning of the estate's history. I did not believe the present Sir Wadsworth shares in his ancestor's unfortunate proclivities. Clearly, I was mistaken," she said tightly, reluctant to refer more specifically to what she had seen the previous evening. "As a result, I should still like to leave. Now," she repeated.

He crossed his arms over his chest. "If we leave, you will go quietly? The injury you sustained could have been far worse."

"As though that would have mattered."

"Actually, it does matter. I'm to keep you in good health, for the next day or so."

She approached him in the darkness. It took courage, he conceded. Her soft breath fanned his throat where the top two fastenings of his shirt lay open. He was surprised to find his body tightening in response to the scent of lavender floral water.

"And what comes afterwards?" There was pain in her voice, a strangled quality that spoke not just of her injury and incarceration but of something else.

"Why make the situation more difficult for yourself, Miss Woolcott? Oftentimes, knowledge can be distressing." What a liar he was—knowledge was everything. Knowledge was power.

He sensed a renewed tension in the confining space as Miss Woolcott began facing the implications of what she'd seen upon her arrival at Wadsworth's estate. As far as he was concerned, not much had changed since he'd left England five years earlier. The lives of the aristocracy were still devoted to, in no particular order, hunting, whoring, and billiards. From his vantage point, the middle-aged rutting—a confirmed group sport among the male upper classes—was as ingrained as cannibalism in pigmy tribes or riding to hounds among the gentry.

The best he could hope for, when the Wadsworth debauchery concluded, was not to be forever haunted by the specter of sagging jowls, swollen paunches, and worse, bent over their pleasurable labors. He surmised that the female guests were harvested from the countryside surrounding Wadsworth's Eccles House or let from the demi-mondaine or the theater.

Miss Woolcott had yet to back away from him. "I am assuming," she said, "or rather hoping, that this was all a misunderstanding. That Sir Wadsworth had no intention of inviting me to his"—she paused—"*soiree* and that, in my confusion and shock, I panicked and, as it turns out, unreasonably struck out at a footman before I could think . . . before I knew. . . ." She trailed off, unable to convince herself to continue.

He made a low sound in the back of his throat. "Whatever gives you most comfort, Miss Woolcott. It doesn't truly signify. You're here now."

"Why?" That one word whispered through the dark.

"I don't know why." It was a lie and it was the truth. They both knew it.

The dark was strangely liberating for Julia. "I find that difficult to believe. Your tone leads me to surmise that you're not the type of man who does anything on a mere whim. Why not simply put me in a carriage and allow me to return to London?" She was standing so close to him, her skirts brushing his knees, that he could simply encircle her neck with his hands and end it there, if it were not for his overly precise instructions and the convincing tableau he was to construct.

He laughed, an incongruous shot in the dark. "You're in no position to inquire, Miss Woolcott."

"I'd hazard a guess that being one step away from certain death entitles one to ask questions, sir."

"Certain death? That's a trifle melodramatic." Only it wasn't.

"Is it?"

"You're convinced that someone wants you dead. Now why is that?" Miss Woolcott knew far more than she was willing to disclose.

"You can hardly expect me to believe Sir Wadsworth invited me to join in . . . in his . . . peculiar . . . gathering."

He decided to continue the game. "Why is that so improbable?"

Heat emanated from her, from the masses of fabric, crinolines, and whalebone that encircled her body. She could be developing a fever, courtesy of the wound no doubt beginning to suppurate on her lower leg.

"I am a woman of a certain age and disposition, hardly the sort to participate in . . ."

"Participate in what, precisely?"

"Whatever it is that you must keep me in good health for." She took a step away from him and into the darkness. "Please let's dispense with this unfortunate misunderstanding," she added, suddenly all crispness and efficiency, lying to him and most of all to herself. "I shall tell no one about your involvement, rest assured. After all, I don't even know your name or circumstances."

It would be better to keep her compliant, he decided. The truth would come, right at the end. He closed the space between them and took her arm. She flinched away from him. "Let's have a look at the cut on your leg, shall we, before we decide upon anything else."

He pulled her none too gently behind him, his hand reflexively finding the seam in the wall a few feet before them. Sliding his fingers beneath the hidden hinge, he felt the clasp release. The door swung open, the soft light of dusk as harsh as the noon sun after an eclipse.

He watched Julia Woolcott turn her face to the light pouring through the casement windows, her eyes squinting against the assault, and he wondered suddenly how he could have ever considered her plain. Her violet eyes were set wide and tilted between arced brows. She had a straight, assertive nose, a subtly clefted chin, and a mouth too wide for true beauty. Her features communicated a wary vulnerability and an unsettling intelligence. The mahogany hair that had been strictly scraped into a low chignon fell loose.

She tried not to favor her leg but he could see the spasms of pain tighten her features. Soon, the pain would be gone, he silently promised her.

"And now?" she asked, not bothering to struggle from his grip.

There was no answer that she would want to hear. He knew she remembered what she'd attempted to forget—the women and the men in the glittering salon with its unforgiving chandeliers illuminating every dark corner of lust and licentiousness. It was important she be seen that evening, at one of Wadsworth's infamous country-house weekends, that there be witnesses to her outrageous behavior as a more than willing participant.

A spiral staircase waited at the end of the hallway, leading to a suite of rooms, a copper tub, appropriate clothing. He would ensure that her wound was taken care of, that she was costumed and prepared in a few hours' time. There would be no more mistakes. No more struggles.

He would see to it himself.

Julia wished the staircase would go on forever, despite the jolts of fire at every step she took. She watched the broad shoulders looming before her, leading the way to what she was certain would be her doom. A large hand still spanned her arm, and she imagined those fingers could choke the life from the most powerful of men. Despite his voice and disengaged manner, she sensed a heavy undercurrent. His size alone prompted claws of fear to tear at her belly.

A pulse pounded in the back of Julia's eyes as she wondered what her sister would make of her present predicament. *You're ever so bookish, Jules. Put down your spectacles and come riding with me!* Rowena, just a fortnight ago, exhorted Julia to rouse herself from her ink-stained studies. How many governesses had paled under the onslaught of that headstrong willfulness?

What Julia would do to have her small, tightly constrained world returned to her. A life punctuated by visits to the vicarage or closely chaperoned outings to London with their aunt. She was the careful, patient, older sister who spent most of her time attending to detail, on the printed page or on her copper plates. In this, at least, she had some small advantage.

Julia's eyes swept over the broad back and the arrogant tilt of the head in front of her. Dressed simply in trousers and a white shirt, he was not what he seemed: a wayward rogue of Sir Wadsworth's unsavory circle. She recognized the man was of another sort of Englishman, with his aggressive jaw, the slight hook of his nose, and the gray eyes whose intensity was unseemly. Built like a fortress but with the sleek movements of someone half his size, he was no ordinary man subject to a quotidian world.

That he was sent by Montagu Faron was a certainty. The name soured on her tongue. Unbidden, Meredith's alarms rang in her head.

The man stopped, on the landing, and she nearly tripped on her skirts and catapulted into his broad back. She froze and moved as far away as his grip would allow. She was gazing up at an enormous hall, two storeys high, with vast oriel windows facing gardens on both sides. Four colossal fireplaces framed priceless chairs and banquettes, richly panniered in dark red velvet. It was the room she had glimpsed the evening before. Luscious silk damask curtains, lined in bronze and white brocade stripes, had been tied back with huge silk tassels to better frame entangled limbs and flashes of skin. It was empty but she sensed they were far from alone.

Walking down corridors she realized the house was ostentatious, even by the standards to which she was accustomed at Montfort.

Moments later, after being abruptly left alone by her captor, she surveyed the vastness of a room dominated by a raised four-poster bed. He had left her there without a word, and she reveled in the luxury of being alone and unobserved. A fire roared in the corner in front of which a mobcapped maid filled a copper tub with water. Not meeting Julia's eyes, she carefully placed folded linens on the rosewood vanity table. The young woman looked vaguely familiar and Julia wondered whether she had glimpsed her freckled countenance in the debauched scene the evening before. Dismissing the thought as unproductive and heeding the need to collect herself, she watched the maid's plump backside retreat from the room and then quickly divested herself of her soiled clothes, ripping at the stays pinching her ribcage, struggling out of her sorely used chemise. Layer after layer was removed and thrown in a heap, until she stood in her plain white cotton shift and silk stockings.

Leaning on the edge of the tub, she carefully peeled down her stockings, wincing as the gossamer fabric clung to the crusted gash on her calf. She shuddered at the memory, at her loss of control, at the recollection of lost hours in that hideous, cork-lined room. Where had it come from, that feral panic, so unlike her customary calm demeanor?

She lingered but briefly in the fresh, warm water, as she had no desire to be interrupted by the man she was convinced had been sent by Faron. She would be able to think more clearly when she'd bathed and had something to eat. Swallowing more nervousness, she wondered why the strange man, as she now called him, would leave her to her toilette for so long. Darkness would come soon, she saw by the fading light spilling through the tall, mullioned windows. The fire had made the room overly warm and she longed to throw the windows open wide but was certain they were locked.

She dried herself quickly and took up the fresh muslin shift the maid had left on the four-poster bed. Her leg began to throb again, weeping a thin stream of blood, as the shift dropped over her head and skirted her legs. Fresh weariness invaded each and every muscle of her body. Lowering herself to the edge of the bed, she smoothed a palm over the cool sheets. Perhaps she would allow herself just a moment to close her eyes and sort out the madness of the last twenty-four hours.

None of it made any sense. The pulse continued to pound behind her eyes like a hammer on a blacksmith's anvil. Even if he were connected with Montagu Faron, why would Sir Wadsworth invite her to a sordid country-house weekend? Meredith had been frantic with worry at the invitation, urging Julia to ignore the summons with its elaborate script and aristocratic seal. Questions crawled into every corner of her mind, forming a thick web of confusion. And fear. Pulling the feather pillow over her head, Julia buried her face, and her uncertainties, in the softness.

When she opened her eyes again, it was dusk, the air thick, heavy, and eerily still. For a moment, she thought she was back in that horrid place, Sir Wadsworth's perverse chamber. She wasn't certain what had awakened her. She lifted a hand to sweep aside the tangle of her hair, then froze.

She surged upright, fists twisting into the sheets, unwelcome pain shooting through her calf. "What are you doing?" she asked, knowing very well whom she was watching—certainly not a serving maid, but *him,* dark hair falling across his brow, as he finished winding a clean linen bandage around her bare calf. "How dare you!" She tried a fresh assault while attempting to pull her leg beneath the counterpane, despite the numbing pain.

He ignored her and leaned forward to strike flint to steel and light the bedside lamp. In the dim glow, his features were drawn, pulled taut across his cheekbones and shadowed by a day's growth of black stubble. "I dared," he said, "in order to keep the wound clean. It didn't require stitching. Consider yourself fortunate."

In the lamplight his eyes were brilliant, and she could see they were an unusual shade, more gray than green, but not decisively either color. They were deeply set in a long face punctuated by a wide, spare jaw. Her eyes swept closed when she again felt the gentle pressure of his fingers on her leg, where a pulse throbbed fiercely and with rhythmic intensity. Not exactly in pain but something else. She couldn't stop time by closing her eyes so she stared at the opening of his shirt, the same one he'd worn earlier. She fought the urge to leap from the bed and seek haven in the farthest corner of the room. She was a woman nearing her third decade, educated better than most men, but nothing had prepared Julia for this.

She was all but naked and alone with a man for the first time in her life. She bit her lower lip to halt her traitorous thoughts and to keep from crying aloud. The last thing she wanted to admit to herself was what she'd always known. Her life with Meredith had been a prison, albeit a gold-plated one, built to keep evil out, to contain a malevolence that threatened, however subtly, every waking hour. It had required a watchfulness as unrelenting as the queen's royal guard. Against all good judgment and dire warnings, Julia had forced her way out, providing the crumb on the trail that had allowed the man—and Faron—to find them.

"Sir Wadsworth's invitation was a ruse, wasn't it?" she blurted out. Heat swept up her neck and flooded her cheeks.

He released her leg, placed it back under the sheet with cool efficiency, and settled into a chair by the bed with a confidence that Julia found appalling. "You are searching for answers, but you will find none, Miss Woolcott. You'll discover I'm a man of few words, a predilection which, trust me, works in your favor. Now, would you like something to eat?" he asked, gesturing to a tray at the foot of the bed.

She would get little from him, that was clear. She tamped down her anger with herself by pretending to eat, picking at the morsels, eyes lowered to her plate of chicken, cheese, and bread. The situation was untenable. Impossible. Rage seeped into her consciousness against the backdrop of guilt and self-recrimination. She would simply not allow it. She chewed mechanically, the food in her mouth tasteless.

He was quiet for the moment, watching her profile, watching her eat. Lamplight cast half his face in shadow.

Suddenly, she wanted to lash out. "Would you at least tell me your name?" she demanded when she could stand it no longer, lifting her eyes to his. "It doesn't have to be real—I would not even expect it to be."

She was pretending to brush the crumbs away from her lap and into her cupped hand when he abruptly stood. She jerked her head up to see him move to the fireplace mantle and pour two glasses of wine from an opened bottle. Because she was too anxious to keep her thoughts from straying, she found herself distracted by the way his shoulders moved beneath his shirt, and by the stretch of his back narrowing to his waist in perfect proportion to his long, muscular legs.

With an impartiality that surprised her, she conceded that her captor was a beautiful man. Her eyes, so accustomed to peering through a lens, were startled by reality. Her mind raced ahead, searching for something of use. He moved with an expansiveness that was unfamiliar to her, fluid but powerful, as though more accustomed to the outdoors than confinement in drawing rooms and parlors. His tones were educated and well modulated but told her little more than that he was not from the lower classes.

He turned toward her, placing a glass on the tray. "Drink your fill. You appear as though you need it."

Her fork clattered against her plate, her nerves stretched taut. "Need it for what, sir? You prevaricate, and your insinuations are becoming tiresome. Name or no name, there is little you can do to convince me of this charade involving Sir Wadsworth. It's simply preposterous, your keeping me here against my will."

He inclined his head a fraction of an inch, fixing those pale gray eyes upon her. "Alexander," he said.

At last, like a wretched bone thrown to a dog. Surname or Christian name, it probably didn't matter.

"You're the one making insinuations," he said softly, watching her carefully.

She pushed aside the tray, leaving the wine untouched. Her

fingers moved unsteadily to the high neck of her shift. "I have little enough information. While you—"

"Really?" His tone stilled her fingers on an ivory button.

"You know my name," she snapped, thinking of the invitation that had arrived at Montfort. "Of that, at least, I'm certain."

He arched a brow. "Miss Julia Woolcott, amateur botanist, photographer, and recently published authoress of a monograph entitled *Flowers in Shadows: A Botanical Journey.*"

Julia could not keep herself from flushing. She was inordinately proud of her work. It was unseemly, indeed. Had she been able to hold her pride in check, she would not be there, at that moment, with that man. She tamped down her frustration. "A mere trifle, as you are most likely aware. There are possibly hundreds of women devoted to this respectable pastime. I am someone of no rank or importance. A country mouse."

An unidentifiable expression crossed his face as he leaned forward to clasp the back of the chair. She found herself unaccountably staring at his hands, large and long fingered. "Ah yes," he said, the corners of his mouth twitching. "Botany is an acceptable womanly pursuit that fits within a woman's sanctioned role as helpmeet of man, educator of children. Botany poses no danger of inflaming the imagination, unlike, shall we say, a radically new creation like photography."

Julia would curse the moment of weakness later, but she couldn't deny the pull of curiosity. "And what do you know of it? I believe that dabbling in the fine arts is generally acceptable among ladies of leisure," she countered. He wore no rings and carried no timepiece, she noted, before returning her eyes to his.

"Daguerreotypy requires a special knowledge of chemistry and a certain manual dexterity, hardly ladylike accomplishments."

That had not stopped any number of women from completing outstanding series of photograms of plant specimens. "And what of it?" She sat up higher in the bed, pulling the sheet closer around her shoulders. "This discussion is not helpful in the least. It brings us no closer to resolving this situation."

He smiled slightly.

More impatient than ever, she pressed on. "If it's money you want in exchange for my freedom, I can arrange—"

His gray eyes widened speculatively, the pupils flared.

Julia froze. Dread filled her chest. Trying to keep calm, she studied the man the way she would any of her projects, placing him in an imaginary frame, looking for useful details, but finding none.

"You should not have changed the subject," he said, his tone even. "There is no possibility of negotiation." His gaze stripped away every last layer of reserve she possessed. "It's for your own good," he said softly.

The lamp glowed low, throwing his solid, hard body into shadowed relief on the wall. Unwillingly, she inhaled his scent of smoke, forest, and desert. An exotic, contradictory combination and far outside her ken. Who was this man sent by Montagu Faron?

Julia swallowed the thickness that welled unexpectedly in her throat. Memories of a childhood spent in blissful but willful ignorance, cocooned in the warmth of Montfort, flooded over her. She blinked rapidly at the pain in her heart, at the sense of sudden, poignant loss. At that moment, it seemed the entirety of her life was a palimpsest, fragile truths built upon layers of secrets and lies.

Meredith's warnings rang in Julia's ears. Meredith had never before spoken directly of her past, or of the shadow that Montagu Faron had cast over her life. It was the unholy power of secrets—what was left unsaid.

Julia had made a fatal error in ignoring the threats. But Faron would get no closer to her aunt or her sister despite her own lack of judgement, her uncharacteristic impetuousness.

Staring into the shadowy depths of the room, Julia had never been surer of anything in her life. Meredith, who had given her shelter, given her back her life, was under threat of this man. Faron. Her gaze rested on the bank of windows, each and every one surely locked against her, and she came to a decision.

"I shall do it," she said abruptly, bracing her back against the pillows, bracing herself for battle. "I shall attend this debauchery." Her words shattered the silence like stones dropped into a pool.

Alexander's eyes narrowed, his gaze holding hers. "Why the sudden change of heart? It's difficult to believe you're suddenly keen to accept Wadsworth's invitation."

"My motivation should be of no interest to you." She was tired of hiding—she, her sister, and her aunt so fearful of stepping out into the world. There was always a threat, something, someone—Faron—holding them back. She remembered the argument with Meredith, her aunt's insistence that publication of her photographs would lead to unwanted attention. Guilt and then a fierce protectiveness flooded Julia's heart.

"Fair enough," he said, finally looking down at her with a cynicism that was galling. He didn't trust her.

Laughable, given the situation, she thought, tensing her shoulders. As though she could trust herself or even begin to explain her actions. Ignoring Meredith's warnings. Accepting Wadsworth's invitation. Launching herself at the footman. It was all a form of madness.

She shook her head silently and slanted a look at her adversary, his hands resting on the back of the chair. She expected him to reach for her at any moment. Nothing about him suggested inaction.

"At least we can dispense with force," he said with a trace of a smile in his voice. "I'm much relieved."

"I'm sure you are," she said, suddenly suspicious. She eyed the tray at the foot of the bed. "I take it the wine was not laced with opiates?" Despite the mockery in her tone, her stomach tightened further.

"Entirely unnecessary, as it turns out," he said lightly, straightening away from the chair. She noticed again how tall, how broad he was. That this Alexander was anyone's lackey, even a man as powerful as Faron, was preposterous.

She stared at him, her suspicions lending her courage. "So what will it be? What is expected of me?" She forced out the words, pulling the sheet over her shoulders. Her mind cringed at what was in store for her. "Attend a few hours of this wretched evening, feigning enjoyment?"

"You may surprise yourself," he said, appearing unmoved, as far from mortification as the sky was wide. He was utterly at ease in the outrageous, dangerous situation.

Blood drained from her cheeks. "I'm not entirely the country mouse you take me for, sir. I have heard of this unfortunate taste for licentiousness among the upper classes."

"Truly? I'm amazed."

Unreasonably irritated, she said, "I have read de Sade, Laclos and the like. My aunt saw to it that my sister and I received a thorough and comprehensive education. She does not believe women should be kept in ignorance of the world."

"Your credentials are impressive."

"You would mock me." She wished she could order him to quit the room. As though that would do a whit of good. "I am simply well read," she said, hating the pinched tone of her voice.

"Clearly," he replied, and miraculously retreated from the massive bed. He strolled toward the windows hung with heavy damask curtains, casting a quick glance to the courtyard below. When he looked up again, he said, "If you permit me to say it, you are an unusual woman, Miss Woolcott. Shy and retiring on the one hand and yet ready to take up a letter opener upon the slightest provocation."

"Provocation? I should say in self-defense."

"You appear to be a creature of extremes, Miss Woolcott. You have just assured me of your familiarity with what many would deem salacious texts, yet you cringe like an untried maiden at the specter of carnal behavior."

Carnal behavior. The room might as well be spinning out of control. Taking a deep breath, Julia schooled her features into passivity. She prided herself on her breadth of knowledge. "I am, of course, familiar with Ovid and Catullus." She had the uncomfortable sense that he meant to test her.

His glance was assessing. "One cannot hope to learn everything from books or from the Western canon of knowledge. We seldom think to include the knowledge and wisdom of the East."

Needing to defend her scholarship, she sat up straighter, ignoring the numbness in her leg. "Of which you have some small knowledge, I am persuaded to believe?"

"Yes, some small knowledge." He shoved both hands into the pockets of his trousers and looked at her expectantly. For one moment, she believed she'd seen a glimpse of something personal in his eyes.

She gave an unladylike puff of derision. "Here we sit discussing the merits of ancient texts whilst Sir Wadsworth's evening unfolds below. I assure you, if you're at all concerned, I shan't dissolve into vapors at the first glimpse of"— she broke off awkwardly at the sight of his arced brow—"at the first sight of a well-turned ankle," she concluded. "I am hoping to make short work of the evening and then make a hasty retreat. I take it you're to be my escort."

"Something like that."

Julia could not trust herself to meet his eyes. Instead, she glanced at the ornate ormolu clock on the fireplace mantel. "Let's be done with it, then, sir," she ground out. "Send me a serving maid and the clothes you promised and give me twenty minutes more."

It was the only way. To become the hunter and not the hunted.

She wrenched her eyes back to the window. Not for the

first time, she was aware of an acute need to watch him, to study his face, the gray eyes that gave nothing away, his preternatural calm. This lackey of Faron's required her unadulterated attention.

He was her link to Montagu Faron, her escort to his underworld.

Chapter 3

"**H**e sleeps at last."

The man known only as Sebastian nodded. He was long and angular, with a high, domed forehead and narrow shoulders. "This episode was not as acute as a fortnight ago," he said more to himself than anyone else in the room.

They both knew to what he referred. A detritus of broken glass and crockery crunched underfoot, the aroma of a spilled astringent pinching their nostrils. As for the rest, little enough damage had been done. Two rectangular tables lined the room, topped by rows of microscopes, most of which were double-barrelled. Each instrument had a lamp by its side, the beam adjusted so as to illuminate a prepared specimen. Minute and beautiful shells, dredged up from a sea bottom of unfathomable depths, glistened like jewels in their scientific settings. Glass cases were mounted on the walls, from floor to ceiling, replete with intricately constructed creatures, some vegetable, some animal, some dyed with carmine to better display their transparent bodies.

"It was not such a struggle this time," said Giles Lowther, the larger of the two men. He crossed his arms over his barrel chest. His booted foot nudged a broken beaker aside. Subduing Montagu Faron was never an easy task, a sobering reminder that twenty years earlier one of the world's finest minds had been destroyed. Whether there were lingering outward injuries was difficult to determine, as Faron was never without his leather mask, shielding the world from the facial tremors that overtook him with unexpected ferocity. For decades, no one had seen his face.

Sebastian grimaced, for a moment looking away from the chaos inside to the ordered park outside, which had been designed by one of Louis XIV's esteemed landscapers. "I shall have the laboratory set to rights in no time," he said, making a swift accounting of the disarray with an abrupt glance. "Difficult to understand, this mania. He was perfectly lucid just this morning." They both knew that the voices in Montagu Faron's head clamored for his attention, the crashing of cymbals destroying the former orderly music of his mind. In the past, primitive societies would have said the voices came from God or the Devil, but as acolytes of a great man of science and reason, they both knew differently.

"Perhaps it was the daguerreotype in the library. An all too potent reminder," said Lowther.

"Since this business began, he has been most savagely beset by his demons." Sebastian lowered his head to examine a flake of coal on the floor, laboriously filed down with sandpaper until it had become as thin and transparent as a sheet of notepaper. He straightened, putting a bony hand at the base of his spine. "You saw to it that Strathmore received the proper directives?"

Lowther nodded. "To the letter."

Sebastian leaned his hip on the table at his side. He flicked a glance over a small dish at his elbow displaying a frog, its foot spread out and pinned to show the circulation of its blood. He pursed his lips in contemplation of the amphibian. "I fear this is simply the beginning. Faron will never be satisfied. He is manifesting all the signs of morbid obsession, I'm afraid."

"And we're to do his bidding, as always. Although I don't quite understand Strathmore's involvement."

Sebastian continued addressing the moribund frog in its distressed state. "You and I both. What I do know is that Faron has been following Strathmore's progress these years past with feverish intensity. As we both realize, that intensity is prompted by envy, curiosity and, quite possibly, a desire to punish."

Alexander Francis Strathmore was known as England's preeminent adventurer and explorer, conversant in at least nine eastern languages, discoverer of Lake Tanganyika in Africa, chronicler of exotic mountain ranges and rushing rivers, a man with a reputation for being both fearless and relentless in his quest for knowledge.

Everything that Montagu Faron had been and was no longer.

Lowther exhaled sharply. "I begin to understand. However, why would Strathmore allow himself to become involved in these desperate machinations? The man has everything he could possibly desire."

Sebastian flicked a finger over the frog dismissively. "You believe so, do you, Lowther? Then you have not learned as much as I from Faron." He added abruptly, "Think on it. Clearly Faron has something that Strathmore covets."

Lowther held up his arms to indicate the room and its contents. "You are suggesting something of a scientific nature?" he asked.

"Whatever else?" Faron was wealthy beyond belief, damned by a family fortune that gave him unrivaled power and had led him down the darkest of paths. Sebastian leaned away from the table with its scientific offerings that many believed blasphemed the work of God. "What we have here is a Faustian dilemma," he continued, "wherein a man will sell his soul to the very devil to gain the knowledge he craves."

"What knowledge are you suggesting?"

"I'm suggesting that Strathmore knows Faron has the original Ptolemy maps."

"I have yet to set eyes on Ptolemy's *Geography,*" said Lowther, refering to the ancient Greek astronomer and author of an eight volume treatise on physics, mathematics, optics, and geography. Ptolemy was renowned for having created a world map one hundred and fifty years after the birth of Christ, but it was believed that none of his maps had survived.

Sebastian knew otherwise. "The volume exists, believe me, including the world map." Scholars in the fifteenth century had recreated Ptolemy's map using the instructions in his work which explained how to project a sphere onto a flat piece of paper using a system of gridlines. "And it is not a replication but the original," he emphasized.

"The original? How is that possible and how did Faron come by it?"

"Who knows? But we can be certain Strathmore wants it. He wants it enough to do anything to get it. From what Faron has told me, Ptolemy compiled his geography of Africa based on the writings of Marinus of Tyre who recorded the Greek trader Diogenes's travels over land from Tanzania. In it he described two great lakes and a snowy range of mountains from which the Nile, purportedly, draws its source. He also made the first recorded rendering of the Mountains of the Moon."

His heavy brow furrowed, Lowther said, "Understandably irresistible to a man like Strathmore. But the question remains—why has Faron taken such an interest in Strathmore, baiting him with promises of the map?"

"He has his reasons. He always does," said Sebastian, who had first heard of Faron while studying at the Sorbonne in Paris. "And he requires someone without scruples who will conclude this situation with the Woolcotts."

"A further mystery—this Woolcott situation. Why a man with the vision of Faron occupies himself with such seemingly petty concerns, stemming from some perceived injustice perpetrated years ago—although it is said that his injuries stem from—"

Sebastian interrupted. "As I said earlier, Faron does nothing without purpose." Lowther was English and could not begin to understand the complex mind of his French master.

"If I might ask," began Lowther carefully, "does this matter involve Faron's . . ." He searched delicately for the right word.

"Injury?" supplied Sebastian. Without waiting for Lowther's nod, he continued. "Suffice it to say, your tracking down the Woolcotts at Montfort was much appreciated. Faron has been at a loss for many years, unable to determine their whereabouts."

Lowther did not fail to notice that Sebastian had not answered his initial question. "Faron has demanded that Strathmore furnish proof of Julia Woolcott's death. Clearly, he is serious about the matter."

"Without doubt," agreed Sebastian tersely. "At least when he is lucid, Faron knows the measure of a man." He paused deliberately. "You may count on it—Strathmore will not disappoint."

Alexander Francis Strathmore, the younger son of the Earl of Dunedin, gave Julia Woolcott an hour to prepare.

Procrastination was not in his repertoire but for some reason he preferred to ignore the evidence of the entertainment underway in Wadsworth's opulent halls below. The subdued hum of crystal and china hung in the air, a backdrop to the troop of silent servile feet making their way through polished hallways. Dinner had been served unfashionably early, to ensure plenty of time for the main course the assembled guests were slavering for.

Not that Strathmore gave a damn. Whatever Wadsworth had planned would hardly be shocking to a man of his experience. Boredom was the more likely enemy. He loosened the unfamiliar tightness of his cravat, shot his cuffs, and hovered in front of the heavy oak door, behind which Julia Woolcott stood prepared. Bloody hell, it was like serving up the proverbial sacrificial lamb to the angry gods. Embarrassingly easy.

Worldly, Miss Woolcott was not, despite her self-proclaimed bookishness. Damned irritating, that. He'd never liked bluestockings or whatever they called women who spent more time with their heads in dusty volumes than was wise. That was it—*on the shelf.* He wondered whether the term was still in use. It had been some time since he'd observed his own culture, whereas he could discourse at length on the sexual practices in Somalia, the politics of the Sufi order, or the geologic formations underlying the Nile.

Strathmore paused again, crossing his arms across his chest, straining the superfine of his evening coat. What the hell was going on with him? He'd made a life out of being a rakehell, exploiting his unhealthy curiosity and unsettling ability to learn exotic languages and dialects, to scale mountains and cross deserts, to absorb more by living in a place for one month than others would perceive in years. He'd been summarily exiled from Oxford and dishonorably discharged from the East India Company. He was more at home on an expedition disguised as an Afghani physician than at a country house weekend, for God's sake, saddled with a spinster with nerves as thin as parchment.

Yet something nagged at him. Why had Faron chosen Julia Woolcott? There had to be a reason, though he was damned if he knew. Or if it even mattered. Miss Woolcott was a small price to pay. He allowed images of staggering mountains, cobalt rivers, and sultans' palaces to shimmer in his mind's eye, effectively overriding any lingering and inconvenient spasms of conscience.

He gave the door a sharp knock and, not waiting for a response, pushed it open. He took two steps, then stopped. Julia did the same, reaching blindly for her discarded nightshift, crumpled at the foot of the bed. But Strathmore had already received an eyeful, taking in the startling length of slender white thighs, delicately turned calves, as well as the full, lower curve of her buttocks. Her unbound hair fell like a shimmering curtain into a tumble that reached clear to her hips. Arms as slender as reeds clutched the nightshift to her breasts. Her violet eyes blazed beneath raised brows.

It was then he knew that he would not kill her. The realization was as blinding as the sun at high noon in the Kalahari desert.

"This," she seethed, gesturing violently from her neck to her hips, "is impossible!"

He knew exactly to what she was referring. The midnight blue silk of her gown, if one could call it that, fell in a diaphanous array around what was a totally and unexpectedly lush female form. The acres of gray wool and the muslin shift of the night before had done little justice to the long slender legs and narrow waist now displayed to his eyes. Desire, as unexpected as an oasis in a wasteland, shot through him.

Julia's eyes widened and her lips emitted deep gusts of outrage. "No shift, no petticoats, not even a corset," she hissed at him, turning and affording him a magnificent view of her backside. He had thought her too thin, and she was, except where she wasn't.

He took a moment to consider. True, he hadn't had sexual relations since his return to England but celibacy didn't trouble him, at least not since his time in a monastery in Tibet, a transformative experience during which his mind had been trained to rein in an unruly body. So what was it, precisely, that caused him to hesitate?

His eyes slid up her body to her elegant face, which save for the generous mouth, had hardly hinted at such erotic beauty. She eyed him expectantly over one pale, exposed shoulder.

"That's the idea," he said, making his voice pleasant. "A certain dishevelment is what's required. Although I can absolve myself from guilt—I had no hand in choosing your garments."

"Then who did?" Her reproachful expression indicated her notice that he was thoroughly clothed.

He felt the pull of his black evening coat across his shoulders—a trifle too small. Since he was no longer accustomed to full evening regalia his London valet had done his best to outfit Strathmore in a short time.

For some reason he found himself staring at Julia Woolcott's lush full mouth, as he stood stiffly, legs braced wide and thighs tensed, just inside the door. Incapable of moving and feeling like an intruder was not at all what he'd intended. He had never claimed to be a gentleman and had long ago made peace with the hypercritical and largely illogical societal standards of his class. It could not explain why he was suddenly undone by the outraged histrionics of a nervous female who should have at least five children and was instead staring at him as though he was the very devil. Which he was, in fact.

Faron. The name pulsed silently through Strathmore's mind. The assignment was relatively simple for a man who had crossed a desert on foot, had lived for six months with a tribe of Bedouins, and could recite the Lord's Prayer in Sanskrit. More than anyone, Strathmore knew the random nature of life and death. He needed to distill his goal to its essentials. He parsed it out to himself. Ensure that Julia Woolcott met a spectacularly sordid end. Earn Faron's trust and gain entry to his inner circle.

But he would not kill her.

There was no time to examine his motivations. "No doubt Wadsworth's hostess for the evening chose your gown," he said finally. Before she could protest further, he offered her his arm. She looked as enthusiastic as a cat approaching a tub of water.

"The hostess is not his wife, obviously," she said. "I can't be seen in public like this."

"Then you've changed your mind."

She slowly turned to face him, her arms covering her breasts. Her lips met in an unforgiving line. "I didn't say that exactly. What I would require is at least a chemise. My own is soiled and would not fit beneath this garment." He saw the problem—the sheath she was wearing was so tight it wouldn't allow but the finest layer underneath.

In fewer than thirty minutes, it wouldn't matter. Because she would be naked anyway. But Strathmore didn't think it was the right time to apprise her of that eventuality. He recalled that Miss Woolcott could be surprisingly volatile. Keeping her calm and compliant would make his task all the easier. In a fluid motion and before she could dissent, he slipped off his evening jacket and placed it over her shoulders.

It enveloped her instantly and he bit back an expression of regret. He'd enjoyed the sight of those slender legs outlined in silk the color of midnight. He did not want to begin to imagine her breasts. It was a disturbing juxtaposition, the elegance of her face and the sumptuousness of her body.

Startled, Julia clutched the lapels of his jacket.

"Better?"

She nodded but her eyebrows rose cynically. "Of course. I'm feeling much more comfortable like this."

"We can always say you are chilled," he supplied.

She cleared her throat, her slender fingers whitening against the dark superfine of his coat. "Before we depart, perhaps you can enlighten me as to the evening's . . . program."

Perhaps the opiates would have been a better choice, he thought darkly. Instead, he said, "You strike me as an intelligent woman, Miss Woolcott, so surely you must surmise the tenor of the evening, judging from what you saw last evening."

Her chin moved up a fraction. "We shall take dinner with the other guests . . ."

Except that they had already finished with the charade of food. Strathmore guessed they would be deep in their cups and ready for their play to begin. Miss Woolcott's inquiries highlighted his dilemma now that he'd decided he would not kill her. As was his norm, he made a quick decision. "Indeed," he lied crisply.

"Who are these guests, *Alexander,* this august circle of Wadsworth's?" Dwarfed by his jacket, she said his name carefully. Her tone was light but her words flickered with tension, reminding him that he didn't know her and couldn't presume her mood or predict her actions. Hers was an unusual temperament, equal parts volatility and reticence. Why she was important to Faron, or more specifically, why her death was important to Faron, mattered little, he reminded himself. The story, like so many other stories, was ultimately insignificant.

The large four-poster bed with its heaped pillows loomed in the background. Strathmore had already dismissed the idea that Julia Woolcott was the Frenchman's former lover. His instincts were infallible, and the woman had clearly known no man. That she would come to a sordid end disturbed him, and suddenly, he fought an overwhelming urge to quit the opulent room and the baroque plans awaiting Julia Woolcott at his hands.

Her low voice cut through his thoughts. "I have decided my wisest course will be to make the rounds, meet Sir Wadsworth's guests, and then plead a headache as an excuse to bid a quick good night and make a hasty retreat."

He glanced at her sharply, the back of his neck tightening. The ticking of the ormolu clock on the mantle seemed louder. "I shouldn't have thought you interested in the identity of Wadsworth's guests, Miss Woolcott."

"Then you supposed incorrectly," she said stiffly.

How utterly resolute she looked, despite her absolute fragility. He could crush her if he so chose. Swathed in his coat and barefoot, she seemed no older than a child and she exuded a ridiculous vulnerability that set his teeth on edge. It occurred to him she might be foolish enough to search for Faron among Wadsworth's coterie. Why? He said carefully, "As I mentioned earlier, knowledge can be dangerous. At evenings such as this, discretion is highly advisable."

"Discretion? In this instance, isn't that the same thing as looking for a curate among a den of thieves? Since you are so reluctant to divulge the reason for my being here at Eccles House, I have little choice but to find answers on my own."

Her gaze sharpened and he was suddenly beset by an image of her behind the camera's lens. He had, of course, witnessed examples of the craft of daguerreotype, but his experience had not included encounters with women brandishing lenses, shutters, and related paraphernalia. With one hand still on the lapel of his evening coat, she continued to examine him with what he could only call a practiced eye, reflexively coiling her hair into a simple knot at the base of her neck. The woman was not in the least vain, he noted, and recalled his mother, whom he hadn't given a thought in years. Outrageously beautiful, monstrously flighty, and monumentally empty-headed, Lady Alicia Broughton Strathmore had led his father in an evil dance.

Miss Woolcott fastened her hair with a final twist of her free hand, not bothering to look for a mirror. "You are, I take it, exceedingly comfortable with the mores of such events," she said, "but then, of course, why else were you chosen to be my escort?" She huffed away from him, sweeping up a pair of slippers from a cushioned settee. Still clutching the lapels of his coat over her breasts, she slid her narrow feet into first one and then the other shoe.

Why indeed? Strathmore smiled tightly. He was beginning to believe she might prove more valuable to him alive than dead. Perhaps Julia Woolcott would lead him to Faron. The strategy held a strong appeal, suddenly.

"Let's be done with this, shall we, Miss Woolcott?" He proffered his arm, his muscles tensing against the cool of her hand where it rested on the cambric of his evening shirt.

"And all will be well?" She turned her face to his, her skin as finely grained as silk, her wide eyes as shuttered as a camera's lens.

"You have my word," he lied smoothly. And judging by her small smile, they both knew it.

"Here you are at last," boomed a surprisingly little man, almost as rotund as he was tall. "Keeping our Miss Woolcott to yourself, you devil. Now you know that is simply not permitted."

Reluctantly, Strathmore handed Julia to Sir Simon Wadsworth, who proceeded to settle her into one of the salon's deep chairs. Around them elegantly attired couples perched on sofas or chairs, some braced against the richly paneled walls, all sipping from delicate crystal flutes filled with champagne. To the last one they exuded a look of louche boredom, unimpressed, despite the lavish surroundings and the impeccably attired footmen catering to their every whim.

After several discreet introductions, Wadsworth fixed his eyes, underscored with heavy, purple pouches, upon Julia. "Now, my dear, I heard of the contretemps yesterday which, I take it, has been resolved to everyone's satisfaction. Unfortunate that you missed yesterday's entertainments."

She bowed her head slightly, feigning embarrassment. "Most assuredly," she murmured. "I was overcome by the strain of travel," she demurred then lifted her gaze to glance admiringly at her surroundings. Her gaze fixed on the hall's enormous panels, each depicting a different scene from Greek mythology. There was winsome Persephone, a beauteous Diana, spear raised. And in the far corner, Hera staring off angrily into the clouds.

Wadsworth chuckled meaningfully. "The strain of travel? I thought perhaps a little lovers' quarrel? Adds spice, does it not?" he continued. "Regardless of the reason for your absence yesterday evening, I am pleased that you're quite recovered, dear girl."

"Miss Woolcott tends to high spirits at times," added Strathmore and then for good measure, "It's her penchant for drama that attracted me to her in the first instance, I believe."

Wadsworth's eyes bulged with anticipation. "A highly spirited filly, eh? Hot blooded? But clearly not an actress, what with that innocence about her. From the countryside, eh?" he speculated, clearly pleased. The countryside, in his experience, offered discreet but reliable entertainments. Governesses turned out on the doorstep because of an ill-advised affair with the scion of the family or even, he licked his lower lip in anticipation, fallen daughters of ministers, or young widows impoverished by hard times. This one had that look about her, a debauched innocence what with those lips and legs. "I encouraged everyone to find an escort with the proper, shall we say, temperament for our little soiree." He leered enthusiastically, his short-sightedness an excuse to move in closer to Julia. "Well done, *Strathmore.*"

Julia's shoulders stiffened. Whether from first hearing his family name from his unflattering description of her temperament, or from Wadsworth's proximity, Strathmore wasn't sure. But he did know, instinctively, that it was his opportunity to set the groundwork for what was to come. Word would get back to Faron that Julia Woolcott was given to fits of pique, perhaps even possessed of an ungovernable temper.

Julia lowered her lashes, hiding a blaze of awareness. Strathmore. The name meant something to her as it did to most of England. Although it was most likely his older brother who came readily to mind, not the younger scion who had decamped for exotic climes over a decade ago.

"I much appreciated the invitation from Lord Strathmore," she said, coolly addressing Wadsworth. "It does one good to get out and about, does it not? Rather than rusticating in the countryside as is my tendency. Please do tell me a little about Eccles House and your guests."

Julia did not know what she was asking. Wadsworth launched enthusiastically into a lascivious tale about the estate, which had hosted, not quite one hundred years earlier, a colorful array of rakes, libertines, courtesans, and adventurers who had enjoyed despoiling the manor house with alarming regularity. "Indeed yes, my great grandfather's guests raced through the dark forests of the countryside for frenzied couplings or libidinous meetings in ruined abbeys, erotic gardens, and underground tunnels. I should be pleased to be your host at any time, my dear, should you care to see some of the more interesting follies."

Julia remained amazingly composed. "What an interesting family, sir. I do recall hearing of your great grandfather who, it has been written, fornicated his way across Europe on two

Grand Tours, causing scandals from St. Petersburg to Constantinople." She added serenely, "As I understand it, he was also a member of Parliament."

"We do try to keep up the tradition," chortled Wadsworth, whose family continued to hold the seat though he never bothered to attend Parliament. "Why, I recall old Edgar, as we in the family call him, would use Eccles house for all manner of carnal misbehavior." He warmed to his subject. "From what we know, he would gather his guests for twice weekly bacchanals and my goodness, there are stories of aristocratic women traveling from London to join the frolics dressed as nuns. Comely local nymphs were enticed, so it is told, to lie quite bare on the altar of lust." His jowls trembling, he continued heartily. "And of course there were the caves."

Julia tilted her head to one side inquiringly. "The caves? I do recall hearing of abandoned chalk mines in the area."

Wadsworth, thought Strathmore with a twinge of irritation, was more than pleased to oblige his captive audience with an excruciatingly detailed explanation. "You are quite the scholar, my dear," sighed Wadsworth admiringly, his cheeks ruddy with enthusiasm. "My great grandfather had ordered the caves built in the 1750s, converting a chalk mine into elaborate tunnels and grottoes going down over three hundred feet. He was very imaginative, I must say, with a bridge built over a subterranean river which they christened the Styx, naturally, and an elaborate entrance with a façade to evoke the nave of a church. Quite an exemplary effort, and as I offered earlier, I should be delighted to be your escort should you choose to experience some of our unique sights first hand, my dear."

"Most kind of you to offer, sir. But I do believe the evening's entertainments hold enough excitement for the moment, as do your guests with whom I should like to become better acquainted."

Strathmore experienced an unexpected flare of temper. Julia Woolcott was indeed looking for someone. Faron. Dangerous for her, of course, but easier for him. He tamped down his inexplicable irritation.

"Indeed yes, my dear, I should be more than pleased to make introductions. As I am certain Lord Strathmore has informed you, we hew to a certain protocol that requests we do not divulge names once we leave the estate. We endeavor to keep our diversions private. To protect the innocent." With that last statement, Wadsworth let out a bark of laughter.

Strathmore tensed, watching Julia survey the room. Faron had chosen her for a reason—and she, no doubt, knew it.

"That includes you as well, Strathmore, despite the reputation that precedes you," said Wadsworth, continuing with a bonhomie that made Strathmore think of a snake charmer he'd once met in the Sindi province of India. "You've been outside the country for a time. Up to all manner of interesting diversions, no doubt."

"I've been away some years," Strathmore said, accepting a glass of claret from a passing footman who glided by as discreetly as a ghost. He preferred brandy but finished the claret in one mouthful. It had been some time since spirits had warmed his belly.

Wadsworth chuckled. "Indeed, indeed. I've been keeping abreast of your explorations, young man. Is there any truth to the rumor that you infiltrated the walled city of Ethiopia, Harar to be exact, a land forbidden to foreigners? That would make you the first white man to enter and leave alive."

Strathmore nodded. He didn't add that he and his followers had been hunted through the desert back to the safety of the coast, barely surviving the trek. If Miss Woolcott was surprised at the revelation, she let on with only a slight tightening of her full lips, which curved in seeming appreciation of Wadsworth's prattle.

The older man, flushed with brandy and anticipation, continued. "More specifically, we've heard tittle-tattle about your latest project, the news of which has already made the rounds in select circles. Although I should suppose the Royal Society won't be quick to invite you to discuss it publicly." Wadsworth stroked his belly, tautly encased in blue velvet. Then he turned to the elegant blonde who had appeared behind him. Her delicate fingers clasped around her flute, she sipped slowly, all the while keeping her gaze glued on Strathmore with heavy-lidded eyes.

"Quite a rousing read what, Felicity?" continued Wadsworth, with a wink toward the blonde before turning back to Strathmore. "Is it any wonder I saw fit to invite Strathmore to my little gathering?"

"You have found me out," said Strathmore smoothly, assuming the characteristic air of a man who took without asking, a man as at home in luxury as he was in a bedouin tent. He knew his size and demeanor alone commanded the attention of the room, precisely what Faron had intended. Two other gentlemen drifted into their circle, scenting new prey, their gaze all but pinning Julia to her seat. She almost looked relieved, her eyes darting around the room as if to reassure herself the evening was proceeding along rather pedestrian lines. No one had yet divested themselves of clothing or flung themselves buck naked on one of the overstuffed divans lining the wall.

A narrow-faced, balding man, who introduced himself only as Robertson, gave Julia a lingering nod before lifting his flute high as if to toast the revelries to come. "I have not read it myself although I have heard that your translation captures the flavor of the original brilliantly, Strathmore," said Robertson, snagging another flute of champagne from a passing footman and offering it to Julia with a familiarity that bespoke intimacy. She released the grip on Strathmore's evening coat to accept the drink.

Wadsworth's smirk widened. "Expect you'll be able to show us a thing or two, eh Strathmore? Living with savages does have its benefits, I should say." Like an orchestra's conductor, Wadsworth lowered his numerous chins to cue laughter all around. Strathmore didn't have to confirm that Julia had paled beside him, her eyes glowing with an abnormal intensity.

She took a sip of the champagne and then said, "Clearly, the younger son of the Earl of Dunedin is a talented man."

"You pay me a great compliment," Strathmore murmured, acknowledging to himself that she knew very well his family provenance. "You'll have me blushing any moment now." She stole a sharp glance. Their eyes met and he had the distinct feeling she had been awaiting the opportunity to glare at him. "Of course you know of my illustrious family," he murmured with hushed intimacy meant to send a shiver through her. His fingers closed over hers on the arm of her chair.

That she knew his identity was of little import. Even he had difficulty attaching himself to his family name. From a young age, he'd thought himself a foundling, tall and dark while his older brother was slight and fair. He had little in common with his father, the absent-minded wraith, who frittered away his time on gentlemanly pursuits, forever unable to capture and hold the attention, or the fidelity of his beautiful wife.

The blonde hanging over Wadsworth's rounded shoulders sighed with admiration. "Do tell us more about the translation of this exceptional compendium," said Felicity Clarence slowly, a strange half-smile twisting her thin red lips. Her sloe eyes narrowed on Strathmore. "From what I understand, there are several chapters on the stimulation of desire, types of embraces, caresses, kisses, marking with nails, biting, slapping by hand *and*"—she paused with the drama familiar to an actress—"on copulation." She leaned over to present the full thrust of her smile and heavy bosom. "Or better still, you could demonstrate." Her eyes glittered like diamonds. "Later."

The man at Robertson's side, who called himself Beaumarchais, concurred. Tall, with a lacquered elegance that extended from the brilliance of his pomaded hair to the patent shine of his shoes, Beaumarchais gave a guttural sigh. "A superb suggestion, my dear. Who knows what the night will bring?" he said, directing his words at Julia. But it was the lifting of his dark brow, the insolent drifting of his eyes over her form that prompted the subtle yet defiant uptilt of her chin.

Strathmore felt another unfamiliar spurt of irritation. Julia's face was unreadable when Beaumarchais's gaze seemed to linger on her breasts hidden in the shadows of Strathmore's evening coat. Normally, he was slow to anger, but something in the cool hauteur of Julia's face set off a series of small explosions in his chest. He clenched his jaw, the annoyance a foreign emotion. Wadsworth droned on while Strathmore began contemplating the more concrete details of getting through the evening successfully. He reached for another drink—brandy—and studied Julia over the rim of his glass, then drained it.

He was getting soft. He'd already decided that he wouldn't kill her and now he was hesitating fucking her.

God damn himself to hell and back. He was not an unlucky man but for some unforeseen reason, all logical thought had fled him the moment he'd laid eyes upon a dreary spinster who trailed in her wake the aroma of musty books, copper, and iodine. He was acting like some damned Lothario, strung as tight as a bow, because of a woman who conjured, of all things, feelings of protectiveness. He nearly spewed his last gulp of brandy onto the carpet. Protectiveness? He knew better than anyone women's capacity for cruelty. They truly were the stronger sex.

He considered Julia Woolcott, meeting her eyes for a moment, like the glancing of fencers' foils. She was untried, his gut told him. He hadn't expected that. He hated virgins, never had one before in his life, not even when he was offered the youngest daughter of the Sultan of Perak, and he was not about to start.

He pretended to listen but didn't hear the words tumbling from Miss Woolcott's lips as Beaumarchais and Robertson leaned over her like two slavering dogs with a bone. He listened as Beaumarchais regaled her with details concerning Wadsworth's cache of lewd memorabilia including erotic drinking vessels and phallic sculptures made of precious stone. Robertson invited her to join him the following day to discover the contours of Wadsworth's secret garden wherein the shrubbery resembled the female form, with two hills topped with pink flowering shrubs and a tightly cropped triangle of forest.

Strathmore forced himself to straighten away from her chair. Nothing marred the serene innocence of her expression. No coquettish guile. No flirtatious smile. Only the concentrated, intelligent gaze that, he convinced himself, hid more than it revealed.

Fuck. What was he going to do?

Somewhere in his peripheral vision, the sinuous Felicity hanging on his arm, Wadsworth clapped his meaty palms, his pronounced jowls and heavy joviality urging his guests to be seated. The heavy double doors dividing the salon, embossed with cavorting nymphs and satyrs, began to open slowly, as if by unseen hands.

Chapter 4

The light dimmed. The aroma of burning wax scented the air. Julia shivered. Strathmore's hand held her arm in a firm commanding grip as he eased her back into her chair. The huge double doors parted, candlelight falling upon and then playing with a set of flowing curtains.

"Follow my lead." His breath was hot in her ear as he stood beside her. She didn't have to turn her face toward his. His image burned behind her eyes, hitching her breath as when he'd first appeared on her threshold in his elegant evening clothes, clean shaven, stark featured, his gray eyes unfathomable.

"I am quite willing to go through with this, Strathmore," she said stonily, her mind focused on the goal of gaining purchase into the world of Montagu Faron.

"That remains to be seen." His voice was low, unassailable with a hint of aggression coloring his usual inexpressive tone. Suddenly, she was all too aware of the diaphanous dress clinging to her body in the most tenuous way, reminding her of why she was there. She glanced around furtively, at the intense profiles of the men and women in the room, their mouths slack with lust as they watched the scene unfolding before them.

Julia swallowed hard, counseling herself to become the observer, the eye behind the lens as she watched a group of three men and two women embracing on an oriental carpet.

They were slick with some kind of unguent, offering their nakedness to each other to caress and play. Their bodies were like the Greek and Roman statues she had seen at the National Gallery in London, the men taut and rippled with muscles, the women subtly rounded with high, bouncing breasts.

She watched, her muscles tensing with each movement and each caress, unbearably aware of Strathmore's strong hard hand at the nape of her neck, conscious of the fleeting stabs of pleasure, invading her senses. Her mouth dry, she watched the two women twisting and bending to give the men purchase to every orifice of their bodies. She tried to avoid the obvious—the hard upthrust appendages of the men, the shadowed hollows of the women.

Was it a dream? Or a nightmare? Her exposure to the opposite sex had been limited to a string of tutors, one paler and more harmless than the next and Randolph Codger, the son of the local vicar. She forced herself to focus on the memory, anything to take her mind from the abomination taking place in front of her. She and Randolph were more excited by their passion for William Gruber's Stereopticon view camera they shared than a passion for each other. She recalled one furtive kiss, after a Christmas reverie, buoyed by mistletoe and rum punch.

She kept her eyes half closed. Her gaze was riveted on the scene before her, setting her mind reeling, the memories of Randolph Codger dissipating like dew in the heat of the salon. It was nothing like she had ever read, nothing like the books in the library at Montfort. Even the specter of marriage had never hinted at such unholy fusion of writhing bodies. The prospect of matrimony had never been on the horizon. Meredith's disquiet dictated they rarely move in London circles, which didn't allow much opportunity to meet possible matches. If she and Rowena had harbored such desires deep in their hearts, they would never have let their dear aunt know. Julia had lost herself in her studies and photographic pursuits and Rowena in her love of the outdoors.

She had boasted to Strathmore just hours earlier of her sophistication. How absolutely absurd. She flushed at the memory and at the two women offering their breasts to the men who began sucking them noisily while they rooted their hands in the women's nether regions. They appeared as one twisting, sinuous beast, one body merging with the next.

Julia's pulse pounded in a combination of burning shame and desire. Need, as unfamiliar as rain in a parched desert, flooded her chest. She yearned to regain control. Watching was unimaginable, unconscionable, impossible—as the two men grabbed one of the naked women, slick with oil, and pushed her to her knees.

Julia squeezed her eyes shut. When she opened them again, the woman was being serviced from behind while she attended to the other man with her hand and her mouth. The remaining man and woman, beautiful and naked as Adam and Eve, walked hand-in-hand into the room toward the spectators.

Toward her. Spots danced before her vision and she felt faint, she who prided herself on her quiet, cool reason, her unflappable calm.

She bit back a moan of pleasure and shock. Worse, she was blindingly aware of Strathmore so close to her she could feel the heat from his body. She licked her dry lips. Good lord, he was watching her every reaction, from the pulse jumping in the hollow of her neck to her thighs that she squeezed tightly shut in an attempt to halt the flow of sensation raiding her body.

She dared herself to take in the scene immediately around her. Robertson had seated himself on one of the settees and pulled the naked woman onto his lap, immediately latching onto her breasts. Julia jerked her gaze from the sight only to see Wadsworth and Felicity join the nude man in one of the alcoves. Before she could look in the other direction, Julia saw Beaumarchais make his way toward her, already loosening the complicated knots of his cravat until it billowed like an unmoored sail behind him.

She made a sound of alarm at the back of her throat. Suddenly, she was pulled violently to her feet.

"Play along." Strathmore's breath was hot at her ear and on the soft skin of her neck. He covered her mouth, and she let him. He kissed her with an urgency that startled her more than the bacchanalian scene transpiring a few feet away. He cupped her head and drew her mouth to his in a slow kiss that sent shock waves from the top of her head to the soles of her feet.

She could scarcely absorb the sheer sensuality of it, and her legs spread to receive him—the flawless connection of their two bodies, hip to hip, groin to groin, perfect complements. Breathing was an impossibility. Pulling back slightly, he brushed his lips over hers, back and forth until he felt them tremble. He kept his hands on her shoulders, using only his mouth to arouse her. "Give me more," he said so quietly she thought she misheard. "We must be convincing, unless you want company." Then he took her lower lip between his teeth.

Julia was dying, the breath robbed from her lungs. She was convinced bursting into flames would be next, as Strathmore's lips feathered their way to the base of her throat. He directed his attention to the sleek slope of her shoulder, and she thought his evening coat slid to the floor. A loud roar hummed in her ears as heat shot through her veins, and whether Beaumarchais or the devil himself was at her heels, she didn't care.

"I shall try." Her voice was husky close to his ear. She felt her fingers curling around his waist in exquisite anguish. Instinctively, she drew his head to her breasts amazed to see that with one flick of his fingers, the clasp on her gown gave way, allowing the silk to fall from her shoulders to linger on the upper swell of her breasts. She couldn't believe simply one hour earlier she had cowered behind the heaviness of his suit coat and now she was directing her aching nipples toward him.

Strathmore drew back, resisting, playing some ungodly trick to keep her in languorous suspension, his eyes flickering with need as he took in the swelling of her breasts against the silk.

"Oh yes," she breathed, dissolving when he pressed his lips to the base of her throat. She wrapped her arms around him possessively, and instantly his mouth came down on hers with a violence that spoke of some submerged exasperation. She felt his hands down her back, stroking her buttocks as he maneuvered them against a wainscoted wall on the far end of the room, the weight of his body illogically reassuring and alarming at the same time.

Thoughts no longer mattered. Reason had flown through the high mullioned windows into the dark night air. Everything was mired in sensation, an incandescence that glowed from the depths of her abdomen to her highly sensitized skin.

Coming back down to earth, not gradually but abruptly, she felt another pair of hands—strange hands, not Strathmore's—grasping her buttocks. She drew back from the arms that held her, turning her head away to see Beaumarchais, his palms sliding insinuatingly over her waist and backside.

"I believe I know what kept you two so long from dinner," Beaumarchais said unctuously, his grasping fingers slicking over Julia's silk sheathed hips. The candlelight gleamed on his pomaded hair, brushed back from a narrow forehead. "You have had your fill of each other, surely. Now is the time to share, no?"

Before Julia could register the demand, Strathmore slid his body between her and Beaumarchais. "As a gentleman, perhaps you should ask the lady," he said smoothly. Other voices, as though coming from a long way away, intruded. All the while Strathmore's hands grasped her hips in a show of possession as he pulled her tightly to his body. "What would you like, darling?" he asked for the benefit of their audience when he knew exactly what she craved.

A thousand champagne bubbles burst in her head. *You,*

she wanted to answer. The rest of the room dissolved leaving only the two of them in a nimbus of light. Her lips parted but no words came.

Wadsworth and Felicity, her dress pooling around her waist, her torso completely naked, followed in Beaumarchais's wake. The small, rotund man had his arm around her shoulders, slipping down over a pendulous breast to finger a rouged and swollen nipple. Felicity arched her back against him and ran her hands over his generous waist like the enthusiastic actress that she was.

"Well, my darling, what shall it be?" prompted Strathmore. "Remember," he murmured in a low growl, placing a hot, lingering kiss on the skin of her neck, "we are not alone."

It was almost as though he wanted her to declare it, state her need publically to the people crowding around them, the musk of sex scenting the air. How could she ever have believed she could find her way to Faron through that thicket of depravity? Confused, hovering between an incendiary desire she had never experienced before and a pulsing revulsion mixed with dread, she forced herself to form the words.

"I want . . ." she whispered. What did she want? And did it matter? What had taken her there and why? Faron. She thrust the thought aside. "I like . . ." she tried again.

"To take your pleasures slowly, isn't that right my pet?" supplied Strathmore, coolness in his eyes despite the heat surrounding them, despite the heat of his hands on her shoulders, sliding up her arms, smoothing the midnight silk and, with dexterous fingers, covering her bare shoulders.

The small coterie moved closer, a bath of fetid breath and unslaked lust. Julia burrowed further into the warmth of Strathmore's body and watched as he flicked his gaze over Felicity who returned his glance with sharp appetite.

"Alas, my friends"—the words rumbled from his chest while his eyes lingered deliberately on the sultry blonde— "my sweet Julia has suddenly developed a certain possessiveness. Most unfortunate."

"She will change her mind soon enough," said Wadsworth, his arm still resting about Felicity's shoulders, his eyes bulging like a carp's, upon Julia.

Strathmore made a low sound in the back of his throat. "You would not wish to see her upset, trust me Wadsworth. Speak with your footman if you'd like to know more. She exhibits a nasty temper when provoked, like a veritable wildcat in a temper."

Beaumarchais's lips thinned. "Then why did you bring her as your guest, Strathmore, if she won't play?" He narrowed his eyes. "She's a good enough looking piece, young, firm-fleshed from what I can see. And those legs, a man can't help but wish to see what heaven lies between them."

Julia's head swirled. Despite the vastness of the hall, the walls were closing in around her, robbing her of air. She took a deep breath, sagging against the hard chest and arms that held her. It had to be an illusion. She was an actor without a script in a mad piece of theatre. Nothing was real. Except Strathmore.

If only she could follow the thread of his logic, if it indeed did exist. *Wildcat, temper, possessive.*

"You'll get your chance, Beaumarchais." Strathmore's assurance, and his words, burned through the thin silk of her gown. "She will prove much more biddable if I indulge her for the moment. Take the edge off the lady's appetite, as it were, prepare her for the main event."

The image was obscene. Julia turned in Strathmore's arms, forcing herself not to bolt from the room like a child fleeing from monsters. Desperation washed over, suddenly clearing her mind. Strathmore wanted to be alone with her. Alone. Without Beaumarchais, Wadsworth, and the others.

At that moment, it was like savoring the sweetest salvation. She lowered her lashes and pursed her lower lip, hoping she was the picture of hot-blooded truculence. Sighing long and loudly, she improvised, *"I want you, Strathmore. Now."* It was a voice that was not her own. Her heart pounded wildly. "You know how much more tractable I am when I'm given free reign." The last three words were delivered in what she hoped was a sultry tone.

Strathmore gave a short laugh and dropped a casual, stinging hot kiss to her lips. "We're not finished here, my darling, that's true, but you know I cannot deny you when you're in one of your intriguingly volatile tempers. I still bear the scars of last night's passion, you'll recall."

"We have never even started," growled Beaumarchais too close for comfort.

Desperation made her brave. She had eyes only for Strathmore, cutting Beaumarchais with a chilly glance. "You know how I get . . . and you know what I want," she directed a pout at Strathmore with the imperiousness of an empress. Forcing her movements to slow, she languorously swept her palms down the front of her breasts, past her waist to the apex, just above her thighs. And held his gaze.

For a moment, she thought she'd almost had him convinced. A slow fire glinted in the gray of his eyes before he turned to Wadsworth and his coterie. "Believe me ladies and gentlemen," he said slowly, his voice lower than usual, "we shall all be better off if I first slake the lady's prodigious enthusiasm. After which, I'm certain, we shall continue our play with renewed vigor and appetite."

"By God, you had the whole afternoon with her in your rooms, Strathmore." Felicity spoke in a high breathy voice.

Something about the woman pulled Julia's nerves taut. "And it clearly wasn't enough," she said throatily, deliberately dismissing the older woman. "With Strathmore"—she emphasized pointedly, wondering if desperation could make an actress of her after all—"it can never be enough." She didn't have to feign the rising anger in her tone.

Strathmore smiled wolfishly, the picture of a man with his hands full of demanding woman. "Hush, no need for one of your outbursts," he said pulling her closer for the benefit of their intimate circle. With the fog of desire and revulsion beginning to lift, Julia felt the cool air on her bare skin just as Strathmore tilted her face toward him for a kiss. He began moving them, a slow languid dance, toward the hall's entranceway. Miraculously, the small crowd parted.

"Perfect," he said, sounding like a caress in her ear. "Now say something. As though you're angry or quite thoroughly mad." Together they edged their way through the room, stopping at intervals so he could kiss her—small, delicious incursions, his lips on hers.

"I don't know what you mean," she said, just as Felicity's arm snaked around Strathmore's waist.

"Strathmore, my love, you are entirely too hasty," pouted the older woman, her crimson-tipped hand extending downward to caress his chest.

Strathmore ignored the questing fingers but Julia did not. For the second time in twenty-four hours, she wondered at the woman she had become. And whether she was acting at all. "I should advise you to desist, madam," she said, each word as distinct as a knife's thrust.

The buxom blonde's sloe eyes widened. "My, my, Strathmore, your kitty certainly has claws. Wherever did you find her? You are welcome to her for the time being." Felicity took quick measure of the situation with the sharpness of a fishwife. "But please do hurry back," she said, recovering her composure, lips curved in promise, "as I shall make it worth your while."

Julia did not have a moment to react. Wrapping a firm arm around her waist, Strathmore marched them both from the hall. Candles blazed and the chandeliers floated past, a blur of light in the dark.

When Julia looked around again, he had deposited her in a music room, with a piano at its center surrounded by a half dozen gilded settees. Glancing at the double sets of French doors, her world began to right itself, fueled by a sudden overwhelming urge to flee. The thought crept in beneath the panic, despite a small voice that told her the evening at Eccles House was not yet finished.

For a moment she'd forgotten Strathmore's presence. Heat rushed to her face at the thought of what she had witnessed and what they had done. Her hands fluttered around her neckline, hastily securing the fragile ribbon that held her bodice in place. She'd scarcely taken one step toward the French doors when her body was jerked backward. There was nothing at all amorous about the grip.

Julia tilted her head back willing herself to look into the deep set eyes above the strong cheekbones, dark hollows carved beneath. The mask had slipped. It was not Alexander Strathmore, passionate lover.

"This is hardly necessary," she said frowning at Strathmore's large hand encircling her arm.

"You're mistaken, Miss Woolcott. It's more than necessary." The formality of his tone after what had transpired just moments ago made her feel as though she'd fallen into a deep, dark well. In the brief, silent impasse that followed, Strathmore's grip did not loosen.

"Very well. What now? I can tell you're eager to tell me of your plan. You do have one, I suspect," she said. She decided to appeal to his sense of reason, even as her pulse beat in time with the overwhelming need to get away from him.

His eyes narrowed. "Perhaps you'd like to rejoin Wadsworth's guests."

"Indeed. With a desire beyond my wildest dreams. Isn't it what one would expect from a tempestuous wildcat?"

He smiled. "Don't tell me you're offended, Miss Woolcott. The gambit worked, didn't it? Otherwise, you'd already be splayed like a ripe peach for the delectation of at least several gentlemen. If you don't believe me, we can rejoin the gathering." To his credit, the last words were delivered with a trace of irony.

Unsuccessfully, she tried to wipe out the outrageousness of the last hour. Worse, she could not reconcile the man manacling her wrist with the man she had touched, tasted, and all but devoured with a desire that scared her. "That's utterly ridiculous and you well know it. I'm hardly here out of my own free will."

"Then follow my lead and I shall extricate you from this situation."

She shook her head, exasperation mingling with a desperation to understand. "Why ever would you do that? I'm here *because of you*, after all. You're the one who invited me to Wadsworth's little party, as I gleaned earlier this evening. I should like to know why the youngest son of the Dunedin duchy, vaunted traveler and explorer, would find it in his interests to forge a liaison with a woman of a certain age with no reputation—"

"A country mouse," he supplied bluntly.

She glared. She was not herself. Truly. She licked her lips, trying to recall the quiet, even-tempered Julia, preoccupied with books and daguerreotypes, she had once been. Although it hardly seemed relevant anymore. All of the torturous, serpentine debauchery began and ended with Faron. She would do well to remember that.

Strathmore watched her closely, his eyes on her mouth.

She flushed. "Very well, then. Why all the subterfuge? Why do we not simply leave? I don't believe Wadsworth has barricaded the doors to keep us here with him."

"You will simply have to trust me."

"Not very likely," she snapped. "But since we find ourselves at yet another impasse, what is it you have in mind?"

"What is required is a lover's spat. A loud, violent one, if you please."

She gazed into those cool eyes and gave a reflexive tug at his hand at the same time. She could think of no other way to respond to his illogical demand. "You are not making any sense, sir. They expect us to fall into each other's arms not engage in fisticuffs." She gave another small tug of her wrist for emphasis unable to reconcile his calm demeanor with the heated nature of their exchange.

"It's not what they want that I'm interested in. It's what I want."

She stilled, suddenly exhausted beyond all reason. "Which

is what?" Never mind what he wanted. She didn't know what *she* wanted anymore. To launch herself back into Wadsworth's debauchery, to follow the thin skein back to Faron, or to flee through the French doors a few feet away?

Strathmore let go of her wrist with an unnerving suddenness. With fluid motions, he leaned over to push aside the right leg of his trouser. A black pistol appeared unexpectedly in his hand which he cradled with the familiarity of a lover. "Prepare yourself," he said bluntly. He looked briefly up at the ornate plaster moldings encircling the ceiling. "Pity." And shot three perfect holes into a trio of rosettes.

A shower of fine dust rained down upon them. It confirmed what she had instinctively known. She was next. He was going to kill her. She turned toward the French doors but his words stopped her more effectively than any bullet ever could.

"Do you want to find Faron?" he asked.

Shock bolted through her. Her throat constricted with emotion, rendering her silent.

"Do you want to find Faron?" he repeated. The door rattled, the handle moving slowly. She realized with dismay she had moved back beside him.

The door opened slightly. A low whisper hissed through it. "Whatever's the commotion, Strathmore?" The voice belonged to Wadsworth, a little slurred from brandy and champagne.

Julia was mesmerized by the pistol sitting so casually in Strathmore's hand. "There's been an unfortunate occurrence, Wadsworth. Simply give me a moment or two."

"I should say so. Those were gunshots we just heard. Sure of it."

Strathmore lowered his voice and held her gaze with his own, daring her to contradict him. "I shall look after everything, Wadsworth, rely on it." He motioned her toward the French doors. Before they could slip through the opening, she felt a hard hand lifting the hem of her garment. Without saying a word, he quickly unwound the strip of white linen from her lower calf. Stained with streaks of drying blood, the bandage was tossed across the piano bench.

"I shouldn't advise entering at this moment," said Strathmore. It was the voice of command. The door creaked shut. The shuffle of footsteps could be heard echoing down the hallway.

Julia's leg burned from his touch, the silk of her skirts brushing against the freshly exposed wound. Sanity was becoming a distant memory.

"You're very quiet." He slanted her a glance. "And you haven't answered my question."

It had happened only three times in her life—a stone in her throat, holding back all words. When she had first arrived to live with Meredith, she had not spoken a word for a year. And once, when Rowena had nearly been taken from them by fever, she had felt the same suffocating thickness lodge in her throat.

She felt the room darken, her mouth opening abruptly. Then she closed her lips at whatever she wanted to say, her brows coming together in frustration. Strathmore studied her for a heartbeat until some sort of realization gradually lit his eyes. As though he understood something about her that she didn't want him to know.

"It's the only way," he said. "You are most likely feeling the aftereffects of shock so I will cut to the chase. We haven't much time." He didn't have to gesture to the closed door behind them for her to understand. "I am looking for Faron. As I surmise, you are, too."

It seemed to be both an acknowledgement and a warning. When she still didn't respond—couldn't respond—she focused on the door behind him, the handle turning slowly and ominously. She pointed mutely.

Strathmore took in the situation instantly. "Now is the time to scream, Miss Woolcott," he said tightly.

"Do what?" The words finally came, hoarse and tentative at the same time. It was some kind of macabre test. He aimed his pistol at the door. A charged second followed. He kept the pistol trained on the door and expertly wedged the back of a chair under the doorknob. With a quick move, he removed the pin anchoring his cravat and jammed the lock with an expert thrust.

"Give us a moment, will you, Beaumarchais?" He made his voice low and furious. "Miss Woolcott isn't herself."

How could he possibly know it was Beaumarchais lurking behind the closed door? Julia's mind spun.

"Is the lady unwell?" It was Beaumarchais's voice.

"I shall manage."

Time was suspended as they both listened to receding footsteps. Julia swallowed hard, convulsively, before finding her voice. She needed to leave. "Your honesty is timely, sir," she said aware of the French doors behind her as well as an overriding and competing compulsion to know him—the man who could bring her closer to the shadow that threatened her family. "What is your connection to Faron?"

"You mean our mutual connection to Faron." His response was curt and distant.

Very well, then. The throbbing in her lower leg kept time with her rising pulse. "Did he hire you? Promise you something in exchange for harming me and my family?"

"This is not the time for this discussion. But clearly we want the same thing—otherwise neither of us would be here this evening."

"Who arranged to hire you, then, if it wasn't Faron?"

Strathmore hadn't the time or patience for discussion. "Look here, Miss Woolcott. If I were to fulfill my obligations you would be dead by now."

"You are to kill me," she said in a rush, and took two steps backwards.

"However, I decided not to." It was a simple declaration. His face was in partial shadow. There was no regret, anger, or weakness in his expression.

Panic accelerated her thoughts. She glanced at the piano, the blood-stained bandage and then at Strathmore. It was all beginning to add up with a strange logic. "So we are to make it appear as though a murder has taken place. Hence, the directive that I scream bloody murder, as it were."

"It's a way out, although you don't appear grateful." Strathmore, the infuriating man, seemed distantly amused. It was Julia's turn to make a quick decision.

"We have yet to quit this place successfully," she said, "so gratitude is not yet in order. Against my better judgment, I have no choice but to wait for your explanations. I can see for myself that we have no time."

"And I for yours," he said, the words taut.

Julia's thoughts were a pattern of images and emotions, fatigue making it difficult to shape them into coherence. She barely recognized herself. She had left her home against her aunt's wishes, attacked a footman and, dear lord, pressed herself into Strathmore's long hard body with a flagrancy and need that was completely foreign to her. And she'd listened to that same man declare his intention to kill her.

Delirium. There was no other explanation. She tried to imagine looking at the tangle of events through the frame of her camera. The lens never lied, she told herself. What she saw was Strathmore at the center of the composition, the axis that would lead her to Faron. She felt a sickening dread that Faron would not desist, that her involvement in the debacle was just the beginning, that Meredith's and Rowena's demise stood at its tragic end.

She said, "I shall follow your lead."

He didn't bother to reply, gesturing to the floor by the piano bench. "Lie face down, turned away from the door. The story is that we argued, you produced a pistol, shot wildly in anger"—he gestured to the splintered plaster overhead—"and proceeded to shoot yourself whilst aiming for me.

"Clearly, a lover's spat," she said wretchedly as she crumpled to the floor, favoring her injured leg with a quickly stifled wince. The carpet against her cheek was soft, the oriental pattern swirling around her like a whirlpool.

"I tried to staunch the blood," Strathmore continued,

gathering up the discarded linen from the piano bench before bunching it at the indentation of her waist.

Julia partially closed her eyes, willing to shut out the sheen of his booted feet as they rested by her head. She heard him step away, remove the chair from underneath the doorknob. A quiet click as the lock turned and then Strathmore's low growl. "Have my carriage sent around."

Julia slowed her breaths, watching through her lashes. Four pairs of eyes appeared at the door, staring at the scene— the woman on the gleaming parquet floor, bleeding onto the carpet. Whether they were breathing hard in lust or shock, she couldn't tell. But Robertson had gone so pale the spots on his face were as vivid as the scarlet waistcoat he wore.

"There has been an unfortunate accident," Strathmore said. He ostentatiously waved the pistol in his hand as evidence.

Wadsworth's eyes, beneath the purple pouches, were the size of billiard balls. "I say, old boy, this is entirely unacceptable. I should have expected that you could manage the woman, histrionics and all. I can't have this type of scandal getting out," he blustered, his multitudinous chins wagging in disbelief.

"Is she dead?" asked Beaumarchais abruptly. He was to the side of the doorway, outside Julia's sight.

"I presume so," said Strathmore with supreme unconcern and to no one in particular. "I shall see to it that nothing mars your evening or your reputation, Wadsworth."

"Perhaps I should have a look myself," said Beaumarchais. Julia held her breath.

"I don't think that's a good idea." For emphasis, Strathmore added, "I find myself quite unaccountably irritable. Any untoward movements will put you at risk of seeing one of your body parts summarily removed." There was a collective inhalation of breath. The threat was casually delivered but hit its mark.

Felicity gave a high, tinkling laugh, totally at odds with the tension in the room. "All's well that ends well. Miss Wool-cott was not to my liking in the first place."

"The feeling was entirely mutual," Strathmore said. "And in part responsible for Miss Woolcott's uncontrollable outburst of jealousy."

Julia clenched her teeth.

"I do have that effect on men, I'm told," Felicity purred, choosing to interpret the words as a compliment, not in the least concerned or discomfited by the drama unfolding before her eyes. "Whenever you find yourself at loose ends, Strath-more—"

"She shot herself accidentally?" Beaumarchais interrupted, impatience tightening his tone.

"There was a struggle—I tried to take the pistol from her," Strathmore said just as curtly. "I presume my carriage has been brought around."

The discussion came to an abrupt end. Cool night air rushed into the music room as the French doors opened. Strathmore scooped Julia from the floor, holding her fast, his arm snug beneath her knees and her shoulders. She kept her breathing shallow and low, trying to ignore the half-cocked pistol riding hard against Strathmore's thigh or the rise and fall, rise and fall of his chest against her back.

Surrendering was all she could do.

Chapter 5

Strathmore narrowed his eyes on the fork in the road ahead. He instructed the driver to follow an alternate path, a longer, more circuitous route to London. He needed time to think. The carriage wheels jolted over uneven country roads as the driver negotiated the turn on two wheels.

A soft rain began to fall, leaving rivulets on the small window framing the dark countryside east of London, which Strathmore knew to be pockmarked with abandoned chalk mines and gently rolling hills, seemingly forever mired in mist and fog. The air was heavy and damp, the layers of his high cravat clamping like a wet vise around his neck. Damned English climate, worse than anything he had ever endured in Bombay or Tanzania. A man could survive in dry heat but it was the endless rain that could drive one mad. He loosened the layers of silk before turning his eyes on the still figure of Julia Woolcott.

Silence blanketed them like a shroud, relieved only by raindrops hammering the coach roof, reminding him that neither was willing to breach the divide. Julia Woolcott feigned sleep. He didn't blame her.

She was supposed to be dead. And for all intents and purposes, she was. It had become patently clear to Strathmore as the evening at Eccles House wore on that Beaumarchais was Faron's conduit, the man who would deliver the news of Julia Woolcott's demise not only to his master but also to her family. Word would get back to her aunt and sister, a cruel revelation that Faron would obviously relish.

There was the rub—why? Not that Strathmore could afford to care, to discover why the Woolcotts had at one time raised the enmity of the powerful man. He would do well to remember his only aim was to gain access to Faron. He had already infiltrated the first ring of the man's circle and accepted the murderous assignment to prove his worth. All that remained was for Beaumarchais to be convinced the deed had been done.

Strathmore would await the summons from Lowther. For the interim, Miss Julia Woolcott would simply have to be his guest until such time when she could resurface, alive and well.

Across from him she sat still, too still. He traced her profile, that straight nose, the wide mouth, distinct in the semi-dark and he realized he had already memorized her features. She was pretending, her breathing too deep and even, her eyes with their thick lashes open to mere slits. He'd thrown a lap rug over her body, more for his own benefit than for hers.

It was too tempting to slide in next to her and pull her into his arms. He'd played fast and loose at Wadsworth's country house, his actions arising both from instinct and years of intrigue in inhospitable places. Or so he believed. Typically, he preferred a brutal honesty in his affairs, yet there was an unpalatable truth lurking behind Miss Woolcott's wide, blue gaze. There was something about her, a vulnerability she desperately tried to hide, that made him question his judgment, his ambition, and his unaccountable attraction to a woman that threatened all his plans.

She was not the sort of female who typically caught his interest. His palate was accustomed to the worldly, the experienced, and above all, the eager. The bored diplomat's wife, or the seasoned concubine. Mewling virgins, nervous spinsters, and prim bluestockings had never held the least appeal.

He crossed one booted foot over the other. She had a surprisingly remarkable form, a body made for carnality. Reluctantly, he remembered the length of her white thighs and the curve of her breasts encased in barely-there midnight silk. And her response to his touch—bloody difficult to reconcile. It made it all too easy to imagine angling her head back into his palms and brushing her lips with his own for another sweet, dark taste of her mouth, her tongue. He eyed the small expanse of silk clad shoulders rising from the enveloping lap rug, envisioning how he would drag his fingers slowly over the midnight fabric, pulling the flimsy bodice gently down to expose her skin to his fingers, his palms, his lips.

White heat coursed through his veins. It had been too long.

The hardening between his legs offered more proof than he needed. Celibacy. That was the root cause of his unease. Nothing else. Certainly not the untutored and surprising ardor of a starchy, bookish virgin. He adjusted the length of his legs in the confined interior of the carriage. His time would be better spent thinking about Faron.

The sound of the rain continued, mingling with the rumble of cobblestones beneath the carriage, telling him that they had arrived in London. Julia still didn't stir when the coach pulled to a stop, nor did the tempo of her breathing change. All Strathmore heard was the drumming of the rain on the coach roof. He decided it would serve his purposes to carry her quickly into the town house.

The white residence glowed in the dark, one of the many in the Dunedin Duchy collection, secluded by Regent's Park from the front and by a mews to the rear.

With studied indifference, he drew Julia into his arms and carried her from the carriage. With a murmur of thanks to the coachman he entered via the servant's entrance, nodding briefly to his steward before proceeding up the staircase to the main floor. All of the Dunedin family retainers were unquestionably loyal, and Baxter was no exception. He followed Strathmore on soundless feet into the library where he quickly lit several lamps, stoically ignoring the limp body in his master's arms. Strathmore instructed him to prepare one of the guest rooms and to ransack one of the many ward-robes for suitable clothing. For his own sanity, that bit of silk lying against Julia Woolcott's white skin had to be replaced.

Bending low, Strathmore placed Julia on a settee, tucking the rug around her, all too aware of her breasts rising and falling against his chest in a gentle rhythm. He'd realized the inherent danger in taking her there, but he had little choice.

"Could you really have killed me?"

Despite the heaviness in her voice, he could tell she was completely awake and Strathmore found himself looking into wide blue eyes. He backed away, a man who had never backed away from anything in his life.

"No," he said honestly. He'd killed out of self-preservation but never out of mere convenience.

She sat up straighter against the cushions, pushing the hair back from her face and, once again, he was struck by the woman's singular lack of vanity. In the depth of her eyes, he saw not fear exactly but that same vulnerability that had made him question each and every one of his actions in the past twenty-four hours.

"I need to go home. To Montfort," she said simply.

"You're supposed to be dead. That was our agreement."

She gave him a slight shake of her head and made an im-patient sound. "My aunt and sister will be devastated to learn the news. I can't allow it."

"You would renege on our agreement, honorably made?"

She regarded him with blank-faced surprise for a long in-stant. Then a type of resolve, almost despair, settled over her face. "Hardly honorable, and made in the heat of the mo-ment. I refuse to allow my family to suffer unnecessarily," she said haltingly. "At the very least, I must let them know. Warn them."

Sorrow lurked behind her wary gaze. Julia Woolcott was an unusual woman, possessing an elusive quality Strathmore couldn't quite determine. He thought briefly of his mother and so many other women he'd known before he left Eng-land. Flighty, temperamental, gossipy and vain, not unlike the yapping lapdogs they kept close at hand. While Miss Woolcott, with her blend of innocence and determination, demonstrated not only a passion for her work, but also for her family.

He turned abruptly to the small rosewood table that Baxter had set up with a brandy decanter and two tumblers. He splashed himself a liberal draft, drained it, then refilled his glass and poured one for Julia. A silent but persistent warning clamored at the back of his head.

It was not right—jeopardizing everything. Miss Woolcott was not a damsel in need of salvation but rather a burden, in all truth, *his burden,* unless he could rein in those sudden and inexplicable impulses. He was nothing if not a practical man.

He pressed the brandy snifter into her hands and leaned on the arm of the settee.

"We could make this work to our advantage, Miss Woolcott."

She studied the crystal glass cradled in her palm. He ignored the clean, delicate line of her jaw, the elegant sweep of her neck.

"It had occurred to me," she said simply, lashes sweeping upward, eyes underscored with fatigue, "that you have a connection with Montagu Faron. Whether any of this can work to my advantage, as you put it, is unclear. However, you can hardly fault me from wishing to pursue any connection with Faron." She took a tentative sip of the brandy before continuing, weariness in every line of her body. "I surmised that you, or someone amongst Wadsworth's circle, were somehow involved with him."

"We keep coming back to my involvement. What about yours? I know fear when I see it. You are afraid of Faron, yet you refuse to tell me why."

Julia studied him closely, frowning a little. "Even if I knew, sir, I shouldn't tell you. Until you honor your agreement to provide me with an explanation as to your role in this saga."

The brandy settled low in Strathmore's belly, its warmth unfamiliar after a number of years' absence. Imbibing spirits was punishable by death in many of the regions he had called home in the past five years. He wondered briefly if the alcohol, rather than Miss Woolcott, was responsible for loosening the reins on his ambitions.

"Montagu Faron has something I want," he said with a directness Julia was beginning to find familiar.

"Which is what precisely?" She stopped short before continuing. "What would be of such value to you that you would kill for it, if necessary? It's difficult to reconcile your possible motivations for involvement in this affair. Forgive me if I have cause to wonder who you are exactly—the younger son of Dunedin or the renegade explorer whose various exploits even managed to amaze Wadsworth's jaded guests?"

"The specifics are not pertinent at the moment."

"Then what is?"

"That you follow through on your promise to remain dead, bizarre as that might seem at present."

"Do you intend to chain me here?" she asked tonelessly. "I assume this is your London residence."

"I doubt that will be necessary as I believe you'll find the safety of my town house far more pleasant than once again becoming a target for Faron."

She drained the last of her brandy, her fingers resisting slightly when he reached to take the glass from her. Deliberately, he pressed his fingers over hers. Their eyes met, and somewhere in the blue depths he saw again a reservoir of pain and secrecy shuttered tight.

"What are you hiding, Miss Woolcott?" he asked softly.

Her lips quivered, then compressed. She pulled her hand away from his and leaned forward, gripping the edge of the rug as if to keep herself sitting upright. He noticed the soiled hem of midnight silk splayed over the mahogany floorboards and wondered at her inner strength.

"How does your leg fare? You should have the injury seen to shortly. I'll have Baxter look for someone to prepare a dressing."

"My injury is the least of my concerns." She lifted her chin. "I'm more concerned about what you want of Faron."

It was the elemental question he was not prepared to answer. The raking of her eyes over him reminded him of what was at stake. "Do you recall, when I warned you that knowledge can be a dangerous thing?" he asked. It seemed like a lifetime ago. "Nothing has changed."

"Everything has changed," she insisted, the rug slipping to reveal a gaping neckline where only a filmy piece of silk saved the swells of her breasts from spilling into the golden lamplight. He steeled himself at the sight, like a wayward schoolboy.

"Faron is intent upon harming my aunt and my sister, and I shall do everything and anything in my power to stop him. I am beginning to fear that means attaching myself to you, sir, like a limpet."

He'd absorbed many threats in his days abroad, but nothing like that one. Yet wasn't it precisely what he wanted? Miss Woolcott at his side, his to use? She had knowledge of a man who was ultimately unknowable, but who clearly had a soft and vulnerable underbelly when it came to the Woolcotts.

Julia rose abruptly from the settee and strode heedlessly to the window overlooking a courtyard below.

Hell, she was transparent as glass. "Don't even consider it," he said. He shoved his hands into his pockets, wondering desperately whether Baxter had yet located appropriate clothing for his reluctant guest. Her long back curved away from him, rigid as a washboard, with the rug draped around her shoulders like a stole. "There is no escape. At worst, the fall would injure you and at best kill you."

"I'm merely illustrating that I refuse to stay behind, passive and fearful, whilst I could be doing something . . ." She turned her head, eyes looking up to his. The troubled reserve had fled and fires were banked there instead. "I have had enough of Faron and his omnipresent threats and machinations. I fear this attempt on my life is merely a prelude, a desire to punish and torment my aunt and sister for God only knows what lunatic reasons." Truth rang in her words.

"What are you proposing, Miss Woolcott?" He was tempting fate, but then he never feared risk.

Her words were etched in steel. "You wish to find Faron as do I."

The situation had the ring of the familiar, of an uncomfortable though necessary alliance. He'd seen the same expression several years earlier in the hard eyes of the Sultan Seyyid Majid, who had, in exchange for firearms, offered Strathmore a caravan to guide him to Kampala. And that journey had not ended well, he remembered with a cynicism born of experience.

Strathmore's voice was deeper than usual when he finally answered, knowing he was making a mistake. "You are proposing an alliance."

"I am."

"An alliance is predicated on an exchange, Miss Woolcott, so it behooves me to ask what assistance you could possibly offer, other than staying well out of sight."

For a brief moment, Strathmore thought she was not attending to the conversation when she said, "Where is my camera and its accompanying apparatus?" A non sequitur. Her eyes darted around the room before she rushed back from the window to stand by the settee, almost tripping over the rug in her haste. "Damn. I suppose it's all been left behind at Eccles House."

Strathmore shook his head. "I fail to understand. Your camera is of little use to me, Miss Woolcott."

She appeared deep in thought, cursing inventively under her breath, the smothered oath coming as a surprise. He saw the shadow again, the tension about her mouth, the suppression of some emotion. "It's of great importance to me," she said finally.

Of course, her collection of photographs. "I'm certain there are other copies of your monograph available," he offered, "although I still fail to see the relevance here." He was a man who'd grown accustomed to having control of a situation and perilously found himself without it.

Julia took a sharp breath, released it, then tipped her head back in thought. "If we could send a messenger to Eccles House somehow, and have my belongings returned"—she looked at him sharply, as though considering his worthiness in the endeavor—"it would be of great help."

"And why might that be?" He hoped she heard the impatience in his voice but, if she did, she ignored it.

"For our alliance," she said simply. "I realize I shall need assistance locating Faron, and in apprehending him. You are precisely what I need—a man who is by nature and experience adventuresome, practical, and physically capable," she continued as though reading from a laundry list.

Strathmore did not feel the least flattered. He was confused and he looked away from her. He tamped down his impatience. "I'm pleased that you believe I may be of service to you, but I still don't understand what your photographic accoutrements have to do with any of this."

"My part of the alliance." She rubbed her hands together eloquently and stared up at him, aware that she had lost him some time ago. "Please let me ask—do you know what Montagu Faron looks like?"

As a matter of fact, he hadn't a clue, and his expression said as much.

"Just as I thought." Then she added, triumphantly. "But I do, or at least I shall, once I have access to my traveling case."

He went still, clearly surprised. "You're still not making any sense. But go on."

"A daguerreotype of Montagu Faron. I have one—given to me by my aunt."

Strathmore was suddenly aware of the hissing fire in the small grate, coaxed to life by a few reddening embers. Possibilities bloomed in his mind. "Interesting in itself, but how might that help if we have no way to locate the man?" Restlessness made the statement curt. "You've seen the likeness?'

"Not precisely." She crossed her arms over her chest, fidgeting with the ends of the rug. She frowned and a shadow passed over her face. "My aunt gave it to me before I left Montfort, and I placed it among my copper plates, in my case." She was thinking aloud.

While he was thinking faster. Montagu Faron was a recluse—no one had clapped eyes on him in over two decades. As to his whereabouts, it was a further mystery, and not a detail Giles Lowther would readily reveal. Just yet.

"There is just one caveat," she added, "one little problem." She stared momentarily into the grate's glowing coals.

"Which is?"

She hesitated a fraction. "It remains undeveloped."

"What remains undeveloped?"

"The daguerreotype," she explained. "The process involves a silver-coated copper plate which is sensitized with chemicals. When the portrait sitter is ready, the photographer removes the camera cover and times the exposure of the plate with a watch."

"You are losing me here," Strathmore admitted.

Julia brushed an impatient hand through her hair. "That preliminary step has already taken place but the photographer did not develop the exposed plate. In other words, the image on the silvered plate has not yet been brought out in a fuming box."

"So we have no image."

"Only the potential for an image," she corrected.

"How did you come by the plate and how likely is the image to have survived?" The muted hiss of the fire grew louder.

Julia hesitated for a moment, as though reluctant to reveal the source of a hidden treasure. "Meredith declined to give me details as to how she came into possession of the plate. All I know is I have the option of developing it, if need be."

"Well done, Miss Woolcott," Strathmore said. "Although of little immediate help to us. Nonetheless, I shall have your belongings sent for immediately. In the interim," he continued, beginning to unbutton his jacket as he made for the door, "I suggest you make yourself at home and ask Baxter for anything you may need." Shrugging out of the sleeves, he slung the coat over his arm.

She nearly tripped on the damned rug again, following him closely, her knees very nearly touching the back of his own legs. Proximity between them, he decided, was not a good idea.

"I don't believe we understand each other, sir." She hesitated briefly, as though his nearness was disconcertingly invasive. "In exchange for Faron's likeness, I expect that you will allow me to send a message to my aunt and sister. At the very least."

He kept his back to her, addressing her reflection in the gilt mirror hanging over the fireplace mantle. "I've already said that's impossible, Miss Woolcott. I don't know how much more alarmist I can be. Understand that by contacting your family you could be doing them greater harm."

"That is a risk I'm willing to take"—her chin notched up a bit in the glass—"and something I am to decide. Besides which, you owe me some conciliation."

"You could have been dead today," he said more harshly than he'd intended, then turned around to look at her. "That's a fair exchange, I should think."

She took a step back and swallowed hard, her eyes large above faint blue shadows. "I am grateful for that, make no mistake. However, should I consider relinquishing what I know of Faron, I need to ensure your assistance."

Strathmore gave a deliberately enigmatic smile, his hand on the door. "Should you consider? What you might consider is that we're even now. Your life and your virtue intact, Miss Woolcott, in exchange for the daguerreotype and your compliance."

His dismissive tone was deliberate, with enough disdain in his words to guarantee that her eyes darkened with anger. Well and good.

"I hardly think that fair."

"Really, Miss Woolcott?" He hooded his gaze. "Your murder today would have been the least of it. I think they call ravishment a fate worse than death, no?"

Scarlet suffused her pale cheeks. Her eyes darted to the chaise and back, wavering somewhere on his chest. "I should ask you . . . I should hope that we both will forget . . ."

His response was a short laugh at the irony of such a possibility. Dark blue eyes lifted to his and, to his great disappointment, he was beset with an urge to snatch the rug from her shoulders and wrap her in it before sending her safely home to her bloody aunt.

"At the very least," she continued, her gaze holding his. Her voice rang with the curt tones of someone who had considered every possibility of escape and finally realized the futility of such a plan. "At the very least," she repeated, "I beg of you to get word to Meredith—"

"That's not possible. It's imperative that Faron believe you to be dead."

She gave a small shake of her head, as though to dislodge a recurrent nightmare. "I fail to see the logic in any of this. You are using deception for your own benefit."

Julia Woolcott was not far off the mark and he should be drowning in self-contempt. Instead, his only focus was on the stiffening of her body when he moved closer to her, out of fear or desire, he had no idea. The air seemed to vibrate between them with a collision of wills and something else that he was loath to identify.

Christ, the attraction between them was bloody inconvenient and as primal as the ocean tides. It was impossible to deny, and yet Miss Woolcott was more than able to shut it out while he was fast losing ground to an inexplicable, uncontrollable hunger entirely out of character for him. He was closer to his goal than ever before and all he could think about was the heat in his groin.

Enforced proximity didn't help. He was done with discussion. "You may have the run of the house as long as you do not leave the premises. Baxter will to see to your comfort, Miss Woolcott."

The mirror reflected her growing anger, the straightening of her spine. "You intend to keep me here. Entirely unfair, Strathmore! While you," she huffed, hoisting the rug more securely over her shoulders, "you go about your business. I warn you, once you secure my belongings, you have absolutely no right to go through my possessions without my consent."

All he wanted to do was get the hell out of the room and away from the temptation to seize her by her shoulders and kiss her into silence.

"I bid you good evening," he muttered. It emerged as a growl, and Julia's eyes widened as he swung around and left the room. The slamming of the door in his wake did nothing to relieve the heaviness in his nether regions. He could only hope a brandy would be more effective in easing his confusion and guilt.

"Now that was certainly anticlimactic, darling. Too much claret this evening, perhaps?"

Beaumarchais did not glance away from the gilded four-poster bed in one of the many ornate bedchambers at Eccles House, despite the fact that Felicity followed him to his chair before sliding onto his lap and fastening her plump arms around his neck. The lace neckline of her wrapper gaped as she nestled closer against his chest and played deftly with the ivory buttons of his shirt. A long fingernail traced lazy circles over his chest.

"It's the business with Strathmore, isn't it?" she murmured. She was pouting and coy, disappointed that everyone's attention had been taken away from her and what she did best. Deliberately and provocatively, she pushed back a sweep of blond hair that fell to her rounded shoulders. "The little party just wasn't the same after that splendid man left the scene."

"Hardly fit for civilized company," Beaumarchais replied, lifting his glass, then scowling when he found it empty.

Felicity purred her disagreement as she pressed her rouged lips to his neck. "So refreshingly unlike the typical Englishman, thank God. I'd forgotten just how much that appeals to me after a steady diet of milquetoast countrymen. I can't imagine what he's like in bed. I heard when Strathmore turned to learning India's languages, he hired a tutor to instruct him by day and took mistresses to teach him by night." She sighed theatrically into the linen of Beaumarchais's shirt. "Such a shame I hadn't the chance to sample the wares."

"You seem overly impressed."

"Wadsworth made it known that Strathmore has crossed the Arabian desert, lived in disguise among Arabs with a mixture of stamina, courage, and high intelligence seldom found among Englishmen. Then there's that delightful translation of the erotic arts," she murmured.

"Only a fool would try such a thing. Deserts, explorations, and the like. Whatever for!" Beaumarchais snorted inelegantly, gesturing to the lavish appointments surrounding them, a jewel box boudoir with blush-pink watered silk wallpaper and profusion of gilt. "You're surely not lusting after a man without a title. That wouldn't be wise for a woman of the theatre. You do still act, Felicity? Other than on your back, that is."

Felicity knew enough to ignore the slight. "I have Wadsworth—and other paramours—to shower me with the trinkets I love," she replied, as her palms slipped beneath his shirt and kneaded his ribs. "Besides which, I hear that Strathmore is very, very wealthy in his own right. Something about a trust that he came into when he reached his majority from a mysterious source." She gave a tinkling laugh. "Surprise, surprise, it's not his pay packet that I'm interested in, my darling." Her fingers drifted over his belly to unhook the top of his trousers.

Beaumarchais' fingers halted her straying hand, interfering with the determined exploration.

Felicity's eyes narrowed. "You are preoccupied—perhaps it's not the claret." She wriggled more deeply onto his lap. "It's that woman, isn't it, the one with Strathmore." Heaving a sigh, she thrust out her lower lip like a fussy child. "She spoiled everything."

Beaumarchais resisted the nearly overwhelming urge to thrust Felicity from his lap. "You're hardly expected to understand, woman," he said harshly.

Felicity shrugged her shoulders, the movements of a voluptuary. "So she is dead—by her own hand, the silly thing. Although, I can understand how one might become overly covetous of a man like Strathmore."

"I don't trust him."

"Strathmore? Why ever not?"

Beaumarchais stared at the ornate escritoire where he had one hour earlier penned a quick note to Lady Meredith Woolcott, informing her of the unfortunate demise of her niece and ward. With copious, painful detail, as per his instructions.

Yet something was not right. "I simply don't trust him—enough said." Unceremoniously, Beaumarchais pushed Felicity from his lap, shoved himself from the chair and began tending to the opened buttons on his shirt.

With feathers finally ruffled, Felicity made little effort to mask her pique. Her mouth thinned as she watched him dress. "I shan't have it." She gave a little stamp of her slippered foot. "An emaciated little nobody causing so much trouble." She lowered her heavily kohled eyes, then readjusted a stray blonde curl so that it wound wantonly against her splendid bosom. "Although, on the bright side, at least she's out of the way, quite permanently, leaving Strathmore's dance card somewhat more open."

Beaumarchais neatly tucked his shirttails into his trousers and snatched his swirling cravat from the back of a nearby chair, looping it around his neck. "You are so obvious, Felicity. It isn't a wonder that Wadsworth keeps you in his stables," he said, retrieving his coat and moving toward the door.

Felicity accepted the comment as a compliment. "I do have my talents." She tightened the sash on her wrapper, which only emphasized her impressive decolletage. "As you've just reminded me, we have unfinished business—if you're up to the challenge, Beaumarchais. I'm certain Strathmore would be," she added coyly with just enough cruelty to make it interesting.

Beaumarchais made for the closed door. "Now is not the time, madam." His tone was dismissive, yet all the while he registered the actress's unbound enthusiasm for Strathmore. Her insatiable appetites might prove useful when the time was right.

Felicity was correct, he thought crudely, slamming the door behind him. She did have her talents.

Chapter 6

Julia was mad with worry. After a night of fitful sleep, she awoke with anxiety in her heart as heavy as the dampness that coated the windows of her bedchamber. Barely aware of the pale green damask walls and feminine furnishings of her surroundings, she made quick work of her ablutions with the help of a silent maid. Requisite garments had miraculously appeared through the quietly efficient auspices of Baxter. She smoothed down the rich velvet nap of a morning dress that protected against the chill. It was a trifle short, skimming her ankles, and required a few tucks from the needle of the maid around the boning of the bodice. It was a lady's dress and Julia wondered briefly to whom it had belonged. One of Strathmore's mistresses?

What did it matter? Clearly she had no moral compass at all, wasting precious time thinking about such silliness when she should be concentrating on Meredith and Rowena. A feeling of helplessness washed over her, an awareness as sharp and piercing as the pain in her lower leg. They would be distraught with grief and unprepared for what was to come.

The Wadsworth debacle was Faron's opening salvo, Julia was convinced, and there was no place left to hide, not even at Montfort. She had been kept in the dark far too long, complicit in the secrecy that Meredith deliberately cultivated to keep her wards safe. But the stratagem was no longer working.

To calm her jagged nerves, Julia spent the next several hours exploring the London town house, searching for something that would give her a hold over Alexander Francis Strathmore. But there was nothing in the house that reminded her of the man. Not the delicate cornices decorating the high ceilings nor the rather pedestrian collection of books in the library, which featured no exotic literature from the mysterious east, no vast atlases marking the furthest reaches of the world.

The room of clover-shaped and sashed windows overlooked a quiet residential street. Through a gentle rain, she could see the discreet entrances of similar dwellings, the comings and goings as regular and unthreatening as the sun rising each day. She could hardly rip open the sash and careen out the window, or hail a passerby with screams and exhortations.

She was as much a prisoner there as she had been in the dark, cork-lined room at Eccles House.

The library was meant to be impressive, with shelves upon shelves of books with their gilt-edged spines. Despondent, she settled halfheartedly into an armchair with a collection of poetry when the door opened. Looking up, she saw Baxter framed in the doorway, his long arms holding two familiar bandboxes.

"Your luggage has arrived, madam," he gravely explained, depositing the packages on the table just inside the door.

Julia dropped the book in her lap and then picked it up again, smoothing the pages nervously with her fingers. "Thank you. And the rest?"

"In the carriage house," he replied.

Her camera and its accompanying apparatus had arrived. She rose from the chair and lifted one of the boxes from the table, knowing without looking what was inside.

"Will that be all at the moment, madam?" Baxter courteously asked, reaching for a tray of tea things to carry back to the kitchen.

"Thank you, yes." She hesitated a moment. "Would you please have these two boxes sent to my room, Baxter?"

"Most assuredly, madam."

"And Lord Strathmore? Where is he?"

"Occupied at present. In the drawing room with Lady Strathmore," he acknowledged, smoothly rearranging the china neatly in the center of the table before sweeping up the two boxes as requested and withdrawing.

Julia felt the heat race up her spine and down to the pit of her stomach. *Strathmore was married.* He had a wife. The knowledge settled into the pit of her stomach. As if the situation were not sordid enough already, her skin smoldered at the memory of his touch.

Strathmore was married. The words hammered in her brain. She felt on fire, mortification and shame blending now with her nerves, already taut as wire. How could it have happened? How could he have allowed it?

Images spiked through her brain, triggering lascivious memories and shivers of emotion. Adultery had never crossed her mind. Her life had been sheltered, calm and ordered, but now she found herself thrust into a world which called for an immorality that made her head spin. She took a deep breath to calm herself. Gathering her skirts in one hand she strode from the library, through the high-ceilinged hallway toward the drawing room. Her mind a blur, she became aware of the voices, one high and feminine, the other distinctly Strathmore's. The wide double doors of the drawing room stood open and she hovered on the threshold.

Even in profile, Lady Strathmore looked every inch the aristocrat, resplendent in a plum satin morning dress with fringed shawl, her only ornamentation two strands of magnificent matched pearls. Her honey colored hair was immaculate under a plume of trembling ostrich feathers.

"My dear, the least you could have done was let me know you were in the country, never mind London." In the harsh morning light, her skin was slightly creped, irritation marring a smooth, high brow. Her posture was perfect, her gloved hands elegantly importuning.

"I didn't realize that you cared," said Strathmore tonelessly. He was standing at the window seeming to examine the low hedge framing the town house.

Julia hadn't seen him since the previous evening and her gaze was mesmerized by his physical presence. The delicate appointments of the room seemed dwarfed by the breadth of his shoulders beneath his coat, his musculature a compelling reminder of his strenuous physical life. He didn't belong in the town house. He was an outsider in his own home and, clearly, to his wife.

"Of course I do, darling." Lady Strathmore curved her lips into a smile.

Despite the civility of the exchange, the tension in the room was explosive and thick. It was not unusual for married couples to live separate lives, but there was something very wrong, more like fissures than cracks in a smooth façade. Julia's eye for detail focused on the rigidity of Lady Strathmore's narrow back and Strathmore's tight jaw line. She struggled to make sense of it while her stomach pitched. Her inventory of sins was ever expanding, adding eavesdropping and adultery to the growing list. Hanging back, she wondered whether it was imprudence or a sense of self-preservation that kept her from announcing her presence.

"Spare me the bromides, Madam," said Strathmore. "I should ask you to leave." It was an order that disregarded entirely any familial connection.

"I haven't seen you in over five years and this is how you receive me?"

Strathmore's shoulders moved in a negligent show of dismissal. "I wasn't the one who let you in. I believe it was Baxter who displayed such lack of judgment."

Lady Strathmore's mouth arranged itself into a grim, straight line. "This is outrageous," she accused. "I am your mother. Nothing can change that."

The hard knot in Julia's stomach loosened. *Mother.* She craned her neck closer, ashamed at the tide of relief flooding through her. Lady Strathmore was a beautiful woman—and far older, on closer inspection, than the man standing across from her. His silence bordered on rudeness.

"I beg your pardon," she finally said. "This is hardly the reception I should expect from my son, gone from his home for an indecent period of time."

Strathmore turned from the window, his glance withering. "Hardly a home. And you're the last one to speak of decency."

Lady Strathmore smoothed the fringes of her shawl in response to the implied criticism. "Your concerns are bourgeois beyond belief, Alexander. Mine has never been the hand that rocks the cradle." She gave a little flutter with a delicately gloved hand. "I married a duke. I am now a dowager duchess who will not countenance being asked to justify her behavior."

"You give yourself too much credit, madam. Your behavior past and present interests me not in the least," Strathmore said. "As for my bourgeois sensibilities, I have traveled much of the known world, where I have seen more evidence of familial connection in the most primitive tribes than in our own illustrious family."

"Really, Alexander! What an insulting comparison!"

Strathmore raised a disparaging brow. "This discussion is now beyond tedious. And I am far beyond willing to dredge up the past."

Lady Strathmore bristled. "Whilst we're discussing family"—she sighed dramatically, clearly eager to make a point—"not even an inquiry from you about the duke, who is, after all, your brother, or the duchess, his wife."

"They're keeping well, I'm sure."

"As one would expect," Lady Strathmore said. "William does not spend his time gallivanting the world over in search of lord only knows what. It's positively humiliating, what with all your highly irregular obsessions. One moment it's strange rock formations and the next, a peculiar tribe from some desperate place. You were always a strange one, even as

a boy—this fixation with sciences and physical geography—
positively unseemly, and quite *vocational.*" She spoke with
total iciness. "Unlike well bred young men, Greek and Latin
were not enough for you at Eton or Oxford. How often were
you thrown out until finally—"

Strathmore looked unimpressed and pulled a heavy gold
watch from his vest pocket. "You have precisely three minutes to leave, Madam."

Lady Strathmore pursed her lips. "I have indulged your
need for adventure, intrigue, or whatever it is that you do,
biding my time in the hopes that you will one day outgrow
such irresponsible fantasies and realize that your duty ultimately lies with the family. If it were not for that damned
trust, giving you all manner of freedom, you might have
found yourself more closely tethered."

"Apt choice of words." Strathmore again sought the windows and what little comfort the scene beyond provided.
"This is all entirely hopeless, as I imagined it would be."

"I thought there had to be a reason for your coming here,
aside from maternal obligation, of course."

"You are ever so nasty, Alexander. Nothing has changed.
Furthermore, if you won't show me proper filial affection,
then at the very least please explain these horrid rumors cir-
culating," she demanded in an acid tone. "I was not pleased
to learn of the incident this morning."

At that, Strathmore threw back his head and laughed, the
sound hollow in the large room. "You never disappoint,
madam. Now we come to the real reason for your visit."

"It's all very unsavory," she said, the ostrich feathers on
her hat trembling in agreement.

"Nothing to concern yourself over."

"A small matter, in your opinion, no doubt. A small matter of a strumpet, your strumpet evidently, and at Eccles
House amid the worst possible sort. And the whispers of intemperate behavior, suicide? You should have realized that
set ran wild. Word spreads so quickly . . . no doubt why the
Duchess of Whittaker penned me a quick note this very

morning to warn me, like the good friend she is. Do you have any idea how difficult this is for me?"

"I hardly think you're a stranger to indiscreet behavior, or sordid country house weekends. So spare both of us the outrage."

"Good Lord, desist in attacking me, Alexander." For several moments, the duchess convulsed beneath an onslaught of discreet coughs, which did nothing to temper the bite of her tongue. When she recovered, she asked, "You will never forgive me, will you?" Her gray eyes, identical to her son's, were the color of a frozen lake. "You are many things, Alexander, but I never thought to call you a prig."

Something compelled Julia to look away from the scene, to trace the black and white marble tiles lining the hallway where she stood. The mutual animosity burned so deeply it could not bear excavation.

When she looked up again, Strathmore was shaking his head. "I've been called far worse. And now you have two minutes to leave the premises." The watch in his palm caught the sunlight and flashed a subtle green prism on the wainscoted wall.

In a show of distress, Lady Strathmore placed a lace-gloved hand at her throat, but her tone was both spiteful and assured. "Who is she? The dead girl. Some savage you picked up in one of those benighted regions of which you appear so enamored? By the way, I expect you to clean up after your own mess. I shan't have unsavory gossip adhering itself to the family name."

Strathmore's eyes returned to the watch held in his large, steady palm. "One minute," he said tonelessly to no one in particular. "A strange concern on your part, madam. I wonder how you plan to discount the fact that you killed your husband. My father. As far as scandal goes, that's a piece of unsavory gossip that has clung to our family name these past two decades."

Blood rushed to Lady Strathmore's face, emotion eating away at her patina of arrogance. "You blame me?" Her slender fingers gripped the huge pearls at her neck. "Your father was a weak, hopeless excuse of a man—and you dare blame me?" Her voice rose an octave.

Strathmore snapped the watch shut and slid it into his pocket. "Your time is finished, Lady Strathmore. I can have Baxter, or if need be two footmen, escort you out."

Julia turned away, frozen, her hand on her mouth. Repulsed by the bitterness scorching the drawing room, she framed the scene in her mind's eye, so accustomed to capturing images on her copper plates. Strathmore and his mother were facing each other, their profiles a declaration of their shared blood. The delicacy of Lady Strathmore's features was misleading, as was the strength of Strathmore's jaw, the prominent nose.

And the eyes. The eyes were the same, Julia thought—gray, cold, and merciless.

She spun on her heels, the black and white tiled hallway offering the path of least resistance. Down two flights of stairs, past the unblinking stare of a footman, through the kitchen entrance, and out to the carriage house she flew. She couldn't begin to assimilate what she had just heard, nor did she want to. Her mind leapt ahead in self-defense, focusing on her camera waiting for her amid her trunks and boxes. She would get to it first, before Strathmore, the undeveloped daguerreotype of Faron the only bargaining tool at her disposal.

She was loathe to admit it—but she needed Strathmore, the dark and complicated man that he was, to begin unwinding the twisting lies and secrets that lay behind the perfectly manicured lives that Meredith had created for her and Rowena.

The scent of horseflesh and hay were reassuringly familiar, natural light spilling in from two overhead skylights. Ten stalls were neatly divided over a slightly inclined floor covered in hard Dutch brick laid on edge. The door to the harness room gaped open, revealing a fireplace and boiler and a partition wall boarded for harnesses and several saddle trees.

Silence—save for the shifting of hooves and the occasional quiet nicker. She leaned over the stall to stroke the strong neck of a Belgian warm blood, its velvety nose nudging toward her. The large head lifted, its ears came up and its nostrils quivered in soft answering snorts. The heat coming off the animal was soothing, the balm she needed before contemplating the neatly stacked tower of trunk and boxes. Strathmore, busy with Lady Strathmore, had yet to note the arrival of her belongings.

She relaxed for a moment, leaning toward the horse, then heard quiet footsteps behind her. From the corner of her eye, she saw Strathmore standing at the door, bringing with him an undercurrent of impatience. She pretended surprise, forcing the images of the drawing room and Lady Strathmore from her mind.

"My apologies," she murmured. "I wasn't expecting anyone to be here."

He took a step toward her. "Damned right."

She glanced over her shoulder and her heart tripped when her gaze met his. "You're angry." She couldn't account for the honesty tumbling from her lips.

It was beginning to rain again and she stilled her hand against the horse's neck, gentling him. She averted her eyes to the skylights overhead where fat raindrops splattered against the panes. A flash of white blue briefly illuminated the stables. A chorus of neighs followed.

Strathmore crossed his arms over his chest. "You constantly surprise me, Miss Woolcott. I didn't expect that you were given to eavesdropping."

Her head snapped around. He drew nearer, and she could see that his mouth was tight, his eyes calculating.

"I hadn't intended to listen in," she began, wondering how he'd known she was listening. "Not that there is any excuse for my lamentable behavior. Of course, I'm meant to be deceased, so it made no sense to make my presence known."

Strathmore took a step closer, and her lungs drained of air, her limbs of strength.

The horse recognized him, stretching its long neck to greet his master. Strathmore reached out instinctively, rhythmically rubbing the animal's nose. "I regret that you witnessed the exchange," he said abruptly.

Julia said nothing, wondering what it was like to be Alexander Strathmore, long estranged from his family, judging by the cold hatred that had enveloped the drawing room like a shroud.

"Lady Strathmore is a difficult woman," he said, filling in the silence that was punctuated only by the steadily increasing patter of rain overhead.

"I cannot really imagine it," said Julia honestly. "I cannot imagine my life without Meredith and Rowena. They mean everything to me."

"Then you are among the fortunate few, Miss Woolcott."

The admission was startling—coming from him. Strathmore continued caressing the animal and Julia was spellbound by his hands, large but beautifully made. Those same hands had . . . she stopped herself cold.

To halt her wayward thoughts, she rubbed her palms over her upper arms. "Family relations oftentimes can be strained," she said. She didn't remember her own mother or father, her past a blank slate, her whole world a cocoon circumscribed by Meredith and Rowena. She had never wanted anything more. Until now. And only because their lives were imperiled.

Lightning flashed in a staccato outburst. Strathmore could take her closer to that threat. She knew little enough about what lay beneath the surface of his façade of explorer and adventurer extraordinaire, but she had just gotten a glimpse in the drawing room. She didn't want to ask the question bubbling beneath the surface, whether it was true that Lady Strathmore had murdered her husband. The very possibility was horrendous. Julia would rather test nature's fury than question Strathmore on the matter.

The rain filled the silence that stretched like a rope on the verge of snapping.

"Are you an equestrienne, Miss Woolcott?" Strathmore said finally, startling her with an abrupt change in subject.

The tension momentarily dispelled, she let her eyes drift admiringly over the glossy coat of the Belgian. "Actually, no. I love horses, or at least my pony, Squire, who is as safe and comfortable as a rocking chair, but it is my sister who is the amazon in our family," she admitted honestly. "She is an excellent horsewoman while I, if you have not already noticed, am almost entirely without grace, continually tripping over my own feet."

"How is your wound healing?"

She flushed. "All is well, thank you. Baxter's poultice is helping immeasurably. Another example of my clumsiness, your point is well taken. Rowena is chiding me about it constantly, exhorting me to join her riding or in her explorations of the outdoors. But these pursuits are hardly my forte." Nervousness was causing her to chatter on.

"Your sister is important to you." It was a statement, not a question. Strathmore studied her over the ears of the horse. "Yours are other talents, I gather. The study of literature, history, botany, photography . . ."

"The latter rather than the former," she confessed, pleased to have the conversation steered onto more even ground. "Botany is readily available as subject matter for photography although I must confess to an interest in landscapes and portraiture as well. There is as much to be learned in the lines of a sunset or in the set of a brow as in the folds of a flower or leaf."

Strathmore listened carefully, as though mining her words for subtext. "How did you become immersed in daguerreotypy, Miss Woolcott?"

His tall frame seemed taller in the shadowed room, his presence perilous to her shaky resolve. She wondered for a moment whether to answer truthfully, or if it would help to qualify her response.

"Come now. You can tell me," his voice was quiet and without inflection, as he continued stroking the horse. "It's only fair that I should know something of you." *After what I heard eavesdropping,* she silently finished.

The Belgian snorted in agreement. Julia hesitated. "I was a rather peculiar, awkward child. Quite withdrawn, and not interested in the usual childhood pastimes and games."

Another clap of thunder was followed by a slice of lightning. The horses stomped their disapproval.

"Go on," said Strathmore, leaning against the stall door.

It occurred to her that they were very alone and, suddenly, his virility struck her like a blow, his muscled arms and broad chest filling her vision. She followed the lean, hard outlines of his torso with her gaze, words flowing to cover her painfully acute awareness. "I was a peculiar child," she repeated. "I always stood back, watching, observing, with very little interest in joining the play of the other children in the village, or even with my sister. Either my head was buried in a book or I elected to spend inordinate amounts of time alone."

She focused on the memories, anything to dilute the intensity of being so close to Strathmore. It was to be expected, her reaction to his presence, after the incidents at Eccles House, their enforced intimacy. The rain pounded on the skylights overhead, keeping time with her pulse. "As a result," she forced herself to continue, "my aunt retained many tutors for me, encouraging my studies. It was one of the last of these, a Mr. Masters, who had worked originally with Daguerre and Niepce in Paris a decade earlier, who introduced me to the process. He taught me everything I know about photography and it has been a passion ever since," she declared with a truthfulness that startled her.

"Your aunt is not only a wise but also an unusual woman."

Meredith was that and more. Julia's throat closed with emotion and she could only nod.

"To have taken on two wards was quite a responsibility. What was her relation to you and Rowena?" he asked evenly.

If only Julia knew the answer to that question. Not that he would believe her if she told him her life before Meredith did not exist. They were back on uneven ground. The thunder was a rumble in the distance, the rhythm of raindrops a background murmur.

"You have an enquiring mind, sir," she said lightly, "although that is to be expected from a man who spends his time in exploration of foreign shores."

He gave her a faint, hard smile, ignoring her reference to his own particular obsession. "I merely thought I could be of greater use to you in locating Faron if I had some prior knowledge of your family's relationship to him."

"You believe Meredith knows him." As did Julia, but she was unwilling to say so.

"Obviously—she gave you the daguerreotype. We can only wonder why it remains undeveloped, Faron's visage hidden from view. He clearly believes in remaining mysterious."

"Meredith counseled me to develop the plate only if necessary. We don't even know if the image will come through after the time that has elapsed," she confessed. "My aunt clearly suspected Faron was behind the invitation to Eccles House. Although how she could have known?"

"Only you can answer that question. If you're willing to try."

The carriage house was silent, the raindrops gradually ceasing their rhythm, the horses settling down with the cessation of the storm. "I would ask of your interest in Faron before I would be willing to disclose information about my situation."

"I've already said that he has something I want."

"Then you must know more about the man than you are willing to relate."

"That may be so, but there is little to gain in sharing the information with you. Other than placing you in grave danger—yet again."

Desperation warred with impatience. "I do not need protection, sir. Perhaps if we were to put our heads together—"

"What would you have done had I followed through—decided to kill you?" he asked abruptly. "There would have been little you could do to protect yourself."

"Then why didn't you?" The challenge slipped out before she knew it. "Kill me and be done with it. Gain Faron's trust—for whatever it is you want so desperately."

He didn't hesitate. "When I make up my mind, I do so quickly."

"So what changed it?"

Something flickered in the dark gray of his eyes. "The realization that I could get away with it—the double cross, as it were. Besides which, I relish a challenge, preferring to take a fork in a road rather than the direct way in."

Was he referring to her or Faron? Julia wasn't precisely certain. "Getting away with it, as you put it, requires that I remain dead and out of sight. And whilst I do that, how do you intend to proceed?"

He shook his head. "No need to involve you any further, Miss Woolcott. The image of Faron that you have in your possession might possibly be helpful enough."

"And if I refuse to disclose the whereabouts of the plate?" Julia did not know whence her courage came, other than a fierce determination to protect Meredith and Rowena.

"Then I believe that's what one calls an impasse," he said straightening away from the stall door, shoving his hands into his pockets. "Generally unhelpful."

"I'm surprised you have yet to ransack my belongings," she said, feeling unaccountably belligerent, her eyes on her trunk and boxes piled near the tack room.

"You need me, Miss Woolcott," he said bluntly, "more than I need you, daguerreotype or not." He dismissed her trunk with a glance. "You admitted it yourself, several times."

She jerked her chin, unwilling to admit even to herself that his very physicality, his obvious intelligence and penchant for arrogance, were precisely what she needed if she was to eliminate the danger to her family. Alexander Strathmore had crossed deserts, scaled mountains, exchanged words with long-lost primitives. For his own reasons, he wanted to locate Faron. He was one of the few men equipped to do so.

"That may be so, sir," she said, taking a step back and standing straight, attempting to intimidate him with her resolve.

The weather was clearing and watery light slanted through the skylights. She was struck anew by his stark power, the gleam of his black hair, his hard profile etched against the milky light. Again she thought of those searing moments at Eccles House, while a radiating heat bloomed in her chest.

Alexander Strathmore was a compelling man who surely had scores of women falling at his feet. She remembered the scorching looks that Felicity Clarence had cast his way. It had very possibly stretched Strathmore's own acting abilities, having to feign passion for an arguably plain woman, awkward and unversed in the arts of . . . *well*, the arts of Felicity, for want of a better description. Julia felt mortified all over again.

She desperately hoped he couldn't read her thoughts. Despite all the awkwardness between them, Strathmore was correct in his assessment of her situation, that she needed him more than he needed her. He waited for her to continue. "You are quite right," she admitted finally, "I do need you. Your assistance," she amended quickly. "I shall share the image of Faron with you on one condition."

He went still, clearly surprised. Then he tilted his head to the side and gave a disbelieving laugh. "Miss Woolcott, your conditions interest me not in the least. You can keep your daguerreotype. And please do not give me reason to caution you again about the dangers of attempting to find Faron on your own." It was both an acknowledgement and a warning.

"You mean before he finds me—or my aunt and sister—again?"

"A defensive move is most likely your safest option."

"As opposed to offensive?" As though a country mouse could mount an attack on a man as powerful as Faron. Perhaps not alone, Julia thought, but if she were to harness the talents of Strathmore . . . "How will I know that you have found Faron, unless I give you something in return?" she asked. "You have absolutely no reason to come back to me—"

"That's correct, no reason at all." His tone struck Julia like a blow. In that moment, the sun broke through the skylights overhead, framing them in a shared nimbus of light. Her heart thudded heavily but her mind skittered ahead, scavenging for possibilities.

"Have you no sympathy? The lives of my aunt and sister are at stake."

"Yet you refuse to tell me anything more about it."

"Because I don't know anything more," she confessed, well aware that the truth could hurt her.

His gaze shifted beyond her, to her trunk and collection of boxes. "I don't believe you. You're hiding something, Miss Woolcott." Causing her to hold her breath, he added, "I see it in your eyes."

He might as well have called her a bounder or a rakehell. "That's the most ridiculous notion I've ever heard," she said.

"Is it?"

"If you'll excuse me, I believe I'm finished here. I'm sure someone will deliver my belongings to my rooms." She gathered her skirts in one hand and turned to leave.

"What are you afraid of, Miss Woolcott, other than, of course, Faron?"

She should have kept walking. Instead, she stopped, as if in some unknown, secret part of her being, she knew the answer to that question. It had everything to do with Strathmore, and her confusing, inexplicable desire—craving—to be with the man. To touch him again, make him respond to her as a man responds to a woman. Were those her true motives, buried beneath her concern for Meredith and Rowena?

She felt on fire, anxious under the pressure of her feelings, wishing she could speak quickly and leave, but wanting to bring resolution to her suddenly ungovernable emotions. Damn, she was confused, her fear for Meredith and Rowena mingling with a desire as exotic to her as manna from heaven. As always when the weight of life became too much for her, she lost her willingness to speak, words scuttling away from her, lost in her mind, cotton batting lodged in her throat.

Biting her lower lip, she turned toward him, intending to force out a quick adieu and flee to her rooms to collect herself. Answering his question was proving more difficult than she'd imagined, his probing had lifted the scarred corners of a deep wound she was reluctant to examine.

"Are you staring at me because you are afraid to respond to my question, Julia?" His use of her name was terrifying, testament to the strange and improbable intimacy that yoked them together. He smiled, disarming her, stripping away another layer of her defense before she could snatch it back. "You become strangely quiet when pressed," he said.

He was close, too close, not simply contracting the space between them but trespassing upon a place deep in her soul. The last of her resolve threatened to crumble when he captured both of her hands in one of his. Sparks, a combination of pleasure and pain, danced up her arm and along her spine at the brush of his thumb over the back of her hand.

"I could help you, Julia, if you would but let me." A finger beneath her chin tilted her face to his. Her lips parted, but no words formed on her tongue. Her complex desires were reflected in his eyes, trapping her there. Escape became impossible.

Her eyes closed at the first brush of his lips, his mouth warm and compelling, sliding over hers with a languor that made her arch up against him, searching for more. The breadth of his hand at her back molded her to him, making her forget all reason and any argument, her fear disintegrating when he drew her bottom lip between his teeth. He traced the lush fold with the velvet of his tongue. "What is it that happens when your eyes shutter, your expression stills, as though you are going to a place far away, known only to you?"

She felt boneless, a moment away from melting into a puddle at his feet. She was as powerless to stop him as she was to stop the yearnings of her body. His breath skimmed along the skin of her throat. "You may trust me, Julia. I spared your life. I can help you if you'll help me." His hands at her back arched her nearer until Julia helplessly sank her fingers into his hair, cupping his head between her palms. She was watching them, watching herself with an anguish that burned, every inch of her body and every corner of her mind desperate for his touch, yet dreading it all at once.

He kissed her more deeply and her own mouth, lips, and tongue matched his strokes, a slow, torpid battle that neither could lose. Her breasts were heavy, a taut fullness that left her panting for more. Her lips parted to welcome the deep thrust of his tongue, her thighs resting between his, the heat beneath the voluminous fabric and heavy whalebone as startling as licks of flame.

She felt his hands maneuvering beneath her skirts and along the stockinged length of her inner thigh. She twisted her head away, gasping for breath, for reason, and for words.

He supplied the voice for her thoughts. "I know you believe this unfair," he said as her skin pulsed with his heat. His hand spread over her thigh and his fingertips brushed against the lace at the tops of her cotton stockings. "But I know when you are at your most vulnerable, Julia. You remember as well as I our encounter at Eccles House, however much you'd prefer to forget," he murmured against her lips, his hand cupping her thigh and caressing the curve of her buttock. "I have a most vivid recollection of your offering me your breasts."

A liquid flame poured through her, an exquisitely painful amalgam of desire and shame. She cringed against him, the desperate humming of her mind grappling for logic and reason. It was then she looked up at the skylight, where a shadow passed over them like a cloud over the sun.

The hard muscles under her hands went rigid. They heard a footstep above, the roof of the carriage house creaking under its own weight. The rectangle of light still enveloped them but also threw a hulking, cloaked shadow against the wall.

Strathmore tensed as the fine nerves at the back of Julia's neck prickled. Without saying a word, he edged them back against the wall of one of the stalls.

The shadow grew and Strathmore's eyes sought the source. A face, shielded by a tall hat, appeared in the window, and then shifted slightly, as Strathmore suspected it would. Julia's lips parted wordlessly as Strathmore threw his body atop hers, in perfect time with the retort of a pistol, the noise exploding in the silence of the carriage house.

The horses went wild. Julia and Strathmore went down hard, rolling into a bale of hay just as the bullet struck the stone masonry a few feet away from them. Splinters of glass glanced off Strathmore's hands and shoulders. He pinned Julia to the ground beneath him, craning his neck to see the shadow above them disappear as quickly as it had come.

Julia struggled under his greater size and weight, trying to roll onto her side, the snorting and stomping of the horses forming an unruly background chorus. A heavy piece of parchment descended from the broken skylight overhead, landing a few feet from their grasp.

"Get off me!" She turned her head in profile so as not to make eye contact, no doubt battling both fear and mortification.

He swallowed his irritation, remembering the intricate charade that accompanied so-called intimate relations in England. So bloody complicated when it should be so very simple. "Are you hurt?" Strathmore was reluctant to move; the length of her body beneath him seemed to meld with his own. When she didn't immediately answer, he followed her gaze to the white piece of parchment lying tantalizingly close by. She freed a hand trapped between his chest and hers and stretched for the paper. But his arms were longer. He closed his hand over the missive. "Are you alright?" he asked again.

"In all probability I'm fine," she said, "unless you have succeeded in crushing me." She simmered beneath him, angry at herself, him and, the note in his hands and not in hers.

To hell with her. He'd saved her life twice and all he had to show for it was her pinched, outraged response. He pushed himself upright, ignoring her and his cockstand for the moment. He seemed to have a raging erection whenever Miss Woolcott was near.

As for the crumbled parchment in his hand, he didn't have to look at the script to know whom it was from.

The recent escapade, the shards of glass, and the spent bullet underscored that his ruse had failed. Faron's people knew Julia Woolcott remained alive and that he had not delivered on his promise. However, it was clear the single shot fired from the skylight above had deliberately missed its mark. A provocation and a warning, a signal that more was to come.

Julia had pushed herself to her feet, brushing her bodice and skirts with surprisingly steady hands. It occurred to him that he should have helped her rise, but he was predictably reluctant to touch her again, the ache in his groin not even beginning to dissipate.

Her hair tumbled around her face, and her eyes were wide with misplaced fear. With an instinct honed over the years of amorous encounters, he knew that she was afraid of her response to him, overwhelmed by sensations for which she had no name. It was a response that he could and would continue to use to his advantage. Because there was no doubt, Julia Woolcott was hiding something, not only from him but from herself. Montagu Faron, he'd wager, was at its center. The man remained a cipher, remote, mysterious and dangerous— particularly to the Woolcott family.

The flames of ambition burned higher. Strathmore was adept at reconnaissance—byzantine mountain passages and perilous terrains a temptation more seductive to him than a king's ransom. It was the unknown that interested him most, snagged his attention, and played him along like the most accomplished seductress. He was not about to surrender.

"That note"—Julia began tightly—"I'd like to read it."

"I'm sure you would."

"It's the very least you could do," she said with forced primness, leaning on the bale of hay to get her bearings. She smoothed the lace collar at the neckline of her dress, trying to lessen the imprint of his hands on her skin.

He brushed the dust and a shard of glass from his knees. "The very least I could do," he repeated, looking for a small kernel of apology in her subtly delivered scorn. "Are you not concerned that you were very nearly shot and that I saved you from a wayward bullet?"

"I refuse to indulge in a fit of the vapors. Meredith always counseled us to keep our heads. But it is the very least you could do after . . ." Her voice trailed off.

"So I'm to understand you are referring not to the fact that I saved your life," he said, "but that I should in some way compensate you for my unwelcome advances upon your person—which is absurd, as you very well realize."

Her eyebrows shot up. "Hardly absurd! Simply because we found ourselves in an awkward situation at Eccles House, you have no reason to continue with this . . . with this . . ." She freed herself with some difficulty from his gaze, and frowned down at his hand and the crumpled note.

"Hypocrisy does not become you, Miss Woolcott," he said with grim humor, shoving the note into his pocket. "You constantly remind me of your erudition and yet you continue to deny what is plainly and obviously nature's intended course. Despite your having read Catullus and de Sade, you are reluctant to admit that pleasure stimuli create a craving between the male and female, a very basic way of explaining why crocodiles go to the bother of having sex despite the anatomical challenges posed by their muscular tails and why lions mate continuously for three to four days at a time."

She opened her mouth and closed it again. Then blurted out, "Crocodiles and lions? You are comparing what we just did with *animals?*"

"We are animals, Miss Woolcott, mammals more specifically. Furthermore, in my travels, I have found the sexual compulsion is something humankind shares across all tribes and clans—if they are willing to admit to the fact."

"Ahh, yes, of course. I had forgotten what an expert you are."

"You are so rigid, Miss Woolcott, I sometimes believe you might shatter into a million pieces."

Julia tilted her head back, a hand to her forehead. "You are truly conniving, do you know that, Strathmore?"

It was not the response he'd expected.

"You expect me to accept your palaver when in reality I know why it is that you are forcing your attentions—"

The thought was repugnant. "Hardly forcing. I'd be more than pleased to parse out your extravagant response to . . ." He was unable to finish.

She batted away his explanations with her hands. "Precisely, Strathmore! You are using your knowledge of these things"—she paused—"to overwhelm me, to rob me of reason, to have me do your bidding. All of which has less to do with our animalistic tendencies and everything to do with your own coldly rational strategems concerning Faron."

A brief, silent stalemate followed.

Her analysis was impressive. "Sometimes," he said slowly, "it helps to have one's thinking processes shut off, to feel rather than to cogitate. In short, you think too much."

"I'm certain you prefer your women not to think at all. It only gets in the way of your ambitions," she said tartly.

"An oversimplification, and unworthy of your subtle intelligence, Miss Woolcott."

"Oh, hell and damnation," she said through clenched teeth, beginning to straighten her hair, sticking pins into the thickness right and left. "You wish to seduce me, I fully realize, Strathmore, not for my person but rather for the information I may divulge. And further," she continued, jabbing a pin into the coil at the nape of her neck, "I don't flatter myself with the delusion that your actions are genuine."

It struck him that he could not honestly respond to her assertion. That he could not be attracted to a country mouse, a bluestocking, an untutored virgin? A siren in a film of blue silk with legs that beckoned and skin like cream?

Christ, he couldn't hope to explain it himself. Except in the reality of the moment, when he wanted nothing more than to throw her against the bale of hay, pull the pins from her hair and complete what had started those first moments in the dark, cork-lined room at Eccles House.

No doubt he'd simply been without a woman for too long. His mind worked efficiently, coming to his rescue. He would seek to remedy the situation. Because authentic enthusiasm was the greatest aphrodisiac, prostitutes had never appealed to him and he had been away far too long from England to have a mistress at the ready in some town house off Grosvenor Square. There were other options to be considered.

Her next words interrupted his plans. "Do you appreciate how ridiculous this discussion is when we have more important matters to resolve?" She paused significantly. "Such as the message in your trouser pocket. Who is it from—Faron?" Her dark blue eyes were on him, an unidentifiable expression fleeing from them, neatly setting aside the physical matters raging between them.

There was nothing she could do about it. To test her, he pulled the note from his pocket. Lowther's assured and confident signature stared back at him. A meeting the next evening at Gordon Square.

"Oh, tell me what it bloody well says." Her voice was rich with resentment.

He made a sound of mock disapproval at the oath. "Why should I, Miss Woolcott? Remind me again, if you please." Strathmore made sure his smile was provocative. "Your penchant for cursing is startling, by the way."

She blinked and then straightened her spine, unmistakably putting distance between them. "The daguerreotype."

He shook his head. "Nice to have but not necessary. We're not even certain that an image exists after all this time. What else?" It was a goad intended to ensure she knew her place in the complicated and very dangerous dance.

"Nothing else. I know nothing else."

He didn't believe her. "But you do know that Faron's people have learned"—he glanced up at the skylight—"that you're alive."

Her face lit up with a smile, and he was struck by its beauty. Her full mouth, the mouth he'd tasted just moments before, curved into unadulterated pleasure. "Then I can let Meredith and Rowena know I am well and warn them of Faron's intentions."

"About which you know nothing," he said.

"Which is precisely the reason why I am accompanying you wherever you go from this moment onward." She glanced at the note in his hand. "You have another meeting, do you not? With the man you mentioned previously. It's obvious."

Her mind was quick.

"How would that help? Your accompanying me—other than to flaunt my failure."

Her eyes lit up at the possibility.

"Don't look so keen, Miss Woolcott."

She ignored the sarcasm. "I might recognize him, or something may jog my memory." There was a slight hoarseness to her voice, a plaintiveness touched with desperation that told him she was telling the truth. He'd suspected whatever she knew lay buried deep, requiring an excavation that would be both profound and painful.

"Would you tell me if it did?"

She glanced at him ferociously, and he could see love blazing in her eyes. He stepped back from the force of it. "If it would help Meredith and Rowena—then yes."

For only a moment, he saw ambition and love balanced on an imaginary scale. It wasn't very often he was compelled to take a good look at himself, at what drove him to undertake risks few of his countrymen would dare and for results that were elusive at best. For the first time, he didn't like what he saw. And so Alexander Francis Strathmore found himself giving in to Julia Woolcott when he said, surprising himself most of all, "Very well, we meet with Lowther tomorrow evening. As always—"

She interrupted with a small smile. "Yes, I can guess. I've heard it several times in the past few days. As always, *follow your lead.*"

But Strathmore was left wondering exactly who followed whom.

Chapter 7

With no small amount of anxiety, Meredith Woolcott ran her long fingers through the dry soil of a dying potted orchid. The damned thing needed water. For the past twenty-four hours she had done nothing but watch the rain-soaked landscape from the windows of the drawing room at Montfort. As she watched the orchid die she felt the spirit drain from her with each minute that passed without word from Julia.

She compressed her lips at the pain that was almost physical, eating at her like the sharp teeth of an invisible gremlin. She should never have let Julia go, innocent and infinitely fragile Julia. Shaking her head, Meredith wandered restlessly over to the wide-sashed windows which afforded a magnificent view of the estate. Fog and mist enshrouded gently rolling green hills, and her eyes strained to see through the thickness to the horizon.

If anything happened to Julia, she would never forgive herself. The words were whispered, a promise, as stale and fevered an exhortation as she had ever made.

Her eyes scanned the expanse of green, expecting to see Rowena on her horse, knowing that the girl rode equally joyfully in the rain or the sun. Hers was the more resilient nature, a gift of fate, that she had been so young, not really more than an infant, when she had first come to live with Meredith.

The burden of knowledge had always rested with Julia. A little girl who chose to sit wordlessly, day after day, in the nursery where no amount of cajoling or pretty toys could move her from her haven of silence, until the day Meredith had spied her from the doorway, pulling books from the nursery shelves, opening them with her tiny hands. As her rosebud mouth moved while she read the words silently to herself, her world began to blossom.

Meredith remembered dismissing the hovering nurse and reading to Julia, instinctively aware of the prodigious curiosity and appetite for learning that her young charge exhibited. Gradually, like a flower opening to the sun, Julia began to venture beyond the nursery rooms of Montfort. Finding herself in the kitchen, in the stables, or in Meredith's private library, she watched steadily and carefully, like a small woodland creature, the floured hands of the cook kneading dough, the mesmerizing flick of a horse's tail in the stables, or the gardener at work in the rich dark soil of the gardens.

So many years ago.

Meredith's heart swelled with love and worry. She was neither a weak nor sentimental woman, a rarity in an age freighted with dependent women, entangled in the ties that bound them as wives, mothers and widows. All the more reason she detested the feeling of helplessness, her inability to do much more than wait. It did not sit comfortably with her, the unfamiliar tightness in her chest. She had done so well for so long. In a strange twist of fate, she had been made wealthy in her own right, wealth that had allowed her to protect herself and her wards from the evil that she had had a hand in creating.

Her profile was outlined in the misted pane of glass, dark shadows scored beneath her eyes. She pulled a handkerchief from the sleeve of her dress, wiping a few traces of earth from her fingers before twisting the fabric into a tight braid.

Meredith had regrets. All too many. But she did not lament retaining Harold Masters, scientist and scholar, upon the recommendation of her old friend, Henri Daguerre. Masters was the last in a long line of tutors hired to instruct Julia, who had quickly outgrown a series of governesses versed in little more than French and pianoforte. Who could have predicted that Julia would fall in love with the newfound discovery of daguerreotypy, with its ability to fix the world on copper plates? Meredith smiled to herself. She should have known that Julia, the eternal observer, with her wide eyes and fathomless gaze, would find herself entranced with the mechanisms that could capture the splendors and details of nature and reality.

Meredith pulled the flimsy fabric in her hands taut. She thought of the monograph, *Flowers in Shadows: A Botanical Journey.* Dear God, why had she permitted its publication? And why had she allowed Julia to accept Wadsworth's invitation and the use of Wadsworth's conveyance? Rather than her own? The girls had never strayed far from her orbit, a sacrifice without doubt, but one necessary to their continued well-being.

Her eyes scanned the horizon, looking for Rowena tacking the expanse of gray and damp hillside. Her younger ward should be back from the stables. The knot of worry hardened in her stomach.

Meredith stepped back from the window. Those overriding and dark presentiments did not suit her disposition one whit. She would send Marksbury to Eccles House. She had barely made the decision when the door to the drawing room slammed open. In two strides, Marksbury was in the center of the room, chest heaving, perspiration running down his face and dampening the tightly wound cravat at his throat.

Meredith's heart stopped beating.

"Forgive me for the intrusion, Lady Woolcott," her secretary stammered. "However, I have no choice but to burst in, unannounced. I don't know precisely how to relay the news."

Meredith felt the blood drain from her face. It took all the courage she had to achieve a measured tone. "Calm yourself, Marksbury. What is it? Is it Miss Julia?"

The man's eyes bulged with disbelief. "Once again, I must

ask your forgiveness. I realize that I am not at my most co-
herent at the moment. But it concerns not only Miss Julia."

For a fleeting moment, Meredith Woolcott stared dumb-
foundedly at her secretary. *Montagu Faron.* She twisted the
handkerchief in her hand into one more knot before tossing
it to the ground. "What is it? Out with it," she ordered,
aware that her voice was high-pitched and strained.

"Miss Rowena . . ." Marksbury thrust a hand through his
hair and turned to stare out the windows, afraid to meet his
mistress's panicked gaze.

Behind Meredith, as though in another world, a world
she'd left behind, there were the usual familiar sounds, the
chime of a clock, the crackle of a fire, evidence of a well run
household, a universe unto itself.

When Marksbury could bear to form the words, he said,
"It's not simply Miss Julia . . ."

"Rowena ventured out, riding," said Meredith, lying to
herself because she could not abide the truth. "Please gather
yourself together, Marksbury."

"If it were only so. I regret . . . ," said Marksbury.

Meredith Woolcott steeled herself. "Regret." She paused.
"Regret what?"

Marksbury's voice trembled and his next words were muffled, as though coming from far away. A note with a piece of
fabric fluttered from his clenched fist to the floor.

The fragile serenity of the drawing room fractured into a
hundred sharp pieces. Meredith sank to her knees, holding
her head in her shaking hands, her skirts ballooning around
her. She did not have to ask who. Or what. Or why.

The abyss yawned before her, the maw of the devil.

She knew.

Giles Lowther paced in the downstairs parlor of his rented
rooms above Whites. Despite having been born in the capital,
he'd never liked London, its eternal grayness and low squat-
ting buildings an inexplicable affront to his sensibilities. Having spent most of his childhood and youth abroad, he felt

more at home on the continent than he ever had in his place of birth.

He watched the clock closely, when he was not going to the window or the front door at least a dozen times, waiting for Beaumarchais to return. It was essential to know that the world was unfolding according to plan. Not his, precisely, but Faron's.

Lowther clenched and unclenched his fists, his mind further disordered by the complications that had overtaken all his careful machinations. He shifted from foot to foot, his riding boots gleaming in the firelight that burned low in the small hearth.

Where the bloody hell was the man?

It wasn't enough that Strathmore had been unable or—interesting thought—unwilling to murder the woman. Disappointing to Faron on the one hand but intriguing in other ways. Lowther recalled Faron's eyes glinting behind his mask with something close to appreciation at the news. He seemed to savor a nugget of knowledge he had mined from Strathmore's actions, a clue to the man's true character that he would store away for further use.

Being the genius he was, Faron had simply moved on to the next level of his labyrinthine scheme. The plan had always been to ensure that Meredith Woolcott would suffer, in the most exquisitely attenuated way possible.

Lowther wondered if there was something else at play. Faron, at his most lucid, did everything for a reason and his interest in Strathmore was intriguing. He could have dispatched any number of loyal acolytes to Eccles House to ruin Julia Woolcott and yet he'd chosen to inveigle Strathmore in his plans.

Why? Lowther turned the question over in his mind, expecting the discreet knock on the door when it came. "Enter," he said.

Beaumarchais complied, droplets of rain shimmering on his top hat and cloak, neither of which he bothered to remove. They dispensed with formalities. Lowther turned to pour coffee from the low side table. He detested the English tea habit, the murky hot water with its milky cast.

He looked up, handing Beaumarchais the cup and saucer. "Well, what's the news?" he asked without preamble.

"The message has been sent to Montfort."

"Well and good. However, you and I both know it won't take long for Meredith Woolcott to discover the truth of the matter."

Beaumarchais pursed his lips. "That her ward is indeed alive."

Lowther nodded, looking into his coffee cup as though to divine some meaning from the brown depths. "Have you seen to the other set of instructions?"

"Of course. Need you ask?"

"After the last mishap, absolutely." Lowther was aware of the other man's fingernails tapping against the porcelain cup. A sign of nervousness, never good. "Are you certain there will be no irregularities this time?" He stared pointedly at Beaumarchais, watching as his eyes darted around the room. He had never understood what Faron liked about Beaumarchais who seemed to be nothing more than a dissipated rogue more concerned with his own vanity than lofty, complex pursuits.

Beaumarchais returned his gaze with thinly veiled venom. "I did not choose Strathmore for the assignment in the first instance, as you will recall. And I was the one who recognized early on that he had experienced a crisis of conscience." The last three words were said contemptuously. "Who would have thought that a man who has lived among savages for the past five years would find himself reluctant to ruin and then dispatch the chit."

Lowther smiled thinly. "So sorry to disappoint, Beaumarchais, but I'm afraid Strathmore is still part of the overall plan."

Beaumarchais was perplexed and put down his cup and saucer noisily. "He can't be trusted, clearly. So why involve him further?" He flicked raindrops impatiently from his arms.

"I think you heard me." Beaumarchais opened his mouth to ask for more details, but Lowther cut him off. "Never mind Strathmore at the moment. I shall look after him."

Beaumarchais bristled at the slight. "I don't like or trust him."

"That's entirely immaterial to me. Of absolutely no account."

"And as a result, I chose another man for this latest purpose," Beaumarchais said petulantly.

"Very well," Lowther replied coolly. "Whoever it is that you've chosen, please assure me that we will be successful this time."

"I did not choose Strathmore," Beaumarchais repeated.

"So you've said," replied Lowther. "Although it does you little good to remind me repeatedly." He glanced at the clock on the mantel before taking a final look at the dregs of his coffee. "I am late."

Beaumarchais narrowed his eyes. "Oh, do allow me to accompany you, sir. You might discover that you require assistance on your mission."

Lowther wondered whether, for all his irritating qualities, Beaumarchais might prove of further use. Highly unlikely, he thought cynically, deciding to swallow the bitter dregs of his coffee after all.

Chapter 8

Torrington Place was a strange, domed structure, out of place in London's Gordon Square. To the back of the lumbering Queen Anne edifice, at the corner of Euston and Gower streets, sat a smaller building on the edge of a park, bordered by tall, densely planted trees and smaller clumps of bushes.

Under the hissing glare of gaslight and the torch in Strathmore's hand, a path strewn with pine needles and leaves led to two metal doors curiously decorated with lions' heads and unicorns. Behind her, Julia heard Strathmore's carriage clatter around the corner, leaving them standing alone on the front stoop. No light glowed through the handsome curtained windows of the residence.

"Is this where he lives? Lowther?" asked Julia. "Although it seems that no one is at home, the place looks quite forlorn." Pine needles crunched underfoot, and she was relieved to be wearing her own sensible boots and boucle cloak rescued from her trunks earlier in the day.

"We're early by several hours. I thought it best to investigate the premises before Lowther's arrival," said Strathmore. He produced a key from his greatcoat, inserting it into the heavy oval lock and easing the door open.

Julia shook her head in amazement, pushing back the hood of her cloak. "How did you get that?" She pointed at his right hand, illuminated by the light of the torch.

"It pays to be prepared," he said briskly, pulling her into the hallway and closing the door behind him. "We must find a place to stow you safely out of sight, before Lowther's arrival." The remnants of reluctance were in his voice. He had agreed to allow her to accompany him as long as her presence remained undetected.

The torchlight illuminated a handsomely proportioned atrium dotted with unlit sconces bracketing shadowed entranceways. A mustiness like dried leaves permeated the air. "We assume that he already knows I'm still alive. So what precisely is the point?" Julia kept her voice low. Turning around in a half circle, she examined her surroundings, her booted feet in their low riding heels silent on the polished parquet floor. "Besides which, I should like to get a close look at the man. It may help in some way." Yet at the same time, she didn't want to awaken what her memory might hold.

Strathmore's look was assessing. "You have the purported daguerreotype of the man we're looking for."

She had been reluctant to share it with him. "You doubt it is Faron's likeness?"

He shrugged under his greatcoat, the torch sending an unsettling beam of light skittering across one wall. "We can't be certain, despite your aunt's assurances."

She was uncomfortably reminded of those intimate moments in the carriage house. And of every uncomfortable moment they had ever spent together. "That's the reason you didn't press the matter," she said tightly. "And why you agreed to allow me to accompany you this evening. At least you believe that I may be of some help to you. I do have a particular talent remembering people's faces, given my interests."

They both knew that he was pressing for something entirely different, using whatever devious means at his disposal to arouse her attraction to him. Well, it would not happen again. She was mortified at how easily she melted at his touch, like one of her copper images, blossoming in the light.

What must he think of her, a pitiful spinster thirsty for a man's attentions?

He was watching her carefully. "I still believe that you're hiding, Julia. If not from me, then from yourself," he offered so softly he might have been talking to himself. His shadow loomed, as unaccountably frightening as her conviction that she had given him a glimpse into her life. From their first moments together, he had pushed the door open and she was aware that she didn't even know what lay beyond it.

There was no response she could readily give, so she swallowed her fear and uttered the words heaviest on her heart. "At the very least, I insist that after this rendezvous, I send a missive to my aunt and sister, letting them know the truth."

"Which is what exactly?"

The question hovered in the air between them, destined to remain unanswered.

Julia looked around the hallway wordlessly before returning her eyes to Strathmore's, preferring to focus on the exigencies of the moment rather than the emotions that raged between them. "You are quite correct in that we should take the time to explore and find a suitable vantage point from which I can observe undetected," she said, deliberately neutral. "Perhaps a wardrobe might do, although I don't know where we might find one in a salon or drawing room."

The chill of Strathmore's gray eyes in the shadows reminded her again how freighted with tension their conversations always were, emphasizing the improbability of their burgeoning physical intimacy. Julia had never allowed herself to believe such a world of blazing carnality existed. At least for her. And with a man such as Strathmore. It seemed impossible.

He looked at her hard. "I'm sure we'll find something suitable. The owner of the house, Dr. Grant, has unorthodox tastes pertaining to furnishings, as you will see."

And Julia did see. Following behind Strathmore, she found not a traditional drawing room but what could only be called a life-sized curio cabinet, holding floor-to-ceiling bookshelves crowded with dusty tomes and interspersed with jars holding unidentifiable objects. In the center of the chaos stood two long tables displaying what appeared to be blanched bones and other curious creatures.

Sharing none of her surprise, Strathmore moved to the curtained window that stretched across the far end of the room, and opened it outward onto the park. A gust of damp wind filtered into the stale air along with the dimmest of gaslight from the lone lantern at the edge of the park.

"Who is this Dr. Grant and how do you know him?" asked Julia peering at what appeared to be the skeleton of a dog's head.

Closing the window and letting the curtain swing back in place, Strathmore shone his torch onto the glass topped specimen. "That's the complete skull of a Tasmanian wolf, a large marsupial carnivore from New Guinea. Dr. Grant and I have crossed paths through our association with the Royal Society."

"I surmise this Lowther fellow knows him as well. Or were you the one who chose Dr. Grant's residence for this rendezvous?"

Without answering directly, Strathmore said, "Since Grant is away in Australia, I knew we could meet here in total privacy."

Julia stared at what appeared to be a zebra encased in glass. "Remarkable," she said under her breath. "I had never thought until now of taking photographs of such specimens. It would make flora and fauna so much more available to a wider audience."

Julia found Strathmore standing by her elbow, disturbingly close. "Indeed it would," he said. "I have often thought it would be useful to have a camera available at certain junctures in my explorations."

She traced a trail of dust on the glass with the tip of her gloved finger. "At present the apparatus is cumbersome, making travel difficult. Only think of the jumble of boxes and trunks that I took to Eccles House. However, only recently I received a letter from Mr. Masters speaking of new advances that will soon make the entire process less unwieldy and time consuming."

"You continue your connection with Masters."

"He introduced me to daguerreotypy and since that time we have formed a close working relationship. He is very knowledgeable and continues to be of help in my pursuits."

"You never thought to wed the man?"

She looked up at him, startled. "Wed the man?" she managed to say calmly, even as a sense of unreality began to seep into her mind. She was imagining that tone of possessiveness in his voice.

"It would seem a suitable match as there are no dynastic ambitions to get in the way," he said flatly.

"Women can and do lead fulfilling lives without husbands and children," she bristled. She gestured to the encased zebra. "Why is it that only men should have an interest in the wider world, in the pursuit of knowledge and study?"

"Why indeed," he said with dark irony. "Clearly, you and your aunt and sister are doing remarkably well without the encumbrances of a man to lead the family."

"We were doing quite well. Aunt Meredith is the most capable individual I know."

"You are impressively loyal, Miss Woolcott. But have you ever wondered what your aunt is keeping from you and why?"

Always questions—which she could not answer. He acknowledged her struggle with a faint smile and it blunted the edge of her frustration. She wasn't any more pleased at being there with him than he was to have her. It was a staggering insight, the contrariness of it all—that the pursuit of Montagu Faron had brought such opposites together.

She was so absorbed in the clamor of her thoughts she had missed the echo of boots on the path outside the drawing room. Strathmore hadn't. He touched her arm, glancing about the room. He had obviously visited Dr. Grant in the past because he made his way unerringly to the far wall lined with bookshelves.

"Lowther's not alone. There are two of them."

Startled by the realization, she followed him wordlessly. He pushed the edge of a bookshelf and swept her backward into the space behind it before she could protest. It was a closet, a hidden storage space, and he pressed them inside, pulling the bookcase all but closed, leaving a sliver of an opening. He held her close, his arm hard beneath her breasts as they sank back in the darkness. The scent of cedar filled their nostrils as Lowther marched into the room.

He had lit the sconces in the hallway, spilling light into the drawing room, illuminating the jumble of curios, the lifetime collection of Dr. Grant. Julia's eyes widened at the man who followed close behind him.

"I don't believe we have finished our discussion," Beaumarchais said, grimacing fastidiously at the little mound of bones in a cabinet to his immediate left.

"To the contrary. You need not have accompanied me here. It was a moment of weakness on my part, clearly," said Lowther dryly.

Ignoring Lowther's irritation, Beaumarchais forged onward. "I need more information if this Woolcott business is to be completed satisfactorily."

Julia remembered where she was and tensed against Strathmore, Beaumarchais unexpected presence igniting searing images of those hours at Eccles House. The picture of craven overindulgence with his smoothly oiled hair, Beaumarchais concerned himself with adjusting the fit of his brocade greatcoat, absently fingering the two stiff-upward points of his cravat.

In the sliver of light, she could see that Lowther was a tall, barrel-chested man, with a retreating hairline, ascetic nose and high brow. There was nothing familiar to her about his features. Julia sank back against the hardness of Strathmore's chest, which rose and fell steadily behind her. She tried to ignore other sensations—the pistol in the waistband of his trousers or the hand that had tightened ever so slightly around her waist.

The situation was quickly becoming untenable. More specifically, her reaction to Strathmore was becoming untenable. Her head was at war with her senses. She was tempted to dissolve into his hard warmth, radiating like a hot summer's day through the damp boucle of her cloak. Mesmerized by the reassuring evenness of his breathing, she briefly closed her eyes, shutting out Lowther and Beaumarchais, taking in Strathmore's scent like the addictive drug it was turning out to be. She had never been so close to a man, and certainly never a man like Strathmore with his assertive physicality that, in the dark, filled her entire world.

She kept her eyes closed, fighting the urge to surrender, to renounce her quest to unearth Faron and simply allow the white heat of desire to take her away. She resisted the inexplicable and mortifying impulse to place her hand over his at her waist and drag it down around the curve of her hips, past her buttocks and between her thighs. To seek and find all the hidden, secret places in her body that craved to be stroked, savored, and seduced when he was near.

Her eyes flew open at the outrageous thoughts, only to see Lowther turn and stare directly at the hairline opening of the bookshelf. She held her breath, tightening her spine against Strathmore.

"It would help to know," Beaumarchais was saying, watching Lowther survey the gilt-edged spine of a book, "what possible reason Strathmore might have to please our mutual friend."

"You don't like the man, that's clear," said Lowther distinctly, brushing a blunt-fingered hand against a title and then letting it drop again. "Did he best you at something, perhaps steal a woman? You are such a peacock, Beaumarchais," he continued. "Besides, I thought we'd finished with this discussion earlier at my apartments. What other reason do you have to follow me here?"

"I don't trust Strathmore."

"Your repetition is becoming tedious. I shall ask again—why should that be of concern to me?"

"Don't you wonder why Faron is so intrigued with the man? When he could have hired someone far more suitable for the assignment of tormenting Meredith Woolcott."

Lowther could not possibly be standing any closer to the bookshelf, hovering for agonizing seconds just inches from the hidden storage space. Julia's breathing became shallower, swifter, as Strathmore shifted his arm up from her waist until it brushed the underside of her breasts. She did not know which terrified her more—the prospect of discovery or the exquisite agony of Strathmore's unbearable proximity.

"Perhaps you should rephrase your question—why is Strathmore eager to do Faron's bidding when he has the world on a string?"

Lowther scanned the bookshelf with watery blue eyes, and Julia noted when they narrowed speculatively. Sliding a large book from the shelf, he turned to Beaumarchais, rifling through the pages until he found what he was looking for.

"What do you know of the Nile, Beaumarchais?" he asked.

Strathmore shifted slightly behind her, easing his leg aside so his pistol wasn't digging into her backside. Instead, she felt the hard muscles of his thigh nestling directly into the folds of her skirts and suddenly she regretted her decision not to don crinolines and hoops. Only her chemise and outer skirts separated her from the hard, unfamiliar body warming hers.

"Not very much, I'm pleased to say, other than what I learned at the Sorbonne in my youth," confirmed Beaumarchais with a certain amount of smugness. "And I know next to nothing, I happily confess, about the flotsam and jetsam Grant keeps littered about here." He confronted a series of glass beakers, picked one up, turned it about in his hand, and put it down again. "Damned odd fellow," he muttered with a sniff.

Lowther cleared his throat impatiently. "You were asking about Strathmore."

"And you're going on about the Nile."

"That's what Strathmore is after. And what Faron can give him."

"I don't understand," said Beaumarchais bluntly.

Lowther slammed the book down on top of a glass-plated shelf. From the corner of her eyes, Julia thought she spied a map. Her mind was suddenly sharp and alert and she wondered how Strathmore would react to her learning more about his plans regarding Faron. Her body pulsed with a strange desire for the man who, for the moment, was just as vulnerable as she.

Lowther jabbed a finger on the pages opened before him. "The Nile has been an obsession that has driven many explorers to their deaths. Finding its source has become known as the Great Prize. Because of the river's maze-like tributaries, the source of all the water is hidden from view," he explained, tracing a finger along the edge of the opened book. "Many believe that finding its source would provide tremendous hydrological power to the discoverer. The rumor is that there are great lakes in Central Africa that are the true source of the Nile."

No response from Strathmore, aside from the fact that the rise and fall of his chest was all but undetectable. Julia made no attempt to ease away from his body. The two of them were riveted on the scene unfolding in Dr. Grant's strange drawing room.

Beaumarchais fingered his cravat carefully. "You mean to say that Faron has information as to the source of the river and Strathmore will do what he must to engage the man, even if that includes responding to some of his more outrageous and baroque requests," he said slowly, understanding dawning.

Closing the book definitively, Lowther waved away the accompanying cloud of dust. "It took you long enough, Beaumarchais."

"Why would Faron entertain Strathmore's interest? Have you ever thought to inquire?"

Lowther frowned. "I had heard something about Strathmore's last journey having taken him to Lake Tanganyiaka. Presumably Faron finds himself intrigued, although that is simply conjecture on my part."

"There's not more to it?"

Lowther looked halfway impressed at Beaumarchais's insistence. "How can one ever know with Faron? He has been following Strathmore's progress, intercepting and reading his missives to the Royal Society. When he discovered that Strathmore had also taken on the Mountains of the Moon, he became particularly excited, almost agitated."

"I don't understand."

"The area is unpassable. Like Nero's centurions, Strathmore became bogged down in the swampy marshes of the Sudd." He waved Beaumarchais toward the door. "All the more reason for you to leave now. Strathmore is hardly a man to be trifled with."

"Nor Faron—as we're both well aware," warned Beaumarchais. With a last glance at the zebra in its case, both men turned toward the door of the drawing room. The conversation continued in more desultory terms regarding Beaumarchais's haste to return to Paris and the unfortunate weather in London.

All the while Julia's head buzzed. She had been correct in surmising that the stakes of the game were high for Strathmore. She'd wager the man never did anything except for grand ambition. She felt the gooseflesh rising over her throat, the flush warming her skin, an inexplicable pleasure coursing through her body at the thought, her desire for him growing rather than waning.

As though he read her mind and sensed the heating of her blood, he shifted his arm up from where it looped her waist and slid a large hand across one breast, gently, lazily, as if they had all the time in the world and would never be discovered in the dark recesses of the storage space.

Julia bit the inside of her cheek to stifle a moan. She tipped her head back against his shoulder, her spine arched ever so slightly into his touch and her backside pressed into his groin. A part of her never wanted to exit the dark, heady space behind Dr. Grant's bookshelves, to delay forever the reckoning that would surely come as night follows day.

The footsteps and voices receded as Lowther and Beaumarchais left the drawing room and the zebra in its glass case behind. It was the moment Strathmore chose to give her a small and totally unexpected push.

Julia tumbled from behind the bookcase as though out of a dream, Strathmore close behind. His arm still around her waist, he broke her fall, their booted feet hardly making a sound on the parquet floor. The moment was suspended in time as they gazed studiously away from each other and across to the zebra staring serenely from inside its case. They listened carefully to fading footsteps. Lowther and Beaumarchais were making their way down the hallway to the front door.

Strathmore motioned her over to the window, which he efficiently and silently opened, introducing a gust of damp air into the musty room. Outside, the high shrubbery beckoned.

"Out you go," he said.

Julia was inclined to argue but disagreement required time they didn't have. Placing her foot onto the sill, she angled her body out the window, easing herself into the shivering pointed leaves of a mulberry bush. Strathmore was close behind, using his arms to lift himself out, the frame scraping his shoulders as he dropped to the ground.

They crouched low, watching the receding figure of Beaumarchais, who moved briskly down the walkway toward Gordon Square to enter a carriage waiting at the corner. Presumably, Lowther remained in the house, waiting for Strathmore's appearance.

"Hold off a moment until Beaumarchais disappears. Then a carriage is waiting for you on Gower street."

The spiky needles of the mulberry bush brushed against

Julia's cheek. "The Nile," she whispered more to herself than anyone else. "That's it?" The realization was staggering now that she examined it under the light of the moon and away from the heady sensuality that proximity to Strathmore induced. "You believe Faron knows the source of the river? And that's why you're doing all of this?" Anger mingled with desire. The bitter irony of it all. Strathmore thought nothing of snuffing out a life, her life, in order for him to feed his blind ambition.

That's what she was left with. In the course of three days, he had told her nothing of himself save his name, and even that she had wrenched from him. More significantly, he had promised her nothing, other than to spare her life. He would not help her ensure the safety of her family.

"This is neither the time nor the place." The resonance of his voice, a low growl, conjured an intimacy she'd prefer to forget. The knowledge that he stood just inches from her, their arms touching, reignited a peculiar and unwanted restlessness, pooling heat low in her belly. Her awareness of him was exhilarating, painful, confusing and, always there. How could she ever explain it?

"It's all simply an adventure to you, isn't it? To achieve your ends, to make your damned discovery, you are willing to do just about anything, even make a pact with the devil, as you've clearly demonstrated. And you won't even give me an explanation."

"I owe you none." He turned around to face her directly, his chest just inches away. Strength of will alone kept her from retreating into the bushes. He seemed immense, his shoulders all but filling the window frame behind her.

"When is the right time, Strathmore?" Once you find yourself with Lowther again, how long will you honor our agreement? If Lowther issues you another challenge in exchange for what you covet so deeply, how do I know that you will not comply?"

His warm breath fanned over her. "You don't. It's enough for you to know that I spared your life."

"Who is to say you will do so again? Whereas I shall do anything and everything to protect my family. Including protecting them from you."

"You exhort me to trust you and yet you do not trust me."

"Precisely. Despite your pitiable strategems to convince me otherwise."

He bared his teeth in the gaslight. "The very least you can do is be honest with yourself, Julia. You seem to be enjoying my *stratagems.*"

A tremor passed through her. She was forced to lower her eyes when his gaze burned brighter than the gaslight behind him. She compressed her lips to still her rioting emotions. "Must you always make reference—"

"You're the one constantly making reference."

"I do not." The disavowal sounded childish even to her own ears.

"The hell you don't."

She lifted her eyes to his, surprised to find a barely tempered rage in his face. A flicker of triumph burned in her chest. "For whatever reason, you delight in tormenting me. Perhaps you are not unlike Faron after all. For that matter, the resemblance is quite striking."

"You delight in dishonesty, Miss Woolcott. With yourself most of all." His hand caught the back of her head, holding her still while one thumb flicked over her trembling lower lip. "You are perpetually in hiding. From Faron, from me, and most of all from the truth."

She lifted her chin defiantly, unaccustomed to the aggression swelling deep inside, eager to test his limits, to stir in him the savagery that so many said was lurking just beneath the surface. "You have been away from civilization far too long, sir, that you fail to recognize the truth when you encounter it. The failing is yours, not mine."

"Christ, you have no idea," he growled, his mouth lowering to just a breath above hers. "I don't know why I bother myself."

"Precisely," she breathed.

"Don't be so quick to agree for once." The last was an ominous threat and should have served as a warning.

His mouth descended over hers, hard and unforgiving. She stiffened with indignation, yet all words, all anger left her when she felt the heat of his mouth. She could gather no resistance as his fingers laced into her hair and she opened her lips to the first incursion of his tongue. Somewhere in the back of her mind she knew she was lost and she could no longer deny that she wanted it, whatever the cost.

Her fingers twisted into the lapels of his greatcoat, losing themselves in the wool and then the linen covering his chest. His mouth released hers in a rush of breath while the gaslight swam in the miasma of darkness and her head fell back beneath the onslaught of his lips on the exposed skin of her neck. It was madness, with Lowther waiting for Strathmore, with the threat of discovery, and the sharpness of the mulberry bush scraping her right cheek.

Pushing it all to the side, she felt his silky hair spring against her sensitized fingertips. She pressed his head closer as he lowered his mouth to her lips once more, the heat of his breath inflaming her as his miraculous sleight of hand parted her cloak and the modest wool shawl covering her bodice. Parting the fabric, his lips swept the highest curves of her breasts, before he cupped and nearly pushed them from her bodice. With a soft murmur, he slipped his tongue into the exposed valley, drawing a long, lingering breath from her.

"Tell me," he murmured, drawing back infinitesimally as his thumbs teased the swelling peaks until they ached. "Tell me now that you don't want this." His lips traced a path along her neck before catching her full bottom lip.

She couldn't speak. She forced a swallow, summoning every last shred of rational thought available to her. Dear Lord, the situation was impossible. She turned in his arms, as far as he would allow her. "This always happens. Between us. It isn't right." She took a deep, steadying breath. "And it isn't the truth."

"And what if it is?"

"It can't be."

"Go back to Gower street," he said while her fingers awkwardly rearranged her bodice and shawl. He pulled the cloak securely around her shoulders. "We shall finish this tonight."

"What do you mean?" she asked, even though she knew exactly what he meant, her mind screaming denial while her body said otherwise. Something in his eyes told her he knew exactly the confusion that was overtaking her.

"You continue to lie to yourself."

"And your arrogance continues to astound me."

"It shouldn't. A moment ago I could have taken you here on the cold ground and you would have welcomed it."

The gaslight shimmered and her hand shot out to deliver a stinging slap to his jaw. Her stomach heaved when she saw that he barely flinched, didn't register the faintest response. What was becoming of her that she could not control her emotions, that she should resort to such actions?

She swallowed hard, the lump in her throat precluding further words. Aware of Strathmore's cool, unflinching regard, she pushed aside the shrubbery and propelled herself onto the pathway as if chased by fiends.

She took a few steps, the tall trees and buildings swimming in her vision. Then she began to run, the dampness fanning the heat flushing her face, cooling the tenderness of her lips. The choice was not hers. She had to keep Strathmore close—to dance with the devil. Because the farther away from her he was, the more dangerous he would become.

Chapter 9

Strathmore stepped from the darkness of the late evening and into the dimly lit hallway.

"Welcome, Lord Strathmore," said Lowther, leaning out of the shadows and into the yellow light of the sconces. "I wish I could congratulate you on a job well done, but we both know otherwise."

Strathmore gave a swift incline of his head. The scent, taste and feel of Julia Woolcott lingered, but he ruthlessly put her from his mind.

"I prefer to use my time wisely. So let's get on with this."

"I intend to, never fear." Without hesitation, the older man brushed by him in the hallway and into the drawing room, pausing only to glance over his shoulder contemptuously. "I should have thought following my instructions concerning Julia Woolcott would have been child's play for a man of your experience."

Of all the reasons Strathmore possessed to despise Faron's lieutenant, none had ever proven half so compelling as the cavalier manner in which Julia's name spilled from the man's lips. For a short moment, Strathmore imagined what it would feel like to have Lowther's thick neck clamped between his hands.

"It should have been so simple." Lowther waved a fist in the air, his head cocked. He leaned against one of the glass topped tables, at ease in the unusual chaos of the room, fold-ing his arms over his barrel chest. "You may count yourself fortunate that I reported your failure to Faron with a certain tact and diplomacy. He can be somewhat unreliable these days."

Strathmore jutted his chin toward the atlas which contained the map of Africa and the Nile. It lay closed beside Lowther's elbow. "Faron would like to meet with me as much as I would like to meet with him."

Lowther gave a one-sided smile. "So you believe."

Strathmore offered no reply.

Lowther drew himself up with supreme self-satisfaction, as though entirely in control, one hand smoothing his vest contemplatively, the other pushing aside the atlas with a careless shove. "You probably don't realize it, but Julia Woolcott is only an instrument in the universe of Faron's making. Completely disposable once she has served her purpose."

Strathmore gritted his teeth into a smile. He forced the words from his throat. "Is that so? You never did tell me the reason for Faron's obsession with the Woolcotts."

Lowther regarded him through narrowed eyes. "And you never told me the reasons behind your obsession with discovering the source of the Nile."

"It's what I do."

"Ah yes, the penchant for exploration—which leads, of course, to a fixation with the Big Prize. I can't help wonder why you do it, risk everything, leave your family behind, sacrifice comforts and endanger your life—all for what? Not to mention involving yourself with the Woolcotts."

"You contacted me, as you'll recall."

"With an opportunity that Faron sensed you could not refuse," said Lowther loftily. "The man has a keen and enviable understanding of human nature."

"Only one among his many talents, I hear."

"You surmise correctly. But tell me, Strathmore, why didn't you finish up with Miss Woolcott? I've heard that you had your hands all over her at Eccles House. Was that purely for effect?"

Strathmore's eyes glittered. "It was required, given the circumstances. We were not invited to attend high tea, as you'll recall."

Lowther's features hardened. "Then what in bloody hell happened? And why are you keeping Miss Woolcott at your town house here in London? With you."

"Before I answer that question," replied Strathmore, strolling over to the bookcase from which he and Julia had watched undetected, "I should like to inquire as to why you saw fit to send a none too friendly emissary to my town house. With a pistol. I thought you trusted me."

"Trust is not the issue."

"For the moment, it appears as though Miss Woolcott met a particularly sordid end at Eccles House. Information that, I take it, you delivered to Montfort. That was the point, was it not?"

Lowther pursed his lips before pacing around the room. "Theoretically, yes, the desired effect was achieved. However, Faron likes to see not only the spirit but also each letter of his dictates fulfilled." He paused, sending Strathmore a stern look. "The emissary sent to your London town house was intended to emphasize that point."

Strathmore shoved his fists into his trouser pockets lest he find his hands around Lowther's throat. He could not account for the simmering rage that lent his voice a hoarseness he hoped would be mistaken for contempt. He was usually slow to anger but since meeting Julia, he could not rely on the customary discipline of his cool nature. "You promised to get on with it, Lowther."

"I did, didn't I?" With his hands behind his back and his chest leading like a ship in full sail, Lowther continued his pacing. "I hazard a guess you have developed an unfortunate affection for Miss Woolcott, which rather complicates the situation."

Strathmore grunted and tried his best to thrust haunting memories from his mind. He casually surveyed the bookshelf behind Lowther's back. "You are obviously not the judge of character that Faron is. Circumstances led me to take a different course of action regarding Julia Woolcott."

"From my understanding, she is a rather peculiar, sheltered young woman. Hardly the sort to take up with the set at Eccles House—which is precisely the reason Faron thought to have her killed in such a dramatic and sordid manner. It would cause her aunt the greatest pain. Diabolical, no?"

Strathmore didn't trust himself to answer. "Why come to me with the proposition in the first place?"

Lowther arced a brow. "You and the great man have so much in common. Your various interests, to begin with." He added slyly, "Of which you are totally aware. Otherwise you would not have taken up the assignment with such alacrity. It's your very enthusiasm, that thirsty ambition, that has convinced Faron you deserve another chance."

Leaning over one of the glass cases to survey its contents of dung beetles, Strathmore said, "How generous. I take it you have another assignment for me. To prove my worth to Faron."

Lowther snorted. "You're very clever, my lord—which is precisely what has me worried." He momentarily stopped his pacing, giving Strathmore a strange look. "Beaumarchais warned me."

Strathmore's head snapped up, his suspicions confirmed. "No surprise to me. Although your acolyte looked more than comfortable enjoying the entertainments at Eccles House."

"Beaumarchais is a curious sort of rogue and his sole qualification is as a hanger-on whose loyalty can be purchased with money and favors. As you no doubt have guessed, he is a notorious philanderer with an unhealthy and possibly destructive fascination with actresses and the like. I needed a pair of eyes and he, of course, was more than eager to supply them."

"You trust him?"

"As much as I trust anyone. It has served me well to have Beaumarchais in my pocket." He paused, sending Strathmore another odd look. "As I have you in my pocket—although I concede that your price is of an entirely different nature from his." Lowther extracted his pocket watch with a flourish. "Ah, look at the time." He slapped the watch closed in his palm. "As it turns out, you don't have much time to spare, Strathmore."

"Imagine that," Strathmore muttered.

"You want this badly, don't you? This Nile business. A crowning achievement for the intrepid explorer and discoverer, Lord Strathmore."

Strathmore scowled at the glass-encased zebra. "This is becoming tedious."

"You will admire the particular genius of my request, once you hear it."

"Of your design or Faron's?"

"You doubt my abilities in these matters?" Lowther pursed his lips in disapproval. "I have decided that since you've initiated a liaison with Julia Woolcott—and don't try to deny it, Strathmore—we shall challenge you further. To test whether you can fulfill your promise to Faron as well as your promise to the young lady in question."

"I made no promises to her."

Holding up a palm in protest, Lowther said, "Hear me out. You will see that my proposition has a particular elegance. You can prove yourself both to Faron and our Miss Woolcott with one supremely gallant gesture."

Strathmore suppressed a curse. He sensed Lowther would tip his hand soon.

"I believe the time is upon us for action," Lowther continued tonelessly. "As you well know by now, Miss Woolcott has a sister, to whom she is very close."

A chill sliced through Strathmore.

Lowther smiled for the first time, his gums peeling back over his teeth. Their eyes locked. "Don't think you can play me for the fool again, sir. As it is you've pushed me to limits no other would ever think to attempt. I shall not disappoint Faron—nor will you."

"This isn't necessary," Strathmore said softly.

"I say it is."

Strathmore went rigid, fists clenching against his thighs to keep from smashing Lowther's grin from his face.

"Simple, really, for a man like you." He held up a fleshy palm. "Save the obligatory speeches. Words, I'm afraid, won't suffice this time. Never fear, you will have ample opportunity to convince me you are a man worthy of the great Faron. You should thank me, Lord Strathmore. Your opportunity beckons." Lowther's gaze darted to the curtained windows. "Oh dear, I do believe that my carriage has arrived."

"Miss Woolcott's sister." Strathmore narrowed his eyes. "What have you done with her?"

"Nothing yet." He paused for effect. "She has been kidnapped. You have three days to find her. Simple enough."

"Or you plan to have her killed."

"Not precisely," Lowther replied, a maniacal light settling deep in his eyes. "I'm not going to kill Rowena Woolcott. Because if you get to her first, and I'm sure that's entirely within your abilities—that particular honor will be yours."

Julia stood in the library of Strathmore's town house, waiting. It was well past midnight. Through the window she stared at the puddles dotting the cobblestone drive, fighting demons she wished she'd never had to confront. *Had she stayed at Montfort*—but that was impossible.

As for Strathmore—she needed only to say his name. He was like a damned opiate, no matter that he was simply using her, no matter that he would do anything to achieve his own ambitions, and no matter that such a man should stir only disgust and contempt in her, and not the mindless, overwhelming desire so fierce she shook with it.

Backing away from the window, Julia felt a chill seep into her bones. The rain had begun again, but it was unable to drown out the small voice that flared in the recesses of her mind. She was ashamed to admit it, but she wanted him. She needed him, in so many more ways than one. Alexander Francis Strathmore.

The house was quiet, most of the servants already abed. Julia found him on the first floor in a small study off the main hallway. He was standing with his back toward her, in front of a dying fire, and she knew he sensed her presence. They both pretended otherwise and she took the time to memorize every dark angle of his shoulders, imagining the clean sweep of his jaw, the slight hook of his nose, his wide mouth. She already knew that mouth to be capable of igniting a firestorm within her and those beautiful hands were capable of sending her into a realm she had never before imagined.

The fire bathed him in a warm light, reflecting in the sheen of his dark hair. He turned his profile toward the doorway, the shadows casting his features into brutal angles. His chest expanded with his breathing, drawing Julia's attention. They did not acknowledge one another. She stood poised on the threshold, her whole body tense with wanting. She would not lie to herself. She wanted to feel that sculpted hardness pushing against her breasts, to smooth her open palms over his ridged belly, the impressive bulge in his trousers, and the iron of his thighs. Her mouth was dry as thoughts of Montfort, her fears for her aunt and sister, receded into the night.

She might never have the chance again. Strathmore exuded an overwhelming, compelling masculinity far outside her ken. A breath escaped her lips and his gray eyes finally sought hers. Something leapt in their depths, mirroring the dying embers of the fire, before his expression shuttered closed.

Her gaze went to the fire, then to the floor, and then slowly lifted to him. She knew what she had to do. Her feet moved awkwardly over the parquet floor until her fingertips brushed his shoulder. In one swift motion, his arm snaked around her waist, and he drew her between his parted thighs.

"Strathmore," she said, the name a plea.

"Don't." He ground the word out. "I know why you're doing this."

Julia struggled to retain her composure beneath his intense gaze. "No, you don't. You are always telling me not to lie to myself—you said so this evening at Torrington Place. Now I am taking your advice to heart. I do not lie when I say that I want you, Strathmore, with no reservations and no hesitations." She stopped herself and then added with all the honesty her heart could bear, "But only if you want me."

Darkness glittered in his eyes. "You only believe that you want me."

"Why are you challenging me? I know what I want. You said only tonight that we must finish this."

"Not what I meant."

"I don't believe you."

"You don't have to do this to ensure that I'll help you find Faron."

"This has nothing to do with him."

"You have no ulterior motives?"

"None," she answered with her heart in her mouth. She held her breath and felt the world tilt beneath her feet. She wanted him to touch her as no man had ever touched her before. "What I'm feeling is natural, overwhelming. And inevitable. Isn't that what you have been telling me since the first moment we met?"

His hand caught in her hair and forced her eyes to his. "You should be more careful, Julia." For the first time there was hesitation in his voice but she ignored it, reveling in the feel of his hard thighs straining against her.

"I need you," she said softly.

"But in what way? And why? To get to Faron?" He stared at her, and then let her go so suddenly she stumbled back against the low damask-covered chair. Glaring at her, he said softly, "Know this. I want you. For yourself. And that too has nothing to do with Faron—which makes me the bigger fool." Before she could respond, he strode out of the study, slamming the door.

Julia didn't wait but charged after him, running down the shadowed hall, her blood pounding in her ears. She bunched her skirts in her fist, his last words echoing in her soul, until she collided with him on the stairs.

"I believe you," she said simply, almost out of breath.

"In the morning you will wish that you hadn't." He forced the words through a tight jaw.

"I don't want to talk about that now."

He turned toward her then, his hand grasping hers, his fingers wrapping painfully around her wrist. Nothing softened the severity of his features. No seductive smile. Not even a flicker of conceit at a game easily won.

"I won't say this again," he said softly. "If you pursue this, I shall take you to my bed. And you will regret your decision."

She had known from the first moments in the cork-lined room at Eccles House that it would end that way. His words made it real. It was exactly what she'd been obsessed with since he'd first touched her. She was strong enough to see the truth, and refused to lie to herself. "I don't want to think about regret right now. Although I know," she whispered awkwardly, "that I am not the most beautiful of women, or what you are perhaps accustomed to."

His eyes lowered and she felt as if she would explode under his scrutiny.

"You know nothing of me or my reasons, Julia, but know this. I want you. *You.*"

Julia stopped breathing as he closed the distance between them. "Christ, I want you like no other woman I've known," he said. His fingers slipped from her wrist to her neck, caressing a slow path up her spine. He drew her nearer until his mouth pressed against the side of her neck. "You have no idea how beautiful you are. How you have invaded my thoughts, my blood. At first I thought it was the situation, seeing you at Eccles House, so unaware of your own sensuality. But it is more than that, and I still don't fully understand what it is you do to me."

She knew who he was—a strong man, a reckless man, who had traveled the known world, powerful and heedless, taking what he wanted, treading where others feared to go. She knew he had taken his pleasure with many women, women far more exotic and skilled than she could ever be. And yet he desired her. Julia Woolcott.

Nothing else mattered. Suddenly she was in the midst of a wild delusion, but she didn't care. She tilted her face to his, her lips parting in unspoken longing, as though she could deny herself no longer. His lips met hers, tasting of warm brandy, and she leaned into him, pliant and supple as all resistance fled her body. His name spilled from her lips without volition when he swept her into his arms and carried her up the staircase and down a wide hall. He didn't stop kissing her, and only paused to push open his chamber door, then kicked it closed behind him.

Julia barely felt her feet touch the ground as he pressed her back against the door. A small smile of satisfaction curved her lips when he leaned his forearms on either side of her and lowered his mouth to hers once again.

She felt a shiver of fear at his touch, but he was too quick for her and dispelled her trembling by slowly drawing her into his arms. "Are you sure you want to do this, Julia?" He placed his hand under her chin, tilted it, and gazed into her eyes, studying her face.

It came to her again that they were strangers, that her senses were spiraling out of control. She felt weak when he placed his lips upon hers, ran his tongue sensuously between them. He traced her mouth with his wicked tongue, and with such subtle persuasion she stifled a whimper. One kiss followed another, on the side of her neck, on the lobe of her ear, on her shoulder. Then he raised her hand and placed it over his mouth and kissed the palm, licked a slow path to the inside of her wrist.

She struggled to find something to say, to tell him that she was falling, drowning in sensation already, and she knew they had scarcely begun. Images flashed through her mind. The naked men and women at Eccles House, their bodies slick with oil, offering themselves to each other.

Strathmore did not let her hand go when he stepped back from her. There was no doubting the passion in his eyes, the warring emotion in the tense line of his jaw, or the way he swallowed hard before he said, "We shouldn't be doing this. You have never been with a man and I have no right. As much as I want you, tell me that I'm not wrong about that."

"It doesn't matter," she whispered, hoarsely. "Or perhaps it does because I may never get a chance again . . . to know this . . . to lose myself." The words would not come, her confession of need and desire. Any further thoughts of piecing together sentences completely vanished when Strathmore placed his hands on her waist and rocked her into his arms. Desperately, she closed her eyes, hoping he wouldn't change his mind, unable to hide the restlessness she felt when he caressed the swell of her breasts beneath the prim wool of her gown.

"How lovely you are, Julia, don't ever forget that." Miraculously, the tiny buttons of her bodice gave way, revealing the simple corset and shift she wore beneath. "I want to see you naked. Your beautiful body."

Questions were left hanging unanswered in the air. When he kissed her again, her lips parted and she settled more deeply into his arms. "Answer me, Julia."

Her heart pounded. "Yes, I want to be naked for you, free and open, to learn . . ." Once again, the images of Eccles House heated her blood. She knew it was desire talking, and suddenly she wanted to tear off all her clothes, to feel his hands on her naked bottom, her bare hips, allowing him to play with every hidden curve and crevice.

Strathmore sensed the turmoil beneath her inchoate yearnings. Placing an arm around her shoulders, he walked with her into the room, the candlelight throwing into sharp relief the dark blue walls lined with books and exotic sculptures, darkly mysterious stone carvings next to glittering scimitars. The carpet beneath her feet was of a great age, patterned in a faded turquoise color with sweeping gray ferns. There were deep, comfortable chairs in black and blue silk damask and a mountain of cushions cascading from a low divan onto the floor. Also, tables of dark, rich woods, a heavy screen, and a large four-poster bed, draped in heavy damask and lined in plum-colored silk. It had been turned down to display crisp white linen.

Julia had not found Alexander Strathmore in the rest of the town house, but she had found him in the dark, exotic richness of his bedroom. They stopped at the foot of the bed. He tilted her chin up and looked into her eyes. "Words only go so far, Julia. You know that more than anyone else. Prove to me you want this."

She waited for him to move, to make a gesture, to feel his hands upon her. Then understanding dawned. Much had been said between them—lies, subterfuge, deception—none of which had a place in that dark, masculine room. Her actions would speak louder than any words, telling him it was her decision alone.

She moved behind him and slid her hands across his shoulders, his jacket sliding easily from his arms. Dropping it carelessly across the divan, she allowed herself to rest her head against his back, caressing his wide shoulders under the white linen shirt he was wearing. She walked around to face him again. He raised his chin and she understood, undoing the ivory buttons at his neck with aching deliberation. Holding herself back, she resisted spreading the fabric across his chest to expose the hardness of the muscular body underneath.

He held up his wrists wordlessly, never taking his gaze from hers. She removed the studs with surprising deftness, before sweeping the shirt from the waistband of his trousers. Her hands trembled and she was afraid he would stop her. She was drunk with desire. To hide her intoxication, she moved behind him again and raised his shirt, running her hands over his strong back. Slowly he reached around, grabbed her hand and pulled her in front of him. They stood for an instant, their breaths coming in tandem.

All she wanted at that moment was his hands on her breasts, his fingers biting into her flesh. She felt out of control, as far from Julia Woolcott as she had ever been.

"Don't stop now." Despite the simple words, there was an intensity in his voice she had never heard before. She pushed back a wave of awkwardness, imagining what she looked like, dressed in her wool and taffeta day gown, with its high lace collar and boned bodice, looking every inch the unmarried, unwanted maiden. She found it quite shocking, and didn't want to look into a mirror to see the two of them, he half-naked and she fully dressed.

"It must be your choice, Julia," he said. "You need only to believe that whatever we do sexually, you will always be safe with me. I will never let you come to any harm."

His eyes darkened as her fingers trembled on the row of buttons at the back of her gown, her own breathing hoarse and tortured to her ears. Her fingers parted muslin and traced soft cotton up her spine until the fabric parted, cool air on warm flesh. Julia heard herself murmur something when he slid both hands inside the back of her dress, molding her flesh and then sliding the material from her shoulders. It fell to the floor in a rush, matching her sharp intake of breath.

Her eyes fluttered closed as she stepped away from him, determined to prove to him that she acted of her own free will.

Chapter 10

Julia Woolcott stood in front of him in her slippers, with their demure pink satin straps, wearing only her undergarments. Her chemise, beneath her corset, came just to the tops of her long thighs, and hidden from his view were her breasts, tantalizingly high and firm, the raspberry nipples visible beneath the thin fabric.

Alexander Strathmore shook his head, trying to calm the pounding in his ears, a burst of passion and depravity mixing in his blood. What was it about the woman? He had been fooled by the elegance of her features, the reticence and reserve marred only by those full lips—until the evening at Eccles House when he had been given a glimpse of the sensual side of her shockingly erotic beauty.

The irony was she hadn't a clue. He held back, taking in the slimness of her waist, her narrow hips. He tested himself, slowing his breathing, walking slowly around her, enchanted by her bottom, high and round and beckoning. He caressed the cheeks, separating them, running a finger provocatively along the smooth skin. Unable to resist, he bent to lick a spot.

Julia swayed beneath the assault, beneath his unwavering gaze. She took a nervous step away from him, instinctively tried to cover herself. He stopped her with a hand on her shoulder.

"I am unaccustomed to this," she said.

"I shouldn't doubt it. Do you wish to continue?"

He could see the starkness of desire and insecurity clouding her eyes.

The cream of her shoulder warmed to his touch. "You have a beautiful, perfect body, Julia, made for erotic play." He took her face in his hands, feathering light kisses onto her lips. "There is no shame in this. I can't stop looking at you." He touched her cheek, the bridge of her nose, returning to her mouth. She slid her tongue between them and licked his lips, nibbling at them, giving in to him and to herself.

At that moment he wanted nothing more than to loosen his trousers, flick them open, and release the tension in his iron-hard shaft. He hadn't had a woman in months, he told himself, but that was no reason to explode like a randy schoolboy.

Mercifully, she stepped back from him, releasing him only momentarily from his own personal hell. Languid blue eyes beseeched him, desire mingling with courage, driving her hand to loosen the satin ties of her corset. She let the stiff material slip from her shoulders and down her arms to fall on the floor. He was mesmerized, watching every naïve and innocent move with a focus usually reserved for a target caught in the crosshairs of his pistol.

She let one chemise strap fall and then the next. The small eyelet hooks gave way with agonizing slowness. The cotton slid off her breasts and down around her waist, her hips, her thighs, and slowly to the floor. Driven by shyness or desire, he didn't want to know which, she closed the distance between them, placing her arms around his neck.

"I know there is no shame in this," she breathed into his chest. "And it's what I want. With you." Her fingers fluttered on his shoulders.

He didn't answer but picked her up in his arms and laid her on the bed, quickly shrugging off his shirt and his trousers until he was naked beside her. She didn't look away, and her fingertips angled toward him as if she wished to run her hand over the length of his body.

"You are the one who is beautiful."

He had been called many things in his life, but beautiful wasn't one of them. He grinned, hoping the levity would take inches from his erection. He was a big man who wanted to be between Julia Woolcott's legs. And she was a virgin. Damn it to hell.

He pressed his lips to hers briefly, holding back, before letting his mouth trace the indentation between her ribs. The scent of warmed lavender flowed over his tongue. His tongue darted into her navel, her breathy inhalations the only reply he needed.

Her breath caught when he slid his hands over her hips, his warm, large hands caressing the length of her bared thighs and calves. A sigh followed and she sank her fingers into his hair just as his mouth brushed over the tenderness of her inner thighs. He remembered what she had seen at Eccles House and her highly vaunted literary interests. "Surely this isn't so unusual, Julia," he murmured into the chestnut curls at the apex of her thighs, finding her soft and wet.

"I'm not certain," she moaned as he parted the moist folds, breathing in her scent.

"Not certain of what you're feeling?"

She was so tense, so on the verge of an orgasm, she could not answer, save to open her thighs further, allowing him to savor her. He grasped both her hips to bring her to the touch of his mouth and tongue. With fluid strokes he roused her, tasted her, sending her over the edge. She tensed, her hands in his hair, suspended in eternity, until she let out a small tortured cry.

The sound filled him with a strange lust, stoking his desire to bring a surfeit of pleasure. He slipped fingers of each hand on either side of her center until she was completely open, entering her for the first time with his tongue. He probed, madly and deeply, making a feast of her.

Her fingers dug hard into his shoulders until, unable to keep silent, she came again with a low keening wail. He kissed the inside of her thighs, then worked his way up her body, his lips tracing a wild path. He nipped her flesh, reaching her breasts, the dark pink nipples and nimbus, stirring in him a lust he had long forgotten.

Julia Woolcott shared his hunger. Bone melting satiation shone in her eyes as she slipped her arms around her neck and drew his mouth to hers. "Thank you," she panted. "Thank you. I never knew. Would perhaps never have known."

He silenced her words with a kiss to her forehead, the high curve of cheekbones, the sweep of her jaw. He was aware that she welcomed his hips against hers and the hard, hot erection between her thighs. It was ridiculous, outlandish, unreasonable—but he had never been so hard in his life.

Alexander Strathmore, who had sampled every erotic game available in the east and west, was famished for her sex. The virgin, far from a sophisticated temptress or exotic seductress, had simply exploded in his arms, responded to him with an ardent, honest simplicity that was dangerous.

He hated himself for it, but he could no longer wait. He parted her thighs, licked the arch of her rib cage and the succulent side of a breast, his fingers going where his tongue had been before, to that small, tight place drenched with need. With gentle, caressing fingers, he opened the deep rose of her inner lips, pushing himself up on his elbows and easing himself slowly into her. With one hand caught in the heavy silk of hair that fanned the coverlet, he cupped her head, drawing her mouth to his, eager to absorb her slightest whisper of pain.

She was too small, too tight around him. But he was too far gone to stop.

His hand at her lower back, he lifted her hips toward him and thrust. Shallowly. Then more deeply. And then again, staring at the intricately carved headboard to gain some semblance of control. He counted the rollicking satyrs, the rosy nymphs, and the frolicking unicorns. Fighting for control, he paced himself in a gentle, coaxing rhythm until she opened around him.

His incursions slowed to extract the most tantalizing pleasure for them both, increasing the tempo until he felt her orgasm once more, warm, wet, and slippery as silk coating his hardness. Her body went taut and she called out in a frenzy of passion when he chose his moment to impale her to the hilt. His fingers bit into the slender hips where he held her. He paused, watching for any sign of pain or discomfort. Her response was to raise her hips more closely to his, urging him on. Her eyes closed as he began a new rhythm, fast and merciless, his body slick with power and need, drumming into her until he knew nothing else.

The world disappeared, leaving only the dictates of his body, and the bone-crunching, mind-numbing passion that finally released them. He tore out of her body just in time, releasing his seed on the smoothness of her thighs.

They slept then, not so much from sensual excess as from a reluctance to permit the real world to intrude. When he awoke again, he was relieved to see no light behind the heavy damask curtains. The candles had burned low, telling him that he'd slept for only an hour.

Julia lay on her back, both hands flung over her head, her breathing as innocent as a child's. Only the smear of blood on the pristine whiteness of the linen beneath her dispelled the illusion.

Strathmore bit back a curse almost at the same time as he unwisely allowed his eyes to travel over her body. Impossibly, she still held him in thrall, as though he had not just come with a fierceness that made his teeth ache. The dark allure of her nipples drew his hands and mouth inexorably to her breasts. She murmured low in her throat, her eyes opening slowly before shuttering again with a languorous sensuality that stunned him.

She smiled at him then, the lushness of her lips widening when he sucked deeply on her nipples, opening his mouth and devouring as much of them as he could. She writhed beneath him, lost, transported and he paused only to tell her, "You are incredible, Julia. More than I could ever imagine." He alternated between licking and massaging. She turned her body toward him, her lips trailing his shoulder before she gave him a little bite, and then tensed to come in several small orgasms.

The shudders of ecstasy barely subsided when she breathed soft, unclear murmurs into his chest. Urgently, he placed pillows beneath her to raise her to an angle to allow deeper penetration. Her nether lips were swollen and slick but the gentle urging of her hips told him what she wanted. He drew her legs apart and took her swiftly, unable to stop himself.

Her eyes flew open. He was rough and her reaction was instinctive. She used her inner muscles, milking him, squeezing every fiber to cling to him, easing off and on again. He caught her around the waist and lifted her high against him until her breasts dangled inches from his mouth. He captured one swollen nipple between his teeth, and drew it slowly against the roughness of his tongue, again and again. Startled, she mimicked his movements, rising and falling on his hardness, finding her own rhythm, until wordlessly they came together just as she collapsed upon his chest.

The night continued, an endless, mindless fog of sensuality. Exhilarated, drained, stunned, and horrified by their mutual, seemingly insatiable need, they finally slept.

Bright sunlight stung Julia's closed eyes. Reluctant to face the day, she burrowed her head into the pillows, her body entangled in bed linens and lingering erotic dreams. She felt, rather than knew, she was by herself, the cavernous space in the bed hers alone.

Her body ached in places she'd barely known existed. Heat rushed from her cheeks to her toes when she thought of the previous hours. The last thing she'd remembered was Strathmore bringing a moistened cloth to the bed, sponging between her thighs, slowly and sensuously, until the cloth was tossed aside and she felt his skin against hers again, heard their breaths, absorbed the heat of their bodies melding, becoming one.

She turned her cheek on the pillow and smoothed her palm

over the depression in the cotton beside her, inhaling Strathmore's elusive scent of forest, smoke, and desert. The cotton was cool, as though he had left her some time ago, igniting a small flame of anxiety in her chest which she tamped down, wanting to have those moments to savor her newfound discoveries.

She was not ashamed, not humiliated, not in the least discomfited by what she had discovered about herself. She had wanted to make love with Strathmore, and had known it from the first. Anything more complicated did not have room in her thoughts or emotions while she lay satiated in the tangled linens.

Julia rolled over on her back, staring at the low-burning lamp on the bedside table and listened to a clock strike somewhere in the town house. Slipping from the bed, she gave only a passing thought to the stiffness in her limbs, the swollen tenderness of her lips and the streak of blood left behind on the sheets. She felt set free, unshackled as a captive released from prison, with a newfound confidence that allowed her to believe anything was possible. With Strathmore at her side, Montagu Faron would have little chance.

Behind the patterned screen sat a fresh tub of warm water and she eased into it with a grateful sigh, her body flushed with lingering pleasure. Soaping herself slowly, running the washcloth over her legs and the rapidly healing wound on her calf, she refused to let the bone-wrenching bliss melt away. After the water had cooled to the point that her skin began to pucker, she rose from the tub as though reborn, wrapping a linen towel around herself as a knock sounded.

"Strathmore?" A welcome smile curved her lips as she curled onto a divan in the corner of the bedchamber, relaxing against the silken pillows. The door opened and she allowed her eyes to drink in the man who was her lover. The thought brought a flush to her cheeks as she watched him walk with his usual economic grace to stand by the bed.

"I would love to move as beautifully as you," she said

with simple honesty, aware of her own native awkwardness, her propensity to bump into things. Fully dressed and shaved, he paid little attention to the tumbled sheets or the wild disarray of her hair.

He shook his head at her words. "It's all your imaginings, Julia, how you persist in seeing yourself. You are an elegant creature if you just admitted it." His smiled faintly, almost reluctantly. She had expected some awkwardness but there was a studied neutrality in his voice, an abrupt contrast to the uncontrolled murmurs and hot words of the night spent in his arms. His expression was closed to her and she was struck anew at how broad and tall he seemed against the sun-lit windows. In his customarily plain black trousers, white shirt and jacket, sans cravat, he seemed ready to back out of the room at the first opportunity. His arms hung at his sides, not reaching for her as she so desperately wanted him to do. The reality of the situation hit her with a staggering finality. She had made love with that incredible man throughout the night, and everything and nothing had changed.

She pushed herself up and glanced around the sumptuous-ness of the room, the heavy woods and rich fabrics bathed in sunlight. Resisting the urge to hold out her hand to him, she instead tightened the towel around her breasts. Her eyes sought his only to find the customary gray shadows keeping her from going any further. He was as distant and dangerous as he had ever been.

That was their reality, after all. She had pushed it from her mind again and again over the past wondrous and terrifying hours and had given no thought to tomorrow, to her aunt and sister or to Faron. A flame of anxiety ignited in her chest, the embers burning higher.

"We have little time to spare," he began, the expression in his voice telling her things she didn't want to know. "It's im-perative we discuss certain matters."

Frowning at the hollowness of his voice, Julia crossed her arms over her chest. She had been naked in his arms, but at that moment, she was overwhelmed by a feeling of self-consciousness, of being an actor who was fumbling for her lines in a play.

She cleared her throat, a bid for honesty making her brave. "The night may be over but I meant what I said last evening, Strathmore. I was not lying when I said that I wanted"—she paused awkwardly with a covert glance at the bed—"that I wanted this."

"I believe you."

"Then I don't understand."

"There is nothing to understand other than that you are getting what you wanted. You are going home. To Montfort."

Her fingers traced circular patterns on the towel gripped in her hand. "I thought we'd agreed that what happened last night has nothing to do with this situation involving Faron." His silence chilled her blood. "Is that not what we agreed?" she asked again.

"Circumstances dictate that you return home where you will be safe."

She watched him in the strong sunlight, his face devoid of the passion that had etched his features only hours before. "How have the circumstances changed? Yesterday, you wanted me to remain hidden, to stay here at the town house. As a result, I am staying with you. And pursuing Faron, as we agreed."

"We agreed on no such thing."

He strode to the chair where her cambric shift lay spread like a ghost against the upholstery. His strong fingers wrapped around the fabric and he studied the cloth caught in his hand as though trying to divine some truth from its delicate, feminine pattern.

It took everything Julia had not to run to him, to press those same hands against her flesh.

A dark cloud hovered in the room, her instincts clamoring for her attention. "You learned something last night, before we . . . before we . . ." She tried bravely, attempting to actually have a conversation rather than a stilted, cold exchange. "We did not have a chance to discuss your meeting with Lowther." Suspicion reared its nasty head. "That was deliberate on your part, I'm beginning to suspect."

His gaze shot to hers, then narrowed. "The faster you get dressed, the faster we can get you home." He tossed the gossamer garment back in the chair.

A knife's thrust would have hurt less. Julia knew she had decided to live for just one night in his arms, and she had expected nothing from him but honesty, however brutal. But she recognized equivocation when she saw it, even when it emanated from a master such as Strathmore. Consumed with the stirrings of wounded pride mixed with simmering anger, she slipped from the divan, chin held high.

"What are you not telling me?" she demanded. "You are obviously reacting to something that occurred or that you learned at your meeting with Lowther. Do not expect me to believe that you gleaned nothing from the rendezvous."

All but naked, she felt her breasts sway with every motion under the thin linen towel and she knew a surge of confidence when his gaze fastened upon her and his jaw tightened. She paused deliberately, one breast just brushing his arm.

"We haven't time at the moment. It's imperative we get you back to Montfort."

"Time was not of the essence last evening, you'll recall," she said, holding out her hand for her shift. He thrust the undergarment at her without a reply and watched for several moments while she deftly slipped it over her head, let the towel drop to her waist, and began securing the hooks over her breasts. She stared angrily at his stone-hard profile outlined against the sunlight pouring in from the windows.

He ignored the challenge and flipped his pocket watch open, glanced at it, and stuffed it back into his pocket. He turned toward her. "Last night, Julia, has nothing to do with this morning."

"Clearly," she said, retreating a step and casting about the room for the rest of her clothing. "There is something you are not telling me."

"It can wait."

"I don't think so," she said stubbornly despite the cold despair that filled her stomach. "Let us pretend, that last evening never happened and let us continue as we left off—as we both promised to do. In the spirit of such compromise"— she swallowed hard—"I expect you to tell me what I deserve to know. After all, this is as much about my family as it is about you and your blasted ambition."

Her hands shook as she finished closing the last hook on her bodice. She spied her underskirts on the floor next to the oak commode. She pulled on the skirt, let the linen towel fall to the floor, forcing back unchecked anger. Her attempts at modesty were baffling, after what the two of them had done and shared together. Nonetheless, she felt as though she was donning armor. Pulling her dress hanging on the screen, over her underskirts, she struggled to knit the bodice together with its tiny and suddenly frustrating hooks and eyes.

When she turned to face him, fully clothed, she had difficulty warding off the chill emanating from his gaze. "You believe you deserve to know," he said, "but what are you not telling me, Julia? Holding back about Faron at this moment is a very dangerous thing."

She sighed, not attempting to hide her impatience. "Why do you always turn the tables when I ask a question of you? There is nothing to tell. I have nothing more to say about the matter."

"You place yourself and your family in grave danger with your willfulness. You are too strong for your own good." He met her swift glance with one of his own. "What I want from Faron, as you are quick to remind me, has to do with ambition, nothing more. But what you want from Faron has, I sense, deeper implications."

Though he hadn't moved from the center of the room, Julia felt a great need to inch away from him, to escape the probing tone in the gravel of his voice. Yet her feet remained rooted by the dressing screen, her body freighted by some invisible force he cast about her. Or perhaps some part of her wished to remain in the bedchamber, beside him, to shut out the past and present and never have to hear, or live with, the truth.

"You do not believe a woman can be as strong as a man?" she asked.

"Stronger." For a moment, the specter of his mother hovered in the air between them.

"Then why do you persist in badgering me about this matter, insisting that I am hiding some dark secret?"

"Aren't you?" The words were bleak. "You've a deep sadness in your eyes, a vulnerability that lifts only when you speak of your work or your sister and aunt. It's that vulnerability, masquerading as strength, that keeps you from discovering what lies behind the torment Faron seeks to unleash upon your family. Do you not see that?"

She turned away from him before she could give any visible sign that his statement had struck home. One hand gripped the dressing screen as she felt the familiar tightening in her throat, cutting off a torrent of emotion. She looked down at the floor, the rug's exotic pattern swimming before her eyes. Silence, as always, was her best refuge.

One hand closed over hers on the dressing screen while the other arm snaked around her waist. His closeness was exhilarating and terrifying at the same time, a force she could not negate.

His voice was so close to her ear that she shuddered. "What happened to you, Julia, so many years ago before you first came to live with Meredith? I have to know. How else can I make it right for you? How else can I protect you from Faron?"

She wanted to say nothing and everything. But her lips refused to move even though a part of her yearned to open her heart and memories to the man, to confide the depth of the darkness stalking her soul.

"You may trust me, Julia. I can do this for you." The ferns in the carpet swam as though under water and she tasted salt on her lips. She flinched when he pressed a linen handkerchief to the wetness of her cheek.

She took it from his hands, inhaling his scent from the smooth linen before she tightened her lips against the emotion that threatened to drown her. She saw the faint glimmer of pain in his own eyes, and her heart twisted in response. The words would still not come but something inside her cracked open, her hand beneath his relaxing its relentless grip on the screen.

Staring at him silently, she took in the starkness of his features, letting her body communicate all she wanted to say.

"If it is honesty you want," he said slowly, retrenching, trying to capture some remnants of the intimacy they had shared in the bed behind them, "then I shall tell you something that lies buried deep within me." He paused before adding, "So much of who we are begins in childhood."

Julia swayed toward him, wanting desperately to hear a truth, any truth, from this man, to plumb his soul and in some way bind him closer to her. Her eyes burned fiercely, mutely urging him on.

"You caught a glimpse of my mother," he said with a levity that sounded strained. "I'm sure once was enough to discern there is little love or respect lost between us." His eyes drifted over her head as though looking into a past that was long dead to him. "Where and why the enmity began, I couldn't say. It doesn't seem natural, a mother rejecting a child, even in the cold aristocratic circles my parents inhabited. Admittedly, I was a wild child, difficult and recalcitrant compared to my biddable older brother, Oliver, and it seemed as though my mother always detested me, could hardly bear the sight of my face for more than a moment"—he smiled grimly—"which, of course, did nothing but encourage my bad behavior."

Julia parted her lips, her eyes following his every expression.

"It became clear to me at a young age that my mother thought nothing of receiving her lovers at Dunedin, a never ending parade she flaunted in front of my father, a quiet, intellectual man several decades her senior, who preferred his books and horses over the London life my mother embraced with hedonistic abandon. Of course, she also loved the comforts and security provided by his title and wealth but resented his seeming indifference to her increasingly flagrant indiscretions."

Strathmore dropped his hand from Julia's, relinquishing her waist, before he continued. "One evening, my mother appeared in the schoolroom, and asked me to summon my father and to accompany him to her chambers in the west wing of the house. I can remember the aroma of her heavy perfume, the softness of her arms as she pulled me toward her in a rare display of affection. I immediately ran to my father's study and with the enthusiasm only a child can generate, dragged him to her rooms."

Julia almost asked him to stop, curling her hands into fists at her sides.

"She was in bed with another man," Strathmore said starkly. "I can't remember what happened immediately afterward, as I ran from the scene to cower in the nursery. In the morning, when I arose, I bolted down to my father's study, where I found him. He had placed a gun to his head, neatly and precisely blowing his brains over the books and papers on his desk.

Julia placed a tentative hand on his chest, feeling the tears burning in her eyes. His hand trapped her, though his gaze remained averted.

"I was consumed with hatred—hatred for my mother and hatred at the weakness of my father. I was promptly shipped off to Shrewsbury, England's strictest school for boys, most of whose students were considered well beyond reform. I saw my mother only once during the next five years. My interest in geography and the sciences took me away from the chaos that was the Dunedin family life. After awhile, I divorced myself from my past entirely, leaving Oxford after only two years to explore the reaches of the world furthest from my family. At twenty-one, I was fortunate to benefit from a trust that has supported my explorations."

Julia wished she could hold him closer and give him the comfort he needed.

As though reading her thoughts, he tipped her chin up. Warm fingers curled around her nape and his gaze burned into hers. "Don't feel sorry for me, Julia. That's not the reason I told you this story. Children in factories, in slums, and in indentured service or worse, both in England and abroad, face far harsher realities than I ever did. My childhood was positively ideal in comparison. What I simply want to demonstrate is how our earliest experiences shape our later lives and why, in my case, my work is everything to me, like a fever in my blood. There can be nothing else. It is something that took me years to understand. I am not prepared to lose it now."

No home. No family. No life. Julia's heart contracted and she knew why he was telling her, exposing a wound that was an infinitely more personal act than the physical intimacy they had shared hours before.

"Exploration is what I am. It's what I do. I push beyond my limits, go where no one else dares to go. It is what has led me to Faron—a very dangerous man—who has what I want. Who has the power to feed my unquenchable hunger for discovery because of what he knows."

His thumb traced the underside of her jawline, the rhythm as mesmerizing as the rise and fall of the ocean's waves. "I am being as honest as I can with you. Talk to me, Julia. Why are you silent?"

She could do nothing but smooth her palm over the linen stretched taut against his chest. He caught her wandering hand in his and drew her fingers to his lips. She wanted only to snatch her fingers back, very much aware of the weakness stealing through her, even more aware that only her crumbling resolve would keep her from succumbing to that powerful man.

Strathmore was telling the truth, she was sure of it, and her heart surged with understanding for him. Yet something still held her back. Her throat worked desperately against the dark emotion welling in her breast.

"Tell me what it is, Julia. I can help you."

Her gaze flew to his, then just as quickly darted away. Surely a man as astute as Strathmore would see through the feeble attempts she made to veil her feelings, the attempts to keep the darkness at bay. She knew she should reveal nothing, and that he could see completely into her soul with a frightening acuity.

"You're trembling," he said, his hands cupping her upper arms. "I shared a part of my life with you, a difficult, painful time that I could only overcome once I acknowledged it, honestly and directly in the harsh light of day. I shall ask again—what is it, Julia? It will help if you finally let it out, I promise you."

She shook her head, unable to give voice to words that could catapult her back into the dark tunnel she had struggled so hard to emerge from.

But he persisted. "Now more than ever, Julia. For so many reasons."

Her stomach tightened at the implication in his voice, hinting at the complexity of the situation, the lives held in the balance. She thought of Lowther and Faron, a biting fear gnawing at her stomach, her senses telling her that Strathmore was holding back, waiting, wanting her to bare her soul not just for her own deliverance from the past but for the salvation of others. Meredith and Rowena. She whispered the two names under her breath, her mouth dry. "What are you not telling me?" she murmured in a small, pained whisper. "Please, Strathmore, what are you not telling me?"

"That is a question you must answer first," he said. "Until you do, you will continue to retreat into yourself when you are pressed." He watched her like a scientist observing an insect under glass, awareness flickering in his eyes.

"I do not wish to speak of it," she said. "I can't."

"It would be better if you did," he growled, his fingers digging into her arms.

"You cannot control everything. You cannot control me." The tears flowed then, humiliating as they were, and she twisted her fists into his shirt. "Despite what happened last night, despite what you have revealed to me about your childhood and the choices you have made in your life, I am not someone you can manipulate to do your bidding. I entreat you to stop pushing me. You may have found success with these tactics in the past, but you will succeed only in pushing me further away."

"You don't know what you risk." His tone was harsh despite the gentleness of his touch as he pressed his handkerchief to her cheeks.

"Then tell me what I risk," she said, her voice ragged with desperation. "You say we have little time . . ." A cold fear pricked along her spine.

"When you return to Montfort you will see the urgency of the situation."

"Tell me now."

Strathmore let go of her arms suddenly and stepped away from her. It was as though he had given up, surrendering to the reality of the situation that he could not move heaven and earth and change her mind after all. His voice took on a sharp, crisp enunciation that was underscored with a combination of weariness and impatience. "It concerns your sister."

"Rowena?" The few words changed everything. She raised her chin, looking for reassurance and found none. "No," she said. Her lungs compressed, forcing tortured gasps to spill from her lips. "Don't tell me . . . I refuse to listen." She fought the urge to clasp her palms over her ears.

"There is no better way to say this." Strathmore's voice

was flat, his utterance so final and his eyes so distant Julia was forced to look away. "Rowena has been kidnapped."

An ache blossomed in Julia's chest like a bullet hitting its target, the tears instantly drying on her face. The room was silent, the ticking of the clock muffled by the screams erupting noiselessly in her head. Her throat was raw even though no sound escaped her lips, her body suddenly weightless, the walls spinning around her.

Strathmore should have told her. Immediately. Last night. "Why did you keep this from me?" she asked, stunned. "Answer me!" Only sheer willpower kept her standing. The deep blues of the room spun relentlessly.

As expected, he offered no response. No explanation. As if he could, as if there was a justification or reason that she could possibly accept. The words were bitter in her mouth. "You're a cold-hearted bastard."

Strathmore had his hand on the door latch already, and he half turned at the sound of her words. His response blistered the air. "Nothing I don't already know," he said quietly.

Chapter 11

The coachman pushed the horses hard, changing horses three times during the trip to Montfort. Mercifully, there was no opportunity for conversation on the desperate ride north, with Julia inside the carriage and Strathmore galloping alongside.

A few miles from Montfort, they stopped suddenly among tall old pines on an isolated rural road. As the carriage came to a rest, Julia leaned out the window to see Strathmore on his mount.

Scanning the landscape in both directions, Julia saw nothing but a ribbon of dusty road. She resisted the urge to hit the side of the carriage to push them onward in their journey. The silhouette of Strathmore with his windswept black hair and powerful frame twisted her stomach in knots. For the first time she recognized that hatred and passion could exist simultaneously.

Impatience and desperation made her brave. "There is no need to stop, Strathmore." She drew a deep, steadying breath, placing her hand on the coach's door handle.

Strathmore urged the horse toward her, reaching her side.

"We won't be here long, I trust. We are a few miles from the village of Hawthorne." Julia's cold voice carried in the silence.

The image of Montfort was framed in her mind's eye. The

local stone of its walls glowed golden in the setting sun of her memory, its windows glittering like jewels set in baronial splendor. She wanted to be home, to see Meredith, with an ache that threatened to shatter her fragile sense of control.

And then she wanted to run from Montfort toward Rowena—to rescue her sister before it was too late.

It wasn't too late. It couldn't be. They had three days. How bitterly she regretted her outrageous desire to make love with Strathmore, made all the more shameful in the crystalline clarity of that desperate morning. Every decision she had made since leaving Montfort had left her mired in disaster, the shame of her intemperance almost too much to bear. Why Strathmore had not had the honesty to tell her, to warn her of the impending tragedy—. Her mind shut down, anger and worry crowding out further thought.

Strathmore's mount snorted, its breath marking the cool morning air. "When we get to Montfort, you will remain behind with your aunt. If you truly wish to help your sister, you will try to convince Meredith to tell us everything she knows." Strathmore's voice was clear and distinct in the utter silence, only the metallic jingle of his spurs counterpoint to his stark request.

"You may leave it to me," she said, rage and disgust pervading her tone. "If Faron so much as touches Rowena . . ." Her mind was on the fearful plight of her younger sister and the frustration of a pursuit begun too late. She would do anything, *anything* to ensure her sister's safety, including never leaving Strathmore's side. "I have even less reason to trust you now. And yet I must trust you with my sister's life. The irony is staggering." And all but unbearable.

His eyes darkened to gray smoke.

"How easily you deceive all who put their trust in you, Strathmore," she continued, unable to hold back. Her laugh was bitter. "Don't expect me to believe that you are somehow acting nobly on my family's behalf."

The horse's head swung away from the carriage door,

Strathmore reigning the powerful creature in with a subtle shift of his gloved hands. "Nothing I could say at this point would make any difference."

Tears stung hot at the backs of her eyes and she gritted her teeth against the onslaught of ungovernable emotion. "I refuse to believe you would ever sacrifice anything for anyone. Everything you've ever done has been self-serving. You have confessed as much yourself. Ambition. Nothing else motivates you. You have sacrificed your own family on its altar."

In the morning light, his features were harsher than ever. Despite the rage that threatened to overflow, Julia was beset with other memories, no matter how hard she tried to deny them. Memories of Strathmore in the library, her heated exhortations, asking him to take her to his bed. "Was that part of your ambitious scheme, Strathmore?" she lashed out at him to take the sting of anger from herself. "To seduce me, as I've suspected all along, simply to make me more malleable, more eager to tell you something of Faron, the one man you so desperately wish to impress. Did you even consider telling me of Lowther's plot before you stripped me of my virtue?"

His mouth was grim. "I wanted you," he said. "I thought no further than that. It was the truth last evening and it's the truth now."

Julia's chest heaved with her vehemence, the hatred scoring her tongue. "Such empty words."

In response, he turned his mount away from the carriage, riding toward the dusty country road. "We have wasted enough time," he said over his shoulder. "Let us carry on."

A short time later, they'd arrived at the high walls surrounding Montfort. Servants met the carriage, and Julia and Strathmore were rushed up the stairways and through the corridors of the old baronial castle. Julia's expression was mutinous, impatience in every step, her motions suddenly fluid and without their usual awkwardness or hesitation.

They were ushered into Meredith Woolcott's private rooms an instant later. A series of large chambers provided

THE DEADLIEST SIN   157

luxurious comforts as well as a magnificent view of the surrounding parkland. The ceiling was ornately plastered, the
walls a burnt umber and the floor piled high with carpets.

Meredith was waiting. Julia rushed into her aunt's opened
arms, the urge to rest her burden almost overwhelming.
Shaking with emotion, she breathed in Meredith's familiar
scent of lemon verbena, feeling the steeliness in the line of
Meredith's shoulders, in her attempt to keep control of her
emotions for the sake of her ward.

Too soon, Meredith unlinked her arms from Julia's waist
and took Julia's hands into her own. Her wide green eyes
were the same as always, wise and calm, but with a sorrow in
their depths that tortured Julia's heart at the same time it
fanned the flames of vengefulness in her soul.

"All will be well, I promise you," Meredith said in her
warm, firm voice. "We shall find Rowena." Her gaze slipped
quickly over Julia, reassuring herself that all was well. "I am
so relieved to find you safe and unharmed." Her voice
cracked.

Julia shook with suppressed emotion, watching her aunt
collect herself, dimly aware that Strathmore stood back upon
the threshold watching them. He had yet to introduce himself, and she told herself she didn't care what he thought of
the drama unfolding before him.

Lady Meredith Woolcott, with her flaming red hair and
regal bearing, was most likely not what he expected. A fierce
intelligence shone from her eyes and hers was an ageless
beauty. "I received your missive from the messenger you sent
late yesterday," Meredith confirmed. Refusing to let go of
Julia's hands, she led her niece over to a divan and two high
backed chairs by the set of oval windows dominating the
room. "You cannot imagine my relief . . . after what I had
been told." She stopped to collect herself. "Dear God, I
thought you were dead."

With iron discipline and a straight back, Meredith sank
into the divan, Julia by her side, still unwilling and unable to
release her hands. "Are you certain you are well, my dearest

girl, that nothing untoward has occurred? You must tell me." She paused, her senses heightened. "There is absolutely nothing you should hold back from me. I shall not judge you. None of this could possibly be your fault."

Julia flushed, her cheeks burning. She shook her head mutely as Meredith squeezed her hands before releasing them.

Staring into her own lap for a few moments, Meredith then lifted her head and addressed Strathmore directly. "Thank you, sir, for returning Julia to me unhurt," she said simply, studying his face with her customary intensity. A small frown marred her brow, as though there was something disturbing in his countenance that she could not account for. "My apologies, but have we met?"

"Alexander Strathmore," he returned with a perfunctory bow. "I don't believe our paths have crossed, Lady Woolcott. Your niece is memorable enough and I would be hard pressed to forget yet another striking Woolcott. No thanks are necessary. However, although I don't wish to press you at such a difficult moment, we have little time to lose."

"I understand all too well, Lord Strathmore." Meredith continued to search his face.

"Unfortunately, we do not have the luxury of social niceties."

"I require none," Meredith Woolcott said with a steely edge that belied her elegant bearing. "Simply reassure me that Julia has been well treated."

"I think she can answer that question herself."

"I am well," Julia said deliberately looking away from Strathmore. "You must believe me, Meredith." She shut her eyes briefly and let her head sag against the soft upholstery.

"We may speak of this later, if you prefer, my dear Julia. But now you and Lord Strathmore most likely require sustenance. I have had the kitchen prepare something for you."

Julia opened her eyes, blinking like a wounded animal. "I could not eat a bite at the moment. There is so much to do, to find Rowena." She hesitated. "Please tell us what happened."

"There is little to tell," Meredith tersely replied.

"Lord Strathmore promises to help us," Julia said through clenched teeth. "He has given his word. Have you not, sir?"

She knew what he must appear to Meredith. Dark, imposing, and dangerous in his dusty riding cloak. She had caught Meredith studying him closely and wondered whether her aunt had heard of his exploits. He had yet to take a seat and didn't look as though he intended to.

"If you could tell us exactly when and how Rowena disappeared . . . Was there a message, a warning, anything?" Strathmore asked.

Julia watched her own hand scrunch her dusty skirt into a thousand creases. Meredith didn't say anything for the moment, because if she tried she'd be in tears. Julia could almost hear her thinking that they must be strong, to find a way to journey through this nightmarish maze. When she spoke finally, her voice was decisive.

"If my ward believes she can trust you to find her sister, then I have no choice but to believe her." A few tendrils of her hair had escaped her neat chignon, looking like blood spilled across the magenta silk of her shawl.

"Thank you, madam," said Strathmore, his voice vibrating very low.

In a fluid motion, Meredith turned toward a small mahogany box at her elbow, its mother-of-pearl sheen gleaming on the low table at the side of the divan. She quickly withdrew an envelope and held it out to Strathmore.

"Read it aloud, please," he requested.

"She went for her regular morning ride," said Meredith, barely audible. "She never returned. My man found this note on the doorstep soon after we deduced she was missing."

Julia rested her forehead on her fists. "We know who is behind this. You warned me, Meredith, after all. And I am entirely to blame. Had I not seen fit to walk into what was obviously a trap set by Faron at Eccles House . . ." She let the sentence trail away.

Meredith shook her head, the silence stretching out like a dark pool. "It is you who must forgive me," she said hoarsely. "This has been going on far too long. I only sought to protect you both, but I have obviously failed. I should have done more."

"You did what you could," said Julia, her voice strangled. From the corner of her vision, she saw Strathmore open the creamy envelope, extracting the thick vellum note inside. From where she sat she could see the initialed monogram. *MF.* Strathmore's face remained inscrutable. "What does it say?" Julia asked.

Meredith shook her head wearily, gesturing to Strathmore to continue.

"It says nothing." Between his gloved fingers he held a scrap of tartan, hued in light and dark browns interspersed with white.

"Except for his monogram," said Meredith bitterly.

Julia leapt from the divan, throwing up her hands in frustration. "That's it? A scrap of tartan? We're to find my sister based on a fragment of fabric?" Julia felt as though her head would explode. "He is evil. He is a monster. He is the devil incarnate, a man so diabolical and twisted that he finds the most torturous means to punish the innocent."

"He is a monster. Not born but made, I fear," Meredith said so softly the words were almost inaudible.

"What do you mean, madam?" asked Strathmore quietly, looking up from the tartan with a frown.

"I made him the monster he is. Faron," said Meredith under her breath.

There was silence, a thick miasma filling the spaciousness of the room. Julia sank back onto the divan. "I don't understand," she said, taking in the fierce beauty of her aunt, a woman who was exemplary both inside and out. "You must not blame yourself for the darkness of someone else's soul. That's utterly ridiculous."

"Is there anything you would like to say, madam, that could be of help in this instance?" Strathmore probed quietly.

"Do you ask because you have no further ideas?" asked Julia sharply, casting him a look that could cut glass. "Perhaps this is a scavenger hunt for you, but it means a trifle more to us, Strathmore."

Ignoring her outburst, he quietly urged Meredith, "Whatever you remember can only help us find Rowena."

For an instant Julia thought she saw the glitter of tears in Meredith's green eyes. She rose gracefully to face Strathmore. "It would make matters far worse," she said. "In this instance, the truth will not set us free but rather unleash a force far more terrifying than what we face at present. You must believe me when I say I would do anything to have Rowena returned safely to us. And you must respect my judgment when I say I could do far more harm to those I love by revealing what I have sworn to keep secret."

It was a variation on a familiar theme, one which Julia had heard most of her life. Looking around the familiar room, the years spent together with her aunt and sister unspooled before her. The Christmas tree was always in the corner under the crystal chandelier they had purchased together on one of their few trips to London. The fireplace bellows, which she had tripped over and broken, still resting by the hearth, its repair invisible. Meredith's favored pen, sitting atop her desk. And, dear God, Rowena's brightly colored shawl, thrown carelessly over the Queen Anne chair . . . Julia rose to stand by Meredith's side, taking a slender hand in hers. "I ask you to desist, Strathmore. My aunt knows of what she speaks. Besides which," she continued, not bothering to keep the derision from curling her lips, "I take it you know more about the scrap of a clue you're holding than you are letting on." Her eyes flew to his, but the coldness in their depths was far from reassuring. "After all, this game of Faron's was devised with you at its heart."

Suddenly it was as if they were in the room alone together. A tremor passed through her and she had to lower her eyes when his burned still colder. "An assumption on your part." His voice was devoid of anything at all, as though they were disagreeing on nothing more important than the color of a hair ribbon.

"It all makes perfect, though thoroughly mad sense, a hallmark of Montagu Faron," she continued, her fear for her sister's life making her brave. "Faron wishes to test you yet again, Strathmore, to offer you another opportunity to prove yourself to him as the highly vaunted explorer and adventurer you purport to be. It leads me to conclude the clue you hold in your hands means something more to you than anyone else. Faron would not have it any other way."

His features tightened. "Astute as always, Miss Woolcott."

At some point Meredith had released her hand, aware of the private tension between the large man and her niece, who was exhibiting an entirely unusual assertiveness. Confusion marked her brow as she tried to come to terms with Julia's marked transformation. "I have heard of your exploits, Lord Strathmore," she said by way of dispersing the uneasiness in the room. "And I can understand why Faron might find himself interested in your varied career."

"So what will it be, Strathmore," Julia snapped, gesturing to the scrap of tartan. Despite the anguish writhing in her soul, she kept her gaze level with Strathmore's. He turned to stare out the windows, one gloved finger tapping against the envelope in his hand.

"Is there anything you need, my lord?" Meredith asked. "Access to my library? I have men I can place at your disposal."

Strathmore turned away from the window, his shoulders filling the width of the portal. He twisted his lips into a smile. "I have everything I need, madam, thank you."

Fighting the urge to scream out her impatience, Julia forced her gaze away from his false smile to the bouquet of flowers brilliantly displayed on the occasional table in one corner. Tall, elegant lilies held her attention, the room swimming in their scent. How long would they have to wait for the damned man to—

Strathmore's voice broke into her careening thoughts. "The earliest tartans were made of undyed wool from the indigenous Soay sheep—much like this," he said tonelessly, fingering the brown and white streaks of color.

And so? What has that to do with finding my sister, Julia wanted to shout, but she held her counsel, willing him to continue. Beside her, Meredith stiffened but said nothing.

"This is a sample of the oldest preserved Scottish tartan, which was buried near Hadrian's Wall."

"Which, unfortunately, is seventy-five miles long," Meredith added. "But I don't understand what this Roman fortification has to do with Rowena. Or how it brings us any closer to finding her."

Julia interrupted. "How do you know where this tartan was found?"

"You do remember Dr. Grant's London home?"

Julia nodded, her mind returning to the chaotic and exotic contents of the drawing room on Gordon Square. And the two of them, secreted away behind one of the bookcases, passion barely held in check. Mortified and nauseated with guilt, she turned pale at the memory. "I do. But what of it?"

"Seven summers ago, Dr. Grant and I spent several months on an archaeological excavation. His quest was to add to his collection of specimens, in that case the bones of the *Ichthyosaurus platyodon* which he coveted for the cabinets that wall his study in London. Dr. Grant proposed that I accompany him as I had only recently returned from India and had some time on my hands before I would begin my explorations of the Ruwenzori mountains."

Julia let out an exasperated breath, her agitation stilled by Meredith's calming hand on her arm.

"Faron obviously knows your history, Lord Strathmore," said Meredith. "He is a thorough man when he is intent upon something, leaving no stone unturned."

Strathmore nodded. "He would also know that Dr. Grant

and I spent our time along the River Irthing, which defines the border between Northumberland and Cumbria. There are characteristics of the local geology of particular interest to Grant that are only found on the Irthing's banks."

"We're still talking fifteen miles of river," Julia said hopelessly.

"That's true. However the River Irthing marks a significant transition in the construction of Hadrian's Wall, between the limestone to the east and sandstone to the west. Hadrian's Wall crossed the river on a bridge at Willowford, east of Birdoswald—a Roman fort."

Her mind buzzing, Julia felt the facts slide together like bolts. "Which is where, precisely?"

"A few miles from here. The fort at Birdoswald was linked by a Roman road known as the Maiden Way."

Meredith held back a small cry. "Maiden Way. Faron can be exceptionally cruel."

And exceptionally brilliant, thought Julia bitterly.

Strathmore was already halfway to the door, clearly intent on making his departure. "The fort is situated above a steep gorge carved by the river from the deep glacial till overlying the area. From that point, as I recall, its course as it turns west is lined with other Roman sites associated with Hadrian's Wall."

"I can have my men prepared to accompany you at a moment's notice," Meredith offered.

"No." The denial was stark. "I am meant to go alone. This assignment was clearly designed with me in mind, as Miss Woolcott has noted. Anyone else accompanying me could imperil the life of your niece."

Julia shoved a shaking hand over her hot cheeks. Faron's cunning stunned her. The realization convinced her all the more that Strathmore's involvement in the Frenchman's schemes was more than simply a game or charade.

Her vision cleared, and she was aware of the chill creeping through her bones. Strathmore had been summoned by Faron, as she had been, for the purposes of laying a trap from which her family could never escape. To be close to a man like Strathmore was an invitation to be used by him. Unless, as she had intended from the start, she could use him. Julia would allow Strathmore to believe he was pursuing the quest on his own—but she would never trust him with Rowena's life.

Madness lay that way, she recognized, but madness might well serve as the Woolcotts' only salvation.

Begun one hundred and twenty-two years after the birth of Christ, during the rule of Emperor Hadrian, Hadrian's Wall was built as an easily defensible fortification that clearly marked the northern frontier of the Roman Empire in Britain. The wall was the most heavily fortified border in the empire, dotted with sixteen forts, one of which was Birdoswald.

The fort was situated in a commanding position on a triangular spit of land bounded by cliffs to the south and east overlooking a broad expanse of the River Irthing. Julia had once ridden with Rowena to the site and remembered the harsh landscape and remnants of stone buildings which, as subsequent reading had informed them, had served as a central headquarters, granaries, and barracks when the Romans had occupied the area.

At present, the challenge was how Julia planned to escape the fortress Montfort, which Meredith had surrounded by dozens of men. Her aunt would keep her remaining charge safe, heavily protected and as carefully guarded as the crown jewels.

Pacing the confines of her workroom above the stables, Julia realized she was already thirty minutes behind Strathmore, whose fresh mount would take him to the fort in under two hours. No longer anxious or confused by emotion, she took stock with the coldness of a mercenary soldier, aware that passion had been her sole preoccupation for too long. Her sister was her exclusive focus, her concentration as precisely defined as the view through a camera's lens.

Julia would use her pony, Squire, reliable and steady as an

old friend, to take her to the fort. Quickly pulling on an old riding habit from one of the workroom's cupboards, its velvet crushed and comfortably worn, she made her way quietly down the back stairs and into the stables. The grooms were already abed, save for Meredith's old retainer, Mclean, who had been at Montfort longer than anyone could remember. Vigorously oiling a leather bridle under the light of a lantern, he looked up and then stroked his grizzled cheeks contemplatively as he saw her leading Squire toward the stable doors. Alarm was written on the old man's face.

"I know what I'm doing, Mclean," she whispered with no preamble. "You must trust me in this."

"Lady Woolcott will have my head."

"This is my doing. Not yours."

"This is not anything like you, Miss Julia." His wrinkled eyes held concern. Mclean had known her as a shy little girl. He did not recognize the brazen woman who would challenge the hostile night alone to find and save her sister. "Leave this dangerous business to others. There's little you can do even if you do find Miss Rowena."

"*When* I find her," she said stoically. "Please, Mclean, Lord Strathmore has gone before. He will ensure that nothing befalls either of us," she lied, aware of the bitterness on her tongue. She gave Squire a quick pat with her gloved hand. "Squire and I know the terrain well. We shall be fine. All I ask of you is that you create a diversion. Perhaps call the guards at the side entrance to the stables to help you with some task or another. I only require a few moments and we'll be out the door."

The old man regarded her from beneath a heavy brow. Clearly undecided, he picked up the bridle he was oiling and then put it down again before turning his attention to the rough hewn tool box in the corner. Opening the lid furtively, he grabbed something in his hand before turning his attention once again to Julia.

"Take this," he said brusquely, placing a dark and ugly

pistol in her hand. Julia forced herself not to recoil, recognizing that accepting the weapon might be the only way Mclean would do her bidding. Her palm closed over the metal, which radiated coldness through the leather of her glove. Mclean knew very well she hadn't any experience or knowledge of marksmanship. Rowena had excelled at skeet shooting and had even bested successive groundskeepers in her ability to drill a dime at twenty paces. Whereas Julia was sure she would be unable to hit the proverbial side of a barn.

Nevertheless she said with every bit of confidence in her voice, "Thank you, Mclean, for your concern. I shall do my best . . . if need be . . . for protection," she tried.

Mclean eyed her deliberately. "'Tis very simple, Miss Julia. You are most likely a better markswoman than you believe. Pretend you're looking through one of those cameras of yours—then squeeze the trigger."

Ten minutes later, with Mclean's words still ringing in her ears, Julia left Montfort under a moonlit sky, Squire's familiar gait buoying her confidence. They were in the foothills of the Cheviots but the light frost made her pony's footing treacherous. The landscape held an eerie stillness, only the dogged footfalls of her mount breaking the pristine silence. A small lantern fixed to Squire's saddle illuminated the way, hardly brighter than the milky light provided by the moon.

It would only be an hour's ride, if they continued their pace. The wind stiffened the skin of her cheeks and her resolve. Hands clenched around the reins, she recognized that she had no set plans, other than to do what she must to ensure her sister's safety. Mclean's pistol rested on her lap, beneath the folds of her cloak, cold but necessary comfort.

Scrub pine and alder bushes marked the landscape and Julia surveyed the scene, quartering the area, assessing it as though planning the layout of a photograph. With Squire sure and steady beneath her, she passed Brampton as it merged with the River Gelt, the rushing of water telling her they were near Warwick Bridge, just north of Wetheral. But it was not until they came to the Irthing's banks and the Willoford Bridge that they slowed. They were perhaps a quarter mile east of Birdoswald, her memory told her.

The rush of the water beneath the planked bridge intensified, a white froth along a harsh, rocky shore. Julia slowed to a stop. For the first time the reality of the situation penetrated her consciousness with a steady stream of disquiet. She realized how the past few days had been excruciatingly tense, each agonizing hour passing in a nightmare of apprehension, fear, and uncertainty. Now that she had all but reached her destination, she was unsure of what to do next, almost wishing Strathmore were by her side rather than out there in the night possibly bartering away the life of her sister and the security of her family for his own shallow ambitions.

Sliding her gloved hands over the gun on her lap, she considered her few options. As she had recognized the moment she had first met Strathmore, he was the one man who could take her to Faron. If she were truly clever, she would allow him to complete his assignment and rescue Rowena.

But Julia would be there, observing undetected. If she believed even for a moment that he would forfeit her sister's life to serve his own purposes—Her thoughts stopped cold.

Julia urged Squire toward an outcrop of dwarf trees on the other side of the bridge, one of the few copses in an otherwise battered landscape. In the moonlight the scene was harshly beautiful, but she focused instead on sliding from her pony, her stiff calf reminding her of her recent injury. With a departing whisper in Squire's ear, Julia unhinged the lantern and extinguished the wick. Hiding it under her riding jacket, she began walking toward the rushing river and the steep gorge.

The murmur of the river grew louder but suddenly she heard voices. She slowed her steps, crouching low into the scruffy underbrush, her ears straining to pick up Rowena's familiar tones. A moment later, she heard the muffled echo of a male voice.

"Where is she?" Strathmore was saying, the sound low and controlled.

"I think that's up to you to discover," another masculine voice replied. "Do you think you're up to the assignment, Strathmore?"

Julia crouched lower, almost on all fours, creeping toward the mutterings, the hair on the back of her neck standing on end. A man's broad silhouette loomed against the moonlight. He held a dagger in his right hand. Facing him was Strathmore, a sheen of silver in his right hand, the blade glinting like ancient treasure. Julia wondered wildly why the men were confronting each other with knives rather than pistols.

"Faron thought it would be more amusing to have our confrontation using daggers from his collection," said the larger man, unwittingly answering her question.

"Early Etruscan, how appropriate," said Strathmore without glancing at the weapon in his hand. He stood motionless in the moonlight, tall and calm, although Julia imagined his eyes were vivid with anticipation. Rowena was nowhere to be seen nor heard. "If you are not willing to answer my question, I suppose I'll have to kill you quickly," he said softly.

There was an angry growl from the larger man, and he thrust and lunged with his knife in a straight push for Strathmore's chest.

Strathmore slipped sideways. "You'll have to do better." His tone was insolent, but he ducked as the blade slid by his ear.

Then neither spoke as the slashing blades glimmered in the moonlight. The men fought in earnest, sliding, moving, their breathing becoming more labored by the minute. Julia held her breath as the two well-matched opponents used instinct and superb coordination to gain the advantage. To the untrained eye, Strathmore was outmatched by the larger man's skill but made up for the deficit by attacking with increased intensity, moving brutally fast, meeting every trick with a natural fluidity.

Julia cursed silently at the display of masculine bravado,

her anxiety for her missing sister building as she watched Strathmore, his shirt soaked with sweat, foiling the larger man's thrusts and aggression with his superior physical condition and faultless reflexes.

How long would it go on? And to what end? Her sister was nowhere in sight, lost somewhere in the night while all she could do was watch the hopeless battle, her eyes mesmerized by the flashes of metal in the moonlight. They parried, retreated, and the larger man leapt behind a low stone wall to catch his breath while Strathmore marched toward him with lethal intent.

Strathmore could not die. With his death, Rowena would be lost. Julia began crawling toward the scene, watching as the larger man suddenly lunged and caught Strathmore unaware. Leaping back, Strathmore slid out of range once more.

Before rising to her full height, Julia felt for the outlines of Mclean's pistol pressed against her waist. She imagined clutching it between her unsteady hands and training it on the two moving figures. The impediments to a clear shot were numerous. She told herself she was capable, that her photographer's eye would see her through.

A third figure was silhouetted in the moonlight—Julia Woolcott. She rose from her knees and when she called out, she knew that her voice would be stripped of emotion, her hands amazingly steady. Raising the weapon, she fixed it with her left hand under the iron barrel.

Her objective was to stop that fight to the death—without killing either man. And to assert her control over Faron and Strathmore.

Fiercely concentrating on the crumbling stone wall on one side of the men, Julia prayed for a clear shot. But they moved at blurring speed. Strathmore was infused with bottomless energy, his blade swooping and driving back his opponent, nearly overpowering the larger man with his savagery.

"Are you certain you don't wish to answer my question now?" Strathmore asked, his eyes glittering as he took a moment to savor his victory, and to gather his strength to lunge for the kill.

Holding her breath, Julia narrowed her eyes, focusing on her quarry. Then she squeezed the trigger. The lone bullet exploded in the night, ricocheting twice off the low stone wall, the recoil driving her backwards.

Both men stopped in mid-motion.

"*I'm* asking the question now, gentlemen," said Julia, her voice straining to be heard over the rushing river in the gorge below.

Strathmore stood with his arms hanging loose at his sides, his chest heaving. His opponent was the worse for wear, his left should bleeding, crimson stains creeping down his shirt-front. Wondering briefly whether it was the right decision, she swung her pistol at the strange man, framing him in her sights.

"Where is my sister? I shall not ask twice."

"This is most unwise, Julia." Strathmore said.

"I did not ask for your opinion," she said, stronger than she had ever been in her life. The larger man watched her silently, his head covered by a knitted cap, his features obscured by shadows. "Unlike you two gentlemen, I shall not be held ransom by outdated ideas of fair play, particularly when it comes to my sister. In other words," she said, making each word count, "I shall depend on my poor marksmanship to ensure that I don't hit anything of *vital* importance. Although I can't promise that I shan't skim a knee cap or, heaven forbid, areas of a more private and personal nature."

No answer from either man. "I am not willing to discuss terms," she said, her breath curling into the damp air. "As I've plainly stated, I shall not ask twice."

To make her intentions plain and to ensure the accuracy of her shot, Julia took two confident strides toward the men, who watched her with unnerving concentration. The hard, uneven earth beneath her boots grounded her. When she stopped she was only several feet away from the two men who would take her sister from her. Her ears strained over the sound of rushing water, the back of her neck tightening as her ears struggled to hear a cry, a voice, anything that would let her know Rowena was near. Her eyes scanned the low wall behind the unknown man, wondering whether they might have secreted her away beneath the pile of ancient stone.

Don't worry. Don't cry. I will save you, Rowena. The simple words echoed with a childish rhythm, resonating from somewhere in her past. Her grip tightened on the pistol. She had rescued her sister once and she would rescue her again.

"I am going to ask you to drop your weapon, and turn slowly around, sir, with your back to me, at which point you will begin marching toward wherever it is that you are holding my sister." For emphasis, she pulled the trigger again, a blast hitting the ground by the man's feet. To his credit, the large man didn't flinch but dropped his knife and turned his back to her. He began walking toward the low wall furthest away from them.

"My aim is improving," Julia said. "Practice makes perfect, after all." She wondered how many bullets she had left in the chamber. Strathmore was watching her, the knife glinting in his gloved hand. Part of her wondered why he wasn't interfering, why he was holding himself back in a manner that was totally unlike his usual aggressiveness. Just stay where you are, she begged silently.

Her chest tight, she matched the unknown man, step for step, until he stooped down over the low wall. From her memory, Julia saw the gentle slope beyond that led to the rushing river. The breath rushed from her breast like a deflated balloon when she saw him rise with a bundle in his arms, the slack body and face covered by a cape whose hood had fallen open. In the moonlight, she could make out the features that were as familiar to her as her own—the perfectly white oval of Rowena's face.

Julia's voice was harder and stronger than it had ever been. "Put her down. Now. And then step away from her," she commanded. Her outstretched arm holding the pistol never wavered.

"I'd be pleased to do so, Miss Woolcott," said the unknown man, his voice nothing more than a rasp over the rush of the river nearby. "Because she's not mine to kill."

Thank God, confirmation that Rowena was still alive. Yet the words were meant to provoke, serving as a riddle intended to disturb. Strathmore took a few steps closer toward her until she sensed he was an arm's length from her back.

"Forget the wordplay. Put her down," she repeated.

The man shook his head, a white smile gleaming in the moonlight. "No wordplay. If I do relinquish your sister, she will surely die," he said.

Julia gritted her teeth until her jaw hurt. "You are in no position to make light of the situation, sir."

"You are clearly confused. So I shall clarify the circumstances for you, Miss Woolcott." He settled the bundle more comfortably in his arms. "You see, it is not I who will kill your sister but the man standing behind you—Lord Strathmore."

Thunder rumbled in Julia's ears, competing with the churning of the river. It was all she could do to steady and silence her breath. "Put her down," she commanded with a stabbing sensation in her stomach.

"Why don't you confirm what you know to be true, Strathmore?"

It was then Julia felt the sharpness of the dagger in her back.

"It's very simple," said the unknown man, "Lord Strathmore is to choose between you and your sister. Only one of you will leave here alive." He paused. "You appear to be shocked, Miss Woolcott, which tells me that Strathmore has been less than candid with you."

Julia's throat sealed up like wax and the hand holding the pistol shook, badly.

Chapter 12

Strathmore hoped Julia wouldn't shoot. There was no way she could hit the kidnapper without jeopardizing the woman he held aloft in his arms.

His mind calculated swiftly. "Miss Woolcott can't be depended upon to act reasonably when her sister's life hangs in the balance," he said into the night air, wondering about the man's stamina, the blood stains flowering through the rips in his shirt and breeches. "I know the requirements of my assignment. Although I'm amazed that Lowther believed I would kill Rowena to save her sister. Perhaps his judgment is not nearly as keen as he believes."

Strathmore pricked the back of Julia's cloak, ensuring that she felt the pressure of the dagger in his hands. Her profile was pure ivory, her eyes locked on the man only a few feet away. "I can shoot more quickly than Strathmore can plunge his dagger in my back," she shouted over the wind.

"I doubt it," Strathmore said under his breath but making sure that she heard. Julia Woolcott was prepared to think the worst of him. It was the logical conclusion, one she would not ignore despite the distress, borne of her love for her sister and her hatred of him, that must be ripping her apart. Difficult to reconcile, Strathmore admitted to himself with a coldness that often served him well in the past.

"I think we need to clarify the rules of the game," offered the stranger without sparing a glance at the body in his arms.

"You're clearly good with the dagger you hold in your hand, Strathmore, as you've demonstrated, so it shouldn't take much to finish off the senior Miss Woolcott quickly, neatly, and painlessly. For your troubles, once I determine the deed has been done properly this time, I shall dutifully relinquish Miss Rowena Woolcott, alive and well, if a trifle faint from a healthy dose of laudanum."

There was a sickening silence and then Julia said, "Consider it done."

It was at that point Strathmore decided to move. "Whatever you do, don't shoot," he growled into Julia's ear before thrusting her behind him. He held her tightly, one large hand pushing her to the ground as he heard a series of erratic shots.

Something wasn't right. Another volley of shots, and Faron's man, with Rowena still in his arms, fell behind the low stone wall. For a moment Strathmore's vision blurred. Rubbing his eyes, he brought away his gloved hand soaked in blood. He heard a scrambling around them and the ricochet of rock spitting from the ground. They were surrounded, by a phalanx of dark riders on horseback who held glimmering pistols trained upon them.

He shook his head to clear his vision again, dragging Julia with him toward the figure that had disappeared behind the low wall. He felt a numbing pain spreading up his arm and into his shoulder, filling his awareness and threatening to blot out all else.

Julia was clearly in shock, her eyes blank and haunted as she peered into the night, frantically searching the elusive shadows, barely aware of the half dozen or so men surrounding them. Strathmore looked over his shoulder, aimed Julia's pistol into the air, and kept up a steady barrage of fire until he heard the empty click of the cartridge. From a distance, he heard a series of voices, commands, affirmations, and snapped orders.

He forced himself to move, the two of them running and half rolling down the hill toward the rushing river. He was certain a glimmer of dark liquid on the scrub beneath their feet was blood. Faron's man was wounded and heading toward the water.

Behind them, a merciful silence. Faron was a suspicious man, and his assailants had disappeared as quickly as they had come. That Strathmore remained alive was no coincidence. There were further plans in store. He scanned the darkness, while absently watching the blood drip from his arm. Clearing his head, he stopped for a moment as Julia took great labored gasps of air.

She trembled as he pulled her into his arms. "He'll kill her. He'll kill Rowena," she whispered, clinging to him with the wild strength of burgeoning hysteria. "You should have done as he asked and spared her."

"Taking your life would have solved nothing," he soothed, not really believing his own words. The river was a short distance away and he calculated whether they would be in time to intercept the stranger who had Rowena. He would be weakening, from his earlier loss of blood and quite possibly from a gunshot wound. Strathmore's hands gently stroked Julia's back, although his own brain worked feverishly.

"We can't wait. Dear God, it was probably my bullet that hit him and possibly"—she bit back the words against his chest—"It's my fault." Panic held her frozen in his arms.

"Stay here," he said, "I'll go . . ."

"Can you find them?" Julia whispered, lifting her face to Strathmore. He started to disengage her clinging arms. Her hands tightened on his shirt, oblivious to the stream of blood matting the fabric.

"Every moment counts," he said.

"I am coming with you."

He looked down at her and said, "No."

But she was already running away from him toward the river, turning back in the same sweeping motion, her eyes manic. "She's my sister. And it's my fault."

Strathmore inhaled deeply and then a second later said

harshly, "The track of fresh blood leads over to that low copse a few feet from the river's edge." He pointed and in a few strides overtook her.

In moments, they stood at the water's boundary, a thin streak of pink highlighting the horizon, heralding a new morning a few hours away. The wind had refused to release its grip, the river's chop fighting with the swirling current dragging the water down its winding path. Julia paced frantically, her focus on the glistening drops of fresh blood that came to a stop where the rocky shore met the river.

"The bastard." Her voice rose in white-hot rage, followed by a torrent of obscenities, her back uncompromisingly rigid. "I shall see him dead," she finished in a breathless fury, standing stiff, pale and unyielding, fists clenching and unclenching at her sides.

Strathmore studied the horizon but Julia, despite her fury, had already followed his gaze. In the far distance, a small eddy darker than the larger whirlpool of water, floated with the current. Julia took a deep breath and ripped off her riding jacket, throwing it to the ground before he caught her both arms.

"Let me go. I need to be with her," she said, the fury in her eyes replaced with blank fear.

"You can't fight that current, even if you were the best of swimmers."

"Let me go," she said, terror making her unusually strong. She tore at his arms, the blood from his wound covering her hands and the front of her dress. Closed to reason, she began loosening the fastenings of her riding vest, her features tight with determination. The truth was too painful to absorb.

Julia hated him already and she would hate him even more. He had nothing to lose by saying the words she was loathe to hear. "It's no use, Julia. She's already gone. There is no possibility of survival, drugged as she is, possibly injured by a stray bullet. And the water is too cold, the current too strong."

She struggled in his arms, against the tide of awareness that threatened to consume her. "That's not possible. I won't allow it," she repeated, her eyes glittering, fighting the staggering reality.

Reflected in their depths was a darkness so complete, an absence of light so absolute, he was compelled to steal himself against it. "I am sorry. Desperately sorry," he said.

Julia arched away from him. However long he lived, Strathmore never again wanted to hear such a cry as the one that was wrenched from her lips, poisoning the moon-drenched night like the howl of a wounded animal, primitive and inconsolable.

Julia Woolcott, once returned to Montfort, was ensconced in her old bedchamber, the drapes in the bedroom closed to the sun, which chose to shine brilliantly for three days after Rowena's death. It didn't seem proper the universe continued its march and the spring leaves outside turned a tender green when Julia's world had died. She lay on her bed, face turned away from the windows, curling deeply into the pillows filled with the memories of her years with her sister.

It seemed only yesterday Rowena had sprawled at the end of her bed, holding up a botanical sample for her to examine or bubbling with news from the stables. Julia's mind echoed with Rowena's gentle teasing, her mocking imitations of the curate's prim wife, the restless energy that kept her perpetually in motion, a study in laughter and love.

Julia's tears began to flow in a slow bleeding at the poignant memories, as if her grieving heart was bound at last to mourn in the solitude of her childhood room. The trickle gave way to great heaving sobs followed by a flood of uncontrollable weeping. It was her fault, no one else's.

How would she survive, when she would never see Rowena again? Because of her own heedless pride and recklessness, she would never touch her again, never hear her laugh or hear her teasing, never feel the comfort of a closeness that had enfolded her most of her life. Clutching the pillow with tears streaming down her face, she lay against the lavender scented sheets of her bed, wanting to dissolve into the softness, to travel where oblivion lay.

She floated distraught and mournful for an endless time, tormented by loss. Shadows of people came and went. Meredith's beautiful face, etched with her own private agony. And others. The low gravel voice that belonged to Strathmore, arousing an embittered fury beneath the depths of her grief. What chaos had she unleashed when she had allied herself to such a man? She berated herself for her own folly at wasting precious time because of her own dangerously irrational desires.

And now it was too late. She realized how senseless and trivial her concerns had been. Her photography. Her false pride in her learning and knowledge. Her foundationless trust in a man who was buffeted by senseless ambition, and inexorably linked to Montagu Faron, the evil at the center of the morass her life had become. It was far simpler to let go, the urge reassuringly familiar, to give up the regret, the painful desire to be given another chance. Their prison at Montfort had been a gilded one but she would have done anything to retrieve every moment of her time together with Rowena, to collect and treasure their history, every exchange of words, every comfort she had shared with her younger sister.

Julia wished she could pray, asking like a child in complete, heartfelt sincerity for another chance, another opportunity to set things right. But she didn't believe in prayer, never had. Her dry sobs fell into the dark silence of the room, her grief so intense her breath stilled in her throat. Laying her cheek against the damp linen, she cried, wishing for a return to the past, however imperfect.

Whether asleep or awake, suspended in some nether world, she drifted, weary in spirit, devastated by the stunning realization that her soul had been severed in two because she had failed. Failed her sister. Failed her aunt. Failed herself, most of all. And not for the first time.

* * *

Julia tossed in her sleep, tangled in the sheets, her dreams consumed with fire. Flames danced, their tips licking at her skin, smoke clogging her throat. The paisley wallpaper with its cheerful collision of yellows and pinks mocked her. Whorls of hot mist curled the edges brown, stinging her eyes with acrid ash. If she strained and lifted herself from the pillows, she could see the top of her sister's head, the chestnut curls tied with pink ribbon, her dark lashes crescents against her cheeks as she slept the sleep of childhood, blameless and deep.

Julia saw the flames surrounding the crib, crackling and sparking like chestnuts on an open fire, consuming everything in their wake. Nothing could stop the inexorable hunger, an advance that was amoral in its intentions, devouring the innocent and the guilty with equal voraciousness.

The heat stung her face, flushing her cheeks and singeing her hair. Each breath hauled into her lungs was harder than the last as wreaths of smoke filled the nursery. Her senses slowed, and her body became a heavy stone beneath the sheets as she struggled to rise. Holding her breath, she controlled the panic screaming through her mind. She could still detect the outlines of her baby sister through the bars of her crib. Unnerving images flashed through her mind, one more horrific than the next.

The polished wood beneath her bare feet was unnaturally warm and her lungs felt like they were going to burst as she stepped across the nursery floor. The familiar rocking horse blinked at her with glassy eyes; a spinning top they had played with just that morning lay abandoned in the corner. Julia ignored the pain in her lungs, drawing each breath as though it would drown her.

She was almost at the crib, an obstinate determination warring with pain and fear. The baby's image floated closer, nearer, she could almost touch the white spindles. Smoke closed her throat and burned her eyes but she drew her arms away from protecting her head, moving inexorably toward the crib. The throbbing in her lungs was agonizing, unbearable, a lacerating pain that penetrated her skin, her bones. Darkness closed over her, a hot blanket, smothering and complete.

Julia slept, suspended in a strange dreamscape, startled to discover Montagu Faron across from her, relaxing in a chair where Meredith once sat, reading to her as a child until she fell asleep. Sitting with his back against a bright sun, Faron remained maddeningly indistinct in the shadows, like a half-developed daguerreotype, but somehow lit with an inner triumph. It was a face that Julia finally recognized as her nemesis.

"You," she croaked, her throat lacerated by burns.

He steepled his hands together, staring down at her. It wasn't an evil gesture, merely languid and indifferent. "Why so surprised, Julia?" he asked. "Were you not expecting me all along?"

She stared uncomprehendingly.

"One day you will understand, perhaps, although I am not making promises."

"What is there to understand?" she asked, her eyes cutting like daggers. "Nothing could ever justify what you have done."

Faron laughed, a dry toneless sound. "You are nothing but a petulant child, for all your protestations to the contrary. Your aunt was always a reckless woman who should have known better and taught you to mind your place. Knowledge is a dangerous pursuit."

The words echoed in Julia's mind, both familiar and elusive.

Faron's silhouette didn't move, but the light of rejoicing burned brightly behind his dark eyes. "Meredith is in her own private hell and Rowena is dead," he said simply.

It struck Julia afresh like a physical blow, so violent and brutal she had to drag her breath upward from deep in her lungs. When she spoke it was a pained whisper. "Why? What have we ever done to you?"

He smiled then, and even though she could not make out his features, she knew his expression to be both malignant and delighted. "Better that you do not know. That you accept the lesson life has taught you."

"Then what is the point to all of this? To make us suffer?"

There was malice and resentment behind his suave tones. "If you have the courage and stamina for it, as well as an astounding lack of judgment, you may discover for yourself what lies beneath, Julia, although I shouldn't advise it," he added tranquilly. "As with your sister, you cannot possibly survive."

Julia was once again struck with stark reality. She could not help hoping that Rowena was alive despite what she had seen, the eddy of water, the dark stain of Rowena's cloak floating toward the horizon. In the back of her mind, she'd been planning on leaving Montfort, going back to the river, to search for the sister who could not be lost to her.

Strathmore. A thin thread of hysteria ran through her mind. The man who had deceived her, over and over again, but was her only direct connection to the specter who sat opposite her bed, exuding malevolence.

"Do not entertain any useless hopes," continued Faron. "Your sister is dead, quite dead. As you should be, if it hadn't been for the incomprehensible machinations of Alexander." There was no attempt to hide the enmity. Venom infused each word. "You must accept the facts, Julia. I can see it is very painful for you—as I had hoped it would be. Only imagine how cruelly Meredith is suffering."

Julia pulled a pillow over her head, trying to shut out the coolly detached but poisonous voice. But hiding didn't help. Each syllable stabbed at her very being, a slow bloodletting, leaching her will to live. Tears resumed their flow, streaming down her face. Finally she relented, numb with grief, to a living death where walls kept out the pain. It was just a dream, she told herself, over and over again. It was just a dream.

Two days later, inwardly frozen but wide awake, Julia sat in the hard, straight-backed chair by the mullioned window in the sitting room off her bedchamber. Someone had seen fit to open the heavy drapes and to take away the untouched broth on the tray at her elbow, finally allowing Julia the isolation she craved. If she cared to look in the cheval glass over the fireplace mantel, which she did not, she would see how mourning had sculpted her features, rendering her delicate and pale, her heavy hair falling to her shoulders, her eyes dominating her face.

Grief had carved away any remnant of feeling and she took strange pleasure in the sense of detachment. She was a woman now, no longer the girl she had been a few weeks before. Physical intimacy and death had left their indelible mark, offering her a peculiar self-sufficiency she had lacked heretofore. Fear no longer held her prisoner because there was nothing left on the earth that could make her suffer more than she already had.

It was difficult to determine where nightmares left off and reality began. Her encounters with Faron were the result of her own feverish guilt, she realized, and yet continued to haunt her waking moments.

Rising to pull the curtains closed over the sunlight pouring into the room, she caught a reflection in the cheval glass over the fireplace. This specter was all too real, and she had nothing left to fight with.

"You appear somewhat stronger today, Julia." It was Strathmore's deep, familiar voice. He stood in the doorway, dressed in dark wool, the velvet collar of his topcoat throwing the clean plane of his jaw in sharp relief. In the past, his presence might have engendered immeasurable joy or desire, hatred or fury, but those emotions wilted under the gaze of his cold, assessing eyes. Instead, Julia felt nothing. She sat back down in her chair, turned away from the mirror, and met his gaze calmly.

"You have not spoken a word since our return to Montfort five days ago." He was leaning against the door, favoring one shoulder, showing slight evidence of the injury that could have easily taken his life. The way he was dressed, Julia knew he had come to say good-bye. Her hands slid from the arms of the chair and tightened on the heavy black silk of her wrapper as if the stiff fabric would hold her upright.

"Your aunt is worried about you," he continued. Julia had witnessed Meredith's haunted expression, her hollowed eyes and elegant frame bent from the burden of guilt and remorse. However, there was nothing Julia could do to alleviate her suffering. Words never did anyone much good. A world of silence was far preferable.

Her grip loosened on the silk crumpled in her hands but her heart remained cold at the sight of Strathmore. He had stayed at Montfort after all. Of course, he would want to find out as much as he could from Meredith, and from Julia, about Faron before resuming his quest. Who knew where it would take him except further away from her and closer to the man he was so intent on finding.

Julia no longer cared to decipher the nuances of Alexander Strathmore's character. She watched indifferently as he slowly pushed away from the door and strolled out from the shadows with his customary lithe grace so unusual for a man of his height and breadth. He stepped into the full sunshine by the window and, despite the coldness in her heart, she was struck again by his physical presence. Perhaps it was her eye, trained to the camera's lens, that forced her to acknowledge his tall, broad-shouldered strength, the lean spareness through his torso and hips, his long, strong legs.

Memories rushed back, lucid and searing. She rose from the chair, ready to make a motion indicating he should leave.

As always, he was more than prepared for her remonstrations. "I'm not quite ready to make my exit as yet," he said, easily reading her mind.

It was inconceivable, she thought wearily. Right back where they had started.

"Who are you punishing, Julia? Yourself?" he asked silkily, knowingly pushing her where she didn't want to go. Shaken, she moved back a half step. He followed her, his boots silent on the carpet until he towered over her, power in every line of his body. "You are endangering yourself and Meredith by hiding," he went on in a deliberately emotionless voice. "Shutting yourself away from the people who can help you is not the answer."

You would like for me to speak, to tell you what I know, she wanted to shout at him, angry tears suddenly welling into her eyes, her lips trembling. Help her? His life was a long litany of pure selfishness born of a privileged background that had allowed him to make the known and unknown world his playground. The damned source of the Nile. What did it matter except to those foolhardy men who courted hardship, illness, treachery, violence, and starvation to feed their bottomless ambition? She would never understand it and she would never forgive him. He had known that her sister had been kidnapped before he had taken Julia to his bed. And he had known of Lowther's perverse request that he murder Rowena himself.

Why should one night of feverish coupling make any difference? Julia shut herself off from the kaleidoscope of images that crowded her mind's eye. She was angry that he could still affect her so, with his cool reticence and eyes like gray granite. She held herself stiffly, meeting his gaze directly. He was no longer capable of casting his spell over her.

"Were you not the woman who was willing to take on Faron single-handedly, if need be? The woman who took pride in her learning and independence? What happened to her?" he asked with deliberate cruelty, his eyes on Julia's pale face, contemptuous—as though his sheer will could force her to react.

She bit her lower lip in agony. It was precisely the woman Strathmore described who had caused Rowena's death and Faron's resurrected interest in the Woolcott family. Had it not been for her pride, her own vainglorious ambition to have her monograph published, they would still be safe and protected at Montfort. Wiping away a trail of drying tears with the back of her hand, Julia's look silently accused him.

"I make no excuses for my decisions, nor should you," he

flatly replied to her silent reproach, intently reading her face. "We do the best we can in life with no assurances as to where our passions will take us. Perhaps it is my fault that I have not spoken more fully about my work, or shared with you my fascination with the mystery of one of the most magnificent regions in the world." Strathmore hesitated, his lashes lowering. "Africa is an elusive place where nothing is as it seems. Mesmerizing." He added quietly, "A passion of mine."

Why was he telling her this now? Something stirred deep within her. It was as though he was speaking honestly with her for the first time, with even more candor and transparency than when he had allowed her a glimpse into his boyhood and his father's death. Julia grimaced inwardly. What a fool she was in the presence of such a master of manipulation.

Turning away from him and his compelling voice, she focused on the unlit hearth, staring moodily into its charred depths.

"Bagamoyo is a small seaside town in Central Africa," Strathmore continued, seemingly oblivious to her disregard, as though they had all the time in the world and as though his story would make a difference to her. "It means *lay down your heart*. For whatever reason, I laid down my heart in that savage place. Just one example of how intently the geography and the people of the region speak to me." He smiled briefly at his own folly. "Of course, I understand this is of no interest to you."

Strathmore had a heart, after all, Julia acknowledged with grim silence, concentrating on the snowy whiteness of two birch logs resting in the hearth. He was ultimately unknowable, as vast and untouchable as the pristine and unexplored wilderness of which he spoke. The irony was not lost upon her.

She turned to see him shrugging at her silent indifference. "Faron once entertained similar ambitions, from what I have been led to understand. You will recall once accusing me of not being far different from the man himself. Perhaps you are correct after all. The source of the Nile is a great mystery that even Julius Ceasar yearned to unravel. It remains the greatest mystery of our time."

The nakedness of his ambition was so astonishing and undeniable and alarming that Julia felt a transient moment of fear.

Strathmore watched the tightening of her fists on her wrapper. "All of which takes us away from the matter at hand. I should simply like you to remember that I spared your life once, which you insist on forgetting. Furthermore, despite my aspirations, I intended to find your sister. And I would have succeeded had you not interfered with your suddenly acquired penchant for adventure."

An expression of shock and wide-eyed affront played across her face. His arrogance and confidence in the face of tragedy were staggering. Strathmore was baiting her, deliberately attempting to prod her out of her self-enforced isolation. He raised his large, beautiful hands and applauded softly, smiling in faint derision. "You lie to yourself beautifully, Julia. Not simply about Faron and your past."

He paused, allowing her to fill in the silence with images she'd prefer to forget. The wide bed in the London town house, illuminated by candlelight, surrounded by exotic sculptures, darkly mysterious stone carvings, and glittering scimitars. A warmth suffused the paleness of her cheeks.

"I thought so," he said with a small smile. "You lie to yourself about other matters, pertaining to physical urges you would prefer not to acknowledge. Or at least, blame me for." The words were said softly, drifting across the intimacy of the room, evoking memories of that bedchamber, redolent with the scent of desire and passion. His eyes, unfathomable, held hers for a long moment, recognizing the impact of those memories hovering between them.

It took every effort to deny them. Steeling herself, impatient with the warmth uncoiling in her chest, Julia sank back down into the hardbacked chair, the gesture one of dismissal.

Strathmore looked down at her, his expression neutral. "I

told you something of my childhood, as you'll recall, not to gain your trust for my evil purposes," he said with a glint of sarcasm, "but to help you understand that we always have choices."

For the first time in what seemed months, Julia was tempted to laugh out loud.

"I won't deny that our circumstances may have been quite different," he continued. "Clearly our responses and subsequent actions were." He added softly, "Simply stated, I ran while you chose to hide." His eyes were expressionless, without depth or shade. Feigning sincerity was so simple for Alexander Strathmore.

His assessment was unfair. Monstrously unfair. He was a man, born into a powerful, titled family. While she—

But none of it mattered. Julia turned her head to the reflection of two strangers in the cheval glass above the fireplace. Strathmore was saying good-bye. A thin sheen of sweat covered her body. Desolation swept over her and for a long, terrible moment, she relived the horrors of the past and anticipated the emptiness of the future.

Strathmore's voice brought her back. "You will never slay that demon, Julia," he said, his words a parting gift. His image in the cheval glass glittered in a shard of reflected sunlight. "Until you slay your own."

Chapter 13

A daguerreotype studio was often situated at the very top of a building with a glass roof to let in as much light as possible. A posing chair was placed on a raised platform which could be rotated to face the light.

The upper rooms of the stables adjacent to Montfort had been outfitted for just those purposes. Dust motes danced in the air above the long table dominating the space where Julia's camera obscura sat prominently displayed. The raised platform at the other end of the stables remained at the ready, empty and prepared for the next subject.

Julia looked away, the heavy weariness that she carried within her only intensifying at the sight of three leather bound copies of *Flowers in Shadows: A Botanical Journey* displayed on the far shelf. She focused instead on the sets of iodine and bromide boxes which sat atop the mercury cabinet with the sliding legs that she and Masters had ordered from France two years ago. In the shuttered cupboards, she knew there were plate holders with clamps, additional plates, a leveling stand, and a dish for washing and hand-buffing the finished daguerreotypes.

On the opposite wall was her coveted portrait of Louis Jacques Daguerre himself, taken by an acolyte, and a gift from Meredith to Julia on her twentieth birthday. It was a surprisingly informal image of the French artist and scenic painter who had discovered the first practicable method of obtaining permanent images with a camera. He was posed casually, the top three buttons of his vest unfastened, his head leaning quizzically to the right.

Next to the image was a landscape by Joseph Niepce, with whom her tutor had studied in Paris. According to Masters, Niepce had been an amateur scientist and inventor who had succeeded in securing a picture of the view from his window by using a camera obscura and pewter plate coated with bitumen. Niepce, Julia recalled, had named this picture-making process heliography, or sun drawing. It was only later, through experimentation, that he abandoned pewter plates in favor of silver-plated sheets of copper and discovered that the vapor from iodine reacted with the silver coating to produce a light-sensitive compound.

Julia had not visited her studio since she had left Montfort at Wadsworth's invitation—what seemed a lifetime ago. Her heart twisted at the sight of Rowena's discarded riding jacket, dust still clinging to the worn velvet, hanging jauntily from the arm of a chair. Emptied of tears, she walked dry-eyed to the jumble of boxes that had been hastily deposited at the edge of the raised platform. Her hands shook as she lifted the smaller one from the top of the pile and took it to the table.

Discarding the cover and rustling through a layer of tissue paper, she extracted a polished silver-coated copper plate nestled in cotton wool. In her mind's eye, she pictured the original photographer placing the sensitized plate into a camera placed on a high shelf. When the sitter was ready, the photographer removed the camera cover and began timing the required exposure with a pocket watch.

Julia's experience told her that the plate appeared in pristine condition, although that promised very little. An air of inevitability hung in the room along with the spinning dust motes. Competing voices jostled in her head as she caressed the sides of the plate carefully, looking into its surface as though looking into a crystal ball.

What would she find? The face of the demon that Strathmore had taunted her with? After one week of nightmares and fitful dreams, she felt compelled to look directly into the eyes of the man who had unleashed a torrent of pain on her. The man who had sent her aunt to the brink of insanity, and who had sent Alexander Strathmore to take her life and to murder her sister.

Perhaps looking directly upon such evil would prove her undoing. Regardless, she would know.

Working with surprising calm, she assembled her apparatus quickly in the darkened alcove at the end of the long upper floor, holding her thoughts at bay. Donning heavy leather gloves, she suspended the photographic plate over a dish of mercury before placing it inside a small fuming box where the image was to be brought out.

Keeping her mind deliberately blank, she watched as the chemical emulsion did its work, the outlines of an image appearing as though by magic. It was usually her favorite step in the daguerreotype process, although she took no pleasure in those moments she waited for the likeness to emerge. The acrid aroma of iodine pinched her nostrils, familiar and disturbing at the same time.

Her eyes had adjusted to the dark before she lifted the plate from its bath. Expertly fixing the image in a mixture of specialized soda, she took a closer look at the likeness miraculously unveiled.

With the slowness of a nightmare, the image blurred, faded and then returned. Julia looked at it disbelievingly. The man, wearing a tight waistcoat with its row of military buttons, sported a fashion already twenty years' past but it was not the sartorial detail that held her transfixed. There was something familiar about the image.

The arrogant tilt of the head, the aggressive jaw and slight hook of the nose. Even the breadth of the shoulders, and the sheen of thick, dark hair worn in the Byronic style. Only the eyes were different, inky jet instead of cool gray.

Blood pounded in her ears, awakening emotions in her she had mistakenly believed to have been drained away.

Impossibly, the ghostly image of Alexander Francis Strathmore stared back at her.

From the door at the rear of a discreet gentleman's club in London, Lowther and Beaumarchais stepped into the darkness of the late evening. With curt instructions to his driver, Lowther and his companion ducked into his coach and instantly drew up short. In the gaslit interior, Lord Strathmore waited, all too menacing despite his casual sprawl against the well-upholstered squabs.

"Do sit, gentlemen," he said, leaning forward. He swept a black-gloved hand at the seat opposite him in a show of good manners. "We have quite a journey ahead of us, as I've already informed the coachman."

Lowther at first failed to recognize the tightening in the back of his neck for what it was. Fear. Beside him, Beaumarchais turned an unflattering shade of red under the rim of his top hat, his hands fisting over a gold-handled walking stick.

"Truly, Strathmore. Your time spent amidst the savages has clearly left you with few manners."

Strathmore's white teeth flashed in a grim answering smile.

The coach lurched into motion and Lowther settled his bulk on the seat, reluctantly wishing he had secreted a pistol in his waistband. God only knew that Beaumarchais would be of no help. Instinct told him the man who sat so cavalierly across from him had something dark on his mind. Strathmore had never seemed so still. With those calculating eyes trained upon him as though the world depended on it, Lowther felt caught in the crosshairs of a pistol. All the more reason he forced levity into his tone as the coach sped into the London night.

"If you desired a meeting with me, you need simply have asked," he said. "Commandeering my coach seems a trifle melodramatic."

"Barbaric," Beaumarchais agreed, emphasizing the point with a thump of his cane on the carriage floor.

"You might try asking where it is we're going," Strathmore said.

"I trust in your good judgment, so do forgive me if I'm not overly concerned." Lowther thought it best to be politic.

"Most unwise," Strathmore said easily, although Lowther was hardly deceived by his neutral tones. "Gentlemen, I'm changing the proceedings to which you have become overly accustomed. Typically, it is you who do the commandeering." The gas lamps shuddered with the coach's movements, temporarily illuminating Strathmore's empty smile and the handle of the pistol tucked beneath his overcoat.

Lowther smoothed the folds of his cloak, his unease building. "I'm not a stupid man, and I take it from your tone and unexpected appearance this evening that you are unhappy with the present state of affairs."

Strathmore's smile disappeared. "I'm not here to provide long-winded statements that are meant to provide a testament to my emotions. I'm simply here to present my demands." He stretched his long legs deliberately in the confines of the coach.

Lowther arched a brow. "Your demands?"

"Demands?" Beaumarchais echoed. "Outrageous!"

Strathmore nodded. "I have decided to change the rules of the elaborate game that we play."

Understanding dawned, but too slowly for Lowther's liking. He unbuttoned the top fastening of his overcoat, the fabric straining over his barrel chest. "I had not thought you squeamish about certain matters," he said in what he hoped was a conciliatory tone. Faron would have his head if they lost Strathmore. "Clearly, I was wrong."

Strathmore remained silent, merely staring at the older man.

Beaumarchais spoke with the experience of a qualified rogue. "Don't tell me you've lost your so-called heart to the woman," he said, unable to hold back his contempt. His chest heaved visibly underneath his impeccably tailored satin topcoat. "Good God, Strathmore. I should never have believed it, despite your curious volte-face at Eccles House. You have somewhat a reputation for, shall we say, rather more outré liaisons. I should think after having tasted more exotic fare in those heathenish backwaters the likes of Miss Woolcott would rather bore your adventurous palate."

Lowther held himself in check, swallowing the urge to beat Beaumarchais over the head with his own walking stick.

"Here you are," continued the Frenchman, unaware of Lowther's glowering beside him, "on the brink of having precisely what you desire. Not that I begin to comprehend the allure of that particular chase—all that nonsense concerning the Nile and so on. However, still so very, very close," he nattered on. "Instead, you succumb to the dubious charms of a woman." He snorted again with derision. "Good lord!"

"You're wasting my time," Strathmore replied coolly.

"Am I? Or is it just the truth that you find discomfiting?" Beaumarchais persisted.

It simply defies reason, this sudden and unexpected change in Strathmore, Lowther thought. A turn of events Faron had not counted upon, and his assessments were rarely wrong in such matters.

"The truth has no relevance in this discussion," returned Strathmore all too calmly.

"Really?" Beaumarchais lazily traced a pattern on the velvet-covered seat beside him. "I find that difficult to believe."

Strathmore's gaze sharpened upon Lowther, compelling him to say something.

He complied with a tight smile. "We are straying from the point of this unexpected rendezvous, Beaumarchais. So what shall it be, my lord?" he addressed Strathmore directly. "How long shall we continue driving in circles around London in my well-appointed carriage?"

Strathmore gave an indulgent shrug. "As long as it requires."

"For you to outline your demands," Lowther confirmed, though he'd prefer not to hear them. His regret at the moment was that he'd been caught unaware, and with the ridiculous Beaumarchais in tow. Had he left for Paris when he'd originally planned, he might have been able to avoid that unnecessary and ultimately uneasy confrontation. He forged ahead against his better judgment. "Faron will not be pleased."

"Fuck Faron."

Lowther sat up straighter.

"A young woman is dead," said Strathmore tonelessly.

"Your astonishment strikes me as disingenuous," interrupted Beaumarchais.

Strathmore ignored the comment. "I believe the time has come for me to tell Faron what I require from him. For a refreshing change of course."

Lowther tried to find a more comfortable purchase on the overstuffed upholstery. "You do understand. I am merely the messenger. All this," he said with a wave of his hand, "is beyond my control."

In the dimness of the carriage, their eyes locked.

"You are overreacting, Strathmore," tried Beaumarchais. "I should never have thought—"

Strathmore smiled. "So you choose to believe. If you don't heed what I'm about to say, this encounter will appear mild, indeed."

Lowther shifted in his seat, his eyes on the pistol at Strathmore's side. Not that the man needed a weapon. A fleeting image of his own body lying face down in a river of blood took shape and was gone. "This isn't necessary."

"Yes it is. As I pointed out at our last rendezvous, Faron wants to meet with me as much, if not more, than I want to meet with him. As a result, we'll be working on my terms from now on."

The carriage took a sharp turn, jostling Beaumarchais so he almost tumbled into Lowther's lap. "Don't take me or, worse still, Faron for a fool," Lowther said, pushing himself upright, irritation bright in his eyes.

"Indeed," echoed Beaumarchais, straightening his top hat.

Strathmore leaned out from behind the shadows, his features harsher than Lowther remembered. He recalled what had been said about the man. How he had survived weeks in the desert with little more than what he carried on his back. And the rumor that he had taken on a tribal chieftain in hand-to-hand combat to ransom a group of children from slavery. There was a simmering undercurrent of impatience about him, a dark brutality.

"My instructions are very simple." The words interrupted Lowther's increasingly uneasy thoughts. "And I shall relay them only this once."

The threat was explicit. Lowther crossed his arms over his chest, wise enough to know he had no choice but to listen.

Strathmore continued, speaking very softly. "You will tell Faron to desist in his pursuit of the Woolcotts," he said evenly, watching for Lowther's reaction. "Did I not warn you that my demands are simple?"

The older man shut his eyes for a moment and took a deep breath as a chill ran down his spine. "You don't know what you ask."

"And I don't care to," Strathmore said quietly. "I trust I needn't elaborate."

The rumbling of the wheels over the cobblestoned streets was the only sound in the tense silence.

When Lowther finally spoke, he said, "You are prepared to forfeit your major expedition in search of the Nile's source, then?"

"Not at all," Strathmore said simply, the arrogance of prerogative undeniable. "I shall leave that discussion for the moment when I meet with Faron himself."

Lowther stared, disbelieving, hardly aware that the coach was slowing to a stop.

"I expect to hear from him within the fortnight—and I shall give him the courtesy of deciding where and when we shall meet." Strathmore's voice was moderate, detached. He rose from his seat.

Beaumarchais surged to life. "You are a bloody fool, Strathmore. Julia Woolcott is hardly worth the trouble."

Strathmore's gray eyes flicked past Beaumarchais. "I hate repeating myself. I thought my directives were simple enough."

Beaumarchais's lips curled, his tone taunting, despite Lowther's hand on his arm. "I did notice at Eccles House that Miss Woolcott was a tasty morsel indeed. So fresh and untried."

Lowther noted the telltale hardening of Strathmore's jaw line, the subtle flaring of his nostrils.

Beaumarchais continued, "From what I could see, she is possessed of the most winsomely long limbs and I can only guess at her other fulsome charms, that lovely mouth for one, which you were so reluctant to share with the rest of us that evening."

In an instant, strong fingers twisted into Beaumarchais's topcoat, all but lifting him from his seat with the mere flex of an arm. "You do not listen well, do you, Beaumarchais?" Strathmore's eyes narrowed. "Let me make this abundantly clear—the Woolcotts no longer exist for the likes of you. And I would suggest you watch your back. There are, shall we say, more *primitive* means of making you understand the reason for our little visit this evening." To demonstrate, he grabbed Beaumarchais's walking stick and broke it in half over his knee. He looked over Beaumarchais's head, addressing Lowther, who had shrunk into the upholstered seat. "I trust we understand each other." He tossed the broken walking stick to the floor and shouldered open the carriage door. The night air swept into the compartment as Beaumarchais gripped the upholstered seat to keep his legs from crumpling beneath him. Strathmore disappeared into the night.

The shroud of predawn gray was heavy when Julia stepped from beneath the dripping roof of the stables where Mclean had prepared a coach and four for her use. She drew the black veil of her bonnet more closely over her face as she approached. She kept her face deeply shadowed and averted, unable to put into words what lay heavy on her heart. Her booted feet moved determinedly over the slick cobblestones, making little sound in the quiet of the morning.

Meredith would read her note with some surprise and perhaps even a glimmer of hope. Despondent herself, she was at a loss as how to reach her remaining ward, who had cloistered herself away, refusing to speak or even to indulge in her usual pastimes. Books remained unread and, save for the one fateful afternoon spent in the studio above the stables, Julia had stayed in her rooms, sealed in her own exclusive and self-made hell.

The single trunk loaded into the carriage held her mourning wardrobe and the small wooden box that contained the fully developed daguerreotype Meredith had given her a lifetime ago. It was all she needed for her sojourn in Paris, France where she would reinvent herself as a widow, free to come and go as she pleased.

And ultimately, to find Faron.

That the widow was unwilling to speak, the world would attribute to her all-encompassing grief and unfamiliarity with the French language. Julia had already contacted a solicitor in London to find her discreet apartments in Paris along with a small staff who would interpret her wishes.

The veil of silence was reassuringly familiar, a defense, a warm cocoon that had served as her armor once long ago and would do so again. She did not panic at the thickness lodged in her throat, cutting her off from the world. She welcomed it.

Without glancing at Mclean for fear she would change her mind, she directed the coachman to her trunk, then climbed unassisted into the conveyance that would take her along the eight-hour journey to Calais, with stops to change horses. The coach lurched to a start and her mind drifted along with the miles that sped by, shutting out her memories of Rowena. The pain was too much, a knife where her heart had once lodged.

There were other more pressing matters to consider. Every time she closed her eyes, she replayed the moments in her studio, watching again and with renewed horror, as the image of Montagu Faron flared to life in front of her. What did it signify, the shadows and lines that coalesced into a definable shape, head, shoulders, and all-too-familiar features? Her pulse gathered speed. It was impossible. He was and he wasn't Strathmore.

The back of Julia's eyes burned hot. She blinked furiously and pressed trembling fingers to her throat. She could no longer afford to be the naïvely gullible pawn in the game that Strathmore played, clinging to the remnants of some romantic delusion. She had been irreparably scarred by his betrayal and her own refusal to recognize the truth from the first moment he had confronted her in that cork-lined room. Since her sister's death, not a morning dawned that she didn't awaken with a bleak ache in what was left of her soul and no amount of foolish delusion would ever erase that grief.

But Strathmore had at least left her one shred that made her life worth living. Revenge. It was all that remained, a dry crust for her to gnaw upon. Despite Strathmore's words to the contrary, Julia recognized her own demons well enough to take on the last challenge that would ever matter to her.

Relaxing of her limbs against the seat as the coach devoured the miles, she allowed herself to think of Strathmore. His accusation of her cowardice was an indictment she would readily accept. It gave her a strange kind of strength, she realized with a newfound conviction, rising from the ashes of grief and defeat. Despite Rowena's death—or rather because of it—Julia would never be imprisoned again. Not by Meredith and not by Faron. And certainly not by Strathmore's endless lies and subterfuge.

If there was anything of Rowena's spirit that remained within Julia, it was her sister's simple joy in life. It flowered within her and gave her a rare courage she had lacked. She would not wait for Faron to terrorize what remained of her family. She would go and meet the dragon in its lair.

As for Strathmore—she shut away the memories that still had the power to wound her. She had been wanton and reckless, desiring something that had always seemed out of reach, but she would not allow that history to overshadow what remained of her future. Doubts continued to haunt her. How would she last the rest of her life, she despaired, damning Strathmore's memory and his compelling imprint upon her body and soul?

Julia ruthlessly subdued her unspoken wishes and undefined feelings. For Strathmore, without doubt, she would be too easily forgotten. What had he said so long ago? *Despite your having read Catullus and de Sade, you are reluctant to admit the pleasure stimuli created between the male and female. Hypocrisy does not become you, Miss Woolcott.*

Strathmore's knowledge of the world told him as much and he offered himself to women with a naturalness that justified his facile reputation with the fairer sex. The man had sampled wares from several continents. He would never have been satisfied with the likes of the scholarly Julia Woolcott. She should have taken note, she thought bitterly, rather than endowing their enforced companionship with a hopeless idealism that embarrassed her to her very core. Strathmore was wrong in one matter. She had not hidden from her fate but all too recklessly embraced it. As a result, her education had been short and painful. But she had learned the lesson well.

As for Strathmore's stunning resemblance to Montagu Faron—it was the continuation of a paralyzing nightmare, one she hoped and feared she would awaken from one day. The implications, she thought with sharp agony, could not bear scrutiny.

Dusk had fallen when the coach finally drew to a halt before the country inn in Calais. The quay opposite the inn hummed with life as men came and went like ants. Even at that late hour, they tended to the merchant vessels that plied the narrow channel between England and France.

Julia took little notice of the activity as she stepped down from the coach, averting her face and drawing the black netting securely over it. The aroma of the sea was pungent and strong, the shore of France a distant and imagined shimmer on the channel. Her dress hung limp and soiled, its ruined hem sweeping in the dust as she entered the front steps of the modest inn, eager for rest in a quiet room and decent bed.

Julia moved toward the darkened interior, ignoring the elbows that jarred her progress. She set her sights on the rumpled figure of her coachman approaching the plump matron behind the bar at the back of the large room to secure rooms for the night. The air was heavy with smoke and ale as seamen, merchants, and travelers filled the tables, hoisting tankards in high spirits and boisterous talk. She squeezed through a maze of tables, endeavoring to catch the matron's eye, her gaze sweeping over the crowd in search of a clear passage.

Deciding it was better to wait in the darkened hallway leading to the upper story rooms, she edged her way through the thinning crowd. Her appetite, never keen, had all but disappeared since Rowena's death but she realized she needed to eat and would have a note sent down to the kitchens for a simple meal to be delivered to her rooms. Taking the first weary step up the narrow stairway, she found her waist gripped from behind. Startled, she peered through the black netting of her bonnet at a lumbering seaman.

"Yer, not goin' up there all lonesome, is you?" he asked with a glint in his red-streaked eyes. Julia swallowed the bile rising in her throat, watching in horror as a hairy arm clamped around her waist, rocking her over the stairs despite the elbow she shoved in his bulky chest. "Yer a thin one, ain't ya?" he said, pawing through her petticoats at her hips and buttocks before his hand, with dark-crested fingernails, closed over her bodice searchingly.

A combination of rage and fear erupted from her throat. Julia twisted and spat, struggles that only seemed to amuse her captor, who chuckled throatily in response. The black netting of her bonnet tore, the sound galvanizing her into action. With a cry of rage and humiliation and an uncommon surge of strength, she twisted to drive her fist into the sea-man's neck, knocking him momentarily off-guard. Seizing the opportunity, she lunged from his grip, and up the first stairs, only to hear his grunted curse as he clambered after her, snatching at her skirts.

Her mind reeling, she gasped and turned, shoving her full weight against the onslaught. Her legs bucked and the stairs disappeared beneath her feet. Hauled up against the beefy chest, she was assailed with the scent of cheap rum and sweat, certain that at any moment they would go crashing down the stairs in one gruesome heap.

The seaman grunted his impatience and his arms locked around her waist once more. Ready to drive her nails into his eyes, Julia was suddenly, miraculously freed, the realization so startling that she spun around only to find herself swept up into another set of arms.

The instant recognition was shocking. The scent of forest and desert triggered lush memories, ones Julia desperately wanted to forget. Overcome with a sudden and irrational urge to collapse against the hard chest, she felt her legs going weak as her head burrowed into a clean linen shirt front.

She breathed in the exotic yet familiar scent of Alexander Strathmore and closed her eyes against the onslaught of emotion.

"I believe we're finished here," Strathmore said softly over her head with a decisive click of his pistol. Unwilling to look up, Julia heard the seaman shuffle away from them.

"Didn' mean no harm, me lord."

"I doubt that," Strathmore said so quietly the ominous undertones were unmistakable even to a drunkard up to no good.

"Thought she was a lonely widder, that's all. Needin' some company." The voice faded into the din of the common room, and relief instantly sent warmth into Julia's limbs. She twisted her fingers into the lapels of Strathmore's topcoat, resisting the urge to slip her arms around his waist and hold on forever.

Brushing the ruined black netting from around her shoulders, Strathmore remained silent as she resolutely stared at the ivory buttons gleaming on his shirt front, fighting the fingers beneath her chin, lifting her gaze to his. Strathmore's expression appeared to soften as his eyes, gray and remote as ever, roamed her face. One corner of his mouth slanted upward slightly.

"This is not a good idea, Julia," he said, one thumb brushing over her cheek, his palm smoothing her hair from her forehead. "I suspected that you would do something like this." He turned her toward the stairway, his hand on the small of her back, urging her up the steps.

Julia had yet to look directly at him. She couldn't. The daguerreotype image swam before her eyes, and a tumult of feelings swept over her. The floodgates that had been closed for weeks threatened to overflow.

"I've let your coachman know all is well and I've secured a room for us. You are no longer a widow but my wife, in mourning for a loved one."

For my sister, Julia finished the words for him silently, inwardly rebelling against his high-handedness. There was a sense of finality about their meeting in a rough-and-tumble inn on the rugged English coast. Drained of will after her unsettling encounter, Julia had little choice but to accompany Strathmore, dismayed by the contradictory flicker of gratitude flaring in her chest. Her legs still shook beneath her skirts when she thought of her struggle with the seaman and what might have happened had Strathmore not come upon her in the darkened stairwell.

He had been looking for her. The realization hit her with the ferocity of a thunderstorm in midsummer, and a surge of energy nearly sent her speeding ahead of him to the top floor of the inn. But she knew she had nowhere to run. His presence behind her was implacable as his hand at her waist directed her up the narrow flight of stairs.

Chapter 14

The accommodations were the best the inn had to offer. A small alcove held a simple, narrow bed which gave onto a larger room containing a small round table and two button-backed armchairs. A tall window, the heavy curtains closed, and yellowing wallpaper that was once upon a time either blue or green, completed the basic appointments.

Strathmore briefly glanced away from Julia's slender silhouette standing by the table. She had yet to turn around and face him, offering him no thanks but only her enduring silence. She was draped in invisible armor, deliberately cutting herself off from him and the world.

He watched as she removed the shambles of a bonnet from her head. Her heavy hair had come loose in the struggle, intensifying the paradoxical aura of vulnerability and determination that clung to her. Unbidden, he moved behind her and took the bonnet from her hands, tossing it carelessly on the table.

"I don't have to ask you where it is you're intending to go," he murmured, "not that you would answer me." For the first time, her eyes met his. He was surprised at the heat that burned there before she drew back from him as though he were the devil himself. The translucence of her skin scared him, as did the fineness of her bones more delicately defined than ever.

"You intend to find and confront Faron and yet you look as though you could be buffeted about by the slightest breeze," he said.

Her lips quivered and she brushed past him, moving to the other side of the table, gripping its scarred edge as though to keep herself upright.

"Do not look so astonished at the sight of me," he continued. "My family's solicitors are the best in the country and it took very little for them to unearth your itinerary. Although what you hoped to accomplish in Paris, I'm not certain, given that you do not know the whereabouts of Faron."

The fleeting changes of expression on her beautiful face held a fascination for him that was patently unwise. Her wide eyes raked him over, looking for something she couldn't exactly determine, her full lips widening in frustration. He realized that he could watch her forever. Perhaps not so odd an insight considering he hadn't given the rashness of his actions a second thought since the moment he'd met her.

Strathmore had known when he left Montfort over a week ago that he would not allow Julia Woolcott out of his sight. He had been a man consumed with tracking her every movement, convinced that she would strike out on her own. The slight bullet wound that he'd received the night at Birdoswald was healing quickly—if only his conscience would do the same. Damn Julia Woolcott and damn her family. It might have all been so very simple. For reasons he could not articulate, he wanted answers. He wanted an explanation that made sense to him and to the world he had so carefully constructed for himself.

Worse still, Strathmore wanted her.

Pushing away from the wall, he watched Julia hungrily, recalling the motion of her hips beneath the heavy black of her skirts as she had walked slowly ahead of him on the stairs, her slender shoulders and neck erect as if the coils of her dark hair were almost too heavy for her frame. The scent of lavender and freesia hung in the room, mingling with the aroma that was purely her own.

He was stunningly aware that since he had first met Julia Woolcott he had subsisted almost solely on reckless emotion. While no one would ever accuse him of being prudent or wise, the risks he usually took were heavily balanced in his favor. The memory of his recent encounter with Lowther and Beaumarchais flashed through his mind. Strathmore had effectively jeopardized the last three years of dangerous, back-breaking work to protect the woman who, for some inexplicable reason, meant more to him than she should.

As though Strathmore were not in the room, Julia sank into a chair by the small table, weariness in every line of her supple body. He wondered what she was thinking even as he questioned the wrenching relief he'd experienced the moment he'd found her in the darkened stairwell. And the overwhelming desire to pull her into his arms and breathe in her essence like a man lost in a desert, desperate for water.

He had come so far. He shoved a hand through his hair and stood behind Julia's chair. Her eyes swept closed when she felt the gentle pressure of his palm against the nape of her neck. A pulse throbbed there, keeping time in rhythmic intensity with his own rush of blood.

"Where do we go from here?" he murmured, more to himself than to Julia, his fingers curving around the softness of her neck with a strange combination of tenderness and possessiveness that shocked him. Suddenly frustrated beyond measure, he pulled her from the chair with such fierceness the room spun around them.

Julia's mouth opened to protest, her lips moving against the skin exposed by the open neck of his shirt as she was propelled against his chest—where he intended to keep her. She jerked her head and looked up at him, barely concealing the desperation in her eyes as she searched his face. Then she pushed against his chest to achieve some distance between them.

"Perhaps it is better that you maintain your silence," he said with a hint of a growl in his voice. "If only because it gives me an opportunity to say what I think you need to hear." His voice sounded hoarse to his own ears, a trace of savagery hinting at passions barely tamed, reminding him of his own weakness with her.

He kept his hands firm around her waist, his thumbs moving over the stiff indentation where her bodice met her skirts under the heavy cloak she wore. He couldn't let her go if he tried, he recognized grimly. If only he could mine her secrets, mine the depths of the mystery that was Julia Woolcott. "This has happened to you before," he said carefully, trying to keep his vexation in check and wondering exactly how to begin healing a wound so resistant to ministrations. "The muteness, this unwillingness or inability to speak."

Heat swept up her neck and flooded into her cheeks. He caught her beneath the chin with one finger and tipped her face to his. His eyes lowered to her mouth and her lips tightened in response despite the controlled gentleness of his tone. "You should be aware by now, Julia, that I will finally prove myself not only your protector but also entirely noble of purpose—difficult though that may be to believe. I will not push you, that I promise. However, you will not be rid of me either. Slowly and with patience you did not even know I had, I mean to help you get to the source of your tribulations."

Julia swayed nearer as the pressure of his hands at her waist brought her breasts to brush against his chest. Her lips opened with surprise at the contact, and a glint of satisfaction burned low in his belly. He reminded himself of his promise which, he thought grimly, included managing what Julia Woolcott would call his baser instincts.

As though reading his thoughts, she pressed her palms against his biceps half-heartedly and found herself pulled closer, her hips nestling against him. Unwillingly, her mouth hovered just below his. She held her breath, clearly startled when he bent to press his mouth to the tender spot modestly revealed by the high collar of her cloak.

She stiffened in his arms, her eyes fluttering closed when he lowered his head further to the base of her throat where the high lace collar of her bodice parted under the heat of his lips. Her pulse leapt against his mouth, thundering in his ears. It was absurd, his reaction, his intemperate response to the thought of her silken skin beneath the stiff bombazine, aching for the touch of his hands.

Unbelievable. His jaw set for a transient second while a muscle high over his cheekbone twitched. Up until his meeting with Julia Woolcott, the idea of a woman taking center stage in his life was incomprehensible. Women were purely ornamental and entirely beside the point. He knew his mother had not set the bar particularly high, souring him from his earliest years on the female sex. Furthermore, his years of exotic experiences had unearthed in him an enticing sensuality. If he happened to have the time and inclination, it was easy for him to turn women's heads. A bevy of female admirers was at his disposal both at home and on several continents, although he realized he had never given any single one a serious second thought.

He would not apologize for his past. It was too late for that.

Julia bit her lower lip when he lifted his head and gazed into her eyes. Perhaps she believed she would see triumph there, or an arrogance that would justify her hatred of him. But he made sure she saw neither. He would give her time. He brushed his thumb over her bottom lip slowly, with a supremely controlled patience that told her more than he could possibly say.

"You are tired," he said, dropping his arms to his sides and stepping away from her. "There is always tomorrow," he declared. "The bed is yours as you are sorely in need of sleep." He didn't say that he would be spending the night sitting by the window with his pistol cocked.

A few moments later, he heard the sound of her heels on the floorboards as she moved to the bed, modestly shedding her traveling cloak and a layer of her petticoats before she gingerly lay down on the mattress fully clothed, pulling the thin comforter over her body.

Strathmore cast off his jacket in one shadowy moment and hauled out a chair by the table decorated with Julia's discarded bonnet. He stretched his legs in front of him, listening to the soft sounds of her even breaths.

He blinked into the darkness, entirely awake, still pulsing with lust despite every reasonable argument warring in his brain. Without looking, he imagined that she lay back on the pillows at the farthest edge of the bed, as far away from him as she could get. He sat staring into the dimness, listening to her breathing, strangely content with the moment—to have her near, where he would could protect her.

The night held no fear for him, accustomed as he was to finding himself in harsh environments with every imaginable obstacle presented by man or nature arrayed against him. His ears had become attuned to the hiss of poisonous snakes hiding in the scrub and the ominous chant of carrion birds, the grim reapers of the desert.

After a while the hum of raucous revelry of the common room below faded away. When he moved the heavy curtains guarding the window aside, he saw a sky that hung like a heavy black mantle, offering no indication of the hour. He moved silently over to the bed where Julia slumbered on her side, one leg drawn up over the other, her crumpled skirts heaped around her. Images unspooled in his mind's eye. Diaphanous blue silk against white skin. Long, slender limbs entangled with his. A tumble of chestnut curls and the most beautiful eyes shut tight against a mindless orgasm.

Christ. He was holding his breath. The flames of desire burned with an immoderate immediacy, as he took in her elegantly exposed calves dangling over the side of the bed, her skirts twisted around her hips.

God damn it. He climbed into bed beside her.

Julia feigned sleep. Under the fringe of her lashes, she watched Strathmore sit down at the edge of the bed and quickly pull off his boots. The muscles in his strong back flexed under the fabric of his jacket, which he quickly unbuttoned before stripping it off in a swift move and tossing it over the bedpost. With restless, abrupt gestures he unbuckled his belt. Twisting his pistol in the leather braid he looped it over the thin headboard.

She studied him, taking in the taut muscle and lean power, the pulsing strength, and the unsmiling face. His frame seemed larger and sparer than she had remembered and an unsettling sensation simmered in her chest.

They lay silent, an acre of distance between them. The silence was unnerving. Every moan of a floorboard and rattle of a window pane brought them to a shuddering, intense awareness. Strathmore locked his hands behind his head, his eyes surveying the iron ceiling with its cross-hatched design.

For once Julia didn't want to think. She was so weary, so tired of the despair that pulled taut every muscle in her body as she tried to make sense of the chaos her life had become. Grief and vengefulness was threatening to pull her into a vicious vortex. She should be afraid of Strathmore, in whose face she saw the palimpsest of Faron.

But she wasn't. Her body relaxed as Strathmore's arms came around her, cradling her close—demanding nothing, she suddenly realized. The revelation was a shock, the sudden truth so startling she understood at last that she would never exorcize her connection to him. She remembered the first time they had made love when no words and no arguments stood between them and melted into the seductive rhythm of his long fingers smoothing her hair against the curve of her forehead.

Their breaths found a common cadence, an ebb and flow of silent accord, her head resting against his shoulder, her body encircled by Strathmore's strong arms. The silence flowed around them, and the embers of anger flared briefly before being extinguished through sheer exhaustion.

Her whole world lay behind her closed eyes as she concentrated on Strathmore's hand moving in regular, circular patterns down her back. The small buttons of her bodice gave way, exposing her skin to the cool air. She shivered briefly before he dragged his palm slowly up the curve of her back, his fingers exploring each indentation of her spine. When he reached her nape, he repeated the motion, warm velvet finding its way back down her back with leisurely seductiveness.

A sigh issued from her throat as her hands delved beneath the thin pillows and she closed her eyes. His hands lingered at the upward slope of her buttocks where the tapes of her dress and remaining underskirts blocked his entry. She bit back a soft moan when his palm moved along the sleek, exposed curve of her back, a familiar warmth pooling in her abdomen.

Julia didn't question why she was reluctant to stop him. She didn't move, aware of the slow rise and fall of her exposed back as Strathmore braced his hands on either side of her, his loins resting against her buttocks. His chest was hard against the soft skin of her back and he pressed his mouth to her cheek, murmuring her name.

The feel of his lips on her skin was white heat, his hands parting the fabric of her chemise and corset a welcome release. He reached under the silk and cotton to find the swell of her breasts, and cupped them in his hands. They both knew she was already moist between her legs but her twisted skirts and clinging undergarments remained obstacles.

With her eyes still closed, she put her hands over Strathmore's, trying to move his palms to her nipples, which ached for his touch. He kissed her on the back of the neck, but instead of responding to her pressure, he avoided it, caressing the swell of her breasts with a teasing leisureliness that was suddenly not enough for her. Maddeningly, he skimmed his hands across her flesh, bringing her closer to his hips. Even through the voluminous fabric, she could feel the rigid swelling in his trousers as he pressed himself into her buttocks.

Behind her closed eyes she saw only color as her muscles contracted with shimmering sensations, the slick lubricant of desire flowing down her thighs and inundating her body with bone-wrenching pleasure. Julia knew she shouldn't be responding to Strathmore's deliberate seduction but as the sensations tore over her, all self-control fled.

Strathmore was waiting for her, she realized, too flushed with desire to be concerned about her body's easy acquiescence. It was too simple for him to command her response but she no longer cared. Her own hands slid from under the pillow to wrestle with the tapes and fastenings of her skirt. Unlike his leisurely caresses, her movements were abrupt, her slanting hips communicating what she couldn't say. Soon her legs, clad only in their cotton stockings, closed around his hand. She raised her hips to follow the sensations of pleasure thrumming through her. She trembled under his ministrations, so close to orgasm she felt as though molten gold were running through her bloodstream.

Her face still turned away from him, she felt his hands spreading the moisture over her core, smoothing the soft tissue in a heated pattern while she shuddered against the inexpressible urgency building inside her. His fingers slid over her slickness, probing slightly, penetrating gently, then more deeply. She was dissolving into a sea of pleasure, waves of heat flooding over her. He knew exactly—expertly—when to restrain his stroking fingers or move them slower or faster, deeper or not so deep. She arched into his warm hands, but he held her down, his palms pressing into the flesh of her thighs. The heat spread and blossomed between her legs, strong, steady, and burning beneath the wicked skill of his fingers until with a gasping, incoherent cry, she tensed against him, suspended in pure sensation. She released a hot moan into the pillow, her body melting with a flush of completion.

Every last thought fled her mind. Worries, anxieties, and despair were momentarily cleansed from her being as though she had been washed in a spring rain. Her body and spirit numbed with pleasure, she turned her head back into the pillow and slept.

Julia tossed in her sleep, tangled in the sheets, her dreams consumed once again with fire. Flames danced, their tips licking at her skin, smoke clogging her throat. The paisley wallpaper with its cheerful collision of yellows and pinks mocked her, whorls of hot mist curling the edges brown, stinging her eyes with acrid ash. If she strained, she could see the top of her sister's head, the curls tied with pink ribbon, her dark lashes crescents against her cheeks as she slept the sleep of childhood, blameless and deep.

The flames surrounded the crib, crackling and sparking like chestnuts at Christmas, a ceaseless and ongoing march to consume anything in its wake. Nothing could stop the inexorable hunger, an amoral advance, devouring the innocent and the guilty with equal voraciousness. Bitterness closed Julia's throat, cutting off her breath.

The bedclothes enveloped her like a winding sheet, her limbs thrashing in the bed. She was alone in her nightmare, the cloud curling through the darkened room moving toward her. The cloud thickened, coiling like a deadly serpent, a monster on the threshold ready to devour her.

Julia opened her eyes to strong arms shaking her awake. Over Strathmore's shoulders she saw flames licking around the door of the room, where the heavy wood had begun to bubble with blisters. It took the shortest moment to realize that she was not trapped in a dreamscape. It was real. And yet . . . she looked around the room as though the familiar rocking horse, the spinning top, and the white cradle should be there. Hysteria fueling her blood, she allowed Strathmore to pull her from the bed, her hands shaking in his. Pulling away from him, she fumbled with the tapes of her skirts around her waist. Without saying a word, he propelled them both toward the window, wrenching back the curtains and then cursing at the lack of a balcony.

Julia's heart throbbed as she surveyed the sheer drop. About fifty feet below, there were the beginnings of a bucket brigade, along with a wagon carrying tubs of water on a runner.

"No worries." Strathmore had to shout over the roar of the fire. "We can use the windowsills to climb down." He took her shoulders, his grip firm but gentle. "Julia. I need you to listen to me now. This is important."

His words were coming in waves, difficult to absorb. She looked around again, expecting to see the tiny white cradle and the downy head of a child fast asleep. Smoke seeped through the door and she tried to stem a spasm of coughing, while in the background the fire hissed like a witch, building to a crescendo.

"Julia." Strathmore's voice broke into the space between sleep and wakefulness, past and present, and she shook her head mutely in response. She would not leave without her sister.

Gripping her shoulders more tightly, he forced her to face him directly. "You can't stay here. Trust me, I'll get us out of this," he said. With the thrust of his booted foot, he broke the window pane, repeating the movement until only a few shards of glass clung to the casement.

Cold air rushed into the room, fanning the flames around them. Julia remained rooted to the spot, pushing Strathmore away from her as he tried to secure an arm tightly around her waist.

"I will not leave you here," he said, his eyes shining with intensity as he took her in his arms, placing one leg out on the narrow windowsill.

Julia shook her head, her muscles straining against him.

"What is it, Julia?" Strathmore's voice called to her.

The room spun around her as she fought for breath, the sound almost dying in her throat. From somewhere deep inside, the words formed, spilling from her mouth in a rush. "I can't leave. Not now. Not until I have her."

The hard muscles of Strathmore's arms stilled around her.

His eyes roamed her face, looking for something he would not find. "You did everything you could." His voice held a rough gentleness. She didn't answer, overwrought, gulping for air while he waited, holding her tightly on the precipice of the window, shards of glass glittering around them.

The rush of air from the window whipped the flames into an increasing frenzy, surrounding them in a blaze of heat. "I can't . . ." she said bleakly, in a hushed voice.

"I know." Their faces almost touched. "So I will do it for you," he said without thinking, working entirely from instinct and need. "Lean on me. Trust me. This once, Julia."

"I don't know if I can," Julia whispered, afraid to believe in herself or in Strathmore. But it was enough for him. He lifted her in his arms, maneuvering through the broken glass to the cold stone windowsill. He reached out one hand into the darkness to grasp the sash that levered them both onto the wide stone ledge. Julia squeezed her eyes shut, a strange euphoria overtaking her. She would trust him, this man who had invaded her life and who had the power to wrest the truth from her soul. Her arms looped around his neck as they stood precariously on the edge, the air heavy with smoke. She pictured the limestone crenellations above them as she felt Strathmore wedge them both between two corner stones. With one free arm outstretched, he pressed steadily against the wall, his boots catching the rough texture of the masonry beneath their feet. Carefully, he edged them across the ledge until he grasped the smooth metal of a giant copper downspout.

With his hand still around her waist and his body covering hers, Julia pressed her face against the coolness of the copper, as the stone beneath her feet gave way. Julia prayed the downspout would hold their weight as Strathmore eased them down to the lower ledge. They were only several yards away from the ground. Before Julia could protest, Strathmore pulled them away from the wall, prepared to cushion her fall.

The packed earth beneath them catapulted Julia into sharp awareness.

Daring to open her eyes and lift her head from Strathmore's chest, she found herself amidst a cacophony of noise as people raced by, shouting while carrying buckets overflowing with water. Craning her neck to stare at the top floors of the inn, Julia was transfixed by the inferno.

"Has everyone been led out safely?" she asked hoarsely, her fists opening and closing at her sides. Unaware that Strathmore was still holding her, she took great gulps of air, watching as sparks from the fire shot up into the early morning sky.

"It hasn't spread beyond our room as yet, and mercifully the public house was closed." What Strathmore wasn't saying was what was clearly being revealed by the tall flames leaping from the room they had just vacated—It was no accident the fire had started there.

Shaking with cold and shock, Julia was oblivious when a rough blanket was placed over her shoulders. Strathmore gently wiped a streak of soot from her face before lifting her in his arms and carrying her from the conflagration. He murmured into her hair, wrapping her in his strength and in the rough velvet of his voice.

They were in his carriage in the next instant. "London." Strathmore gave the sharp order to the coachman, snapping down the window shades.

Julia's head shot up as though from a deep sleep, when she was deposited onto the cushions. "I didn't say that I was going with you."

"There's nowhere else for you to go—other than with me," he said, his voice a low growl as he pushed her smoke-stained skirt aside with brusque motions. "You see what happened here tonight. It was no accident. The faster we get to my London town house the better."

"I have no say in the matter?" she hotly retorted, fighting off his hands and the weight of his body as he lowered himself next to her. She could not explain the power he had over her, the might that could make her nightmares dissolve and give back her voice.

"You realize that you are speaking, Julia," he gruffly murmured, smoothing the hair back from her forehead. "That alone should convince you to do what is right, what is necessary, for both of us. Why are we wasting time when we both realize what we need and want?"

"You can't possibly want me, damn you!" Julia said in an agonized whisper, pushing at his chest with all her strength. The carriage swayed as the desperate words hung in the air between them. "You don't understand who I really am. What I am guilty of." Suddenly she lay quiet beneath him.

"We can talk about it. We will talk about it. And it won't make a whit of difference about how I feel."

Julia was frightened to ask the question. "How do you feel?"

Strathmore took her face in his hands. "I want you."

"I don't believe you."

Strathmore's body was rigid with tension. "I don't believe it either. But it's true. There's nothing else that explains my decisions, my actions, since the first moment we met." His voice was hushed exasperation, his gray eyes heated and intense, although his smile was one of certainty. The blanket had slipped to the cushioned seat and he eased it back over her bare shoulders. "You believe I have power over you, but see what you have done to me."

"You can't . . . I won't let you . . ." Julia's voice was hard, her palms pressed against his chest.

One dark brow rose. "Can't? Won't? You are ignoring an irrefutable truth and whether you or I like it is immaterial," he said with impeccable reasoning. His eyes shut for a moment while he took a deep breath. "The evidence is there if you'd only look."

Julia struggled anew against his weight and her own contradictory emotions. "As though we are one of your damnable science experiments or geographical explorations!" She despised his arrogance, his hold on her and, worse yet, the tenderness she had glimpsed at the inn, which had proved her undoing. Strathmore had the capacity to bring her back to life, to make her feel with a vividness that hurt, and she resented him for it.

"Wanting is not loving," she said vehemently, regretting the words the moment they left her lips. Images of their moments in the small bed unspooled in her mind, the memory of the heat, her need, and the searing intimacy. Then, like a fearsome invasion, the image imprinted on the daguerreotype intruded. Strathmore but not Strathmore. Flushing, she reached up to push his hands from her face.

His hands fell away and he looked down at her for a moment before moving to the seat opposite. "Why do you always fight me?" he asked. His thick black hair was disheveled and he crossed his legs, leaning further into the corner of his seat.

"Why do you always disappoint me?" she flung back at him. With her hands braced to hold herself balanced while the carriage sped through the early morning, she shrank further into the blanket covering her.

"What happened back at the inn meant nothing to you? Proved nothing to you?" Strathmore spoke with remarkable softness. "That you were willing, unconsciously at least, to trust me is significant. You can't deny it."

Julia tensed against the supreme confidence. "You are beyond arrogant." His clothes, soot-stained now, did little to detract from his long powerful legs covered in close-fitting twill, his booted feet so close in the narrow aisle between them, she could have reached out and touched the dusty leather. Struggling to ignore the heated feelings, the familiar combination of desire and anger warming her body, she used his own argument against him. "You yourself pointed out that our feelings are simply the product of animalistic tendencies. No more, no less."

"You would use my own words against me. That is desperate." His voice held a trace of amusement, annoying and provoking. "And you continue to lie to yourself even though it does you more harm than good. Do you think, Julia," he said, gazing at her for a moment, "that the enforced silences you endure are something you must live with forever? They are the result of dishonesty, with yourself and your past. You must lance the wound or it will not heal."

"What has that to do with us?"

"You admit to an *us*." The words were so quiet they barely reached her across the small distance separating them.

"I admit to nothing." Julia twisted in her seat, reaching out to unlatch the window curtain. The fine brocade shade rolled up with a snap. "Take me back. I leave for Paris tomorrow."

"Impossible. You are coming with me."

She pulled the shade back down because she had no adequate reply at the ready, aware that she could hardly turn the carriage around by herself.

"You are coming with me because I care for you, Julia," he said, his eyes darkening with emotion. "Why else do you think I would risk everything to find your sister? Risk everything to come back to you?"

Julia slowly turned to face him, pulling the rough blanket to her chin in self protection. She was afraid, feeling her anger and some of her grief drain away, all too aware that he meant too much to her already.

"What else are you not telling me?" His gaze was suddenly assessing.

That you look like Montagu Faron. And I don't know what to do about it. She didn't know what to say. "What about your plan—regarding the Nile and finding its source," she said, deciding it was a good enough feint. "You are willing to sacrifice your ambitions for me?" Her voice was disbelieving.

"My concern, not yours," Strathmore said decisively.

"But I am to share everything with you."

He shrugged, meeting her gaze directly. "Haven't you already?"

A flush of pleasure ran through her. She would never forget how his hard body felt under her hands, how he moved with a seductive sureness and skill to bring her such exquisite sensation. Strathmore had stormed her body and penetrated her mind. A cloud of guilt hovered at the margins of her conscience, guilt at the thought she could feel that way while her sister lay dead. The tendrils of her nightmare clung to the corners of her soul, the heaviness in her heart a constant companion.

He leaned across the aisle and lifted her onto his lap without effort. "I know," he said completing her thoughts. "Perhaps not the details, but enough to realize that you are haunted by your childhood. The details will come," he said reassuringly. He held her tightly in his arms, the blanket around her shoulders the only barrier between the heated warmth of their bodies.

"How can we explain this . . . this tangle of emotions?" she murmured. Her palms slid a small distance across his shoulders. "It frightens me that you can do this to me. I don't know if I like it." When it came to Strathmore, the ground beneath her feet kept shifting, at one moment secure and dependable and the next moment unbearably shaky.

He smiled in understanding of how courageous her admission had been. Her dark lashes lowered as her mind came to terms with the fact that he had come back for her and had been willing to save her life at the Birdoswald fort, even though it had cost her Rowena.

Tipping her face to his, he said softly, "We can't order everything in life. From that first night at Eccles House, I now realize that I was lost. Lost to you. While logic, reason, and ambition fought to maintain the upper hand, something else won the day."

Something else. The innocuous phrase hovered in the air between them. Strathmore smiled into her eyes. "For what it's worth, because I really have no way of judging, I believe it to be love," he added. "I've never said that to anyone before."

His statement fell into the heated atmosphere of her doubts and resentment with stunning impact. "Love?" Her hands fell away from his shoulder and she shook her head, shivering as a premonition of ruin overtook her. "That's not possible." And yet against every modicum of good sense and caution, she knew it to be true.

"How else do I explain my actions? To you or to myself?"

Shattered by the honesty of his words, Julia reached up to touch his mouth gently with her finger to stop him before he said anything more, before ugly reality intruded, robbing her of a gift that seemed impossible. His face was inches from hers, his dark hair brushing her cheek. Her pulse accelerated with the touch of his lips, her eyes shutting against the surging flood of sensation already racing through her body.

"You taste," he said against the softness of her lips, "sweet. So sweet." His breath caressed her body and a flush of arousal heated her flesh. Moments later, the blanket dropped from her shoulders as she lay back on the carriage seat, shoving her skirts and petticoats out of the way with an intemperance that should have shocked her.

It was as though she was ravenous, famished, liberated in such a way she didn't hesitate with the buttons on his trousers or linger to watch him shrug out of his jacket. The breadth of his shoulders under the white linen shirt was miraculous in the close confines of the carriage and her hands traveled over the hard muscles as though they were hers alone.

In counterpoint to her urgency, he kissed her with a slowness that deliberately stoked fires already burning out of control. His mouth was delicious temptation to her, possessive and demanding, moving across her lips with enough pressure she felt an answering heat spread deep inside her. His mouth slowly parted hers, his tongue sliding into her mouth in seductive suggestion. She felt the hardness of his arousal on top of her, finding herself hungry for that same slow penetration.

She reached up to touch his hair, thick, black, and silky, always worn too long for fashion. His skin beneath her fingers was bursting with vigor, bronze and taut over high cheekbones, strong nose, and powerful chin. His eyes, so gray and unreadable, melted her resistance. She reveled in the muscled body, the wide shoulders and strong, perfect torso, wondering how she had ever lived without the feel of his skin next to hers, suddenly as necessary to her as breathing. She wanted to dissolve into him, always—for the rest of her life.

The carriage rolled on. Continuing to play with her lips, her tongue, Strathmore deftly moved her back to his lap. As if by magic, he pulled the thin shift from her body and over her head, rocking her gently, savoring the movement of her breasts against him.

"You are the most beautiful woman I have ever seen." There was a hardness in his voice that had not been present moments before. He was transfixed by her nakedness, caressing her flesh, taking her nipples between his fingers and then tantalizing her with his tongue upon them.

Julia could say nothing, her body speaking for her. She moved from the waist down, slowly back and forth, in sensuous, barely perceptible movements that seemed inborn. With the same velvet undulations, his hands made her skirt and petticoats disappear into a shimmer on the carriage floor. Unable to wait any longer, she pushed her breasts onto his chest, the lower half of her body enticing him with its rhythm as her hand found his rampant erection.

Raising herself enough so she could straddle his thighs, she lowered herself, eyes shut, slowly onto his hardness.

"This is right, no matter what," he said softly as she clung to him, waves of pleasure suffusing her body. He thrust upward at the same time as he exerted a downward pressure on her hips with his palms. His hard rigid length filled her, the only sensation that mattered, obliterating everything else in the universe.

He licked her lips and lightly caressed her nipples as he forced her wider with a slow upward movement, his legs flexing as he lifted her weight. Julia moaned, her head flung back, lifting herself so that she glided with his erection, controlling the rhythm of withdrawal and penetration. With panting breaths, she laced her fingers into the silk of his hair, on the precipice of explosion when his fingers sought the sweetness between her thighs.

He circled her pulsing core as though he had all the time in the world, and Julia thought she would expire, muffling her throaty sobs of pleasure until the sensual patterns of his fingers increased with each of her sighing exhalations. She raised herself one last time, breasts outthrust to his seeking tongue, before she lowered herself on her knees, dissolving on a held breath.

Her pleasure sounded deep in her throat and rose from her parted lips in a sighing moan but Strathmore began the rhythm again just as another climax threatened. His hard length robbed her of breath as he drove in deeply and then withdrew, with a slow friction so exquisite she knew she would die. She clutched his shoulders for balance as he withdrew, leisurely, from her body once more. The pattern continued, the measured penetration, the easy withdrawal. Then the tempo built in tandem with the growing tension in the muscles of his shoulders, until at last his hips drummed against her. Julia urged him on with mad words of pleading and pleasure.

The orgasm crested and crashed down over her body while his hips rose to meet hers, pulsing inside her with a ferocity that was exquisite until he suddenly lifted her from him and exploded, calling her name in a voice raw with passion.

Their harsh breathing drowned out the rolling of the cobblestones beneath the carriage. With heads resting on the back of the cushioned seats, they turned to look at one another. His hand reached up to push her hair out of her eyes.

Julia inched closer to him, nestling her head against his chest, one arm reaching around his waist. It was a simple gesture but freighted with more meaning than she wanted to admit. It spoke of intimacy, of trust and, horrifyingly, of love.

She loved Strathmore, and there was nothing she could do about it.

He gathered her more tightly into his arms, drawing the blanket from the carriage floor to wrap around her. He kissed her throat, her lips, her eyelids, and her forehead, finally returning to her mouth. In silence, they sped toward London together.

Chapter 15

Julia was happier than she had any right to be. Strathmore carried her into his town house through the carriage house, although they were both in a state of undress. Baxter looked on imperviously, standing aside as his master, with his exotic peculiarities, requested bathwater and luncheon served in his rooms within the hour.

With her flushed cheeks warm against Strathmore's shoulder, Julia felt suddenly at home, as far away from her grief and fears as she could be. In the cocoon of the fortress that was Strathmore's town house, the daguerreotype, her sister's death, and Faron seemed as far away as a remote continent. While a dark cloud darkened the horizon, it remained in the distance.

The days that followed were magical. Although Julia doubted she would ever learn everything about Alexander Strathmore, there was a growing but fragile understanding between them. Their never quiescent desire hung over them like a sensual fog, trapping them in its thrall. In only three days, they had coupled in virtually every room of the town house, disinclined to restrict their passion to the night. In the library she had shamelessly enticed him to sweep aside her skirts and take her bent over the settee. In the salon, while she was trying to demonstrate her lamentable music skills, he had spun her around on the piano bench and driven her to the edge of madness with his mouth as he knelt between her legs. And the evening before, they had not survived the first dinner course before dismissing the footmen and—Julia flushed at the memory.

Unbidden, she remembered how Strathmore had undressed her on the daybed that morning, stopping her laughing protestations by slipping her blue kid slippers and pale stockings from her legs with languorous ease. Everything was forgotten as the watery London sun warmed the room. Julia had helped him tug his shirt over his head and watched with the admiring eyes of a lover as he leaned over to pull off his riding boots. His broad shoulders and long torso were bronzed from exotic climes and, when he playfully sprawled across her lap, she stroked the tautness of his stomach.

"You are the one who is beautiful," she murmured, her fingers tracing the hardness of his biceps and pectorals. There was still a hint of doubt in her voice, that a man like Strathmore would find her intriguing.

His gray eyes gazed up at her intently. "Hardly"—he grinned—"when compared to your loveliness, which, for whatever mysterious reason, you continue to deny."

Julia blushed. She adored being with him, and didn't bother to hide her delight in basking in his attention.

"Let me enumerate the ways, in case I've been remiss." He reached up to caress her bare arm. "Your eyes are the blue of a tropical pool, your lips as soft as that pillow over there," he pointed carelessly in the direction of the down-stuffed settee. "And your form, well, where do I begin?" he said with a salacious glint in his gaze.

Julia shook her head. "Mercifully, you decided to spend your life as a traveler and explorer because, dear Strathmore, you would never make a poet. I give you leave to stop trying before you embarrass both of us further."

"Did I mention that you are formidably intelligent as well as inexpressibly lovely?" he asked, continuing to grin up at her, well aware of her discomfort but disinclined to leave off. Julia Woolcott was beautiful—and she was his.

She stroked the hardness of his chest, with a small frown.

"I thought you detested women who spent their time with their heads in books."

He caught her wrist in his hand. "But most bluestockings of my acquaintance don't look like you."

"Terrible man!" She wondered exactly what most of the women of Strathmore's acquaintance did look like. "Were there many?" she blurted out.

Strathmore pretended not to understand. "Many what?" His thumb stroked her wrist enticingly.

"Women." Watching his face closely, it struck her anew that his experience would be vast, given his demonstrable skill at lovemaking, his knowledge of her body—women's bodies to be more exact—prodigious. The previous night had produced an exemplary lesson in diverse sexual positions, culled from the translation she had found in Strathmore's private library, the compendium to which Felicity Clarence had referred with such appetite that night at Eccles House. A procession of dusky beauties, harem slaves, and bored expatriate wives paraded before Julia's eyes. "I shouldn't be so naïve, should I?" she amended in self-defense. "Your recent translation of the ancient Sanskrit text, for example," she murmured, still blushing at the memory of what they had done.

"I am merely the translator and in no way lay claim to having actually tried all of the variations suggested by the original text." He gave her an open smile. "Last night we were merely improvising."

"I find that hard to believe," she said, a flicker of doubt in her gaze.

"But pleasurable?"

"Need you even ask?" Julia trailed a hand down his chest. "I expect that I shall simply have to accept your rather adventuresome past."

"I spend much of my time at work." Strathmore's response was scrupulously honest; the women, and there had been enough on several continents, were suddenly a faceless, numberless pageant. "As a younger son, I was fortunate not to have been led into the marriage mart. My brother had the honor and duty to marry well and produce the requisite heirs, which he has done quite splendidly."

"Fortunate man," she said drily.

His gaze swept her form, lingering on her breasts and slender waist covered in the wisp of silk that he had left her. "You did not marry," he said.

"I already explained why." She felt his hand still on her wrist. "In truth, I never felt the urge, having been curiously content at Montfort." The image of Montfort appeared and as quickly disappeared. "And so here we are," she said, dropping a quick kiss on his nose, wishing to change the subject. Strathmore did not require much prodding, drawing her face close to his before finishing what he had started with his usual profligate and irresistible enticements.

The recollection sent a flush through her body from her head to her toes. Sitting off the small balcony to the back of Strathmore's private rooms, she lounged on a chaise, a book on her lap, as he entered the intimate enclosure. Her eyebrows rose in inquiry when he dropped into a chair with unself-conscious grace.

"I have a surprise for you," he said with a grin, crossing his arms beneath his head and looking at her with a benign expression. She closed the book on her lap. Worry flickered to life at his choice of words. The unexpected, she had recently learned, was rarely a good thing. For the past four days they had been keeping reality at bay, selfishly using the time together to build a world of their own creation, one in which grief, fear, and the past had no place. The exigencies of their situation hung in abeyance for the moment.

"Please let me thank you in advance," she responded lightly, keeping the anxiety from her voice.

"There is a special delivery for you. I've had Baxter put the parcels in the salon—where there is a maximum of light from the bow windows," he continued enigmatically. "Intrigued?"

Eager to maintain the air of lightheartedness, Julia sprang from her seat and sped through the double doors. Aware that Strathmore sauntered behind her, she burst into the salon.

The familiar mountain of boxes greeted her, incongruous amidst the tender green and soft pinks of the room. She clapped her hands in delight and twirled around to fling herself into Strathmore's arms.

"My camera apparatus," she said. "How can I ever thank you?"

Strathmore kissed the top of her head. "Don't get me started," he said roguishly.

"Maybe I will," she said, reveling in the security of having Strathmore take care of her although she knew it was imprudent of her to do so. One day, the house of cards they were so happily constructing would be pulled down by the force of Faron's evil will. As it was, they were simply waiting until the time was ripe to engage the devil himself. Julia buried her head in Strathmore's shirt front, inhaling his scent, willing the daguerreotype image she had secreted in her trunks to disappear, banishing it from her mind's eye.

"I love you," he said suddenly, into the softness of her hair, almost with a kind of violence.

The words struck both fear and exhilaration in her heart. "You are not being realistic, Strathmore," she murmured. "There is so much we don't know about each other. What you don't know about me." She sensed a change in him, an uneasy wariness, as though the gauntlet had been thrown down in a fight to the death. He was on alert, leaving Julia to wonder when the battle would resume. "You don't have to protect me."

The feminine brightness of the salon did not suit her mood. Like a knife to her heart, the thought of Rowena could send her buckling to her knees, the memory of the fire at the inn following close behind, threatening to blot out the impact of Strathmore's declaration.

"I've said it before. I love you. Nothing you can tell me will make a difference."

"You don't know," she repeated stubbornly but not a moment before his mouth stopped her words, covering hers with a punishing kiss of willful possession. His fingers hurt as he pulled her tightly into his body, his hands at the base of her spine.

"I know what I want. And it's you," he murmured, his mouth lifting from hers for a brief moment. "Why don't you tell me what I don't know, Julia. Tell me what happened so long ago." His eyes darkened.

"I can't." Her palms braced against his chest, her soul twisting in agony. He grasped her chin, bent his head, and met her trembling lips with his. She wanted to vanquish the grief but still could not give in to him.

"Talk to me," he murmured against her lips. He crushed her against him, her cheek pressed to his chest. She sensed his frustration. "Tell me what's hurt you so deeply, beyond even losing Rowena." She flinched at the name, lifting her face to his. Her expression told him more than she could ever say. "You've surmised much already," she said quietly. "But here is the truth, as best I know it, if you need to hear it from my lips." The irony was lost on neither of them.

He held her still in the circle of his arms. "The fire," she began. "It is a nightmare and not a nightmare."

"Finally," he bluntly said. "Go on."

"I must have been seven years old because I can remember details of the nursery—our rocking horse, the one Rowena was mad to play with, the brightly-colored top, and the dolls," she recounted with a grim solemnity. "I remember waking up, choking, my throat closing against the thick smoke in our rooms and then trying to rise from my bed to reach her . . . in time."

"And you did, you did reach her in time," Strathmore soothed. He seemed to know what she was feeling and for as many times in the last few days she was overwhelmed by emotions she could not control, outrun, or hide from.

She whispered. "I did. At least I think I did awaken her and bring her out of the fire. I can't remember exactly, and I always felt as though I'd left something precious behind." Her voice was taut with consternation until she took a steadying breath. "Then all I remember is coming to live with Meredith. That she looked after us."

"You would do anything for Meredith, wouldn't you?"

She nodded numbly. "Something terrible happened between Meredith and Faron. I have always sensed it, although Meredith never wanted to burden us with the truth. She believed it would only endanger us further."

"You feel indebted to your aunt. I understand now why you would take on as formidable a foe as Faron."

"I would do anything to protect Meredith," Julia said fiercely. "She protected us. She refused to let me remain in my self-imposed silence. Imagine—taking in two children in such tragic circumstances, after the fire." She paused and took a breath. "I owe Meredith *everything*."

Strathmore was holding back, and she sensed he wanted to ask who had been responsible for the blaze had threatened two young lives. What she didn't discern was the carefully banked rage he so assiduously hid from her, unwilling to mar their growing but fragile intimacy.

"I don't know who was responsible," she said, her cheek against his hard chest. But they both knew that she did.

"You have nothing to feel guilty about," he said carefully, his voice even. "The culpability rests with someone else entirely. We know who was responsible." The casualness of the statement belied his mounting fury, the uncontrolled emotion frightening to a man who, since childhood, had never really cared about much other than the next mountain to climb or riverbed to explore.

Julia took a shuddering breath. "What kind of man is Montagu Faron, to set fire to a nursery?" It was out, the ugly truth hanging in the air between them. It was a question with no ready answer.

"We will find out one day," he said starkly. "We have the daguerreotype should you choose to develop it. Who knows where it might lead," he said enigmatically.

The lie slipped from her lips before she could hold it back.

"I already *did* develop it. But the plate was degraded after twenty years of storage," she continued, the falsehood taking on a life of its own. "I tried, when last at Montfort, after you had already left," she said, the embellishments coming frighteningly easy to her. Dear God, she loved Strathmore so much she was willing to lie to him.

"Another dead end," he murmured softly into her hair. "But let's not think of it right now."

Julia waited for a rush of relief but it didn't come. Instead, she chose the next words carefully, the wound still too raw to contemplate openly. "What does it all really matter when I did fail Rowena, finally and ultimately?"

"You were not responsible for Rowena's death," Strathmore said, ignoring her words, wishing to sweep the burden of the past and present from her shoulders, and to mute his own growing rage. She felt the heat of his skin next to hers as his hands moved to the buttons at the neck of her dress, slowly slipping the first one free.

"I wish it were that simple," she protested, welcoming the touch of his palms against her neck, a balm for the ache inside her which he knew all too well. The image of the daguerreotype floated stubbornly in her mind's eye, a warning she knew she must heed, but could not find the courage to confront. At least not yet, when all she wanted was for Strathmore to hold her forever.

"You are making it complicated, Julia. Let it go. At least for the present." He kissed her lightly on her lips. He looked into her eyes searchingly and she wondered whether he believed her.

"That's all I know and that's all I remember," she said, as he slipped the dress from her shoulders. "I am being completely honest." She reached up and kissed him, her arms clinging around his neck, desperately wishing everything she could not reconcile would drop away. They stood together, their bodies melding.

"You don't have to speak of it any longer." His kisses soothed away remaining pinpricks of anxiety. "I believe you, that there is nothing more you are holding back." His mouth dipped to hers again, while her chemise strap slipped over her shoulder.

"Thank you." The two words were simple and heartfelt as she tried to hold off her doubts and fears, her happiness spilling over to drown an ugly reality. For now, with Strathmore, she was strong and whole.

He lifted her hands to his lips, kissing each fingertip one at a time. "You are thanking me for having your camera apparatus sent from Montfort?"

"Indeed, many, many thanks. I shall give you a demonstration of the daguerreotype process if you like."

"Later," he said with an arrogance that she was beginning to find appealing. "But for now, I'd prefer to hear more of your thanks."

She heard an undercurrent of lightness in her own voice, surprising herself and Strathmore at the same time. "You know precisely what it takes to please me."

The double entendre did not go unnoticed. "Why Miss Woolcott," he grinned, "are you complimenting me on my amorous prowess?"

"I meant the camera apparatus, of course," she said primly, the curve of her smile belying her words, while deep inside, she thanked the gods that he was not asking her more questions about the daguerreotype. Perhaps like her, he was unwilling to break the fragile mood they had created together, reluctant to open the door to ruin and devastation. "Nothing whatsoever to do with your other many talents, of which you are clearly inordinately proud."

They undressed each other then, leisurely, in the doorway of the salon, the rhythm of their movements beginning with a heated ease before quickly escalating into ferocious hunger they seemed unable or unwilling to appease. Kicking the door of the salon shut behind him, Strathmore lay her on the plush Persian rug as, moments later, they gave into the intemperate demands of desire.

"You are exhausting me," Strathmore murmured much

later, with Julia nestled against his chest, both of them oblivious to the threat of servants hovering outside the door or the scratch of wool against their naked skin.

"Not too exhausted, I trust."

"Greedy minx."

"I hear your heartbeat," she said softly, the powerful rhythm of life strong beneath her ear.

"And what is it saying to you?" he asked drowsily.

"I don't know," she said dreamily. "Perhaps it is the drums of Africa. Tell me about your explorations there." She was sated and content, desperate to know every facet of the man she loved.

And he did. He told her about the horrors of slave selling that he witnessed in Zanzibar. About the push to Lake Tanganyika, a journey wherein he studied and made notes on the ethnography of the indigenous peoples while observing the behavior of birds. About the Mountains of the Moon, the mysterious snow-capped giants shrouded by perpetual mist and brooding under eternal storm clouds. About the Nile.

And for the fragile present, as the sun slowly disappeared from the windows of the salon in London leaving the two lovers in the cooling shadows, it was enough.

Lowther threw the letter across the room, uncharacteristically losing control, only moments later picking up the missive to familiarize himself with the instructions. He ironed out the crumpled paper with the flat of his hands and went over the words slowly.

It was impossible to discern Faron's mood, or the stability of his mind, which was more important. However, it was clear that his master was far from pleased to have to cross the Channel and make an appearance at Eccles House. A command performance, if Montagu Faron wanted to continue playing his game.

Lowther preferred not to see the devil released from his den. There was probably good reason Faron was disinclined to join society, show his face, given the ungovernable moods that would overtake him with the unexpectedness of sheet lightning. Unpredictability was not to Faron's taste. Lowther painstakingly read the words again, as if some hidden meaning would be revealed beneath the stark, harsh sentences. Disquiet filled his mind at the perfunctory statements definitively stating a searing displeasure at the recent outcomes of what Lowther referred to as the Woolcott dilemma, or more accurately, the Strathmore debacle.

It brought to mind Beaumarchais. Rage pulsed in time with Lowther's fluent curses, the tempo escalating at the thought of the Frenchman's utter capriciousness which had only provoked Strathmore further. The fire at the inn was beyond disrespectful, an outrageous gesture fanning the flames of the past that were better left buried in ashes. A furious, impotent anger swelled inside Lowther's chest at the thought of the vain, cavalier Beaumarchais attempting to avenge himself against a perceived slight. Lowther replayed the encounter in his carriage, the moment when Strathmore broke Beaumarchais's gold-handled cane in half as though it were a twig.

The extent of Lowther's anger was evident when he broke into Beaumarchais's rooms above Bond Street, a scant thirty minutes later. Ignoring the pained expression of the butler who had reluctantly escorted him up the stairs, he knocked on the door with his own pearl-handed walking stick. "A moment of your time, Beaumarchais, now."

The butler, pressed against the doorjamb, drew back as the two men stared across each other from a table where Beaumarchais was about to indulge in a glass of champagne and mille-feuille larded with custard and cream. With the practical sense of his bourgeois ancestors and in acknowledgement of the provenance of his regular pay packets, Beaumarchais politely said, "Well, of course, Lowther. I am most pleased to make time for you."

Lowther remained scowling and silent while the butler pried himself away from the wall and gratefully shut the door behind him, leaving the two men alone.

"Don't look so grisly," chided Beaumarchais, rising from

his chair, his green watered-silk vest immaculate. "I can see that you are somewhat distressed." He offered Lowther a chair with elaborate courtesy.

"How could you have been so monumentally stupid?" Lowther asked, ignoring the invitation to sit, his scowl deepening, fingering the walking stick to leaven his temper. "Simply because your much vaunted pride is pricked, you decide to have someone set fire to the room where Strathmore and that Woolcott chit are staying."

"I simply had no choice, Lowther. You know that." He returned to his chair at the table where his champagne and platter of pastries remained unfinished. Fussing with the damask napkin on his lap, he reached for his champagne flute just as Lowther's walking stick interrupted the gesture with a decisive feint right in front of his nose.

"One always has a choice if one chooses to exercise restraint—an attribute that seemingly eludes you. Of all the reprisals you might have chosen, why the fire?"

Beaumarchais sat back in his chair, his full attention on the walking stick, understanding that he'd misjudged Lowther's, and very possibly Faron's, reaction to his impulsive course of action. He considered the extent of Lowther's bad humor with the beginnings of trepidation.

"Why did I choose fire?" he asked reflexively. "The truth be told, the choice has a certain symmetry or one might even say elegance, would you not agree?"

Lowther exhaled sharply. "Symmetry," he fumed. "You deliberately alluded to an incident that best remains buried. Furthermore, did you give any consideration that Strathmore may have been killed in the blaze?"

Beaumarchais shrugged. "Don't be ridiculous, Lowther. The man is indestructible, having survived the basest hardships among the most savage of primitives. As for Woolcott, would it matter?"

"Would it matter?" Lowther repeated. "You are immeasurably fortunate Faron did not learn of the incident." His voice was so soft Beaumarchais had to strain to hear it. "As it is, I am reluctant to place in your hands his further instructions and I do so only because it behooves both of us to follow the directives to the letter—this time. Have I made myself understood?" Lowther's fists came down on the table with unexpected force. "So what I expect from you—if you value your continued good health—is that you listen closely to what I have to say next."

Beaumarchais hesitated, trying to weigh how much goodwill he had available to him. It was not simply his physical health that concerned him but the ongoing allowance provided by Faron. He eyed the champagne and pastries meaningfully. As the great man seldom left the confines of his estate, Beaumarchais had become, over the years, a glorified factotum, entrusted to execute many of the great man's more minor affairs. His relatively low standing in the hierarchy of Faron's retinue did not rankle as he preferred to keep his involvement at a more superficial level. The incident at the inn, he had decided, was worth the risk. A man could only be expected to endure so much. Ever since that first meeting at Eccles House, Strathmore had done nothing but belittle him with a careless arrogance that he wore like the mantle of a foreign potentate.

Beaumarchais considered the pearl-handled walking stick lying across the table, just inches from his champagne flute. Satisfaction had a price but he was not about to sacrifice a relatively good and easy life for a moment of impulse. Therefore, he recognized it was not an advantageous time for argument or recriminations. He swallowed his pride to insure his voice did not carry an audible layer of self-regard. "Of course, I understand."

Lowther straightened to his full height, his eyes narrowing. "Thank you, Beaumarchais," he said sarcastically, "for your admirably good judgment. Too bad it comes too late."

Ever practical and eager to put the disagreement behind them, Beaumarchais asked, "What is it then you wish for me to arrange?"

"This shouldn't be too hard to accomplish, even for you."

Lowther was all business. "A weekend at Eccles House—within the fortnight."

"A reprise?" How unimaginative, Beaumarchais thought, to repeat oneself. It did not smack of Montagu Faron. But then again, it was the ever-arrogant Strathmore who was attempting to snatch the baton from Faron. Hardly wise. He smiled to himself with relish.

"Yes, a reprise. Was that not what you meant by symmetry?" asked Lowther with an arched brow.

Beaumarchais thought it best to ignore the obvious taunt. "Same cast of characters I presume?"

Lowther nodded. "However, this time with a few additional twists. I take it that both Strathmore and Faron would like to conclude their association."

"I am surprised Faron has been brought to this juncture by Strathmore." Beaumarchais took a sip from his champagne.

As am I. But Lowther did not say the words. Stepping away from the table with a glare, he said, "Must you always indulge yourself? And at such an early hour?"

Beaumarchais looked over his glass, pursing his lips with satisfaction. "Yes, if you must know."

Lowther sighed with exasperation. "I encourage you to attend to what I have to say next. There are several other details that must be seen to." Faron's instructions had been precise, a complicated orchestration that was to culminate in a crescendo, not that Beaumarchais needed to know.

Beaumarchais relinquished his flute with some reluctance. "I am at your disposal. What shall it be, then?"

"Three challenges."

"As opposed to four, or two?"

"Your sense of humor is in poor taste, given the situation." Lowther grasped his walking stick from the table and tapped it on the floor with impatience. "By now you should know that Faron does nothing without a reason. So it is simply a matter for us to speculate." His walking stick punctuated the floor in an increasing staccato. "For Pythagoreans, three was the most noble number. Let us not forget, Sir Francis Bacon's three tables."

"Yes, of course, Faron's interest in all things scientific and mathematical," conceded Beaumarchais drolly, secretly bored by the discussion. "Although, of course, one might add Aristotle's three dramatic unities to the list. This business is a drama, after all," he drawled, somewhat eager to demonstrate his erudition in the classical tradition. One day soon, Lowther would regret his unfortunate tendency for underestimation.

Lowther eyed him speculatively. "As for myself, I cannot help but recall King Solomon in Ecclesiastes—'a three-ply cord is not easily severed.' "

"Ordinarily, I would not associate Faron with the Bible."

Lowther ignored the remark. "Antiquities then," he said. "There are the last three labors of Hercules."

"Generally considered metaphors about death," added Beaumarchais helpfully.

Lowther looked away for a moment, lost in thought, before his head snapped up to meet Beaumarchais's gaze. "The greatest challenge always remains in interpreting Faron's motivations."

"Never entirely clear, in my experience," said Beaumarchais, wondering abstractly how long the pastries would last before losing their crispness. "To summarize, then" he began somewhat portentously, "you wish for me to arrange the three challenges for Strathmore's entertainment."

"For Faron's entertainment, more precisely."

"Of what nature, might I ask, although I can surmise, given the general ambiance at Eccles House."

"The first must involve a woman," said Lowther abruptly. "To test Strathmore's loyalty to the Woolcott girl for whom he has apparently risked much."

"Easily accommodated." Felicity Clarence would be more than eager to tread the boards, particularly where the virile Strathmore was concerned. "And secondly?"

"The abandoned chalk mines. Arrange for an accident," he said enigmatically. "Let us see how crafty Strathmore truly is when confronted with elaborate tunnels and grottoes going down three hundred feet."

"And should he survive—what is the third herculean challenge?"

Lowther clasped his hands over his walking stick, his eyes narrowing. "That's where Faron truly demonstrates his unique genius." He paused, watching Beaumarchais's plump fingers momentarily stay over his champagne flute, an answering glint in his eye.

"Do tell," he asked softly.

Lowther gave him a long look surrendering each bit of information slowly rather than simply offering the facts. "It's quite brilliant," he said distinctly, aware that he was keeping Beaumarchais from his pastry.

The Frenchman leaned back in his chair. "I'm sure," he murmured.

After several more moments, Lowther relented. "Faron intends to give Strathmore an incredible opportunity."

"Not the bloody Ptolemy maps he so desperately wants, surely."

"Much too simple, Beaumarchais," continued Lowther with something akin to admiration in his voice. "Faron intends to give Strathmore the opportunity to kill him."

Beaumarchais's lips were pursed in an expression Lowther often saw when he was confused, which was often enough. "Truly? Isn't that a trifle perilous even for Faron?"

"He will have his reasons," said Lowther, gripping the handle of his walking stick. "But then again, we are not meant to understand. And we never will."

Chapter 16

A lexander Strathmore swore to himself that he would not leave Julia's side again. She was far enough away from him as it was.

"She's quite the piece," said Robertson, glancing up from his cards to impale Strathmore with a greedy, covetous look. "And quite the delightful handful judging by our last meeting at Eccles House. Although truth be told, she doesn't appear worse for wear given her brush with death."

"Brush with death, indeed." Simon Wadsworth leered in agreement, tossing several coins onto the pile accumulating in the center of their table. Strathmore grunted something suitable in response and matched the wager wondering about the nature of his gamble in allowing Julia to accompany him to Eccles House in what he realized would be a final reckoning with Faron. However, he knew enough about her to know that resistance was futile. Julia would have made her own way to the estate, with or without him.

Strathmore stared at the bald-pated man with the heavy jowls opposite, very much aware that Wadsworth's beady gaze had settled with typical intensity on Julia. Had he chosen to interpret his host's thoughts at the moment, he might have found himself lurching from his chair and wiping the slavering leer from the man's face. Christ, he was besotted, convinced that no man could rest his eyes on Julia without entertaining lascivious thoughts. After days spent in splendid seclusion at his London town house, he was still in feverish thrall to the woman, held hostage by a stinging combination of love and lust that, to his continual wonderment, he had never before experienced.

He followed Wadsworth's gaze as he had been wont to do since entering the salon at Eccles House in the late afternoon with Julia on his arm, only to see her spirited away to another side of the vast room where she sat on a divan surrounded by at least five male guests. She was wearing a simple, square-necked cream silk gown that bared her arms, nipped her waist, and fanned in a sweep of flounce at her feet. As was her custom, she wore no jewels, and her hair was simply gathered to the back of her head, the chestnut waves glowing in the afternoon light. The pureness of her profile was enhanced by the unsettling fullness of her lips and thick crescents of her lashes. She shimmered more radiantly than the glittering diamonds encircling the neck of Felicity Clarence, who was watching Strathmore with predatory intent.

He ignored the sultry actress with a heaviness in his chest as he watched Julia converse in quiet tones with the men looming over her on the edge of the divan. She appeared genuinely immune to the intense regard and the unrelenting attention. But Strathmore knew she was as tightly wound as he, prepared to find answers to the questions that had plagued her for close to a lifetime. It was the sadness he had always sensed lurking beneath her surface. He would have done anything to take the hurt away—he expelled a short breath—or to hurt Faron.

All the more reason for the sojourn in London where he had deliberately cut them off from painful realities, enveloping them in the reassuring warmth of a lover's dream. Losing Rowena had all but sent Julia spiraling into a bottomless chasm. It was enough that she had recovered from her self-imposed isolation and from the muteness that threatened to take her away from him more completely than Faron ever could. They had moved closer to finding the answers to painful questions but Strathmore realized if he pressed too hard, Julia could slip away again. It had become a matter of taking time together, while waiting for what they knew would come—a return to the world of Faron's making.

Strathmore tossed in his cards, watching the other two men spreading their losing hands on the table. "Damned lucky," muttered Wadsworth, his gaze again straying meaningfully to Julia. She was being helped from the divan by a number of eager male hands. Wadsworth's words rang with desire as they all watched Julia maneuver around the ornate occasional table, each movement seeming to bring the curves of her breasts into view beneath the glow of the afternoon light.

Responding to a riposte, Julia laughed low and Strathmore's entire body went rigid in a primal reaction that was pure possessiveness. *She was his.* He had known the truth all along, from the moment he had first touched her. The realization astounded and calmed him, pushing every other earthly consideration he might have had into the ground. The Ptolemy map, the Nile, his ambitions—none of it mattered if he could not have Julia Woolcott. Sometimes life was astonishingly simple.

Strathmore quickly pocketed his winnings and shoved his chair from the table. "Gentlemen. I believe it's time to repair to our rooms and prepare for the evening's festivities."

Wadsworth guffawed. "I'm sure you have some interesting ways to prepare for our supper, Strathmore. See to it this time, would you, that our dear Julia is in the proper frame of mind to share her bounteous charms with the rest of us."

Not bloody likely, Strathmore thought but gave a patently false smile as he turned to reach Julia who was making her way toward him across the shining parquet floor. Although she stood straight and unbowed, he was aware when she took his proffered arm that her expression held a touch of gratitude and relief. Her fingers lingered on his arm and he resisted the urge to keep them beneath his forever. Her smile was as forced as his.

His gut wrenched like a man obsessed. In fact—because all logic had not abandoned him—he knew himself to be not simply a man obsessed but a man in love. Wordlessly, Strathmore and Julia deliberately slowed their steps, each moment agony as they made their way up the grand staircase of Eccles House to their rooms, eager as always to be alone. As soon as the heavy doors shut behind them, he placed one hand on her shoulder, on the soft skin where her sleeve ended. She barely breathed when he slid the other hand around her waist, flat against her abdomen, pressing himself against her back.

She trembled and he drew her more deeply against him, pressing his mouth to the side of her neck, breathing in her warmth.

"Julia." His own voice was unrecognizable to him, harsh. "I love you. I need you to return to Montfort. Nothing else matters to me but your safety."

Her waist expanded against the circle of his arm. "You know I can't do that. Please don't ask me to." Her palms smoothed over the length of his arms until his fingers entwined with hers, still pressed against her gown.

Turning her slowly, he lifted her face into the waning afternoon light. "I made a mistake in allowing you to accompany me. I don't want to make an even bigger one."

Her hands smoothed over his, then up the corded lengths of his forearms beneath his afternoon coat. "You need me here."

"I need you safe." His thumbs brushed in gentle strokes over the soft skin of her arms.

"No—listen." She could barely restrain the heat flushing her cheeks. "I am the one that Faron wants." Her fingers dug into his shoulders.

"Exactly my point." What did Faron want with the Woolcotts? Strathmore was not about to let Julia find out alone. That last meeting with Lowther was the turning point and Faron would not take kindly to Strathmore's demands. Not that he gave a damn anymore.

Julia interrupted his wayward thoughts. "Without me, you will get nowhere."

"That certain, are you? Are you prepared to endure another one of Wadsworth's eccentric evenings in the hope that the proceedings will somehow lead to Faron?" His jaw tightened. If so much as one man laid a hand on Julia . . .

"Don't look so grim. I don't think we should do battle over this, Strathmore."

"You should have nothing to do with Faron. I'll handle it." He straightened away from her suddenly, his features so hardened she drew back in the arms that tightened immediately around her waist. She placed a hand on his cheek, sensing the tension gathering beneath the tightening of his jaw.

"You will be here with me every moment." It was a weak attempt to pacify him.

"You overestimate my abilities."

"The intrepid explorer, Lord Alexander Francis Strathmore? Not possible." She stroked the strong planes of his shoulder, veering in another direction in an attempt at persuasion. "You can hardly participate in Wadsworth's weekend without an appropriate escort."

His smoldering gaze was level with hers. His eyes narrowed. "One of my many worries. I witnessed the near riot your presence caused in the salon this afternoon."

"Hardly. And stop being so possessive," she said lightly.

"You have yet to see possessive," he growled.

"After all, your own reputation in these matters, I gather, is hardly pristine," she reminded him pointedly. "Your history with the fairer sex is well known, according to Felicity Clarence at least, who at our last meeting here regaled the drawing room with evidence of your excesses. As I recall, she could not wait to learn more about that rather colorful translation of the text we consulted just the other night."

"I never said that I was a monk," he said, his mood darkening. "However, all this discussion is beside the point. You should leave Eccles House now. It's simple enough to say you have taken ill or that we have had a disagreement."

"Please be reasonable."

"Not possible."

"You are ridiculously stubborn."

"I was thinking the same of you."

"Yet you still love me?"

"Strangely enough," he said drily, "more than ever."

"You adore a challenge after all."

"Must be true." It was an attempt at lightness. "But I don't believe in placing you directly in the line of danger. The only reason you are even here with me in this room and this house is because I didn't trust you to not slip away and follow me here. You have an annoying streak of independence."

Julia's chin rose. "This is where it all began and where it will all end. You have said as much. I have as much right, if not more, to be here. For Meredith and for Rowena." She refused to let her voice break. "I must do this. I can do this." She amended quickly, "*We* can do this."

He shook his head in disbelief.

"I love you." She had never said the words before and he wondered if her desperation was making her brave. "If you think that I would leave you alone here . . . We face Faron together."

"Even if it is a trap?" It most likely was, and one set off at his own behest, Strathmore knew only too well, recalling his last meeting with Lowther and Beaumarchais in the carriage.

"If we truly love one another," she said with conviction, "we are stronger together."

It wasn't her logic that defeated him but rather but her wide eyes lifted to his. Her fingers began working the silk covered buttons of his vest with a growing confidence. Unable to resist, he bent low and kissed the soft skin of her neck, then freed her hair with a slip of his fingers, releasing the heavy curls to her shoulders. He filled his lungs with the fragrance, watching as she drew her cap sleeve bodice down over her arms as he spoke. "This isn't going to work—distracting me."

"I have learned much these past few weeks," she said,

sweet and provocative simultaneously. Images unfurled in his mind, heating his blood. Strathmore lowered his eyes, as her bodice slipped over her breasts to reveal her tightly laced corset. The flush on her cheeks served to sharpen his appetite. He kept his hands on her bare upper arms, in a show of resistance, redirecting his attention to the sleek slope of her shoulder and beyond to the opulent room, its four-poster bed hung with rich, velvet draperies.

The husky whisper was close to his ear. "I am not leaving Eccles House."

He would not force her, could not force her. Particularly at the moment when she kissed his lips, then his eyes, and then his lips again as she trailed her hand down his stomach. Helpless for the first time in his life, he took her hand in his and drew it lower. His breath halted when her fingers closed around him to find the fastening of his trousers. Once she had him in her hands, she slid from his arms to her knees, between his legs. Under heavy lidded eyes, he saw her sprawled at his feet, half naked, the soft heap of a silk skirt hiked up, leaving a span of slender thigh exposed amidst a flurry of pantalettes, a hint of bottom sheathed in the thinnest cotton.

The weight of his erection, iron hard and straining for her in the cool smoothness of her hands, almost proved his undoing. Her mouth teased him, pushed him into surrender, toward sensual oblivion. A roar hummed in his ears, warping all reason in a rush of blood and a tangle of heavy silken hair wrapped in his hands. Strathmore's last thoughts were of a pyrrhic victory with its devastating costs going not to the vanquished but to the victor.

In the Eccles House dining room a scant two hours later, a moody and smoldering Strathmore sensed the turn of conversation before Julia could possibly respond with anything resembling equanimity. Her gown, if one could call it that, set his teeth on edge, a diaphanous, flesh-toned sheath that revealed more than it hoped to conceal. Another testament to Wadsworth's impeccable taste, he thought darkly. Julia's hair had been returned to a serene knot, only a faint flush to her skin evidence of the tumultuous hours they had spent in their rooms before returning to the dining hall.

It rankled Strathmore that he had lost. Replaying and then brutally forcing the more recent heated moments with Julia from his memory, he cleared the bitterness from his palate with a swallow of red wine from a heavy lead crystal glass. Through a break in the sea of candlelight, he watched Julia turn to Beaumarchais at her right, before lifting a forkful of pheasant to her lips. The Frenchman had arrived late for dinner in a white cutaway evening ensemble and haughty demeanor. As though that was not enough, Strathmore glanced at the woman opposite Julia. Felicity Clarence was oozing barely concealed envy for the younger woman who seemed, inexplicably, to be robbing her of center stage.

To Strathmore's jaundiced eye, Miss Clarence was as indistinguishable from the many women who populated the demimondaine, spending their time either on stage or on their backs for remuneration. The hypocrisy of English society never failed to astound him, all the more since his self-imposed exile. It appeared that at any moment, Felicity's opulent white flesh would snap the elaborate bows and hooks of her crimson red taffeta dress as she directed hard glances at Julia. As expected, Felicity waited until Julia had taken the first bite of her repast to launch her attack.

"My dear girl," she began, leaning slightly over the table with a quick slanted glance in Strathmore's direction, so sly he might have missed it. Taking another draught of wine, It occurred to him the performance might be for his benefit more than anyone else's.

"I do so hope"—Felicity's sultry voice drifted over the three shimmering candelabra—"you are a trifle more eager to join us in our play this evening than when we last parted company. Although I must say, if you'll allow me, that gown does little to enhance your already pallid complexion and frail figure, my dear. Are you quite certain you are recovered from your earlier ordeal? Such drama, but then one supposes drama is necessary to hold the attentions of Lord Strathmore for any length of time."

Felicity lowered her lashes over feline-shaped eyes and darted Strathmore another quick look.

Julia smiled pleasantly. "I am quite recovered. Thank you for your kind concern."

Beaumarchais glanced up with sudden interest. "Indeed, my dear. I trust you are up to some spirited activities this evening. Why I hear our host has moved the venue to one of the caves with its cavernous banqueting hall and cozy little monk cells—for our use, they inform me, should any of us require additional privacy." He finished with a sly chuckle that was echoed by several other men within hearing distance.

"We may be joined by additional guests," Felicity continued, with a thin smile for her host at the end of the table. "Wadsworth does so enjoy a surprise."

Julia's bare shoulders, gleaming in the candlelight, tensed imperceptibly. "What a convivial and generous host so eager to extend his hospitality and to invite yet more favored guests to his estate," she said with an inquiring tilt of her chin. Strathmore knew exactly what Julia was thinking, the hope lighting in her eyes that Faron would make an appearance, as promised. His gut tightened in response.

"It would not be the first time," Beaumarchais supplied. "Wadsworth's august ancestor was known to have entertained King George IV himself in the very caves of the abandoned chalk mines."

"Along with his royal courtesan." Felicity smirked, clearly privileged to have in her possession such an important piece of prurient knowledge. "I hear there still exists a silver snuff box, oval in shape and delicately engraved, which contains a tightly packed clump of hair claiming to be trimmed from the mons veneris of the King's mistress."

"Quite the keepsake!" Beaumarchais took a deep gulp of his wine before giving an imaginary toast to the long-dead King and his revelries.

Felicity dabbed her linen napkin at the corners of her

mouth. "As a case in point, one does so quickly bore, does one not? Particularly for men of the world, men of experience, such as the gentlemen who join us here this weekend." She swept a hand over her low décolletage in case anyone had failed to notice its fulsomeness. "I do so look forward to the upcoming adventure, although truth be told, it does require a particular stamina and appetite. Would you not agree Miss Woolcott?"

Through the candles, Strathmore watched as Julia took a sip of her wine as though she'd barely absorbed Felicity's deliberate baiting. Then her eyes lifted and locked with his.

God damn. Strathmore instantly recognized his inability to control his physical and emotional response when it involved Julia Woolcott. Even in the midst of that nest of vipers, his need for her had become so great, his desire so acute, he wondered if he was the same man who had once crossed a desert on horseback or ever dreamed of holding the original Ptolemy map in his hand.

He wanted Faron out of their lives and Julia Woolcott safely in his. Then he would have a lifetime of her next to him. The image of her disheveled and wanting floated in his mind's eye and, for the life of him, he could feel himself hardening beneath the fine wool of his trousers. An exotic warmth shimmered in his blood stream. He reached for his wineglass.

"I have heard it said," continued Felicity, her eyes riveted on Julia, "that our host knows precisely each of his guests' proclivities."

"I am certain Sir Wadsworth has in his possession such information," responded Julia above the twittering of laughter. "He is the consummate host, after all."

"I don't believe you understand fully the implications of Wadsworth's research," said Felicity. Her smile was smugly malicious. "Your escort for the weekend, Lord Strathmore, if we were to take an example, is a man of prodigious appetites."

Julia's fingers whitened around the stem of her wineglass.

"Of which I know first hand," Felicity continued unabated. "Which makes your erstwhile outburst, what with the pistol brandishing and the like, all the more inexplicable and positively mysterious. What did you expect, Miss Woolcott, from Lord Strathmore? That he should be brought to heel like a whelp newly taken from its litter to do your bidding? Hardly likely or realistic. Trust me when I say," she lowered her voice conspiratorially, "that a man of Strathmore's appetites and experience will never be content with just one woman." She gave a chirp of laughter. "How hopelessly naïve!"

Julia carefully set her wineglass aside. "I appreciate your generous insights into Lord Strathmore's character, Miss Clarence."

Felicity fingered a fat curl resting just above her bosom, expanding with every excited breath she took. "The list of women is seemingly endless, my dear, although completely understandable given the man's prowess. Naturally, the specifics of those on other continents are unknown to us. But once again, only imagine, ten years out of the country," she mused aloud.

Strathmore remained seated, the unfolding scene floating before his eyes as Felicity tried to drive a perceived rival from the field.

"It simply staggers the imagination. The harems, the mistresses he hired to teach him exotic sexual play, the rumors of debauchery that we here, in the comparatively safe shores of this emerald isle"—Felicity's theatrical roots were showing— "find completely shocking. And Strathmore's translation of the sexual mores of primitives . . . that scandalous compendium is simply wicked in its scope and breadth!" Her voice was a hushed undertone that nevertheless carried across the room to the end of the dining table where Strathmore sat. "My dear, I thought you should know so you may enjoy the evening's festivities with a rather more open mind." Her eyes narrowed thoughtfully. "This possessiveness of yours regarding Lord Strathmore is peculiar to say the least, given the man's history and, dare I say it, given your rather meager charms."

Strathmore imagined what Julia was thinking—most of which was true. But it was all in the past, his past, transformed into a blur of memory. Scrubbing a hand down his face, he felt the need to shed his evening coat, a fine sheen of sweat trickling down his spine. The sensation was strangely familiar, an effervescent warmth chafing his blood which was, inexplicably, rushing to the erection between his legs. He moved swiftly, his chair scraping against the marble floor. In two strides he stood behind Julia, the words tight in his throat. "I regret you've had to deal with this . . ."

"A former mistress?" Julia offered quietly, her voice touched with irony, her back to him. "One of hundreds?"

There was no excuse nor reasonable answer. Not a bolstering thought. All he knew was that all of it was irrelevant because of the reality of his love for Julia. More pressing was the gnawing certainty that Felicity's display served as an elaborate ruse, that they were being led into an elaborate trap. Yet all he could do was breathe in the familiar scent of Julia, lavender and freesia, which he would recognize if he were blind. Julia looked up at him and held his gaze, trust blazing from her eyes. She quickly lowered her lashes before anyone could interpret the quicksilver understanding passing between them.

"Oh dear, was it something I said?" Felicity smiled beguilingly at Strathmore, aware of the pot she was stirring. Her thin lips spread into a smile as she watched Julia rise from the table, removing her napkin from her lap, carefully avoiding Strathmore who stood a mere inch away from her. It was as though they were alone, despite Wadsworth's small audience hanging on every word and nuance. Disregarding it all, and with a small nod, Julia walked from the dining room, leaving the assembled guests with gaping mouths and a few awkwardly timed guffaws.

Beaumarchais launched from his seat. "I shall go after

her," he said, smoothing the wings of his hair with elaborate concern. "Should she require consolation."

"Leave her be," said Strathmore with quiet menace. Beaumarchais remained rooted to the spot, the cold authority clear in the low voice. "As for you, Felicity," Strathmore continued despite the waves of heat coursing through his body, "I require a moment of your time. Privately."

"Here, here now." Wadsworth's jowls shook as he tried to move his bulk from the table. "I shan't have our weekend interrupted with such squabbling. Once was more than enough."

Strathmore and Felicity ignored their host's exhortations, and a strange light appeared in the actress's eyes. "I should be more than pleased to accompany you wherever you desire, my lord Strathmore," she cooed. "The music room perhaps?"

He nodded curtly, dismissing the assembled guests with the turn of his back. "I am positively atremble," said Felicity for the benefit of her audience, with a mocking smile and a small wave over her bare shoulders.

The music room was as he remembered, the piano at the center surrounded by gilt-edged divans and the French doors through which he, with Julia draped over his arms, had escaped—it seemed so long ago. Someone had seen fit to light the sconces which flickered wild patterns onto the watered silk covered walls. Loosening his cravat with an impatient hand, Strathmore cursed under his breath, as sparks of desire shot through his bloodstream. It was not altogether an unfamiliar sensation. Something flickered in his memory, a potion he had once consumed at the behest of a bedouin chieftain, just before—

"More wine, darling?" Felicity was pressing a long-stemmed glass into his hand. The realization struck him like a blow to the side of the head. The wine at dinner had been laced with cantharides.

Plump arms fastened around his neck. "What the hell are you doing, Felicity?"

"Don't play coy, Strathmore, darling. It doesn't suit you a whit." The plunging neckline of her gown gaped as she nestled closer against his chest and with a certain deft skill began unbuttoning his white linen shirt to the waist of his trousers. "I can see that you're more than ready for me."

His gaze drifted over the abundance of perfumed bosom that seemed to plead for his touch. One long fingernail was already tracing circles over his chest. "Your musculature is spectacular, darling. But then again, I'm sure you already know that." She purred throatily.

Odd that he had an erection that could drill through rock and yet odder still that he felt unmoved. And phenomenally detached. "Who put you up to this, Felicity. And why?"

She slanted feline eyes at him from beneath a sweep of blond hair which fell in waves upon her rounded shoulders, softening her sharp features as did the pink rouge on her cheeks and lips. As an actress, Felicity Clarence was adept at the tricks that would help her appear younger.

"You mean telling Miss Woolcott the truth? She deserves to know." Her thumb brushed over his bottom lip. "I was hardly lying, darling. Your reputation precedes you—nothing to be ashamed of, certainly in present company here at Eccles House. We more than understand."

"That's not what I'm asking. Who doctored my wine?" In all likelihood Beaumarchais, but Strathmore wondered how much Felicity knew and whether he could make use of whatever information she held close to her opulent bosom. His gut tightened at the thought of Julia alone in the house. The sooner it was over, the better.

"I don't concern myself with such details, darling." Felicity pressed rouged lips to his neck. The heavy scent of attar of roses and musk enveloped him. "You are so unlike the milquetoast Englishman, Strathmore. You can't begin to imagine how much that appeals to me." Unrelenting fingers slipped beneath his shirt, her fingers drifting over his abdomen to unhook the top of his trousers. Her lips curved as one finger traced over the impressive bulge in his trousers.

"Unlike the typical Englishman, indeed, and so remarkably endowed."

Strathmore's fingers wrapped around her wandering hand, halting its journey. Her eyes, staring up at him, widened. "Perhaps you should concern yourself with details, Felicity," he said.

Her fair brows rose tremulously and she forced a sultry smile. "Whatever do you mean, darling? I believe, judging by the evidence in hand, you are as eager for a tryst as I am. As a matter of fact, it's as though you can hardly survive through dinner without bursting."

He smiled grimly. "You get what you want if I get what I want. Simple." Strathmore resisted the overwhelming urge to disentangle the arms wrapped around his neck like an asp.

Running her hands over his hardness, Felicity heaved a sigh and thrust out her lower lip. "Can we not just play, darling?" One arm dropped to grasp his hand, pressing it to one silk-covered breast as extra inducement.

"We'll play soon enough, Felicity." He tried to keep his voice pleasant, all the while wondering where Julia had gone, hoping she had locked herself in their rooms. The specter of Beaumarchais, all unctuous concern, intruded, the knowledge spiking his blood hot and dangerous, more than the aphrodisiacs ever could.

"Dear Lord, you're magnificent, Strathmore," Felicity breathed into his ear, her hand between his legs.

The faster, the better, he thought. Felicity's breast was heavy in his hand, the nipple pushing impatiently into his palm. He forced himself through the motions. "What did Beaumarchais ask of you, Felicity?"

"Simply to augment your wine, darling, with a little extra something," she whispered, her breath coming in small pants. She tugged on the silken ties binding her bodice. "And to arrange a little impromptu interlude with you, after dispatching the wan-faced wraith you insist upon bringing with you to these affairs. I can't imagine how she would ever hold your interest." With a shrug of her shoulders, the dress pooled at her waist, demonstrating that she had dispensed with corset and chemise. Voluptuous with a narrow waist and fleshy hips, her breasts hung full and heavy, her nipples large and dark.

Strathmore thanked the gods he didn't believe in that the aphrodisiacs were having their desired effects because he would not have been able to feign passion without them. A pitiful testament to the man he had become since meeting Miss Woolcott.

Dutifully, he filled his hands with the heaviness of Felicity's breasts, shutting out the memory of silken skin, long limbs, and resilient flesh. "Beaumarchais must have a specific purpose in mind," he muttered into Felicity's ear.

"I think, most of all," she breathed heavily, "he wanted to cause a diversion, to have your little Miss Woolcott all to himself. Though God only knows why."

A diversion. To separate the two of them, thought Strathmore ominously. He shoved a hand into the blond tresses, pulling Felicity closer to him in a show of lust. He crushed his mouth over hers, determined to see the situation to its end, all too aware the hot desire flaming through him had been prompted by his images of Julia. The plan was diabolical, torturous, a flagrant challenge to a man whose love for a woman made it impossible to erase her from his mind or body because she had invaded his blood, his very being. It wasn't the aphrodisiacs that made him want to crawl from his skin with a howl of disgust.

Strathmore opened his eyes. Felicity stepped away from him, her breasts flushed and heaving in restrained passion. The thought of touching her in more intimate places filled him with uncommon dread. He swallowed hard. "What else do you know?" Each word was finely tempered steel.

He was aware of his erection, an attraction Felicity could not resist. "I can see that you're impatient," she said, and he composed himself, his hand deliberately setting Felicity's stroking fingers aside.

"Not as much as you are."

Felicity licked her lips and kneeled at his feet. She arched her back so her breasts jutted upward, offering herself to him. "I don't know much of anything at all," she murmured, languidly stroking his erection.

"You won't get what you want," he said in a deliberate, commanding tone, "in your careless mouth unless you tell me what little you do know."

Felicity stroked him, reveling in his rigid length and full turgid arousal which pulsed through him with a startling autonomy. "There is to be," she said in a small voice, her rapt eyes focused on the casual stroking of her fingers, "a special ceremony to be held in the caves this evening. Beaumarchais requires that your little Miss Woolcott attend without you."

It was as though a bullet shot through his brain. Strathmore watched with a curious detachment as Felicity leaned over and drew his manhood into her mouth with avid enthusiasm. Only to see, across the room, the handle of the door rocking.

Beaumarchais's voice boomed theatrically from the other side. "Why I believe I saw them last repair to the music room. The last door on your left, if you'll recall, dear Julia."

Chapter 17

The image should have been imprinted on Julia's mind and soul forever. The scene spoke of heinous betrayal except that she knew differently in her heart. This was but one more step in a cruel and elaborate dance choreographed by Faron. She fled from the scene in the music room after one agonizing look.

"I take it you have had quite an eyeful, Miss Woolcott," said Beaumarchais, his fine features filled with obvious concern. Julia was barely aware of his hand on her arm, leading her through the narrow hallway, down a flight of stairs, and into the main hall of Eccles House where the mammoth chandeliers blazed in all their ostentatious glory.

Julia wanted to run. She wanted to hide. But she would do neither—finally. Still oblivious to the hand on her arm, she fought through the fog of pain lancing her side, where her heart pulsed for Strathmore. It was enough, she told herself, finally *enough*. The word infused her limbs with a fury and determination to be done with the mad world into which Montagu Faron and Alexander Strathmore had plunged her.

"I'm hardly surprised, my dear," said Beaumarchais at her side unaware that she was scarcely listening. "He is obviously a bounder, what we in French call *un bete*, a beast, with none of the breeding or politesse expected from a man of a certain rank and station. Not that one does not deserve diversions." He continued unabated, leading her into the drawing room off the main hall. "However, I can understand that you have had an upset, all the more reason I should be pleased to offer you a sympathetic shoulder upon which you may exhaust your fit of pique."

Julia was suddenly aware that she stood in a magenta and gold room, richly furnished and grandly proportioned, and overly warm from the heat thrown out from blazing piles of logs in two great fireplaces. On every wall were mirrors in gilded frames reflecting the soaring paneled ceiling, curved like the bow of a ship on which were painted scenes depicting the abduction of Helen of Troy by Paris.

Beaumarchais released Julia's arm, his eyes scanning her person with renewed interest, making Julia suddenly aware of the obscene nature of her gown. The fine flesh-toned silk moved against her body as insubstantial as mist. "I should like to retire to my rooms," she said, forcing her breathing to more normal levels. He made no move to step out of her way, his gaze fastened on the low-cut square of her bodice. The house was silent, the guests who had made an appearance at dinner seemingly vanished.

"Retire to your rooms, my dear?" Beaumarchais repeated as though it was an outrageous request. He arched a thin brow, clearly feeling resplendent in the white evening attire he wore. "I believe Wadsworth would prefer that you rest here in the drawing room. You have all the time in the world, never fear," he said. "After all, we have some unfinished matters to complete."

Julia didn't understand and was about to say so when she was alerted to a presence by footsteps behind her. Looking quickly over her shoulder, she saw Giles Lowther advance into the cavernous drawing room, his reflection—the high-domed forehead, the barrel-chested posture—multiplied in the gilded mirrors surrounding them. He carefully closed the double doors, leaned back against them, and smiled gloatingly.

"I can see the situation is proceeding according to plan for a change, Beaumarchais." He added with a glint in his eye,

"Good evening to you, Miss Woolcott, we meet at last." Swallowing another wave of shock, Julia registered that Lowther would have no idea they had met before, the night at Gordon Square, when she and Strathmore had secreted themselves behind the bookshelves.

"It did go rather well, didn't it?" Beaumarchais agreed. "Now that Strathmore is out of the way for the time being, at least."

"Still with the whore?" Lowther asked calmly, shedding his greatcoat and tossing it carelessly over one of the low ottomans littered about the room. They were speaking as though Julia was not present.

Beaumarchais answered, his voice malicious with mockery. "I think they should just about be completing the first round, if I'm not mistaken. The catharides do have a lingering effect, so I shouldn't be surprised if the exchange, so called, doesn't continue once they find themselves in the caves."

Julia found her voice, not bothering to acknowledge Lowther's presence with a semblance of formality. "You mean you drugged Strathmore?" she asked, her arms suddenly pricked with cold despite the heat emanating from two giant hearths.

"Amazing, isn't it, the potency of the dried beetle," Lowther murmured thoughtfully, adding for her edification, "known in Latin as *cantharis vesicatoria*. But then, Miss Woolcott, I am given to understand that translation is unnecessary, that you know Latin and Greek."

Julia advanced into the room, suddenly brave. She was convinced she had nothing to lose. Wanting to put distance between her and both men, to allow herself time to think, her slippered feet made no noise on the highly glossed marble floor. Something seemed to shudder beneath her, the vibration traveling from the ground with infinitesimally small reverberations. She shook off a sense of ominous dread, instead focusing with unwavering attention upon Lowther. "You seem to know something of me and yet we have yet to be introduced," she addressed him directly.

Lowther contentedly examined the polished toe of his boot. "Let's just say that I am a friend of an old friend of your aunt's, Lady Woolcott." His eyes, small and assessing, met hers calmly. "Once our evening is concluded," he said in even tones, as one might tick off items on a list, "your knowing my name will hardly be necessary."

"All very neat, as requested," Beaumarchais said with a certain smugness.

Julia listened quietly, rubbing her arms against the chill that suddenly descended, although her mind was racing to make sense of the labyrinthine plot that Lowther held in store. Another part of her barely made sense of what she had just heard. Assimilating the implications of the aphrodisiacs, relief flooded back in one intake of breath. Strathmore had been drugged, and was in the caves, the word a sudden threat, turning her to ice.

She consciously willed her hands to unclench her arms before either of the men noticed. "I trust that you intended to separate us. How clever, gentlemen," she said casually, wishing she had Mclean's pistol in her two hands, eager to frame Lowther in the crosshairs of her sights and then to see a neat, black hole blossom in the middle of his forehead. Her hands shook, and once again she imagined the floor beneath her feet shuddered in response.

"Ah, the caves," Beaumarchais drawled, his mild voice suddenly incongruously harsh. "It might well be a fitting end. I fear that Strathmore will not get so far as to enjoy the sepulchral corridors and peer at niches containing moss-covered statues in interesting poses." He looked up at the image of Paris and Helen overhead. "Do you feel what I feel?" he asked.

"You mean the explosions?" Lowther answered with a smile in his colorless eyes. "Strathmore is impossible to kill, unlike a normal man, but we shall see. I'm sure our special guest is even more curious to know whether he will survive the challenge." It was clear that he disliked loose ends. "I trust the corridors beneath the house will hold."

A series of explosions in the caves—where Strathmore was searching for her. Julia absorbed each realization individually as though the message would alter with a change of rhythm, but the meaning was callously fixed, mocking her. She felt cold, chilled to her bones by an icy rage, surging slowly at first but building in a momentum. The mirrors enclosing the drawing room shimmered, and her frightened heart raced. She glared at Giles Lowther, lounging against the fireplace mantel as though the world was his to command. That man had wanted Strathmore dead. That man had arranged for Rowena's death. Tiny black dots danced around the edges of her vision.

"Are you feeling quite yourself, Miss Woolcott?" he asked with mock concern. "We shouldn't want you to faint before meeting our exemplary guest who is, word has it, more than eager to make your acquaintance." He gestured to Beaumarchais, his high forehead gleaming in the firelight. "Please see to it that smelling salts are at the ready, in case Miss Woolcott feels overcome."

Lowther knew that he mocked her, realized she was close to feeling overcome not with helplessness but with a blinding rage.

She actually wondered whether she could choke the life from him with her bare hands. His neck was thick, she considered, burying her fists in the folds of her gown. The thoughts careening through her mind, fueling her monstrous anger, should have felt foreign but extraordinarily felt exactly right. "Do not expect me to ask for whom we are waiting," she said. "I already know."

Lowther cupped his chin and looked at her inquiringly. "You are hardly what I expected, Miss Woolcott, the withdrawn, diffident spinster who rarely ventured far from home. You speak with a confidence and certainty that is admirable and rare in a woman. I trust you will not be disappointed by our guest."

"Doubtful," she said, her suddenly involuntary appetite for violence swift and sure.

Lowther smiled knowingly. "I'm certain you have many questions." When she didn't answer, he continued unhesitatingly, stretching an arm out to embrace the heavily carved fireplace mantel. "Perhaps we should first begin with Lord Strathmore, clearly the object of your affection. Am I quite correct? Ah, I see that you are suddenly reluctant to divulge your true feelings. How discreet of you Miss Woolcott, despite the fact that Lord Strathmore has seen fit to disrupt his plans because of you." He gazed at her speculatively. "Does that make you feel any better? Knowing that Lord Strathmore has recklessly squandered his chance of finding the source of the Nile because of an unreasonable infatuation? Difficult to believe, given the man's history." His expression was contemptuous. "Have you heard of the Ptolemy map, by any chance, Miss Woolcott?"

Her legs were trembling beneath the ridiculous excuse of a gown, but Julia did not give in. "Of course," she said. "Maps lost to antiquity and merely replicated in the Renaissance based on Ptolemy's writings."

"Or so you believe," interrupted Beaumarchais suddenly. He had been watching the exchange between Lowther and Julia with the desultory interest of an observer at a game of whist. He held a thick crystal tumbler filled with brandy, which he had taken from the drinks table at his elbow groaning under the weight of decanters and goblets.

"What of it?" asked Julia sharply. "Might I have some refreshment, gentlemen?"

"Certainly," said Lowther gesturing to Beaumarchais. "The lady requires brandy as fortification." He looked down at the fire for a moment before continuing. "We are in possession of the original map which draws upon some of the most consistent and enduring apocryphal elements in the history of cartography. As you may know, the source of the Nile River has been a matter of speculation for thousands of years. According to Herodotus, the ancient Egyptians believed that the Nile had its source in two great mountains within which were eternal springs. It was believed by some that the Nile's annual inundations was caused by snowfall at its source."

Beaumarchais thrust a heavy tumbler in Julia's hand but she barely looked away from Lowther. "Hence, Lord Strathmore's eagerness to access the map. Nothing I don't already know," she lied, wondering as to the source of her sangfroid.

Lowther pursed his lips, removing his arm from the fireplace mantel to undo the top buttons of his straining evening coat. "All the more reason to test Strathmore's character."

"Why ever would you care—to test his character?" Julia asked, taking a small sip from her glass. Once again, she marveled at her transformation, at her courage, reveling in the recognition that if she lost her life that evening—and it was entirely possible she would—that she was done with hiding. She was amazed that she would confront Lowther, and eventually, Montagu Faron, with the intensity of a lioness protecting her young. They had taken Rowena from her . . . would rob her of Strathmore. Her emotions threatened to explode from her chest, the brandy burning a path to her heart. "Where is Strathmore at present? The caves?" It was a question that demanded an answer.

Lowther shoved himself away from the fireplace as though giving due consideration to her query, his hands behind his back, his pacing an affectation designed to inflame her anxiety. "Strathmore, if you must know, Miss Woolcott," he said with exaggerated politeness, looking at her from under arched brows, "is presently trapped beneath several hundred feet of stone."

Julia did not feign indifference or pretend that she did not already know what the vibrations implied, the tremors beneath the great house testament to an inescapable fate. "You are trying to kill him," she said sharply combatative, "and it won't work."

"You should feel some measure of guilt," purred Beaumarchais from his corner of the grand drawing room. "After all, he went looking for *you* in the caves. It's where dear Felicity told him you could be found."

An icy rage flowed through Julia's veins, a rancor inflating with every breath she took. "You claim that Strathmore is impossible to kill, gentlemen—which I believe to be true also. However," she continued, unsure from where her audacity originated, "as you will soon discover, you and your *guest* will be easier to dispatch because I shall ensure this evening is your last." Her eyes narrowed and she allowed herself a small smile. "You have my word."

The force of the first explosion threw Strathmore against the wall. When the smoke cleared, the entrance to the cave was sealed from the winding corridors he had just exited. Shaking the dust from his shoulders he estimated that in one or two more explosions, his light would be gone. The air in the caves would be limited once the shafts were closed off.

It served him right, following Felicity Clarence down the winding stairs to the caverns beneath the estate that led to the mines long abandoned save for the maniacal whims of an earl over a century before. Torches along the narrow walls flickered, already starved of precious air, and Strathmore knew, without looking behind him, that Felicity Clarence had not accompanied him into the bowels of the earth. It was Julia's face he could not forget, her eyes breathtakingly huge with pain, numb and stunned with shock at the scene he and Felicity had presented in the music room.

Julia would survive, he lied to himself. He had no other recourse. He could not live without Julia Woolcott, and he forcefully held off the specter of her demise. Taking one step after the next, aware of the flickering flames starved for air decorating the narrowing underground passage, he knew he was a short breath away from black oblivion. Frantic thoughts of Julia evoked her image, floating around the hazy perimeter of his mind. His lungs already reacting to the deprivation of air, the face and body of the woman he loved faded like a receding echo down the panicked corridors of his mind.

Julia would not be found underground, trapped in the twisting corridors leading to the caves about which Wadsworth had boasted with such relish. It was all a lie. The thought burst in his head just as another explosion shook the white, chalky walls enclosing him. Leaning and panting against the tunnel wall, he waited for what seemed like an eternity before a third blast knocked him to his knees.

When he awakened, it was pitch black, and pain in his shoulder ripped through him with nauseating force. He compelled himself to move, drawing on thoughts of the past, days spent thirsting in the desert, weeks trapped in the jaws of a storm, his survival instinct lingering in his oxygen-deprived mind. Aware that he was sweating profusely, the pain in his shoulder was an agonizing burn. His body was in shock. Only his strength of will and thoughts of Julia held the darkness at bay.

He pulled himself to his knees and crawled, his shattered shoulder dragging along the roughness of the cave wall, his exposed nerve endings screaming with pain. He pushed himself up until he was standing. How long he stood swaying in the dark, he would never know. Images flashed through his mind. Julia, bravely confronting him in the cork-lined room at Eccles House. Her face dissolving in grief. Her body melding with his. Julia, eyes burning with intensity, insisting that she accompany him to meet with Montagu Faron.

None of those thoughts, he thought with bitter irony, hauling the last pockets of air into his heaving lungs, had to do with maps, or mountains, or rivers. Only Julia.

Strathmore leaned against the wall of the narrow shaft, allowing a wave of panic to subside. He opened his eyes against the darkness, the pitch blackness his current reality. He forced himself to breathe calmly, running through a cold calculation, relying on his instincts to determine the possibilities remaining to him. He thought of the gold mines of Africa, his memory blurring but not enough to erase his recollection of the mines of Wangara, along a tributary of the Senegal River. What were they called? His mind grappled, the knowledge slipping like coins from his fingers. There was always a vertical or near vertical chute into a mine from the surface, a tunnel that was originally used for haulage, drainage, or ventilation or any combination of the three. They were typically six feet wide and a little over six feet tall, and somewhat arched.

He was beset with the nagging realization that Montagu Faron was anticipating his every move, secure in the knowledge that the most recent challenge would not prove to be Faron's downfall. It was as though the man knew him better than he knew himself.

His mouth dry with chalk dust, Strathmore spit into the ground, Faron's name a smothered curse. Using his hands he began a search of the wall nearest his uninjured shoulder, looking for an arch or shaft reinforced with concrete, or log cribbing to protect from erosion and caving. Whether the search took a minute or an hour was difficult to tell. He had to rest finally, his arm throbbing in a steady, pulsing agony. Resuming his search, his open palms traced the arched cribbing with relief. Only six feet away, he told himself, estimating that freedom was no further above his head. Grappling amid the sharp and plentiful boulders at his feet courtesy of the explosions, he began chipping away at the soft stone. He rested every few moments, dozing off as the lack of air took its toll, only a spurt of fear rousing him to wakefulness.

The stones quickly became chalk in his hands, the notion of air and Julia mere inches away keeping him alive. The soft chalk gave way repeatedly but once he broke through, a layer of sand and topsoil poured in. He very quickly realized his left shoulder was useless, and carefully maneuvered himself up the narrow shaft, rising carefully, a fresh pool of sweat following his every exertion. He didn't move one foot until the other was securely placed, aware that he could not risk a fall. His injured shoulder, still stinging from its recent injury at Birdoswald, screamed with every motion.

A night sky, overflowing with stars, greeted his gulping breaths as he hauled precious air into his lungs. His shoulders, breaking the surface of grass and moss, ached with a combination of misery and exultation. Strathmore lay panting, face down, breathing in the sweet smell of earth and sky. He allowed himself only a moment, after which he rose from the ground, painfully turning toward the silhouette of Eccles House, outlined by the light of the moon. He found himself standing in the kitchen gardens, bloodied, covered in chalk, a ghost returned from the dead, a mere fifty yards from the house. His first and only thought was of Julia.

It was as though he had been wrenched from a deep sleep, pulled into consciousness by a new nightmare. With every stride he took, he knew that time was short, the grimace cutting his lean face destined to strike terror in the next person he met. The park was deserted that time of night and he strode from the kitchen garden to wrench open the door of the servant's entrance in record time. A cold sweat covered his body. He might be too late.

Despite the blazing lights, the house appeared deserted. He took the back stairs three at a time, fear he'd never known galvanizing his limbs, pushing open the door to the rooms he and Julia had last shared. The broad bed with its heavy velvet curtains was empty, the dressing room deserted. Dropping his head into his palms for only a moment, he felt the cold hand of dread before he gathered up his pistol from the wardrobe. Shoving the weapon into the waistband of his trousers, he ran, faster than he'd ever run before.

No servant stopped his passage when he hurled himself down the heavy main stairs into the hallway, the heavy chandeliers blazing with light, mocking his frenzy. Forcing himself not to call out Julia's name, he launched himself into the dining room, the salon, each space gleaming with beeswax and a stark emptiness that only served to constrict the panic tight in his chest.

Something was not right. Eccles House was deserted, swept clean of its guests, as though readying itself—for what exactly? He began to understand. Montagu Faron was already on the premises, a man who refused to allow himself to be seen. Looking up, he saw the heavy mahogany entrance of the drawing room closed against him.

With no hesitation, he shouldered open the door, only to see Julia's startled shock as her widening eyes took in his presence. She was alone, her image glittering in the gilt framed mirrors of the room. Ominously alone.

They did not exchange a word. He walked quietly toward her and leaned down, his long coat trailing dustily on the floor. It was only then he saw the tears that had dried on her cheeks. Her eyes raised to his slowly at the touch of his fingers on her cheek.

"I came back—" he whispered, his words meaning to soften the blow. But when her beautiful eyes looked at him in astonishment, he smiled at the face that had changed his life. "I came back," he said, knowing that, with a tightening in his stomach, he had been allowed to escape for a reason.

"I tried not to worry, to believe in you. . . . Somehow I knew that you would survive . . . despite the explosions." She reached out to touch his face, as though he had indeed returned from the underworld for her, and as though she needed to reassure herself that his physicality was real.

For a moment, no explanations were necessary and Strathmore opened his arms as Julia folded herself into his embrace, heedless of the dust, the blood, and his injured shoulder. He held her close, his mouth moving across her cheek in a brushing caress to breathe in her softness. "But we haven't much time. You must go—now."

"Nothing has changed, my love," she said, the warmth of her gaze dissipating in the harsh glare of his commanding tone. "Lowther is here as well as Beaumarchais, promising that I shall meet with Faron—alone. It's what I need to do." Streaked with dust, she straightened against him. "I intend to kill him," she said with stunning simplicity, staring up at him. "I am finished with hiding from Faron. He has taken so much from me already, and dares to rob me of even more. You, Rowena, Meredith. It is not to be borne."

"You don't know of what you speak, Julia. You intend to kill Faron with your bare hands?" Strathmore raked her form, the delicate shoulders arising from the frothy silk of her gown, slender, pale, and rigid with determination. "You have no idea what it is like to take a life. And we are wasting valuable time." He stepped back but did not release her, his eyes scanning the room looking for means of escape. "I shall manage Faron." As he had managed the inconceivable odds of escaping from collapsed underground tunnels. It was what he did best, he recognized, with barely contained cynicism. And somehow, Montagu Faron knew.

"You can't kill him," Julia said, in a pained whisper, her hands clutching his shoulders.

He examined her closely, attuned to the tension in every line of her body. "Isn't that what you wish for? To have Faron eliminated from your life forever. To punish him for the fire that robbed you of your childhood, for taking away your sister, for tormenting your aunt? I don't understand."

Her fingers dug into the muscles of his arms. "There is something I have not told you. Something that has to do with the daguerreotype." A shudder ran through the floor beneath their feet, a muffled turbulence following like distant thunder.

"It can wait," he said, moving them toward the ground floor windows, a less noticeable escape route than the main hallway and front doors. "The explosions in the corridors earlier might be causing some instability in this part of the house," he added tersely.

"No, it can't wait." Julia looked up at him and into his eyes, her gaze strong and unfaltering. "You cannot kill Montagu Faron." Another distant rumble of thunder sounded, the mirrors shivering in their gilt frames.

"*And why ever not?*" The voice, at once strange and familiar, struck sparks off the high, expansive ceiling with its serene depiction of Helen resisting the lure of Paris, her smile secretive and aloof.

The man stood tall in the entrance of the drawing room, his reflection multiplied in the ornate mirrors. The height, breadth, and lean grace were too familiar to Julia. The candlelight threw shadows on the face hidden behind a black leather mask, she wished, despite the hatred congealing in her chest, that she would never have to confront.

The hair was silver and not raven's wing black, and his eyes, a dark fathomless pitch rather than the gray she knew so well. Julia met his unyielding scrutiny with a sharp twist of her head, only to absorb the many reflections in the coldly glittering glass encircling the drawing room. Montagu Faron and Alexander Francis Strathmore stared back at her—seemingly one and the same.

"I apologize for having interrupted what is obviously an intense discussion, and at such a delicate juncture." Even the voice was an echo of the one Julia loved so well—low, with a gravel pitch, the only difference a slight French inflection. "Please finish what you were about to say, mademoiselle, exactly why it is that Lord Strathmore should resist the entirely natural urge to give in to his murderous impulses."

Strathmore was rooted to the spot, his steady gaze chill and dark, but open with contempt. With his black hair streaked white with chalk dust, he acknowledged the man who stood with equal arrogance several feet away from him. Strathmore was the younger and the stronger, despite his recent injuries, but Julia could not fail to notice the gleaming pistol that Faron carried casually in his right hand. Dressed with dramatic simplicity, his midnight blue evening coat and blindingly white cravat, Faron carried himself with a brutal arrogance that was all too familiar.

"You come alone, Faron. Unwilling to show your face to the outside world," Strathmore said levelly, casually moving in front of Julia so his body shielded hers. "I shouldn't wonder given the nature of your activities these past few decades. Setting a nursery afire is hardly the act of a courageous man. Nor is sending a young woman to a watery death."

Faron smiled easily, taking another few steps to stand in the center of the drawing room. "I had my reasons," he said, not attempting to defend himself.

"What did you do to Meredith Woolcott those many years ago?" Strathmore asked the question for Julia's sake.

"The question should be rephrased. What did Meredith do to me?" said Faron. His eyes were obsidian behind the mask. "I do not wear this mask without reason."

"Disfigurement. I shouldn't have judged you as a man of vanity."

"Your thinking is so shallow for a man of your discernment, Strathmore. There are wounds that go far beyond the superficialities of the skin."

Julia watched the exchange with disbelief.

She stepped from behind Strathmore, despite the restraining hand around her waist. "You fiend," she said, endeavoring to keep her voice equally cool but knowing it quavered with emotion. "I shall hate you into hell and beyond. You have no idea of the pain you have caused."

Faron's voice rose in surprise. "But I must disagree! Indeed I do. There's nothing that gives me more pleasure at the moment than causing pain to your dear aunt Meredith. Through you, your sister, and of course . . ." He let the sentence trail off deliberately knowing Julia would not rest until she learned what he'd left unsaid.

Julia swallowed hard, the reference to Rowena a knife to her heart, an emptiness that would never leave her as long as she lived. "I don't expect that you will tell us what lies behind your evil machinations."

"You never know, mademoiselle, it might do you good to learn the reasons behind what happened that night so long ago in the nursery where you and your sister slept." He paused to look over her head to Strathmore, a small smile playing on his lips, before meeting her glaring gaze. "I understand that you suffer from certain episodes, shall we say, stemming from the shock of the fire. It seems that we share something in common, mademoiselle."

"I shudder to think that we share the same air."

He gave her a sly look from behind the mask, and her stomach clenched at the knowledge that he was enjoying her pain. "You and Meredith miss Rowena, I'm sure. Must be troublesome for you, in particular, living with the knowledge that her death should have been yours."

Julia refused to close her eyes against unshed tears watching as Faron's gaze locked upon hers. It was a test, or simply another form of torment Faron believed was his to unleash. Trying to read his twisted mind, Julia was suddenly thrown back to the moment at Birdoswald, desperate at the river's edge, and felt a part of herself die once again. Despite all her hopes, her fantasies, she knew that Rowena was gone.

Strathmore's hand tightened around Julia's waist. "We don't need to hear this, Faron. I shall ask Julia to leave so we may conclude our business as I had requested. Nothing has changed."

"I don't believe Mademoiselle Woolcott wishes to leave. Do you?" Without waiting for her reply, Faron continued. "I'm sure she's eager to hear what you intend to offer in exchange for the Ptolemy maps." The Frenchman turned to walk toward the largest of the drawing room's fireplaces, his back to the flames limning his tall figure in red. Physically jarring, the resemblance was remarkable. She watched the two men circle each other as though they were handling dynamite, neither willing to state the obvious for fear of setting off an explosion. As if to punctuate her thoughts, Julia again felt the marble shudder beneath her feet.

Faron failed to notice. "You have acquitted yourself well, Strathmore. That business with the actress, the tunnel explosions, all child's play in your hands, as I expected, having watched your exploits for some years now."

"Keep your damned maps, Faron." Strathmore's voice was insolent. The two men's eyes met over Julia's head. Both were aware the stakes had just been pushed higher.

Faron's voice was sincerely troubled. "Unfortunate, and entirely unexpected, Strathmore. I should not have anticipated you would throw away the opportunity to have within your grasp the Great Prize."

"You will just have to live with the disappointment." Strathmore's gaze slid over the pistol in Faron's large hand.

Julia tensed as he moved toward the fireplace, a strong arm pulling her to stand behind him.

No. Don't do it. But Julia could not say the words. Faron had killed her sister. Had tormented her aunt and would continue to do so if she did not have the courage to end the nightmare. When she looked up to meet his dark eyes, it was as though he already knew exactly what she was thinking.

"Why the hesitation, mademoiselle? There is no room for morality in this drama. Simply take the pistol from my hand and do what you will with it." He held out the weapon as casually as though he were offering her a flute of champagne. "I had actually anticipated asking Strathmore to do the honors. To give him the opportunity to—."

"You can't. You won't. I shan't allow it." The words left Julia in a rush. She could hold back no longer, the truth ringing not only in her head but aloud, her voice echoing in the high-ceilinged drawing room, hoarse, desperate and altogether too real. "*Because you are his father. Strathmore's father.*"

There was a sickening silence. Then Faron casually lifted a hand to release the mask covering his face and revealed a broad forehead, strong nose, and a wide mouth—so very like Strathmore's—turned down in a frown. Grasping Strathmore's arm, her gown a flurry of chalk dust and silk, Julia turned to him beseechingly, prepared to confess to a litany of sins, one darker than the next, the worst of which was keeping from him the knowledge that had been revealed to her in the daguerreotype. "You can't kill your own father, Strathmore. I know that you would do it for me. For Rowena. But I can't allow it."

Strathmore's eyes remained steadily fixed on Faron, a mockery of a smile playing on his lips. No evidence of shock, no tightening of his jaw, just a calm, neutral expression that lit a flame in Julia's horrified mind. With the slowness of a dream, she grasped the realization that he had known all along.

The flames burned higher, encircling Faron in a glow of red light. "Surely, mademoiselle, you didn't believe that I would evince such sustained interest in a man who was not my son?"

They had both known. Julia felt as though she was emerging from a dark tunnel, burdened by guilt, haunted by loss, feeling hope die. A metaphor for her life, she was the woman behind the camera obscura, refusing to emerge from the darkness and into the light.

Strathmore's low voice was full of mockery. "Forgive me if I choose not to call you father." He shook his head slowly, his thick black hair drifting chalk dust over the travertine floor. "And would I evince such sustained interest in a man who was not my sire?" In the blankness of the room, Julia heard the emptiness in Strathmore's soul.

They felt another shudder beneath their feet and, as if in response, the flames in the hearth shot higher. They seemed to kiss the hem of Faron's jacket. Images flickered to life, dancing amid the flames—first Meredith's face and then Rowena's. Julia blotted out the pain. She had lied both to herself and to Meredith when she first set out to Eccles House those many weeks ago. Honesty compelled her to admit that she had wanted to confront the past the Woolcotts could no longer afford to deny. How strange that she should be the one to finally banish the threat.

"I don't even care anymore about your explanations of what occurred between you and Meredith years ago," she whispered above the spitting of the flames. "There is nothing you can say that will make any difference to me. You tried to kill two innocent children in their nursery—nothing excuses such a heinous act."

"Are you sure, mademoiselle?" His black eyes, mercifully unlike Strathmore's, challenged her. "You choose not to hear how your dear aunt robbed me of what I value most in life?"

"You robbed me of my sister," Julia said, hoarsely. "Nothing, nothing else matters." It was then she moved from behind Strathmore, arms outstretched, charging the Frenchman. The pistol, held casually in his hand, fell to the floor as Julia felt her fists strike his chest, driving Faron into the hearth. Another jolt of thunder shook the ground beneath their feet, and the mirror atop the fireplace mantel snapped to the floor, bursting into lethal shards the size of china plates.

"Get out. Now," snarled Strathmore behind her. "The explosions underground have done damage to the foundation of the house." But Julia wasn't listening, watching flames eating their way up Faron's coat, the desperation in his black eyes widening in incomprehension, as he attempted to wheel backward to put out the flames while encountering sharp shards of glass with every movement he made. Muted blasts of noise hammered in Julia's ears, indistinguishable from the roar of the fire and the thunder shaking the house. She refused to move, mesmerized as Faron's dark eyes flashed with life, his mouth a rictus of horror, unable to scream. He sucked in massive gulps of air, and one hand flew to his chest as though to stop his heart before the flames could do their work.

Strathmore lifted Julia into his arms, and she imagined Faron's scream of desolation cleaving the air, stretching toward infinity, toward hell. Her hands flew up to cover her ears, but the screaming didn't stop, merging instead with the grief and fear festering so long in her heart.

Then she felt only cold, damp air. Silence. And Alexander Strathmore holding her, looking into her face, as though she had flown away from him, as though the past had swallowed her. Behind them, the windows of the drawing room at Eccles House glowed red, but Strathmore's long strides took them rapidly away from the estate.

"Julia. Speak to me." Those were the last words she heard as consciousness deserted her.

Epilogue

Three months later

"Hold still, Strathmore. Perfectly still. Did I say you could move?"

"I am merely impatient for my wife to join me in rather more exciting pursuits."

"This is exciting, my love," said Julia, glancing at the watch pinned to her bodice and away from the man, resplendently and unapologetically nude, seated before her camera obscura. "I estimate only two more minutes and we should be finished here." A rare, hot summer had blessed London, casting the former drawing room of Strathmore's town house in a warm glow. Converted into a studio for Julia's pleasure, the tall windows allowed in a cascade of light.

She smiled at the sight of her husband, the most beautiful man she knew, watching her with those gray eyes lit in a combination of amusement and passion. And a certain vigilance, as though he was loathe to let her out of his sight for more than a few moments. It had worked in her favor, Julia conceded. They had become inseparable since their marriage three months ago in the small chapel at Montfort.

"You are tempting me with that look of yours," said Strathmore. "Not to mention tempting me with how fetching you appear in that gown, although"—he raised his dark brows roguishly—"you would look even more fetching without it altogether. Can't understand the fascination with all the ruffles and furbelows when the natural form is so much more beautiful."

"As you learned amongst the primitives, no doubt."

"We have much to learn together as it turns out," Strathmore said smoothly while Julia slid the copper plate from its mooring, ready to place it in the fuming box for development. "As you will soon see when we leave for north Africa in a fortnight."

Julia's smile was brighter than the sun bathing the room in its glow. "I've never experienced such feelings of anticipation. I can't wait. By the way, you may move now." He rose from the chair, his broadly naked shoulders gleaming like a Roman sculpture. She could still not fathom that Alexander Francis Strathmore was hers.

"I trust this series of daguerreotypes will remain in our private collection?" he asked. He moved to the divan where his discarded trousers lay, pulling them on lazily, his eyes never leaving Julia's face.

"I can't believe the man responsible for translating one of the most erotic texts in the world can afford to feign modesty." She slid the plate into the fuming box and waved a finger in admonishment. "Nonetheless, *I* am the one disinclined to share you—your daguerreotype or your person—with anyone. Just to make that clear, Lord Strathmore." Julia sauntered to the divan, her movements languid and sensual with a newfound confidence. His warm hand pulled them both down to the cushions, his skin burning through the thin fabric of her tea gown.

"I have the most beautiful, intelligent, talented woman as my wife," he growled into her ear. Already Julia shook with the need coursing through her body like silken heat. They had languished for what seemed like days in bed, talked until they were hoarse, pushing away the ghosts of the past to make way for their future together. Theirs was a fierce intimacy that had left them forever changed.

"A wife who is grateful to you for everything," she turned toward him, bringing her lips close to his.

He smiled at her, a slow, sweet smile that was for her alone. "I only wish I had been able to do more. Sooner."

Julia still found it difficult to think about Rowena but knew her sister would never wish for her to live under the suffocating shadow of grief and vengefulness.

"You had another dream, didn't you," Strathmore murmured into the silkiness of her hair.

Julia's lips tightened. "I see her rising from the riverbank, beautiful and whole, the sunlight shimmering around her. I know it's just a dream, stemming from my sorrow and inability to let go but I have this feeling she's still alive. Somewhere."

"She lives on in your heart and memory."

"Lately, since the fire at Eccles House, I have this feeling . . ." she said haltingly.

"Do not concern yourself unduly, Julia. Our journey will prove the best medicine in helping you leave all this behind."

Meredith remained safely at Montfort, the threat of Montagu Faron only a haunting memory. With a strength and determination to forever confront the truth without flinching, Julia had insisted on dispatching Meredith's secretaries to Eccles House to confirm the death of the Frenchman. That they found only simmering ashes was something she did not wish to contemplate. "He is truly dead, isn't he." It was both a question and a statement.

Strathmore paused a moment longer than necessary. "Forget the past, Julia. We have our entire lives ahead of us."

"When did you know Faron was your father?" she asked softly, leaning against Strathmore's shoulder.

The cadence of his breathing didn't change when he said, "Not long after I was first contacted by Lowther regarding the Ptolemy maps. The world of cartography and exploration is surprisingly small. I'd long known of a Frenchman who had twenty years earlier attempted an expedition to the

Mountains of the Moon and failed. My research revealed the man was inordinately wealthy, and endowed with an inquiring mind and extraordinary courage." Strathmore paused to capture her hand in his hard one. "He had also spent some time at Dunedin, I soon discovered. And he was the source of the trust I received when I reached my majority." He did not elaborate, and Julia once again saw the visage of Lady Strathmore, vain, intemperate, and faithless, censuring her son on a London morning not long ago.

"He knew you were his son. I believe he was strangely proud of you," Julia murmured, and then in a barely audible voice said, "I hope you forgive me."

He tightened his arms around her, loving her more than he should. "Nothing to forgive. Faron met a fitting end."

Rowena's beautiful face shimmered briefly before Julia's eyes. Upon their return from north Africa, Julia had promised Meredith a long visit, hoping that living without fear would allow her aunt to reveal what had transpired so many years ago to inextricably link their fate with Montagu Faron.

Strathmore pressed a soft kiss to the side of her neck. "What are you thinking, Julia? Talk to me. *Always*, talk to me."

"About Meredith and Rowena. How when I left for Eccles House that first time, I already knew that I would confront Faron, although I didn't have the courage to admit it to myself. It was the least I could do for Meredith when she had taken on so much for us. For me."

She turned in his arms. "And I am also thinking how wrong I was to ever doubt you when all you wanted to do was help."

"You can spend the rest of your life making it up to me," he said, beginning to unbutton the infuriatingly small row of fastenings on the front of her bodice. "Beginning with accompanying me to Africa, brandishing that camera of yours," he said, separating the lace at her collarbone with annoying efficiency, exposing the soft skin between her breasts. "Of course, if there are other ways you can think of . . ."

Strathmore's fingers were cool and hard against her heated flesh, causing Julia's head to sink into the upholstery with a sensual lassitude. His lips began playing with her mouth. His image burned against her closed eyes, the intense gray gaze seeing her and loving her for the woman she had become.

"Are you happy?" she murmured against his mouth.

"Let me show you just how much," he said, his lazy smile dazzling. And he did.

With heroes like this, who wouldn't want to be in
CLOSE QUARTERS?
Pick up Lucy Monroe's latest book today!

For the first time since arriving at the Sympa-Med compound, Tanya's heart raced at the idea of entering the dining hut. And it wasn't the prospect of eating that was doing it either, but the man she would see.

She hadn't been able to get Roman out of her head since he'd left her earlier. Despite plentiful evidence to the contrary, the idea that he might share the attraction would not leave her alone.

No doubt it was just wishful thinking, but what a wish.

He and Ben were standing beside a table near the one she and Fleur sat at during mealtimes, and talking to the other men in the security detail.

Despite the fact that he was in active conversation with the soldier who had introduced himself as Neil, Roman's gaze caught hers the minute she entered the hut.

She did her best to give him a casual nod of acknowledgment, but ruined the effect with a blush he no doubt took for some misplaced shyness or embarrassment. It wasn't though; the heat climbing her neck and into her cheeks was pure, unadulterated arousal.

Was she going through her midlife crisis early, or something? She was only twenty-eight, but something had to explain the way her nipples tightened to hard points every time she saw the man.

And that wasn't even taking into consideration the heat between her legs. She'd never had such a physically visceral reaction before. Not to anything. Not fear. Not joy. Definitely not passion.

It was just a little terrifying.

Forcing her eyes away from him, she heard Fleur invite Ben to join them at their table for dinner. Roman didn't wait for an invitation to sit beside Tanya on the bench at the long table. The other men all sat at the table they'd been standing by, seemingly unaffected by their colleague's desertion.

Okay, if looking at him affected her, sitting next to him was a stimulation overload. Not only could she smell his subtle masculine scent, but his heat reached out and touched her like a caress to every nerve ending along the side facing him.

She found herself inhaling deeply to more firmly imprint his scent into her olfactory memory. It was such a primal reaction and she couldn't help it any more than she could the need to breathe.

"Are you okay?" he asked, sounding like he knew exactly what was wrong with her.

She was not a mare in heat, controlled by her body's urges, no matter how much she might secretly want to be.

Taking a deep breath, she then let it out slowly, concentrating on getting her voice under control before she spoke. "Of course."

Are you settling in all right?"

He certainly didn't look like he was suffering jet lag, or culture shock as so many newbies did when arriving in Africa for the first time.

"No problem."

One of the kitchen helpers delivered food to their table.

Tanya waited until everyone had been served before asking him, "Is this your first trip to Africa?"

"No."

He took a bite of food, showing neither pleasure nor distaste for the traditional local fare.

It had taken her a while to get used to the lack of spices, or the different spices in most African cooking when she'd first arrived with the Peace Corps.

When he didn't clarify his one-word response, she asked, "To Zimbabwe?"

"Yes."

"It's an amazing country."

"If you say so."

"Don't you think so?" No matter the drawbacks to life on the original continent, Tanya loved so much about the different African cultures she had experienced. And the ability to experience nature at its most pristine was unparalled. "There is so much unspoiled beauty here, both in the people and the land they inhabit."

"And a human-trafficking industry that rivals any other location on earth."

She couldn't deny that, but it was only part of the picture. "The U.S. has its own severe problems with gang-related crime and violent crime overall, not to mention its own human-trafficking issues."

"True."

"No country is perfect, but the people here are resilient. They live and persist in hoping for the future, despite their troubled political past and present, and a terribly debilitating near eighty percent unemployment rate."

"And Victoria Falls is supposed to be one of the most beautiful spots in the world." The words were right, but the subtle sarcasm lacing them belied his sincerity.

She shot him a disgruntled frown. "It is, in fact."

"You've been?"

"Naturally." Did he seriously believe she would have lived here for nearly two years and never made the trek? She couldn't imagine that level of indifference to the beauty the world had to offer.

It would be one thing if she had no way to travel, but she had both sufficient time and money.

"I thought you were too busy providing medical help to the needy." Again the sarcasm.

She would have been offended if she didn't suspect he wasn't trying to annoy her, but simply reacting as per usual for him. "Even relief workers get personal time."

"And you use yours to visit Zimbabwe's top tourist spots instead of going home to family?" he asked, not sounding condemning, just curious.

"I do both."

"How much longer do you plan to stay in Africa?"

"My contract with Sympa-Med is up in six months." She'd thought about taking a year to travel, then going home for an extended visit. "I haven't decided if I will renew it."

"You know I hope you will," Fleur inserted from across the table.

Tanya smiled and nodded. "I want to stay in Africa, keep doing what we do, but I think a sabbatical is in order."

"Sabbatical?" Roman asked.

"We can never help everyone who needs us. The AIDS epidemic has a huge hold on the African continent. Children die daily from it, and from malnutrition and malaria, just to name a few of the big diseases. If you have any kind of heart at all, it gets to you. It has to. I want a break, not to leave permanently. But if I don't take that break, I'll probably burn out. I've seen it before. So, yes, a sabbatical."

"I'm surprised you haven't taken one before," Ben said, his voice warm with admiration and understanding.

Roman stiffened beside her and gave Ben an impenetrable look. "She spent almost two years Stateside training for her EMT certification."

"That was hardly a sabbatical," Ben said.

Tanya found herself laughing. "If you knew how much I dislike formal education and sitting in a classroom, you'd realize it was more a test of my endurance."

"You passed the test," Fleur said with approval and a little humor.

"I did." Tanya turned to Roman. "Considering the fact you chose a career path that took you out of the lab and into the *field*," she said, for lack of a better description, "you probably have more in common with me than either of us knew."

He looked down at her, his steel-gray eyes trapping her gaze until everyone around them fell away. "We definitely have a few things in common."

Keep an eye out for THE BEAST WITHIN,
with stories from Erin McCarthy, Bianca D'Arc, and
Jennifer Lyon, in stores now.
Turn the page for a preview of Erin's story, "The Howling."

The first howl off in the distance barely registered to the bride, since she was so filled with joy and flushed anticipation as the sleigh sailed forth over the light dusting of snow.

The second mournful cry was closer, causing a small pause in the laughter of the six people crammed in together among the furs and robes.

The third voice, a response to the first two, was more feral than sorrowful, more aggressive than beautiful, and the bride reached for the arm of her new husband as the horses threw back their heads nervously and pranced, disrupting the sleigh's rhythm.

Uneasiness crept over the party as the driver whipped the horses, and the sleigh leapt forward, the crisp wind tossing the ribbons in the bride's hair and sending an unpleasant shiver through her. The groom squeezed her hand in reassurance but the group had quieted as the sound reached all of their ears, the unmistakable bounding footsteps of the wolves falling into line behind them in pursuit.

Her fingers dug into the lace of her wedding dress beneath the fur laid so tenderly across her lap by the groom, as the faces in front of her reflected unease, fear. They all knew how fierce the wolves were, they all knew the stories of those who traveled these woods and disappeared, their sleighs overturned, bodies mutilated beyond recognition. She pressed her eyes closed and swallowed hard, trying to gauge how far the pack was from them.

Close. So close that she could hear the snarls and snaps of at least three wolves, maybe more, and she opened her eyes again in panic, head whirling around.

She wished she hadn't.

Everyone likes to be on THE NAUGHTY LIST now and again. Don't miss this sexy anthology featuring Donna Kauffman, Cynthia Eden, and Susan Fox, coming next month. Here's a sneak peek of Donna's story, "Naughty but Nice."

Griff's train of thought was abruptly broken by a loud yelp coming from somewhere in the rear of the small shop, followed by a ringing crash of what sounded like metal on metal.

He gritted his teeth against the renewed ringing inside his own head, even as he called out in the ensuing silence. "Hullo? Are you in need of some assistance?"

What followed was a stream of very . . . colorful language that surprised a quick smile from him. He'd found Americans, at least the ones of his immediate acquaintance, to be a bit obsessed with political correctness, always worrying what others might think. So it was somewhat refreshing, to hear such an . . . uncensored reaction. He assumed the string of epithets wasn't a response to his query, but then he'd never met the proprietor.

He debated heading around the counter to see if, in fact, she might need help, then checked the action. "No need to engage an angry female unless absolutely required," he murmured, then tipped up onto his toes and looked behind the counter, on the off chance he might spy the pot of coffee. "Ah," he said, upon seeing a double burner positioned beside an empty, tiered glass case.

He fished out his wallet and put a ten note on the counter, more than enough to cover the cost of a single cup, then ducked under the counter and scanned the surface for a stack of insulated cups. Oversized, sky blue mugs with the shop's white and pink cupcake logo printed on one side and the name on the other, were lined up next to the machine. He didn't think she'd take too kindly to his leaving with one of those.

"Making an angry female even angrier . . . never a good thing." His mouth quirked again as a few more rather unique invectives floated from the back of the shop. "Points for creativity, however."

He glanced at his watch, saw he still had some time, and took a moment to roll his neck, shake out his shoulders, and relax his jaw. He could feel the tension tightening him up, which, if he were honest, was a fairly common state of late. But then, he'd never been so close to realizing his every dream. And he'd certainly never thought it would come about like this. He fished out the small airline-sized tube of pain relievers he'd bought when he'd landed, but upon popping it open, discovered there was only one tablet left. He shrugged and dry swallowed it. Couldn't hurt.

He crouched down to look under the counter and had just opened a pair of cupboard doors when he felt a presence behind him.

"May I help you with something?"

Hmm. Angry female, due immediately south of his wide open back. And he was fairly certain there were sharp knives in reach. Not the best strategy he'd ever employed.

Already damned, he reached inside the cupboard and slid a large insulated cup from the stack, snagging a plastic lid as well, before gently closing the doors and straightening to a stand. "Just looking for a cup," he said as he turned, a careful smile on his face.

The smile froze as he got his first look at the cupcake baker.

He wasn't normally taken to poetic thought, but there he stood, thinking her clear, almost luminescent skin made her wide, dark blue eyes look like twin pools of endlessly deep, midnight waters . . . and her ensuing gaze that much more probing. In fact, it was surprisingly difficult to keep from looking away, every self-protective instinct he had being triggered by her steady hold on his gaze. Which was rather odd. She was the village baker. And despite the tirade he'd just overheard, he doubted anyone who made baking cheerful little cakes her life's work would be a threat or obstacle to his mission here. "I hope you don't mind," he said, lifting the cup so she could see what he'd been about. "You sounded a bit . . . occupied, back there."

"Yes, a little problem with a collapsed rolling rack."

His gaze, held captive as it was, used the time to quickly take in the rest of her. Thick, curling hair almost the exact same rich brown as the steaming hot brew he'd yet to sip, had been pulled up in an untidy knot on the back of her head, exposing a slender length of neck, and accentuating her delicate chin. All of which combined to showcase a pair of unpainted, full, dark pink lips that, even when not smiling, curved oh-so-naturally into the kind of perfect bow that all but begged a man to part them, taste them, bite them, and . . .

Now he did look away. Damn. He couldn't recall his body ever leaping to attention like that, after a single look. No matter how direct. Especially when his attentions were clearly not being encouraged in any way, if the firm set of that delicate chin was any indication.

"Nothing too serious I hope," he said, boldly turning his back to her and helping himself to a cup of coffee. After all, he'd paid for it. Not that she was aware of that as yet. But he thought it better to risk her mild displeasure until he could point that out . . . rather than engage more of the fury he'd heard coming from the back of the shop minutes ago. Which he was fairly certain would be the case if her sharp gaze took in the current state of the front of his trousers.

"Nothing another five hours of baking time won't resolve," she said, a bit of weariness creeping into her tone. From the corner of his eye, he caught her wiping her hands on the flour covered front of her starched white baker's jacket. "Please, allow me."

He quickly topped off the cup and snapped on the lid. "Not to worry. I believe I've got it. I left a ten note on your counter."

"I'm sorry," she said, sounding sincere now. "It's been . . . a morning. I'm generally not so—"

"It's fine," he said, intending to skirt past her and duck back to the relative safety of the other side of the counter. The tall, trouser-concealing counter. He just needed a moment, preferably with her not in touching distance, so he could button his coat and allow himself a bit of recovery time. It seemed all he had to do was look at her for his current state to remain . . . elevated.

Very unfortunately for him, and the comfort level of his trousers, she moved closer and reached past him. "The sugar is here and I have fresh cream in the—"

"I take it black," he said abruptly, then they both turned the same way, which had the continued misfortune of trapping her between the counter . . . and him.

Her gaze honed in on his once again, only this time he felt like he was the one holding hers captive.

"Okay," she said, her voice no longer strident. In fact, the single word had been a wee bit . . . breathy.

"Indeed," he murmured, once again caught up in that mouth of hers. Those parted lips simply demanded a man pay them far more focused attention. *Step away, Gallagher,* he counseled himself. *Sip your coffee, gather your wits, and move on.*